THE RITUAL

Margery was sobbing, screaming, not believing what was happening, the revulsion mounting from her stomach into her throat, the dreadful stench gagging her, making it more difficult to breathe in the already stifling air.

Then from some distance came a very loud, long, sorrowful, inhuman cry. It rose up and above all other sounds, as if demanding to be heard, so that even the very ocean itself seemed to be silenced.

All was still. She stopped screaming, not knowing why, but knowing she must be quiet, if only to find out what that noise had been. What thing had it come from? She too must be still.

As still as all the others. To listen.

To hear a second cry from the jungle, a scream of agony and challenge, and mad, feral craving. Louder now. Closer now.

Thot spoke, a huge smile slicing through his blood-colored face. "Hear them, oh Nymph of Heaven! You are confirmed. You have found favor with them, made ready as a Holy Vessel. We honor you."

Margery saw a hundred tiny, glowing eyes peering out at her from the jungle. She struggled madly, violently, nearly deranged, but as the sun rose higher and higher, the eyes grew faces, and the faces were not human.

OFFERINGS

T.M.
Minton

LEISURE BOOKS ∞ NEW YORK CITY

A LEISURE BOOK

Published by

Dorchester Publishing Co., Inc.
6 East 39th Street
New York, NY 10016

Printed in the United States of America

**To Marybeth,
for a grand old name.**

OFFERINGS

FOREWORD

The Legend of Pausanias

Where there had been sea, now shore came rushing at the crippled ship, which rode the last enormous wave onto the waiting rocks that glistened in the moonlit surf like polished teeth. With an ear-shattering crunch the jaws of the reef crushed the sturdy hull with one quick bite, wood and metal springing free as if torn asunder by some explosion. Human bodies joined the debris being catapulted upwards, flying furiously through the wind and rain, completing a high, wide arc, and falling fast into the churning ocean and the silence without peace, below.

Whatever life was left afloat moved with the tide until it was beyond the province of the sea, and became that of the earth, as the island pulled this life into itself and let it lay there on its beach, to be dealt with later in the white glare of day.

It came, burning away the dark wet storm. The water that covered all things returned into the sky, and the sun unveiled its brutal heat and bore down with all its terrible strength, as if to punish the intruders who now began to stir on the island's strange black sand that baked beneath aching bodies.

Shielding their eyes, they saw what remained of their ship impaled helplessly on the talons of rock that surrounded the tiny island.

But beyond the reef, out across the water, they could discern another land mass, much larger than where they were now stranded. Aboard the wreckage of their ship were two rowboats, used to spread their nets. There were only five survivors. If even one of the boats were salvageable their rescue was assured.

It was decided among them that three would inspect the wreckage and survey the damage. One would remain behind on the beach, to tend to the fifth, who was still unconscious, his leg nearly torn from its socket. If a boat was seaworthy, they would have to bring it back to the beach first to take their wounded comrade home.

They swam out through the surf, diving through the waves which still broke upon the beach with the storm's residual power, and at last climbed up on to the pile of sharp, slippery rock that had trapped their ship some one hundred feet from the shoreline.

At first glance they saw that the destruction was nearly total, their greatest loss being the nets. But one boat had mercifully been spared major damage, and they yelled with joy to their fellows on the beach. Even a set of oars had been provided them.

Carefully, painfully, they carried the little boat over the treacherous rocks, until it could float smoothly from there to the beach.

They had just gotten past the larger rocks, and were about to hop aboard and ride the boat into shore, when one of the two steering forward turned around to address the one at the rear. He saw no more than a fin slice through the water. Then, the third man cried out in horror, and was gone.

A blossom of scarlet billowed to the surface of the water, then trailed away quickly, following the silent fin that carried their friend with it.

The two remaining scrambled in panic up on to the beach with their boat, and lay on the hot sand, exhausted, breathless and terrified.

From the beach, the guardian had seen the shark moving through the water for the attack, but his calls of warning were not heard above the pounding surf. Now their duty was to themselves, and to their wounded ally. The sun seemed to have set the sky on fire, and it was evident they would have to move the injured man out of the pitiless light.

Just over the dunes, the island's vegetation thickened rapidly into a dense jungle. From afar, they recognized familiar plant life, mingling with exotic flowers and shrubs, and further in, strange, tall trees with orange moss clinging to their branches. All foreboding fled, and they carried the poor, helpless victim away from the shoreline, and into the promising darkness and shelter of the jungle. Perhaps there they would find, at the very least, fresh water, and at best, something to eat, before taking to sea again in their tiny boat.

They hobbled along with their heavy burden for what seemed a very long time, seeing no evidence of the island being inhabited. Then, at last they came to a small clearing in the wood that seemed to them like a little paradise. Nearby was plentiful nourishment,

and ample fresh rain water that had gathered in
pools. The towering trees and dense leafage shielded
them from the onslaught of heat and light, and so,
they were soon cool, and sated.

Try as they might, it had proved impossible to
save their wounded friend. Without regaining consciousness, he died before dusk, and was buried in a
shallow grave, dug with the few tools that had been
left to them.

They welcomed nightfall, and soon the tired men
slept. One heard much movement in the trees high
above their heads, just before drifting off, but the
blackness surrounding them was so complete, that
whatever it had been, passed unseen.

Another awoke with a start just once in the
middle of the dark night, having thought he had
heard a scream echo from deeper in the jungle. The
third slept fitfully, but did not awaken until the first
rays of sun pushed down through the thick greenery
above with needles of light, and the jungle began its
day with the call of birds and the rustle of unseen
animals in the undergrowth.

They were revitalized and stronger after their
night's sleep and, having breakfasted on more fresh
fruits, decided to head back to the beach, and the
rowboat, with a day's supply of food and water.

Looking out to sea, they searched for a tell-tale fin
gliding across the placid water. But the sharks had
glutted themselves on the trio's fellow crewmen,
and even yesterday's last greedy killer had long
since sought other waters.

Pushing off, they skillfully rowed the boat around
and through the larger rocks. At last they were
headed out to sea, each with a silent prayer of
thanks to their God, when they heard the distant
screams of another human being.

At first they looked quickly at each other to see if the other two had heard it as well. Quickly convinced, they whipped their heads around to face the rear of the boat, and the ebony beach of the island.

They were some distance now, but on the shore in the bright light of the sun they saw a naked woman. Her black, filthy hair looked to be five feet long, and in a wild mass swirling about her poor, stupid face. She was shrieking madly, a crazed, demented wail that travelled across the water and crawled into their bones. She jumped up and down, waving her arms in uncontrollable spasms and in so doing, her brown body sparkled in the brilliance of the sun with rapid, blinding flashes, painful to the eyes. Then, she stopped, completely still, listening.

She turned her head over her shoulder, looking up the beach and then behind her, into the jungle. Facing the sea once more, she waded into the water, screaming again, and began to swim hysterically toward the men and the boat.

The senseless woman continued screaming while she swam, and took in much water. She blubbered and gasped, and went under twice. But bent on reaching them, she swam on, now in silence.

The men had been intent on watching the woman in the water. Now one of them looked to the beach again, and signalled the others.

There on the sand, something big, and alive stood, motionless. Its thin pelt shone orange in the glaring sunlight, and in its massive arms it held the tiny form of what looked to be a human infant, whose frail, white hand was pressed against the huge chest. The thing did not move. It watched, and observed the woman swimming away from the island.

Her hands reached out from the sea, gripping the wood of the boat, the long, gnarled nails twisted at the ends of the fingers. The men grabbed her arms and lifted her in, half drowned and still covered in filth the ocean could not wash away. She lay on her back, sucking in air, her rib cage heaving, and her breasts running with milk that already merged with the water and grit that covered her.

The thing on the shore roared.

The woman's eyes snapped open in recognition and terror, and pulling herself over to lean on the edge of the boat, she looked back to the island she had fled. The others in the boat also turned their heads to the shore as they moved further out into the sea, and the creature on the beach screamed again.

It was a horrible sound, like a long, loud lowing; a noise created deep in the lungs and throat, and made of anger and grief.

It had moved to the very edge of the water and while it called to her, it raised its arms straight out and chest high, holding up the new born life, as if to display it. It stopped. It watched, and listened to see if she would respond. When there was no movement in the boat, it called to her again, pleading for itself and its child, groaning in agony and frustration, and the infant began screaming as well, the air vibrating with the mad screeches from the shore.

The thing raised the infant high over its head and opened its mouth in a malicious, growling threat, then cried out once more in torture, and walked, screaming as it went, waist high into the water.

Waiting there for just a moment, it was frozen deathly still. The baby was in its arms, straight over its head, and the tiny voice wailed in short, hysterical bursts.

Then, the thing moved, and suddenly there was

silence as the child's screaming was cut off.

The creature had let go of the child's feet and, grabbing it with both hands around its neck, strangled it as it brought its mighty arms down, holding the little head under water.

The woman laid her hands upon her cheeks and began to moan, and they saw the creature raise its empty hands and start to walk further into the tide. When the water got high and deep, it looked around as if surprised to find itself out that far. It turned back to the land, trudging through the water, until it reached the dry sand, and halted, its back to the ocean.

It seemed to take time, here. To decide.

The last of the woman's reason left her when she watched the thing turn around one final time and walk once again into the surf, the water rising on it higher and higher as it went deeper and deeper. Then, it called longingly to her one last time, and allowing the ocean to close in and over itself, sank below the surface.

PART ONE

MASSACRE

ONE

It was late January, and unlike the northern world, warm and dry. A few scattered remnants of Christmas were still in evidence on the streets and in some of the houses. The Feast Of The Black Nazarene had ended the week before in Quiapo, and but for local festivities on the other islands, the city would not celebrate again on a large scale until Chinese New Year, yet a month away.

But though the excitement of the season had died down, the atmosphere in the uncomfortably warm, crowded little taxi was more intense.

Dr. Dana McKinley looked past the two other women to the far window. They were just passing the Nayong Pilipino. Beyond its entrance, the major cultures of the thousand islands comprising the Philippines were represented in charming miniature. She could see a few of the madly decorated jeepneys

weaving through the tiny towns, loaded with
tourists, and recalled her own first ride in one. They
were hybrids of jeep and bus, ornamented with gold,
brass, mirrors, tassels and paint, their mere presence
promising a good time. But if the cab had arrived
here at the Philippine Village, they were then nearly
at the airport, and the nostalgia was replaced by
longing. Marcus was sitting in the front seat beside
the driver, his white hair blowing in the breeze from
the opened window. The plane wouldn't take off for
another hour, yet she already missed him.

The cab slowed to a crawl, having joined the
legion of other vehicles waiting to unload their
passengers and baggage at their various terminals.

At last, the wait was over, the driver jumping out
to get the bags from the trunk. Lucy was out first,
before the uniformed red-cap could open the door.

"Mabuhay!" he greeted them, but Lucy ignored
him, holding the door for Margery while Dana got
out on the other side. Undaunted, the red-cap made
his way to the rear of the taxi, loading the bags
on his cart as they were handed to him by the
cabbie.

"You certainly brought enough luggage," Lucy
said to Margery, then turned and marched through
the automatic doors into the airport.

Marc leaned into Dana, saying quietly, "Lucy's in
another snit."

Dana nodded. "It'll pass. Besides, Margery's too
excited about this trip to notice."

With that, the three remaining followed the red-
cap and his cart to the check-in.

From where she sat overlooking the main floor of
Manila International, Margery could see nearly the
length of the entire terminal, where thousands of

people scurried in every direction. She wondered how many suffered from the same anxieties she was now coping with.

Did she have everything? Had she packed everything? Would the luggage, the crates, arrive in Port Moresby without damage? It was a long flight from Manila. What if there was some rough weather? If any of their equipment were damaged, Dr. Pemberton would never forgive her!

Stop this, she ordered herself, looking at her watch again. First, he's told you to call him "Marcus," so start thinking of him like that. Secondly, you packed *very* carefully; if anything is damaged, it's hardly your fault; and thirdly, Marcus *would* forgive you.

She looked across the table at her co-workers, who had now become her friends. Dr. McKinley ran a hand through her close-cropped hair streaked with gray, catching Margery's eye. She smiled and said something.

"I can't hear you, Dana!" Margery called back over the din of the busy airport. Lucy sat between them and leaning into Margery's left ear, repeated Dana's words: "She said she wonders what's keeping him!"

"Oh," Margery laughed and yelled, "they're three-deep at the bar. He's probably fighting for the bartender's attention!"

Lucy nodded in agreement and lit a cigarette. Though she knew Dr. McKinley was not fond of cigarettes, especially at such close range, it seemed to hardly matter, since the air was thick with pungent smoke from the crowd of other smokers. Nevertheless, the look on Dana's face had not escaped her.

Through the crowd, Margery at last spotted

Marc, carefully weaving through and around people, tightly gripping a tray full of martinis with both hands, and spilling nary a drop. As he drew closer, she could hear his consistent litany, "Excuse me, excuse me, please," his lithe body twisting and winding its way toward them.

Dr. Marcus Pemberton was perhaps fifty, and looked every day of it. His handsome face, not without a certain boyish quality, had nevertheless the ravaged look that only years in the sun and a life time of hard mental and manual labor can produce. His hair was nearly as thick now as it had been at twenty, but had gone completely silver. His deeply tanned skin contrasted to the bright green of his eyes, and he flashed Margery a grin as he came toward them with the drinks, reminding her once again how like her father he was. Younger, yes, and certainly in better condition, but with the same hearty zest for life, and thirst for knowing what is unknown, especially with respect to the past. The two men had in common a high, rare regard for history, and beneath tough exteriors, a touching sensitivity. Indeed, in her father's case, perhaps too sensitive. Pemberton placed the tray down on the table, then sat to Dana's right, handing over the cocktails. He raised his glass in a toast.

"No," Dana spoke quickly, "let me: to my dear Marcus, and our beloved Margery; success and adventure to you both!"

As the four glasses came together in salute, Margery observed the look that passed between Marc and Dana as she'd spoken the toast. How like her to wish us "success" and "adventure," she thought, and was then reminded of how she herself had changed since joining the Research Center. Six months ago, Margery would probably have thought the toast less than apt. After all, considering the journey that lay before them, surely "safety" and "a quick return home," would have seemed more fitting. But that was before she'd gotten to know and respect these people. Watching them now, looking deeply into each others eyes, she realized that these were lives not ruled by "safety" and "home," and it was part of the reason she'd come to care for them both.

From the loudspeakers about the airport, bells rang, heralding a flight announcement. Dana felt a little ache as Marc broke the eye contact they'd held through the first sips of the cold drink, listening to the perfectly modulated female voice repeat the information four times, each in a different language. Dana's memory momentarily brought her back to Paris, years ago when she'd been there with Marc. The flight announcements at Orly Field were introduced by the first three notes of the song "Camelot." Funny, she thought, the crazy little things one tucks away in one's mind as an echo of the past.

Marc said a quiet "pardon me," and leaned across her to light yet another cigarette for Lucy, who had only just put one out. The hairs on his bare arm tickled Dana's chin, and she felt the ache again, resisting the tempting urge to caress that arm with her cheek.

They'd made love for a long time last night, saying goodbye as lovers do, with their bodies, before the words.

Afterwards, she lay quietly in his arms, her head on his chest, listening to the steady hum of the air-conditioner, the only sound in the room beyond the rapid beating of his heart, which had begun gradually to cease its racing and slow to the normal rhythmic beating that had so often lulled her into sleep.

"Marc," she'd whispered, but at first, there was no answer. She repeated his name once more and he started slightly.

"Hmm? What?"

"I'm sorry. Were you asleep so quickly?"

"Oh, no, no. Just thinking. You know. Little gnawing details."

How well she knew. It seemed the past three weeks had been nothing *but* gnawing details, what with plotting out the trip; how to travel from one spot to the next under primitive conditions; what would be needed for how long, and what it would all cost. Thank God for the handsome grant they'd received from the Archaeological Society. Still, the budget was tight, and time and economy were of the essence.

"I think we've taken care of everything," she said, trying to put his mind at rest, and hers as well.

"Yes, but there are always those last minute things that go unnoticed until you need them." He paused, squeezed her shoulder, and speaking in quite a different tone, whispered, "Am I getting forgetful, do you think?"

"What?"

"Nothing."

Dana had pulled herself up to lean on her right elbow. She repeated her question.

"I worry sometimes, Dana." he answered at last.

"About getting senile? At your age? Marc, you're only . . ."

"Dana, I'm not as young as I was this morning," he stated sharply, cutting her off. "Neither of us are.

We've been after this ... this link ... for so long, now. What if I ... we ... don't find it?"

"Marc, it's there ... we both know it."

"No. We both *believe* it, *feel* it. We have faith that it exists. But if we can't locate it, what's been the use of it all?"

"Then it's for the use of the future, Marc. What we've contributed so far ... what we *will* answer soon ... will help other scientists to dig in deeper. They can pick up where we left off. Oh, my dearest dear, don't think this way, please? It makes it all so unimportant."

"How?" he asked, puzzled.

"I mean, if it only matters that *we* find the truth ... it's too big for that. Who finds it, whatever the noteriety, isn't what matters. That the *truth* is *uncovered* ... that's what matters."

"Of course, you're right," he said, and closed his eyes. But she knew in her heart he wasn't convinced. Dana stayed propped up on her elbow, looking at him.

It was one of the two areas in their working relationship that were sore spots. As they grew older, he seemed more and more concerned with the glory of discovering what might be a missing link in evolution. Sometimes she felt he was in a race against time; that he had to be proclaimed a "great" man before he died. It wasn't fame, she knew. Marc Pemberton was already famous in his chosen field. No, it was more like "immortality," though that too seemed the wrong word. She wondered briefly if there really was something to the theory of male menopause. Lately, he appeared to have a few of the symptoms.

She shivered, and shrunk back down again into

his open arms, pulling the blanket up over them.

Sleep would not come to her. Too much was happening. Earlier that night, she'd wanted to discuss their theory in some detail, to clarify a few elements, but he'd been reluctant. That was the other sore spot.

Since Marc had heard about the Legend of Pausanias, it had captured his interest, and his imagination. Though Dana and Marc had worked together for years, it did occur to her on more than one occasion that *her* work was merely to give credence to what remained to Marc a fable; a myth; a romantic view of evolution. When, in her research, she would uncover some piece of fact that might be termed "evidence" of the actual existence of Satyr Island, Marc would pounce upon it, revel in it, yet always return to the Legend. In a way, she sometimes wondered if he'd be disappointed to prove it true. He seemed so enamoured of the Legend; cold hard fact might destroy his faith, even while making him right.

She smiled. It was not unlike a child who hears that there really was a St. Nicholas, but there never was a Santa Claus, and tries to hang on to the latter, simply because it's more fun.

Snapping herself back to the present, she took another sip of her martini. It tasted good. Even calmed her some.

Aside from the early morning and busy day they'd had so far, what sleep she'd had was not restful.

She hadn't told Marc about the dream. She didn't believe in premonitions, and saw no reason now for herself to have suddenly become psychic. But it had been horrid. Drenched in violence and gore, pain and flame. When she'd woken from it, grateful to be awake, grateful that it had only been a dream, her

first instinct was to shake him awake, tell him about
the nightmare; implore him not to go.

It was ridiculous of, course.

But the dream would not have been so awful if
she'd seen herself in it, with him; with Margery. She
hadn't.

Dana hadn't tried to coax Marc into having her
accompany him on the expedition. Someone had to
run the Institute in his absence. She'd wanted to go;
still did; but she was a realist. She was only thankful
that, of the two assistants in their employ, he'd
chosen Margery to go along, and not Lucy. Not that
Dana looked forward to being left with Lucy,
though they got along well enough. Stated simply,
Margery would just be of more help to Marc out in
the jungle than the other girl, who seemed at times
high strung. But Dana knew how Lucy had hoped it
would be she that was chosen, and how disappointed
she'd been when passed over for Margery. Lucy had
worked for the Institute for nearly two years.
Margery, not quite six months. But it was the right
choice, Dana was convinced.

"Funny, no?"

She turned to Marc. Embarrassed, she said, "I'm
sorry dear. What did you say?"

"You were a million miles away. What were you
thinking?"

"Nothing," she grinned and sipped her drink.
"Now, what were you saying?"

"Just that it's funny we didn't hear from Ben. He
was almost as excited about this trip as we are. I
thought he'd call to say good bye."

"Well, he's a busy man . . . and I said *man*, not
boy. I think sometimes you still have him fixed in
that thick skull of yours as 'that kid from Chicago'."

"Mmm. I suppose you're right. It's hard for me to

think of him as completely grown up. Still, I thought he'd call."

"Did you think to call him?" she asked.

"Well, no . . . but . . ."

"There, Marc, you see? He's a newspaperman. He's very busy. Certainly as busy as you and I. He can't keep your schedule in mind and juggle his own time as well."

"All right, all right! You're so strict, Dana." Marc laughed as he spoke, then continued, "Look, give him a call at that rag he works for. Tell him I said goodbye."

Dana blanched at the word "rag," but she couldn't argue. The *Manila-American was* a rag.

"I will," she assented.

Margery looked down at her watch once again, just as their flight was announced as ready to board. Marc's eyes darted to Dana. "Well," he said, taking her hand, "I guess this is it."

"I guess," Dana grinned, tears rimming her reddened eyes. "I won't see you off at the gate. Let's say goodbye here. It'll be easier, I think."

He nodded and rose, the others following suit. But Margery came around the table saying softly, "Doctor . . . Marc . . . let me say goodbye now to Dana, then Lucy and I can just leave you both alone and to yourselves."

Marc was amused by the solemnity with which she pronounced the suggestion, but was no less touched by its sincerity. "Thanks," he said and meant, stepping aside.

Dana opened her arms to welcome the girl, tears in both their eyes.

"I'll miss you, Dana."

"And I you. Take good care of him . . . and do what he says. He's smart."

The girl nodded, squeezed her tightly once more, then broke away, bolting for the escalator to the lower level. Lucy looked after her, then back to Marc. Quickly, she hugged him tightly. "Good luck, Marc. I mean it!" Then she too ran off in pursuit of Margery.

"Alone at last," Marc joked as Dana stroked his cheek with her palm.

"Be careful, will you?"

"Worried about me already? That's not like you."

"Perhaps I'm getting cautious in my dotage. Just be careful."

He took her in his arms and held her tightly. "There's nothing to worry about. This is what we've worked for all these years. If I find it, it's our victory."

"I know. I envy you. I wish I were going to be there with you when you find it. Just remember, nothing's worth your life."

He held her at arms length and looked into her eyes.

"My life? What ever are you talking about?"

"Nothing. Silly of me. A dream I had. It's nothing. Write or call as soon as you can."

"I will. Now, no more dreams. You stick to facts. Get it all down in that diary of yours . . ."

"Journal," she corrected, laughing.

"Alright, 'journal.' I'll sneak a peek when I get back."

Marc pulled her in to him one last time. They kissed, oblivious of the crowd around them. Then he quickly turned and hurried off down the stairs.

Dana leaned over the balcony and saw him catch

up to Margery and Lucy where they had stopped to hug goodbye. Then, hand in hand, Marc and Margery were off, soon lost in the throng.

"See you on Monday," Dana said, slamming the car door. "Thanks for the lift."

As was her custom, Lucy Case waited until Dana had passed through the gate and entered the house that was the Pemberton Institute before pulling away.

Now on the road home to her little apartment that she'd shared with Margery, she felt free. Alone, finally.

The conversation in the car on the drive from the airport had been stilted and strained. Lucy knew Dr. McKinley was not unaware of the resentment she felt at being left behind.

It wasn't fair. I'm right to feel this way, she thought. I'm more experienced I should have been chosen.

But beyond the jealousy she was aware of another feeling, something she could not put her finger on. It had surfaced when, at the airport, she and Margery had been alone waiting for Marc Pemberton. They'd taken that time to say goodbye and as they hugged, Lucy had begun to cry. Suddenly she knew, even if it *had* been she that were chosen to go with Marc, it would not have changed this feeling.

No, she told herself, that's absurd. She's my roommate, that's all. I'll miss the company at home. That's what it is. That's what it must be.

Still, she wondered just how much of a gentleman Dr. Marcus Pemberton would remain, virtually alone in a jungle with a young, and beautiful girl like Margery. And she wondered too if that thought had crossed Dana McKinley's mind.

She tried to blot the thought from her mind, but it persisted. What was causing this confusion? For that's what it was; terrible confusion . . . and now, the headache was starting again.

Never mind. I will not think of Margery or Marcus or Dana or the job. And who wants to spend weeks in a disgusting, humid jungle with an old man anyway. She's welcome to it, she thought, turning left down the dirt road that would lead to her apartment complex. Only a few blocks away she could hear the pounding of the surf, and the thought of an evening swim struck her fancy just fine. It might relax her. Calm her down.

Letting herself in, she made for the bedroom, ripping off her clothing as she went. She started tearing through her drawers, hell bent on finding a clean, dry bathing suit, cursing as she pulled out brasiers, undies, stockings . . . everything but what she was looking for. She was breathing heavily, angry at being thwarted. A swim. All I want is a swim! Why must everything go against what I want!

Slamming the drawer, she leaned on the bureau, forcing herself to breath slowly; deeply. There were two suits hanging in the bathroom. Surely one of them must be dry by now. They must be!

They weren't. Dammit! The thought of putting on a wet bathing suit made her skin crawl. If it were night, she needn't have worried; she'd gone skinny-dipping before. But now the sun was still in the sky; the beach would still be inhabited.

Dinner. I'll make myself dinner. Yet once in the kitchen, she stood, still naked, unable to decide whether to open the refrigerator or one of the cabinets first. The hell with it. I'm not hungry anyway. Besides, cooking for one wasted so much.

And it would only depress her more. It was Margery who used to whip up something for the two of them when they'd get home from work, while Lucy would make them each a white wine spritzer.

Used to. Used to. STOP IT!

A drink. I'll make us . . . me . . . a drink. A white wine spritzer.

Quickly, urgently, she filled a glass with ice and club soda, then all but ran to the living room where the wine was kept on a shelf in the book case. She spilled a lot of it in pouring and didn't care. Not waiting for the ice to chill it, she drank it down in four gulps, then poured another.

It was hot in the room. She switched on the air-conditioner and sat on the couch, drink in hand.

Perhaps, she thought, I ought to get away. Not now, of course. Dana would never let her have any time off while Margery was away; they were short-handed as it was. But when things had settled down into the old routine, maybe then. But where would she go? In her life, she had never left Manila, or anyway, Luzon.

She'd been born in the northern part of the island, up near Baguio City. It was beautiful there. But despite the mountains of the Cordillera range, despite the pine forests and the smart summer colony that vacationed there (even the President had his summer residence, "The Mansion," there) it was a place she never wished to see again.

Frequently, acquaintances would take their holidays there; some even owned homes in Burham Park, the center of the city of Baguio. Lucy had been invited many times, but always found an excuse not to go.

Her father had been a Major, stationed at the U.S. Air Force Reservation at Camp John Hay. Lucy had grown up an Air Force brat, an only and unhappy child. Her mother was Filipina; a shy, nervous village girl who'd been smitten by the American officer and the uniform. It was this mixture of Western and Eastern parentage that gave Lucy her striking good looks. Olive skin, rich black hair, but blue eyes, and taller than most native women.

That much, she'd told her friends and employers. But there was more to it than that. A lot more.

For the truth was that when she had been nine years old, her father had gotten orders reassigning him back to the United States; Virginia, to be exact. Lucy's mother had protested vehemently. She was frightened of travel; afraid to leave her sister, the only remaining relative she had. The Major had done his utmost to have his orders changed. He'd even obtained two postponements. But eventually, the time came, and they'd had to pack.

The night before they were to depart, Lucy's mother had shot her husband in the head while he slept, then put a bullet through her own brain. Lucy had heard the shots from her bedroom. Lucy had found the bodies. That was when her headaches had started.

For the next nine years, she lived in Burham Park with her Aunt. When she could, she'd spent her time in Wright Park, horseback riding. Horses came to be her only friends.

But she turned eighteen, and came into the money left her by her father. She went almost immediately to Manila, which was only fifty minutes away by air, but a whole world away from the childhood she'd hated. College followed, and after graduation, she'd gotten the job at The Pemberton Institute. Lucy no longer had any contact with the Aunt who'd raised her and as far as she knew, that suited her Aunt just

fine. There had never been any love lost between
them. She never told a soul how she lost her parents.
They had simply died.

In front of her, across the room on an end-table,
the photograph stared back at her. It pictured her
three months ago, squinting into the bright sunlight, her glistening black hair caught by a breeze.
Beside her was Margery, also squinting and
grinning into the lens, her left arm around Lucy's
shoulder.

Before she knew it, the now empty glass had flown
across the room and smashed into the center of the
picture, shattering it before it fell to the floor.

Lucy let out a short, anguished little howl and
buried her head in her hands. She began to cry; then
to sob. Her head hurt so much.

She stayed there, crying, naked on the sofa, for
the next two hours.

TWO

"Ben, if you're after a Pulitzer Prize, go work for the *Washington Post*," Herbert Shiff growled. He picked up the pages of copy and lightly tossed them across the desk.

"I don't like D.C., thanks," Ben answered quickly, letting the five paper clipped sheets lie there before his folded hands. "And I'm not out for a Pulitzer. I'm out to write a good story."

The editor removed his glasses, rubbed his eyes, blinked, squinted, and said, "Look, this last assignment I gave you involved rape, robbery and attempted murder, Ben. You've turned in the basics; the Who, What, Where When and Why of it. Fine. What I want . . . what our readers want . . . is color."

"Christ, Herbert! There are only two colors you're interested in, lately. Yellow and purple!"

The glasses were on again, Shiff staring at him over the rims. But Ben knew he was right, and so did Shiff. Though the newspaper had never been deeply concerned with the "art" of good journalism, it had at least maintained some standards, even if barely paying lip service to ethics. But even that had dwindled since the sale of the tabloid to McNeil, Ltd., a New Zealand corporation whose president had laid down strict new "goals" for the publication; goals that were now carefully adhered to, and looked after by a "company man" installed as Herbert Shiff's immediate superior. So, Ben answered to Shiff, but Shiff answered to "the man."

Neither of them spoke for a moment. From behind Ben, beyond the glass wall that looked out onto the news room, the muted cacaphony could be heard; typewriters clicking away, their bells ringing in counterpoint to the constant jangle of some twenty phones, each with three different lines; voices raised over the din. To a visitor, it might have sounded like a mad-house. To the two men inside the office, it was merely the sound of business as usual.

At last, Shiff nodded and sighed. "I know," he muttered, lighting a cigarette. "Things have changed a lot around here in the last few months."

"You can say that again. And not for the better, Herb."

"Okay, okay. I said I know. But the fact is, Ben . . . and if you repeat this I'll deny having ever said it . . . this piece of yours," Shiff gestured to the stack of papers on the desk, "is too good to print."

"Great. Just fuckin' great," Ben stretched his arms behind his head, staring at the ceiling.

"Hear me out. Word comes in every day from New Zealand for Blair to beef this paper up. Blair comes down on *me* . . . I come down on *you*. It's simple chain-of-command bull-shit, but it's the way things are.''

"So the long arm of McNeil is ruining this paper."

"Ben . . . Ben, let's get serious. We're not sinking much lower than we already were before the buyout."

"That's an excuse? Goddammit, Herb, at least we could fool ourselves into thinking there was no place to go but up!"

"Well, that's truer now than ever before, isn't it?"

The door behind Ben opened, the noise of the city room crashing into the office, just as Ben shouted, "So we're supposed to be happy about turning this sheet into a complete rag?"

The door slammed, the glass rattling within its frame. Herbert Shiff's face had colored, his eyes glued to a spot somewhere over Ben's left shoulder. Ben turned around in his chair to see Geoffrey Blair glaring down at him.

"Hello, Geoffrey," Ben said, grinning.

The short, bald, overweight man glared at him. "Well, if it isn't the American answer to Emile Zola." The New Zealand accent was thick and adenoidal.

"You flatter me," the reporter replied.

"I do not. Zola wouldn't have lasted a week on this paper."

"Then you flatter Zola."

"Ben," Herb Shiff warned, but was interrupted by Blair.

"I came here on other business, but I'm glad you're here, Mr. Ramsey. It saves me time. I can kill two birds with one stone, if you'll forgive the terminology."

"Shoot," Ben said.

"Shooting . . . or firing, won't be necessary . . . yet. However, comments like the one I heard just now are not appreciated."

"Whether or not they're true," Ben returned.

"Truth is no longer the business of this newspaper, Mr. Ramsey, and I think it somewhat naive of you to go on in search of it . . . at least here at the Manila-American. Readership . . . increased readership, is what we're after." Blair turned to Shiff. "Am I right, Herbert?"

Shiff nodded, avoiding Ben's eyes. "I was just explaining that to Mr. Ramsey."

"Good," Blair stated. "Now, first, the story for the Sunday edition that Mr. Ramsey was to do . . . is it ready?"

Shiff reached across the desk and scooped up the five pages before Ben could grab them. "Right here, Geoffrey," he stuttered, but continued before Blair could speak again, "but it needs a little re-writing." Ben began to say something, but Shiff overrode him as well, with, "Not a lot . . . it's wonderful, really . . . just what you're . . . we're . . . after. Ramsey's one of our best reporters . . . just a little clarification on details to keep us from getting sued. I'll have one of the copy boys get together with Legal . . . it'll be ready by the deadline and then some."

Blair smiled. Ben clenched his fists, resisting the urge to hit him; the little man enjoyed his power too much. "Nice and juicy?" Blair asked.

Shiff laughed nervously. "Oh, it *will* be!"

"Fine. As Mr. McNeil's representative, I don't have to tell you how fond he is of good, gutsy reportage." Blair had turned back to look down upon Ben once more. "As for you, Mr. Ramsey, I'm here to give you a very nice opportunity."

Lucky me, Ben thought, but said instead, "Yeah? What?"

"I want another close-up from you, for another Sunday edition. The Canlas case."

"The hostage story!" Ben was on his feet. "That's a day old already! You've got two reporters outside the house now, and nothing's happened since the police were called last night!"

"We will now have *three* reporters on the scene, including you!" Blair screamed.

"Ben! Calm down!" Herb yelled. Ben looked to his boss, then to Blair. He shrugged and said a quiet, "Go on."

Geoffrey Blair paused too long for effect. "That's better," he said finally in a soft, controlled voice. "As you've implied, not much in the way of 'action' has presented itself. Canlas has had his wife and sister at gun-point for over thirteen hours, with the police surrounding the house. You get all the information there is and turn it into a good read for the Sunday Magazine feature. I want it long, I want it graphic, and I want it quick. We print it in three weeks."

"Blood and guts, in other words." Ben said rather than asked.

"In a single word . . . lurid. I said it's an opportunity. A last chance might be closer to the truth." Blair did a ridiculous about-face, spinning on his heels, and fairly marched to the door. He stopped then and turned back to them. "Mr. McNeil has asked me to remind you . . . both of you . . . that he is seriously questioning the wisdom of having kept you both on, rather than hiring his own new people. If there's no news, then make news, and make it good."

The door slammed behind him.

The newspaper men sat staring at each other across the desk. They remained silent for a time, each collecting his thoughts, each searching for words that would assuage the threats they'd both received.

"You see?" Herb shook his head and sighed. "You see what I'm up against?"

"Yeah, but why do you take it, Herb? You're a good editor. You've forgotten more about this business than that son-of-a-bitch will ever know."

"Why do *you* take it, Ben?"

Ben thought for a second. There really was not a great deal of difference between the two of them. "I need the job, I guess."

"Right. And you're twenty years younger than I am. You can still *get* another job, if your ethics mean that much to you. I can't. I *really* need this job."

"He's got you by the balls, doesn't he?"

"And he's squeezing. So . . . what're you gonna do?"

Ben looked at his watch, then back at Shiff. "Listen, can you do what you told Blair . . . give those pages to a copy-boy and have him turn them into a horror story?"

"No problem. I have two kids that would snap at the chance."

"Alright. Then I'm on my way to the hostage scene. I'll dig up what I can and use the best of it."

"Or make it up . . . Ben . . . you heard him. He wants it violent and gory."

"Yeah, yeah, even if it isn't. I'll give him ten pages of slashing and tearing. Maybe I can pass a buzz-saw into Canlas so he can finish off his wife and sister with that!"

Ben stormed out of the office, the news room personnel watching him as he rushed through the maze of desks and phones toward the elevators.

* * *

Traffic was not heavy, the mornings' rush hour long since over now. If nothing else, he could step on the gas, gain some speed and try to enjoy the drive along the coastal highway . . . at least until he turned off at the exit bringing him into the depressed section of the city where Roman Canlas held two women hostage.

It was, as usual, a glorious day, the sun shining clear on the water, birds calling overhead. Hot, yes, but even the heat was good. Cleansing, in a way. And that was exactly what he felt he needed. A cleansing, a purge that would free him from the ruthless, unscrupulous money-grubbers who would do anything to sell a paper.

He analyzed his position. As it was, he had to hope for violence and death to present itself at the Canlas house, thus enabling him to report "the truth." That made him a lousy human being. But the safety of the two women, and even Canlas himself, meant something to Ben. He didn't want anyone hurt. But, if no one was hurt, he'd have to concoct a melodrama to satisfy the blood-thirsty Blair . . . and that made him a lousy reporter.

Maybe Herbert Shiff had been right. Maybe his own ethics would prove to be more important than his post on the paper.

But for now, he needed the job.

The exit suddenly loomed ahead of him. Ben made a quick right turn, thankful there were no other cars behind his, since there had barely been time to signal. Idiot, he thought. He was a good driver, but today his thoughts didn't seem to be behind the wheel. Careful, he cautioned himself. It had taken a long time to get used to Manila traffic, which rivalled any city's he'd been in. So far, he hadn't had any mishaps and he intended keeping it that way. Just concentrate on the road.

Already, it became evident that the neighborhood was not the best. Unlike the bright new edifices that fronted the beach, these houses were in disrepair, and covered in a thin grime that age and industry had wrought.

Steering around a pot-hole in the street, he slowed for a red light up ahead. Crossing the street in front of his car were two young women. Both were dark Filipina girls, both of them lovely. But it was the taller one he had his eye on. Her long, blue-black hair caught the sun and seemed to shimmer as a light breeze moved it from her shoulders. Flipping her head, she raised her arm and tucked the hair back behind her shoulder, the movement pulling the flower-printed shift she wore tight across her small, high breasts, where the shadow of a nipple pressed against the yellow cloth.

He was glad for the red light, which allowed him the time to enjoy what he saw. The girls moved away, the taller one's hips moving gracefully as she retreated down the street, her high heels barely clicking along the stone pavement.

A car honked behind him. The light was green now. Christ, he thought, where is my mind?

He stepped on the gas. Your mind is on sex. And no wonder. It's been a long time. Too long.

Six months ago a brief affair with an English-woman had ended amicably. She was on assignment in Manila as correspondent for her London-based paper. Thinking back on it, he decided that Iris had been one of the best women in his life. Though she swore like a soldier and could drink him under the table, she'd been bright, witty, and great in bed. Ben had been with better looking women, but rarely with one so special. When she'd been called back to London, the question of her staying on in Manila with him never arose. It hadn't been love for either of them, and neither had pretended it was. They'd parted friends, and now, exchanged letters once a month.

Since then, there hadn't been much. An occasional one-night stand he'd connected with at one of the myriad singles bars would take care of his libido, when needed. But the bar scene was not really his "thing." Nevertheless, the image of the beautiful Filipina girl in yellow stayed with him. He thought maybe soon he might have to make an excursion to one of those singles places, if only to be able to concentrate on work again. He smiled. The girl had had a passing resemblance to another girl he knew. Lucy Case.

He'd met her at the Pemberton Institute, a place he'd visited often, and though he'd thought about asking Lucy out, there was something about her that seemed a trifle strange. He'd decided to leave well enough alone. Besides, she seemed to have no interest in him at all.

The Pemberton Institute. Wait a minute, he thought. Wasn't Marc supposed to leave soon on that expedition to . . . to where? New Guinea? Someplace like that.

Ben made a mental note to call Marc soon . . . he couldn't have left already, could he?

He would miss his friend. Friend. Ben was pleased to be able to use that word. For so long, "mentor," "teacher," had been more apt. But they were both older now, and Chicago was long behind them.

Ben admired Marc probably more than any other man he'd ever met. Admired, and in some ways, envied him. Here he was, in mid-life, and on his way to an adventure; a new discovery. Pemberton, it seemed, had never stopped growing; reaching. A man with a dream and a purpose. It kept him young, Ben knew. And, Marc was his own boss. He answered to no one but himself and to his conscience. Oh, sure, he had to keep tabs on how his Institute spent the money from the various grants it would receive; itemize and report the expenditures back to whatever Foundation had shelled out the money. But it had little to do with being "employed" as such, and having to keep some boss happy, no matter how it rubbed against the grain of what you felt to be right and honest.

Whoa, he thought. Boy, this whole thing has really got you by the swingers, doesn't it?

It did. There was no arguing with that. It would be great to get away from this mess. He thought of Marc, there in some remote, unnamed jungle, sleeping out under the sun and the moon, dealing only with the immediate necessities of survival, with no bureaucracy to have to buck. It sounded good. If nothing else, it could get you back in touch with the simplicity of what, in the final analysis, you were: a male animal inside nature's design.

All that aside, Marc had Dana to boot. A great woman on every score. He envied him that too.

Was Marc alone out there? No. Ben seemed to remember some question as to which of the girls he'd take with him. Margery, Ben would guess. Of the two, it would seem she'd probably be more help; unless Dana'd insisted on keeping her there with her. But he discounted the idea as being out-of-character for Dana.

Marc Pemberton. Lucky Marc.

As his car rounded a street corner on the left, he

could see the police barricades and beyond it, the cop cars and ambulances.

Well, gird your loins; here we are.

Inside the darkened bedroom, a cold draft blew in from the closed window, but Mary Pemberton was too weary to move from the overstuffed easy chair she sat in. Merely pulling the folds of her flannel bathrobe more tightly about her, she yawned and put her bare feet up on the edge of the cushion, hugging her knees. The luminous dial on the clock read three A.M. In five hours she would have to leave for work, and the prospects of getting any rest until then were practically nil. Even if she could calm her racing thoughts enough to bring on sleep, the constant coughing and sneezing that came now from the bathroom would certainly keep her wide awake.

The evening had started out badly; but lately, that seemed to be par for the course. They'd been lovers for two years, but it wasn't until Gordon had moved in with her, eleven months ago, that things began to change. For the worse, she at last admitted to herself. This arrangement doesn't seem to be working out.

She shivered as another blast of cold air came at her. The storm windows her landlord had installed (as an "energy saving precaution") were entirely defeated by the gaping cracks around the molding that allowed the invading Chicago winter inside. They'd raised her rent for this privilege, too, making a tight financial situation even tighter. Gordon certainly wasn't helping out on that score.

He'd been out of a job for three months and didn't seem too upset about Mary virtually supporting him, much less eager to find another job. He hadn't qualified for unemployment insurance benefits and his meager savings had been spent long ago. Granted, he was a musician and frequently unemployed, but as she had suggested two weeks ago, some people do *other* things, just to pull in some badly needed funds. Of course, this suggestion had brought on a monumental and truly memorable fight. He'd walked out. She'd been almost relieved. But he'd come back. He had no place else to stay, having already exhausted the hospitality and help from what friends he had left.

She winced as another coughing fit emitted from the bathroom down the hall.

"Gordon, did you take more of that cough medicine I bought?" she called.

"Yes," Gordon gagged as a sneeze forced itself through the hacking.

"Then close the door!"

The walls shook as he slammed it shut.

"Have another cigarette while you're in there!" she screamed full voice.

Before the onset of his cold, he had had severe smokers cough. No wonder, at three packs a day. Damn good thing he was a pianist and not playing woodwinds or brass. He'd never have the breath to blow a note. Though at least those instruments would be cheaper than the upright in the living room, that *she'd* paid for; that *he* rarely played.

At first the coughing hadn't bothered her. But in recent months she'd come to find it disgusting, especially since this cold. More and more, cold or not, it interfered with their sex life.

The thought hit her as something of a revelation, because she suddenly realized what had made her love him . . . or think she loved him. It was his body, and the way he used it. The way he used hers. And that was part of it. Lately, she felt as if her own body was merely being used. The time spent at it was now very short . . . sex, not making love.

That night, she'd come home very tired from work. Her superior's boss had been at her all day. Mary's supervisor drank, to the extent that his work wasn't getting done. So, she did *his* work plus her own. Things were piling up, but since *someone* was getting the work out, the fact that her boss was too drunk most of the time to get anything accomplished went unnoticed. But now there was too much for one person to handle, and the office manager had yelled at *her* for not getting her boss's duties finished.

All she wanted was a quiet evening. She almost looked forward to coming home to nurse Gordon, make some soup, listen to some music or watch a little TV with him. But no. He'd been in the house, cooped up all day. He'd insisted upon going out for dinner. She'd pay, of course.

"It's freezing, Gordon. You'll turn that cold into pneumonia!"

"I'll bundle up. We won't go far. Just around the corner. C'mon. I've got to get out."

He'd coughed so severely in the restaurant she'd been surprised they hadn't been asked to leave. Of course, he chain smoked his Pall Malls whenever there wasn't food in his mouth, pulling wads of tissue from his jacket pocket to blow his nose and dabbing at his watering eyes. But, she'd thought, it will be better when we get home.

It was worse, eventually. He suddenly decided to get romantic. Mary wasn't in the mood . . . which seemed the case more often than not, these days. Besides, it only increased *her* chances of catching the bug. Still, he'd been attentive, gentle, passionate, and at last aroused her with long, slow foreplay, manipulating her with his hands and fingers and mouth.

He'd been inside her, pounding away, driving her mad. It was *very* good for the first time in weeks. She hadn't had to close her eyes and pretend it was a different man moving within her; hadn't had to be careful not to call him by the name of that night's fantasy. She was very close.

Then suddenly, Gordon started coughing fiercely, and sneezed directly into her face. Mary tried to ignore it, tried to keep herself within the moment, straining at the pleasure she was so near. But it was impossible. He continued to sneeze and cough while still pushing at her, and she knew he'd already reached his orgasm and was quite literally only going through the motions. Don't bother for my sake, she thought.

"Gordon," Mary whispered, her hands slapping his hairy shoulder blades, matted in sweat, "blow your nose."

In a second, he was out of her and racing to the bathroom, his erection bouncing ridiculously up and down in front of him. She was reminded of a divining rod.

After he'd been in there for five minutes, hacking away, she'd gotten up, put on her robe and moved to the chair where she now sat shivering.

No, things just weren't working out, were they?

She wished she could speak with her father. But the thought of trying to put the call through, then attempt to talk with him about all that was on her mind while Gordon sulked and made snide comments, decided her against the call. She'd already been through it the last time she'd spoken with him.

The bathroom door swung open and bounced off the wall as Gordon padded down the hallway, still naked, and entered the bedroom. He went immediately to the night table and lit a cigarette.

"Oh, Gordon," she muttered.

"What?"

"Nothing. Feeling better?"

"Much. Chilly in here though, huh? Sorry I slammed the door." He got into bed, his back against the headboard, blue smoke drifting toward the window in the moonlight. He patted her side of the mattress three times and said, "Now, where were we?"

"You can't be serious."

"Well, half serious, anyway. Why not?"

"I think I'm past it for tonight, Gordon."

"Oh." He took a drag of his cigarette. "Something on your mind?"

"No. Nothing in particular. Just thinking."

"About what?"

Mary hesitated, then replied, "My father."

She regretted saying it as soon as the two words had been spoken. Gordon disliked her father, even though he'd never met him.

"Christ," he said in disgust, "again?"

"You know, you make it sound like I've got some kind of father fixation or something. I don't. I just miss him once in a while."

"It's a lot more than just once in a while, baby. Money and your father are all you ever seem to talk about lately."

"Maybe because right now I have neither."

"Don't start on either, alright? I'm sorry I brought it up."

Was it true? Did she think about, talk about, her father so much? Mary didn't think so.

"Why do you hate him, Gordon?"

"I don't. I just resent him."

"But why? You don't even know him."

"I know enough 'cause you keep telling me. Comparing me to him. I'm nothing like him and you might as well start accepting that."

"Oh, you're nothing like him alright."

"You see!" he screamed, swinging his feet to the floor, his dirty blond hair made luminous by the light from the window. "You dig at me every chance you get, to remind me what a great man he is and what a great man I'm not!"

"Gordon, he *is* a great man. And I never said . . ."

"You never have to say! He's twenty years older than I am. He's had time for success!"

Gordon took a deep long drag and went immediately into another coughing fit that wracked his body. Leaning into the night table, he crushed the cigarette in the ashtray, the veins in the well muscled arm casting moving shadows on his flesh. Though she'd said she was "past it," the sight of that arm gave her a brief sexual stir, and she was reminded once again what this attraction, this "relationship," was based upon.

Was it right? Was she being too rough on him? Had she always been? And if not always, then when had she started being so hard? Because in some ways, he was right, she supposed. She did weigh her father's success with Gordon's . . . failure? No, it wasn't failure. He was too young yet for that word to be applicable. But it was her lover's lack of ambition . . . his downright laziness, that was beginning to get to her.

Breathing heavily, he'd leaned back against the headboard once more, his hands behind his head. His cough had subsided again for a time, but she could hear the little wheeze in his throat, now the only sound in the room.

"You alright, Gordon?"

He gasped, pulling in enough air to say, "Yeah, but God dammit, this cold is knocking the hell out of me."

Mary rose and walked over to the bed. He moved over to the left and made room for her to sit on the edge of the mattress. His eyes were closed. She ran a hand along his naked legs, feeling goose-bumps on his skin, and pulled the covers up over him.

"Put your arms down," she ordered. He obeyed, allowing her to tuck the comforter over his shoulders and beneath his chin. "There," she said, "you should stay warm, you know."

He nodded. "Thanks, baby."

"Honey, listen . . ."

"Uh, oh," he laughed.

"What?"

"I hear motherly advice coming, don't I?"

"I guess," she whispered, smiling. "I don't mean to nag."

"I know. What were you going to say?"

"I just don't want to see you end up with emphysema or something."

"Baby, it's a cold. That's all."

"Yes, yes . . . but the cough is from the smoke, Gordon."

"Yeah, yeah. Alright. I'll try to cut down."

"Gordon . . ."

"Mary, I said I'll cut down. Give it a rest?"

She stretched out on the mattress next to him, laying on top of the blankets in her robe, her head resting on the bicep of his extended right arm. "Listen," he said, "what time is it in Manila right now?"

Mary felt herself tense; was he going to start in on it again?

"Why?"

"I just thought, if you miss your old man so much, you could give him a call."

"I'd thought of that. But the call takes so long to put through. It's all the way around the world, practically. And it's so expensive . . ."

"Oh, Mary, stop thinking of money all the time." He squeezed her.

"Someone has to."

Gordon heaved an exasperated sigh. It annoyed her, but she decided not to pursue it. It was late. She was too tired to fight about it anymore tonight. Slipping her hand inside the covers, she gently ran her fingers over his chest.

"Tired?" she asked.

She couldn't see his face, but she knew he was grinning. His left hand covered hers and moved it very slowly down his chest, over his stomach, coming to rest between his legs, where he placed her palm over his partially erect penis. She did not pull away, but began stroking him, while his hand and fingers carressed the soft down on her arms, running over the smooth skin to her shoulder. Pulling her across and over his own body, he kissed her, his tongue gently prodding. She opened her lips to accept him.

"You're insatiable," she murmured with a smile, wrapping both arms around his neck.

"It must be the cold. I should get sick more often, I guess."

Then he coughed. He coughed again.

"Gordon . . ."

"It'll pass, it'll pass. Sshhh," he urged, quieting her, and he was right. The cough did pass.

He untied her robe, exposing her firm body to the moonlight. The comforter still lay as a thin veil between them, separating their naked bodies from contact with each other, though they lay now pressed against one another, and passion rose in her as his hardness pushed at her.

They remained as such for a while, until neither could stand it a moment longer, and she was beneath the blankets with him, filled with him.

He coughed again. His nose was running.

Her eyes stayed closed and from the fog of the day, she summoned a man who had sat on the bus across from her on her return from work. A stranger. She'd never seen him before. But he was naked now, on top of her now, in her now . . . not Gordon . . . but this new man, this new body. This stranger; this fantasy.

Later, once Gordon had at last fallen asleep, she carefully got out of bed, pulled on her robe and went into the living room. Lighting a lamp, she sat on the couch with her bare feet propped up on the coffee table. It was useless to try and sleep now, she thought. It was after four in the morning.

Against the wall across the room, Gordon's upright piano stood waiting to be played. There was a thin powder of dust across the leather seat of the bench that faced it.

What would the space look like if the piano weren't there?

As she began rearranging the furniture of the room in her mind's eye, it gradually dawned upon her that she wasn't picturing the upright in another spot. Not seeing it as moved elsewhere in the living room, but seeing it as gone. Removed. The space before the wall was empty.

For the first time in eleven months she wondered

what it might be like to be once more by herself in this apartment.

Then Mary sneezed.

Oh, no. My turn.

THREE

She listened.

Deep, black night seemed to move in, not from the sky above, but rather from every side, encroaching, slowly penetrating through the lush jungle that surrounded her.

The campfire flickered evenly, no breeze disturbing its steady glow, the sound of its crackling mixed with the dim, far off noises of a hot jungle night, and the soft, white rush of the nearby surf. Now and then, a bird called out, and occasionally, the cry of some unknown, unidentifiable beast broke through the dark, unrelenting silence.

Near her foot lay a small pile of crumpled up, discarded note paper, the refuse of an evening's hard work. Margery picked one up and tossed it gingerly into the center of the fire. The flames flared momentarily, casting long shadows over the camp grounds, illuminating the four large tents that stood like sentinels, fending off the wildness beyond.

The heat of the fire and the heat of the night made her damp, and a fine sheen of perspiration glowed from her high forehead. Her long, straight nose was shiny, and the smooth, taut skin over her prominent cheek bones was tanned and glistening. Her hair was brown, but the bright New Guinea sun had bleached much of it nearly blonde. A few of these hairs had escaped from the roll at the back of her head, and had annoyingly matted wetly against her moist skin. She pulled at them, smoothing them back behind her ears.

From the closest tent, she heard the tinkle of glass against glass, and knew that Dr. Pemberton had mixed two warm martinis, in keeping with his nightly ritual, signifying the end of the work day.

Margery glanced at her watch. It was nearly eleven; a much longer day than usual, but a good day; a rewarding day. She was tired in a good way, and looking forward to her drink. For a moment, she allowed herself to muse on how lovely it would be if it were cold; a freezing cold martini in a stemmed cocktail glass, properly chilled. Then, realizing it did no good to daydream, she turned her head and saw his body silhouetted within the tent, watching as it dropped an olive into each water glass, placed both upon a tray, and pick up the tray carefully with one hand, leaving his other free to open the tent flap and emerge into the flickering fire light.

As he maneuvered his way from the tent and began walking toward her, she was reminded of that last afternoon at the Manila Airport; the image of him politely winding through the crowd of travellers with a tray of martinis. The same ritual, but totally different circumstances in every other way. No longer surrounded by thousands of people; no Dana, no Lucy . . . no air-conditioning . . . not even any ice! My, you're getting spoiled, she said to herself. Still, they were alone, in the middle of nowhere. And martinis they were; makeshift though they may be. It was as if in doing this, Marc brought with him to the jungle a small vestige of what he deemed "civilization."

He placed the tray on the ground beside her, then sat at Margery's feet and, handing her her drink, said, "Thank you, for good work on a long, hard day."

Another toast, she thought, smiling at him, and raising her glass, touched his with hers. The dull, flat "clunk" of the glasses reminded her again of how utilitarian life had become.

She took a sip, winced and coughed. "My God, Marcus! You make these things dryer every night!"

His smile broadened and he popped an olive into his mouth, chewing it contentedly. "We're running low on vermouth."

In archaeological circles, Marcus Pemberton was practically a legend, and Margery had jumped at the chance to be associated with him. She knew he was fond of her, and that he considered himself lucky to have her; he'd told her so, and she believed him. Moreover, she had heard it from his partner, Dr. McKinley as well. Margery was accomplished, knowledgeable and reasonably devoted.

Though she'd only been in Manila a short time, she had not realized how fond of the city she had grown until she'd spent her first night in the jungle. The thrill Margery had felt at being asked to accompany him had paled with the reality of what they were facing now, and in the days to come.

Though the little apartment she shared, back in Manila, was nothing to boast of, she did miss it and its comfort.

Her roommate, Lucy, had shown Margery around the town, and they'd become good friends, after a time. Margery felt she was just beginning to know the city at last, and had begun to strike out on her own; something that Lucy had seemed hurt over. Then Dr. Pemberton had asked her to join him on the expedition. She smiled now, recalling how openly envious her roommate had been. Lucy was sure that they were going to have a great adventure here, while she, Lucy, was 'stuck' back in the city with the everyday, hum-drum mechanics of book research. There had even been some mention as to how lonely she'd be while Margery was gone. If she only knew. This place had to be the loneliest spot on earth.

With a guide and two native men to aid in the heavy work, they had set out from Manila, eager for discovery. But even now as Margery sat sipping her warm martini, it no longer seemed exciting. Perhaps later on, when more of their delving revealed to them the solutions of the mysteries they were trying to unravel, it would once again be fun. Years from now, it might make an amusing anecdote. Anyway, she hoped so.

For now, it was hot, and primitive, and frightening; especially tonight. For whatever reason, there seemed something in the air; an extra "thickness" in the atmosphere; an indefinable quality about the night that filled her with a foreboding she was not accustomed to. Margery thought of herself as a level headed young woman and not prone to an overactive imagination. Nevertheless, she continued, occasionally letting her eyes wander to the perimeter of their camp, searching the darkness for something she felt was out there, waiting.

She wished they had camped on the beach. However, it being largely pebble and rock, this smooth clearing encircled by lush vegetation, had seemed a better idea at the time. Now, she wasn't so sure. The other men were gathered in one of the tents, playing cards, and even they seemed more quiet tonight than was usual.

Her thoughts returned once again to Manila, and the comfort and safety of her own little apartment. She wondered what Lucy was doing right now.

"What are you thinking?" Marcus asked.

"Oh, I'm just a little homesick tonight, I guess."

"I know what you mean."

"Do you miss Dana?"

Marcus looked at his assistant for a long moment, then sipped his drink, characteristically raising both brows as he did so. The warm martinis were hardly a substitute for the nightly ritual he and Dana McKinely had begun back in Manila. After Lucy and Margery would go home from work, it had become a custom for Marc and Dana to take their drinks out into the garden at the back of the house and sit quietly together. The bond between them was unspoken and complete. It was at these times he was reminded that their partnership was a success on any level; as scientists, friends, and lovers. Right now, he missed being able to talk with Dana.

"Yes," he finally answered, "of course. And you?"

"Me?" Margery asked, "What about me?"

"Well, since we're on the subject, is there a man?"

A man, Margery thought.

Well, there was her father, but Marcus didn't mean him, of course.

She was closer to him than anyone; had even

helped him through his collapse—his second—a few years back. She'd only been a child when the first one occurred, when her mother had left them. Her single misgiving about accepting this job was leaving her father. But, he had insisted. Now she was glad he had, but she still worried about him; his heart, his nerves. And like a fool, she herself may have aggravated that situation; jeopardized his well being. She'd told him in her last letter that she'd call as soon as she knew when they were to leave Manila for New Guinea. But with the excitement and preparations, it had completely slipped her mind until after the plane had taken off. Her Dad was planning on retiring soon, and would come over then for a visit to see her, the date contingent on her departure and return to Manila. He could be making his travel arrangements now, if she'd remembered to call.

Yes, she thought. Right now, he is *the* man in my life. Oh, of course, there had been boys—one, especially, in college. But it had been a brief affair, something she passed through during a semester. Nothing more. But no, no man. There had never been a "man."

"Not since I arrived in Manila, anyway."

"You're from Boston originally?"

She nodded.

There was a noise from the jungle; a stirring that made them both look up suddenly. They listened carefully, but all that came to them was the constant sound of waves moving in and out at the shore line.

Margery took a pack of cigarettes from her khaki shirt pocket and withdrew one.

"I'm so jumpy tonight," she said. He held out his lighter to her, saying, "Me too," and laughed, embarrassed at his show of nerves.

"Thank you," she inhaled on the freshly lit cigarette, "Oh, your lighter's gorgeous, Marcus."

He dropped it into her opened palm and stole a brief glance out into the darkness that surrounded them. Sweat stood out evenly on his forehead, and damp rings darkened the cloth under the arms of his shirt. Yet, despite the added heat, he was grateful for the fire.

The lighter had caught the glow of the fire and a small spot of light was cast upon her face. He watched her as she studied it.

"It's really beautiful," she said. It was an oblong shaped pipe lighter, exquisite in its simplicity; a heavy, substantial piece of gold. But closer scrutiny revealed an inscription etched into the metal, across the outer edge. " 'M—FOREVER—M,' " she read.

She gave him back his lighter. Holding it, he grinned, "Can't you guess who 'M' is?"

She thought for a moment, then shook her head. "It isn't me, I know."

"It's Mary. She gave this to me two years ago."

Marcus decided to have a smoke, and reached into his shirt pocket, drawing out his beloved Meerschaum pipe, yellowed with age and frequent use. Dipping it into the worn leather pouch he carried with him, he packed the bowl firmly and lit it. His was a blend heavy with Turkish Latakia tobacco, and as he puffed, the sultry night air filled with the distinct aroma, by now so familiar to Margery.

He exhaled a plume of smoke and she watched it rise and travel out across the camp, into the tangle of trees to mingle and become one with the jungle. Marcus was staring once more at his lighter when she looked back at him. He really *is* homesick, she thought.

"I should have know, Marc. How long since

you've seen each other?"

"Mary? Oh, almost a year now," he sighed absently, slipping his lighter back into his pocket.

"You're due for a visit, I'd say."

"Oh, yes. You're quite right. Soon, perhaps. It'd be good to get home . . . back to the states, I mean, for a while."

"Wouldn't it?" she agreed.

"In fact, if everything goes as smoothly as it has up to now, from here on in, I think we can tentatively plan on a return in, say, a month?"

He laughed at seeing her face beam back at him in a wide, happy smile that made him aware of just how very young she really was.

"Oh, Marcus! You mean it?" Maybe not calling her father was Providence. Maybe *she* could go home to him?

"I don't see why not. Things are moving along beautifully, thanks to your help. You've earned it."

"You're very kind. Thank you," she drew on her cigarette, "and you're absolutely correct. Anyway, it'd be good to see my Dad again."

"And now, I think it's time we called it a night. We've an early day tomorrow."

Just the thought of it made him yawn. He downed the last of his drink.

"How early?" she asked.

"Four."

"Oh, God."

"The men have packed up just about everything. We should be able to break camp and be on our way in the boats by five; five-thirty, at the very latest."

"Are you excited, Marcus?"

"In a way. Stopping here only reinforced my theory. This had to have been the last stop before embarking for the Island. Everything points to it.

So, obviously there have been others in the past, who wanted to get there. The Chief as good as admitted that.''

This was the third trip he'd made to this part of the world, and now his search had widened to the Bismarck Sea, and here to this island of Savong-khai. It was the largest in a cluster of small New Guinea Islands, and it was here that they had found what he had hoped for.

They had arrived from Port Moresby two days ago by air, making an uncertain landing in a makeshift air field. Marcus had been able to contact one of the local Chiefs, and with a hired interpreter, it was he who had intimated that what Marc searched for really did exist; that Savong-khai was the last point of departure to a place Marc had heretofore only suspected of being fact. Just a few hours ago, he had stood on the beach at dusk and looked across the water to the far shore of a land he was now convinced was Satyr Island, whose black sands had already begun to pull the night in and around itself, as if to hide from his inquisitive eye.

Suddenly it was noticeably darker and Margery realized the two aides and their guide had broken up the card game and returned to their respective tents. The only light now came from Pemberton's tent, and from the fire. It seemed a meager defense against the towering blackness that had now moved still closer.

She was very tired and wanted to get to sleep, especially in view of having to rise at such an ungodly hour, and an even longer, more arduous day ahead to face. She was not too certain how sturdy she was when it came to travel on water, nor how sturdy the boats were that they were to travel in, being little more than hollowed out tree trunks.

"Well, good night, Marcus. Thanks, as usual for the 'silver bullet'."

He laughed. That was his pet name for the powerful drinks. "Hope it does the job, my dear. Thanks, as usual, for the company. Sleep well, Margie."

She gave him a little wave. He was the only person she tolerated being called "Margie" by.

Marc watched her walk away from him toward her tent, still puffing on her cigarette. He took note of the sway of her hips, keeping in mind that she was, after all, younger than his own daughter, but still noting how very attractive she was. Sex turned his thoughts once again to Dana and he grinned, thinking of the good time they'd have upon his return.

Marcus brushed the dry earth off his trousers and, placing the empty glasses on the tray, began walking slowly back to his tent, his pipe clenched between his teeth.

At about the time that Marcus Pemberton emerged from his tent carrying the tepid martinis to Margery Croft, three small crafts approached the shore line.

The moon had turned the surf a glittering silver and the silhouette of the canoes showed black against the phosphorescent shimmer of moving water. Swiftly, silently, they cut across the horizon and rode the last waves in, one by one coming to rest on the dark, rocky beach.

There were nine shadows, all male, that crept from the boats and began to move up the beach quietly toward the light coming from the Pemberton expedition. The night sky dimly lit their nearly naked bodies and beneath them, the sharp rocks of the beach had seemingly no effect on their bare feet.

Once they had drawn close enough to the encampment, they split up, separating until they had completely surrounded the five people. They knew to wait until they'd received the vocal signal from the one who led them, and as they moved into their positions, one of them tripped over a large root that had forced its way up through the ground. He landed with a thud, sending a few birds and small crawling animals scurrying in various directions to escape.

The other eight shadows became immediately still, not moving or breathing, their bright eyes fixed on the white man and woman who sat close to their fire, drinking. The intruders did not dare to commence their movements again until they saw the woman reach for a cigarette and the man light it for her with a bright shiny lighter. The small metal object caught the glow of the fire like a tiny star in the man's hand, causing a small pin-spot of brightness to fall on the woman's face. From then on, the watching figures sat quietly on their haunches as the two people in the center of the clearing drank and smoked.

When the white man yawned and finished his drink, the leader withdrew a long, sharp blade from his scabbard, that was slung around his ample waist. The woman stood and stretched as one by one, the other crouching figures followed their leader's suit, and withdrew similar weapons, keeping them low, lest they catch the fire light.

At just that moment, much of the light from the camp was extinguished, and the nine men watched the two aides leave one tent and enter another. Then the man and woman said a few more words to each other, and the woman walked to her tent, still smoking her cigarette. Two or three of the spying faces smiled at seeing the man watch her walk away.

After the white man had risen from the ground,

brushed off his trousers and carried a tray of empty
glasses into his tent, the figures in the jungle
silently crept from the shadows, their weapons held
high at the chirping sound that came as their signal
from The Leader.

Then, they began their work.

Drawing back the flap, she entered the bleak tent
and had a momentary flash of deja-vu. It stopped
her and she stood, thinking back, trying to place the
memory just evoked. It came to her as she struck a
match to light the kerosene lamp near her sleeping
bag. She was walking into a darkened room with her
father, and many voices yelled "Surprise!"
Frightening at first, then thrilling. It had been her
tenth birthday party. She grinned, recalling how
pleased her father had been at really pulling off a
genuine surprise, and her grin widened at the
thought of seeing him again soon. Marcus certainly
did remind her of him; she was thinking more about
her father lately than she had in months.

Her cigarette had almost burnt into the filter. She
looked about her for the little ash tray she'd brought
with her from the apartment, and finally threw the
smoldering butt into the small well of cold coffee
remaining at the bottom of the cup she'd drank from
that morning. It sizzled and went out, turning to
black mud at the bottom of the mug.

"Charming," she said aloud to herself, and remembered once again her promise to herself that she
would *try* to stop smoking. Perhaps when she got
back to Manila, she and Lucy could try giving it up
together.

Yawning, she began to unbutton the damp shirt
she'd had on, wishing dreamily that a lovely warm
bath were possible.

Just then, she thought she heard something—something different, something she'd never heard here before. Like a cry, or a brief scream, that had been quickly cut off; silenced before it had had time to reach full volume. She stopped her action and strained her ears for another noise, but none came.

It was one of the many things she hated about the place. Since she didn't know enough about the jungle to know which creatures were dangerous and which weren't, she remained afraid of them all, and *why* did every single one of them seem to have a special talent for making strange, fearful noises?

The kerosene lamp was beginning to smoke and the fumes were making her sick. She turned down the wick and said a silent prayer of thanks to Thomas Edison.

With her back to the entrance of the tent she removed her shirt, then the brassiere, freeing her small, high breasts, and kicking off her shoes, she took off her trousers and threw them in a heap in the corner, too tired to fold them.

She reached for the light, short cotton nightie and slipped it over her head.

Margery didn't see what stood just outside her tent, only four feet from her, a mere piece of canvas seperating her from what was watching, waiting.

It didn't look human.

Nearly six feet and six inches high, it weighed over three hundred pounds. The dying camp fire in the clearing accentuated the hills and valleys of its muscled arms and legs, shining with sweat, where it was not covered in sparse, coarse auburn hair. Tangled in its scalp were ferns, leaves and other greenery that sprung every which way about its head. Across the broad face, red slashes of paint had been applied in thick masses that scarred its cheeks and mouth.

This was the Leader.

He himself took no part in what had happened—
what was happening now, in the other tents in the
encampment.

He guarded the Woman.

Around him, the others were beginning to emerge
from the tents. Their job was to kill, and to kill
silently. They would hear from him about the
scream. He did not want the woman alerted until the
last possible moment.

The guide and two aides were dead, their throats
cut without a sound. Now, seven men stood before
the Leader. They were all big; not as big as he, but
massive things nevertheless. A few were splattered
with the blood they had spilled. All were nearly
naked, with tusks or feathers protruding from the
nose on their painted red faces; all their bodies
covered with a thin overlay of reddish hair.

On their backs, beneath the left shoulder blade,
they had all been scarred with a small, circular
mark, not unlike a bull's eye, containing three
complete rings.

The Leader became impatient, waiting anxously
for the eighth member of the team to appear.

This last of the killers, who alone wore yellow
paint, was still in Marcus Pemberton's tent.

It was Pemberton who had cried out and his killer
knew that it would not sit well with the Leader. The
yellow man had decided then, to take a few extra
moments there. The last of the many things he did
inside the tent was to discover the small pipe
lighter, and read the inscription. "M—FOREVER
—M".

He used it to set the tent on fire. As the flames
began to catch, he withdrew.

Outside once more, he saw the Leader throw back the flap of the Woman's tent.

Margery had just pulled the nightie over her head and was beginning to tug at the edges until they met all around to fall just above her knees. It was pale blue and the bottom was fringed in pink lace—not my style at all, she thought; in fact, it was horrible. But it was cool.

From behind her, she heard the flap of her tent abruptly thrown back and in that split second, wondered who would be that rude not to ask permission to enter; then thought, of course, that could only have been Marcus, and then, that something must be wrong. She began to turn, when a huge arm came from behind her and wrapped itself around her throat.

Margery Croft was carried through the camp and into the jungle that she hated, terror stricken, kicking wildly and screaming for her life.

Before she was ultimately knocked unconscious, she saw what looked to her to be a huge, orange balding thing with a painted yellow face standing before the tent of Marcus Pemberton, now in flames.

Its arms were held high.

In one raised fist it brandished a shining blade, drenched in gore.

In the other, silver strands of hair ran through its clutched fingers, and swinging back and forth, suspended by those hairs, hung the severed head of Dr. Marcus Pemberton.

FOUR

My Dearest Marc,

So, my third entry since you left.

It hardly seems possible that you're on your way there, considering all the time we spent preparing to get you there.

Since I write this journal to you anyway (and I said "journal," not "diary," darling) you know you're free to "take a peek" (as you threatened to do at the airport) anytime you like. However, I can't be responsible for the shocking things you may read here—not that it will ever be provocative (it's hardly worthy of Mary Astor, I'm afraid), but may be so mundane as to make you lose interest in me entirely. I must try to spice it up for you.

Anyway, here it is Monday again, and I've made it through the whole weekend without you, and so, another week begins. We'll see if we can make it through with business as usual on our own. But, if time seems to be going by so quickly already, you'll be home in no time.

As soon as Lucy arrives (she's late again . . . she must assume that since you're gone she can get away with it . . . I'm not quite the stickler on office hours as you) I plan on having her do another test on the Pausanias scroll. The new solution we'd read about was delivered this morning. Perhaps it will read the acidity of the parchment more accurately than what we've tried in the past. Maybe not, but it's worth the try . . . and will keep Lucy occupied. I'm going to see if I can keep her as busy as I can. I think that's what she needs. It will help keep her mind off living alone for awhile, as well as hopefully keep her from being constantly reminded that Margery isn't here at work . . . or, for that matter, you. I will admit, it's hard for me to keep my attention on things. Twice already this morning I've spoken aloud and asked you two questions. Then suddenly I'm reminded that you're not here, and my mind wanders off, wondering where the two of you are now. How I wish I could have gone with you.

Just before you boarded, you'd mentioned not having heard from Ben Ramsey. Well, you got me thinking about him too, and since, when you and I eventually speak or write, I'd like to be able to give you some news of him, I called him at his apartment on Saturday afternoon. Unfortunately, I didn't speak to him, but I left a message on his answering machine. He didn't return the call yesterday, but I'm hoping he'll call back today. If not, I'll try calling him at the Manilamerican, but you know it's practically impossible to reach him there."

As Dana placed the period at the end of the sentence, she heard the door bell ring at the front of the house. She closed the book and started from her desk in the library, through the living room of their private quarters.

On the way, she caught sight of herself as reflected in the hallway mirror, and was once again struck by the fact that lately, she didn't seem to be too fond of what looked back at her. As yet, however, she'd not allowed herself the time to study the reflection and figure out exactly what it was that displeased her, or, for that matter, what to do about it once she had.

Tucking her red rayon blouse inside her khaki bermudas, she opened the door.

Ben Ramsey stood on the enclosed porch, smiling at her.

"Ben!" Dana exclaimed, hugging him as he stepped in. The cool room was a welcome relief from the hot, sticky day.

"Good to see you, Dana," he replied, returning the hug, then putting an arm around her waist as she closed the door and led him through the living room.

"Can I get you something? Ice tea or a lemonade?"

Ben said yes to the tea.

"Good. You go on back to the library while I get the drinks. The air-conditioning in there is something below hurricane force. I'll be right in."

Marc wasn't in the library as Ben had expected. Must be in the lab, he thought, but knew better than to disturb him. Ben crossed the room, past the shelves of strange books that lined the walls, to the door leading out to the tiny back yard and garden. Through its small window, he could see a pair of work gloves and shears laying on the grass near some freshly dug soil, and knew Dana had been at work early that morning. She was proud of her garden, and rightfully so.

"Here we are." Dana entered with two ice teas on a tray. "I'm glad you dropped by instead of returning the call, Ben."

"Returning the call?"

Dana explained about the message she'd left.

Dammit. The machine must be on the fritz again; he'd never gotten any message. Everything in his apartment seemed to be falling apart; his typewriter was acting up too.

"Well," she laughed, "you're here now. You must have read my mind."

"Hardly. I kept meaning to call, and never got around to it. But I had some free time this morning and I was in the neighborhood. Thought I'd look in on you people."

"It's about time. We haven't heard from you in weeks. Marc even mentioned it to me."

"I've missed you . . . both of you. And I wanted a little heart-to-heart with Marc. I think I need some 'fatherly' advice."

"Don't let *him* hear you use that term. He's getting a might sensitive about his age, I think."

"I'll rephrase it when I speak to him," Ben promised. "Is he around, or just too busy for me?"

"Ben, he's not here."

"Oh. Well, I can call him tonight and . . ."

"No, Ben. He left already."

"Left?"

"Yes. For New Guinea. Remember?"

Shit, he thought. I was right. I missed him.

"Yes, yes, of course I remember . . . *now*!"

"He was wondering why you hadn't called, Ben."

"Why?" Ben asked acidly. "Did he want to know what to bring me back for a souvenir?"

Dana took a sip of her tea, sat down at the chair

behind her desk and leaned back. "Alright," she said. "What's wrong?"

"When did he leave?"

"Last week. What's wrong, Ben?"

"Nothing . . . well, yes, something. I'm just annoyed with myself that I didn't call him right away when I'd thought to do it."

"You're busy. Marc knows that."

"It's what kept me busy that I wanted to talk to him about. And talking with him was, believe me, far more important than what I've been working on."

"Will it wait? We didn't anticipate this journey taking any longer than three weeks."

"Yeah, it can wait, I guess. It's just . . . a sort of moral dilemma, Dana."

"Ben, I won't pretend I understand, so unless you want to clue me in on the problem, perhaps you'd ought to wait for Marc's return. Or . . ."

"Or?"

"You're a strong man, Ben. Maybe you should figure it out . . . whatever it is . . . by yourself?"

She wasn't being curt; he'd known her for too long to think that. It wasn't Dana's style. She was simply direct. It saved time. Besides, she was right. It was his problem. He should be able to work it out on his own.

He'd started the feature story for the Sunday Edition on the Canlas hostage case. But he'd only gotten the first page or so done when he'd ripped it from his typewriter, disgusted at what he was being forced to do. But he needed the job.

Ben took a sip of his drink, Dana silent and intent on him.

"Okay. Here's what's bugging me."

He briefly told her of the instructions and the warning he'd received.

"I feel like a whore, Dana."

"Well!" said a voice from the doorway. "I *am* shocked!"

Ben turned from the seat he'd taken before the desk to see Lucy standing at the library entrance.

"*There* you are," Dana said wryly, glancing at her wristwatch. "I was going to call you in a bit to see if you were going to bother coming in."

"Sorry," Lucy said as she sauntered lazily into the room and took a sip of Ben's ice tea. "Traffic."

"There's a pitcher of tea in the refrigerator, if you'd like a glass of your own, Lucy. And I do wish you wouldn't sneak up on people like that. You startled me."

Ben was relieved to see Lucy, since it meant Marc *had* decided to take Margery with him.

"How's living alone for you?" he asked.

She shot him a quick, impatient look, slammed his glass down on the desk and answered, "Quiet." She turned to Dana. "What do you want me to do this morning?"

Dana explained about the treatment for the scroll.

"Fine," Lucy stated, and left.

Ben got up and closed the door after her.

When he was sure she was out of ear-shot, he asked, "Why do you put up with that kind of behavior?"

Dana grinned. "Why Ben, I thought you rather liked our Lucy?"

"I like her well enough to look at, Dana, but she spoils it for me once she opens her mouth. Does Marc let her speak to him like that?"

"She doesn't speak to him like that. He's a man, you see. Some women aren't above sexism,

Ben . . . though, to their credit, half of them don't know they're doing it. Lucy just doesn't like other women, I think."

"But she and Margery get along so well."

"Not at first. Anyway, to answer your question, Lucy is tolerated because Lucy is excellent at what she's asked to do. We'd have to go a long way to find another like her."

Ben leaned into her, his hands on the desk.

"Still, Marc took Margery with him, didn't he?"

Dana smirked. "Alright, you've got me there. But honestly Ben . . . wouldn't you?"

He nodded, agreeing with her. Though Margery seemed much younger in her ways, much less sophisticated in her bearing, she was a damn sight friendlier.

"Now," Dana continued, "about your problem . . ."

"No, listen. I'm sorry I mentioned it. You're right. It's my battle. It's probably just as well Marc's away. It'll force me into making my own decisions."

She put her hand over his and looked into his eyes. "Don't sell yourself short. Have faith in your own confidence. You're not an indecisive man, Ben. You'll do the right thing, I know."

He shook his head. "I wish I were as sure as you are."

"Look," Dana said standing, "I can't speak for Marc, God knows, but he and I have been together . . . well, a long time now. I think I know him well enough to venture an educated guess as to what he might say . . . though I'm hardly as eloquent."

"Okay," Ben heaved a sigh, folding his arms across his chest, "I'm ready. Shoot."

She paused to collect her thoughts, moving to the

little window at the rear door as she did so. Her back was to him, and she stood now looking out over her beloved garden.

After a moment, she spoke quietly: "Someone . . . I don't know who, but someone once said that total freedom is an indifference to consequence. Freedom seems to be what you're talking about. Not money. Not really even good journalism, though that's the argument, isn't it?"

She waited for his response without turning. He said "yes" and she continued, "So, it seems to me that the question is one of compromise. You either do it, or you don't. But if you don't, you'll lose your job." She turned and faced him. "You're a good reporter Ben. A good writer. There *are* other jobs, better jobs, for you. Why not face the fact that you're good, and go after what you really want?"

The words humbled him in a strange way, as if she'd given him some sort of blessing that he would have to try and think himself worthy of. He bowed his head, digesting all she'd said, then looked up. It was difficult to speak.

"Thank you," was all he managed.

"Thanks for asking."

Ben picked up his glass and finished his tea. At the door, he said, "I'd kiss you if you weren't married."

"Ha!" she laughed. "I'm not . . . never have been . . . legally, anyway. Although I guess after all these years there's something to be said for common law. I've never looked into it."

"I don't think you'll ever have to."

"No. I think not. But if I had a taste for . . . shall we say 'outside interest' . . . an eye for younger men . . ."

"You're not *that* much older," he chided.

"Oh, stop it, now. I'm not a cradle robber. Go on, get out of here . . . flatterer! I'll be in touch when I hear from Marc."

He laughed loudly and opened the door. "I'll call you toward the end of the week anyway. Thanks, Dana!"

Oh his way out, he passed Lucy coming from the kitchen, a glass of lemonade in her hand.

"So long," he said, heading for the front door.

"Oh, Ben." Lucy called.

He stopped and turned.

"Just to let you know . . . I won't 'open my mouth' anymore when you're around. I wouldn't want to 'spoil' things any more than they already are."

She walked on through the living room and into the lab, slamming the door behind her.

Ben let himself out and got into his beat up old Chevy. So, she'd been listening. Christ, what a weird chick.

Nevertheless, he felt better for the talk with Dana. It seemed to restore his brain, his thinking, to the clarity he'd lacked.

He drove off, if not happy, at least calmer than he'd been all week.

"Manila," Barton Croft answered as he grabbed a canape from a tray being passed by a red-vested waiter.

The lawyer looked at him with some surprise, then sipped his flat champagne from the plastic flute and dabbed at the corners of his moustache with a paper napkin. "Vacation?" he queried further.

The four-piece band in the corner started playing "The Way We Were," and though Barton thought the synthesizer was a bit too loud, it didn't stop a

few couples from drifting out into the center of the
large room to dance.

"Oh, no," Barton laughed, trying to be heard over
the quartet. "She's working there now, Martin."

"Working? I thought she was going to college?"

"Martin, she *did* go to college. She graduated
almost a year ago. How long has it been since we've
talked?"

"Too long, obviously. But what's she doing in
Manila, of all places?"

Barton was pleased his old crony had asked, and
hoped it wasn't too obvious the way he puffed up
with pride at any excuse to talk about his
daughter . . . though "bragging" was closer to what
it was. He explained how Margery had landed a job
with the internationally renown Dr. Marcus Pemberton.

"Who?" Martin asked.

The truth was that Barton himself had not heard
of Pemberton prior to the letter Margery had
received accepting her for the position. Of course,
Margery had instantly teased him for his ignorance
and told him all about The Pemberton Institute.
Since then, and in the ensuing months since her
departure, Barton had read his copies of National
Geographic more carefully, as well as looking up a
few things on his own. He'd been surprised and impressed at the very high regard in which the archaeol-
ogist was held. It had become his practice to grimace
at anyone who didn't know of Pemberton's importance, and he did so now, saying, "Why, he's one
of the most famous researchers in the world,
Martin! And according to Margery, onto something
really hot. He's investigating evolution."

There followed a brief resume of Marcus Pem-

berton, all to give credibility to his daughter's
importance.

"Well," the lawyer said, suppressing a yawn as
his eyes wandered the room for someone . . . *anyone*
else to talk with, "now that you're retiring, you've
got the time to go visit her. I've always been curious
about the Phillipines myself."

Barton had already toyed with that idea. But
Margery had written him that there was talk of a
pending trip to do some research ("Jungle expedition" is how she'd phrased it), but no decision
had been made yet as to when ("in the near future")
it would take place, or whether or not she or her
roommate ("Lucy's been here longer and has lots
more experience, so it'll probably be her") would be
going along.

If Margery remained in Manila, he would plan on
leaving as soon as possible; he'd already gotten his
shots. It seemed a slim chance she'd be chosen for the
journey, but if she was, Barton would postpone his
visit until she returned to Manila.

He'd just finished explaining it all to Martin,
when Lawrence Burbage, Barton's second-in-com-
mand at the store, arrived before him after elbowing
his way through the crowded room.

"I've been trying to get over here to you for ten
minutes," Burbage said, grinning. "So . . . was this
a surprise or not?"

Barton smiled. It had been. On the pretext of
taking him for a farewell drink, Burbage and he had
left work early, Barton saying his goodbyes to his
employees quickly. He'd been trying to avoid the
sentimentality of his retirement. But instead of the
elevator opening up onto the cocktail lounge on the
top floor of the hotel, they'd stopped at the ball

room, where over a hundred people yelled out "Surprise!"

The room had been decorated with crepe paper. Over the sumptuous buffet table, foot-high letters in various colors proclaimed "Good Luck Barton!"

He'd filled up, at a loss for words. Still more people continued to come in through the elevators, including those employees he'd seemingly said goodbye to earlier at work, all pleased at the success of their deception.

A month ago, he had announced to these people that he would be leaving soon, and appointed Lawrence Burbage to chief.

He had opened the store thirty years ago, dealing in small, quality pieces of art and sculpture. It had grown, slowly, of its own accord, from a little shop into two floors of store that rivalled the best in the Boston area. Barton was proud of it, and himself. He had weathered tough times and come through, if a little worse for wear. But at sixty, he wanted more time to himself and felt he could get a jump of five years on other retirees, since he had the money to indulge himself.

His wife had left twenty years ago with another man, bringing on a nervous breakdown. But he had recovered with the help of his sister, and had not remarried, choosing to raise his daughter Margery alone. He thought he'd done a damned good job of it. It was she, in fact, that had seen him through the second major crisis; the shop had nearly gone bankrupt. Strangely though, it was only once he'd pulled it through and the business had been saved, that the really hard time came. He remembered thinking, during the worst of it, "If I can only hang on just a little longer—if I can just stay sane until this is over . . ." Eventually, it was, and once done, he'd needed two months to recover. Margery had helped.

He snapped out of his reminiscing and at last answered Burbage, conceding that yes, it had indeed been a total surprise. With that, Barton looked around to see if Harold Baum were present. He didn't spot him, and was somewhat relieved. Harold had been his doctor for the last ten years, and had warned him repeatedly against any sudden shocks. Fortunately, this party had so far seemed to have had no effect on Barton's ailing heart, but he knew what Baum's reaction would have been if he'd witnessed the "surprise." Barton had not let too many people know of his condition; he'd not wanted to be coddled and treated like an old man with one foot in the grave. But now, he questioned the wisdom of such secrecy. Perhaps in the future, he ought to make at least a few more people aware of his precarious health, if only to avoid someone sneaking up to say "Boo!" and killing him in the bargain. He smiled at the thought. He'd been through so much and survived; prevailed, even. It was almost comical to him that something so simple as a prank or a party could trigger another heart attack.

It was Friday afternoon. He surveyed the room. Now more couples were dancing, the champagne having loosened them up; gearing them into a weekend sensibility that would readjust come Sunday night, when thoughts of the work week ahead of them would surface again, and make them ready for Monday morning.

For the first time in years, Barton had no place to be on Monday morning. It was a double-edged sword. On the one hand, he faced it with a slight twinge of melancholy. Clearly, a page was turning in his life, another milestone reached, and he pondered

how he would react to not having to work anymore.
But it helped cheer him to remind himself that he'd
still be involved with the store, at least on an
advisory basis, and perhaps hunt down and bring in
a few items that he knew would sell.

And there was the other side of it. Not *having* to
work, but doing so only *if* he chose, *when* he chose.
He'd even thought of getting back to painting
again, a hobby he'd all but abandoned long ago for
lack of time. Well, there would be plenty of that,
now. Water color was his favorite medium, and he'd
take up his brushes once more, he vowed, as soon as
he returned from Manila . . . whenever that might
be. And who knows? Perhaps I'll find some interesting, beautiful native sculptures to ship back to the
store. Marcus Pemberton might be able to be a great
help, there.

Barton felt a tap on his shoulder. Minnie Fiorello,
the store's accountant, stood with her arms poised,
her hips moving to the geriatric cha-cha rhythm the
quartet was currently pounding out.

"Dance, Mr. Croft?" She'd worked for him for
over twenty years, and still called him 'Mr. Croft.'

"I'd love to, Minnie," he said, and moved her
rather self-consciously out onto the floor.

"So," she asked, the slight whiff of gin coming to
his nostrils, "when are you making the trip to see
that beautiful little girl of yours?"

"She's not so little anymore, Minnie. You haven't
seen her in a while."

"Ah, they're always little to us . . . to me, anyway.
So when?"

"As soon as I get word from her when it's best for
me to arrive. But soon, I think, Minnie. I'll be seeing
Margery again very soon."

"Give her my love, will you? Oh, it's *so* exciting! I'd be so anxious!"

"I am," Barton said with a wide, transparent grin. "I can hardly wait."

FIVE

The three boats slid out of the surf on to the beach almost in unison, coming to an abrupt halt. The scrape of their bottoms as they grazed along the rough rock and sand was the only noise in the quiet night, beyond the steady rhythm of the sea moving in and out upon the shore. Though the constant rocking motion of the small craft had ceased suddenly, Margery Croft did not awaken.

Dawn had not come as yet and there was still much to do before the sun had risen completely. This work was to be carried out in the dark.

They were all very tired, their arms aching from the manning of the oars, even though each one was tremendously strong. But despite their weariness, seven of them were out of the boats almost immediately, running up the slopes of the dune, into the nearby jungle. They proceeded without pause to various places in the underbrush, removing from these hiding places the tools and implements needed for the forthcoming ceremony. Though the half-light of the night sky was their only illumination, they were familiar with these grounds and made ready with ease, even in this dimness. Of the three remaining on the shore, only one watched the carefully planned, time-honored goings on before him. This watcher was the Big One, the Leader. His massive figure stood within the boat. But for a small cloth that covered his genitals, he was naked.

He turned his head, expecting to look at the painted yellow face of his smaller companion. What he saw instead was the circular bull's eye carved into the flesh of his cohort leaning over the figure of the woman who lay prone on the floor of the boat. One large hand had rested upon her thigh, a thumb just now having reached the dainty pink lace that fringed the nightgown.

The Leader had no fear the woman would be molested by the crouching hulk. That was out of the question. But nevertheless, anger rose within him, even at this show of curiosity, and kicking out his foot, he screamed "No!", sending the Other over the side of the boat, and landing upon the sand. For a moment they stared at each other, the red-stained face of the Leader glaring down. Raising one enormous arm, he pointed into the black jungle, saying, "She is *theirs*."

The Other's eyes followed the Leader's gesture to the beach.

With only seven individuals the beach was alive with activity. Every one the large beings scurried about rapidly, moving their sizable bulk around with cumbersome diligence. To a stranger it may at first glance have appeared as if they moved mindlessly through their duties. However, the two in the boat knew that what they observed was not only planned and executed with care and the know-how that came with years, but also performed from the deepest kind of loyalty and motivated by single-minded self-preservation. Their great size sunk them deeply into the sands with every step they took, leaving huge footprints across the landscape, pitting the once smooth beach, their limping, stilted gait accentuated by the difficulty of movement over those sands.

In due course, an area of about thirty square feet had been prepared and on it a small, crude "arena" or playing area had been erected. Sixteen poles had been placed into the sand at equal distances, forming a circle. In the center, four large stakes were driven in deeply, making a smaller circle, and around each of these, strong rope had been tied, with loose ends spreading toward the middle.

Between the two stakes, closer to the jungle, wooden boxes had been placed five feet from each other. Atop each box stood a small vial.

When their work was done, six figures took their places at appointed spots around the "arena." The seventh took a post midway between the two boxes and stood quite still, yet another pole held in his hands. When all had settled down and were in place, he made a soft, chirping noise that signalled action for those down at the shoreline.

The Leader stepped from the boat and stood on the sand beside it, waiting in the dark. The Other bent awkwardly and lifted the limp figure of Margery Croft in his arms, then flung her over his left shoulder like a rag doll.

The wind began to strengthen and the Leader smiled. It blew hot and strong from the water across the beach, and into the thick growth where the jungle began.

The one with the yellow face, the Other, carried his prey up the dune until he reached the arena. Margery was carefully placed on her back upon the hot sand.

From either side, four others moved in and bound her wrists and ankles to the free ends of the ropes. When they had finished, she was staked, spread-eagled, to the beach. It was then that Margery regained consciousness.

She saw the sky first, black, moody and brushed with a web of clouds across a moon that sped along behind them, eager for the end of this night, and rushing toward the dawn. A drop of cold sweat trickled down from her forehead, over her brow, hung for a moment and fell into her opened eye. She blinked and moved a hand to wipe it away, but the hand would not move and she knew then that she was tied down, rope burning into her wrists. She moved her feet but they too had been bound. She suddenly remembered what had taken place a hundred years ago at the campsite—the huge things that had attacked them then surrounded her now, and the most horried of them all was standing above, his hideous yellow face staring down at her.

She screamed.

The Other waited a moment, his massive arms folded in front of him, enjoying the sight of this woman half-mad with fright. He reached down with both his hands and tore the nightgown and panties away, exposing her to the night.

The seven all moaned simultaneously and the Other handed the garment to the seventh, who wrapped it around the pole he carried. Another stepped forward, it was ignited and the pole became a flaming torch. It was handed back to the Other, who stood squarely between Margery's legs and moved it up and down three times in the sand. Margery screamed again, the disgusting yellow face lit bizarrely in the firelight, which grew even brighter as the torch was then passed around the square. All sixteen poles had been lit now, and Margery lay helpless, nude beneath the glaring light.

I'm going insane, she thought as sheer terror washed over her like a sea wave. She was wet with it, her body breaking out in new, fresh sweat, glistening in the flickering glow.

When the circle had been completely ignited, the Leader made his way slowly up the beach. He joined them at the head of the circle, the Other moving to his right as he was replaced by the giant presence with the scarlet face. It spoke in a deep sonorous bass:

"This is the honored Female."

Before Margery could speak the eight other things answered as if by rote, "She is so honored."

It raised its hairy arm to the sky as all the others fell to their knees. The wind whipped at their long hair and the flames rippled crazily, mad shadows appearing and vanishing everywhere and at once.

"Freed of outer garments, separating you from Glory . . . this female is now prepared for anointment. And I Thot, do so anoint her."

The congregation chanted his name "Thot," as Thot took one step forward between Margery's legs and held out his hands to his sides. The Other placed in each one of the small flagons that sat on the left and right boxes. Thot brought them to his lips and kissed the rims, while the congregation began quietly, slowly, to pant in unison, the sounds of their breathing in and out coming to the ears of their victim as if from one huge beast.

The thing held up the flagons to the east, calling across the water to the thin, barely discernable light that had just begun to make itself visible over the horizon.

"Oh, Rising Sun!" it cried out, and all the others gasped, "enflame these holy juices, that they may enflame those whom we secretly serve!"

Margery struggled to be free, knowing it was useless, knowing all she really achieved was burning her skin with friction as the ropes bit into her with every movement. The words weren't making sense anymore, for all she heard now were these creatures around her repeating a word, over and over again, and the word was one she'd never heard before. It sounded as if these things were chanting,

"Gurds . . . Gurds . . . Gurds . . ."

The Other took one of the vessels from the Leader who, grasping the one that still remained in his hand and holding it high, screamed, "The waters of the Female of their kind to glisten as gold upon our chosen Holy Mother!"

Impromptu cries of joy were shouted out among the panting that had increased in volume, while Thot poured the yellow liquid over and between the legs of the hysterical woman. My God, she thought, what are they doing! What is it! Oh, God . . . Oh, Jesus . . .!

The Other took that vessel, now emptied, and replaced it with the second.

"Sacred Scented Blood!" Thot roared, holding this flagon high, "May its carriage, the Wind, deliver the carnal message to those who wait for release!"

He tipped the tiny urn and thick red blood oozed slowly down in a long, thin line, splashing over

Margery's breasts and belly. She screamed in disgust as it hit her flesh, averting her face, her eyes, from the sight of it.

Still louder and more intense the panting from the "congregation" filled the night and mingled with the roar of the flames as they were beaten by the rushing wind, and Thot's voice cried out above it all, "Guide my hands, Oh Coming Dawn, that I may stir these juices on our altar to stir our Lords, and make this Female fertile for the Seed of the Gurds!"

Thot bent over her and starting with her feet, began to mix and rub, working his way up her body while the things that circled them began to alternately moan, the noise mounting louder and faster as Thot's hands moved to her hips and the terror and the movement made the noises more frenzied with mock pleasure, imitated passion, as if this was all done for other eyes that watched from afar. Margery was sobbing, screaming, not believing what was happening, the revulsion mounting from her stomach into her throat, the dreadful stench gagging her, making it more difficult to breathe in the already stifling air.

Then from some distance came a very loud, long, sorrowful, inhuman cry. It rose up and above all other sounds, as if demanding to be heard, so that even the very ocean itself seemed to be silenced.

All was still. She stopped screaming, not knowing why, but knowing she must be quiet, if only to find out what that noise had been. What thing had it come from? She too must be still.

As still as all the others. To listen.

To hear a second cry come from the jungle, a scream of agony and challenge, and mad, feral craving. Louder now. Closer now.

Thot spoke again, quietly this time, a huge smile

slicing through his blood-colored face. "Hear them, oh Nymph of Heaven! You are confirmed. You have found favor with them, made ready as a Holy Vessel. We honor you."

The creatures in the circle chanted, "It is done. She is so honored."

The Other took his torch and the torch at the head of the circle and extinguished both in the sand. Looking out at the horizon, Thot nodded once, and the seven kneeling figures rose together and made their way across the beach in their hobbled run, manning the waiting canoes once again.

When they were stationed at the water's edge, Thot kneeled before Margery. Her head rose just a bit to look at him. His eyes were closed and he held his hands up to either side. The Other approached him from behind and together, they whispered, "Be fertile, Bride."

Thot rose to his feet and the two walked slowly down the dunes toward the first boat. But Thot continued on past the boats and into the water itself, until he was immersed up to his waist. The orange hairs all over his body floated and moved on the water as he began to wash his hands, saying.

"We who serve are thus cleansed of ambrosia, and accept that which is denied."

Another animal scream came forth from the throats of whatever waited in the nearby trees, while the very tip of the sun was making its appearance out across the water, spreading a thread of hot scarlet over the very edge of the horizon. Thot was helped into the boat, and the canoes were shoved off, and into the surf.

There were more and more cries and roars coming from the forest that began at the edge of the beach.

By the time the half circle of the red sun was over the water and the canoes were far out into it, the small island seemed mad with the screaming pandemonium that moved closer and closer to the woman pinioned in the sand.

In the boats, they could hear the cacaphony that rose from the jungle.

Thot said, then, almost to himself, "For as long as men seek to harm you, I will destroy."

The yellow face of the Other stared at the back of his superior, studying the little bull's eye that had been branded there too, as on all of them. From the floor of the boat, the Other picked up something with both of his hands and set it on his lap. The bottom of the cloth covering it was completely soaked now and dyed entirely red. It was round beneath that cloth, and a few silver hairs protruded from the one side where it was not quite completely covered.

On the beach, the sound of Margery's breath was loud in her own ears, and her heart, she knew, would surely give out, it was beating so very, very fast. She saw a hundred tiny, glowing eyes peering out at her from the jungle. She struggled madly, violently, nearly deranged, but as the sun rose higher and higher out of the water behind her, the eyes grew faces, and the faces were not human.

One by one they moved out of the vegetation, as if the light that grew stronger every second drew them from their dark hiding places.

They were not screaming now, but intent on the woman, their nostrils working, their foul mouths puckered and drooling.

They advanced.

Then the largest of them fell upon Margery Croft.

Her final anguished scream travelled out across the water and could be heard, ever so faintly, by all nine in the little boats that glided toward the huge burning sphere of the morning sun.

PART II

AFTERMATH

SIX

Mary was living alone again.

She sat in an armchair, huddled in a blanket. An empty bowl of what had been cream of chicken soup sat before her on the coffee table. A box of tissues rested in her lap. Outside her apartment window, February was at its worst in the Chicago streets, and inside, she was permitting herself just a moment to wallow in a little selfpity.

Gordon had moved out.

At about the time she had finally worked up enough courage to tell him it was really over, he had come home late one night last week, and announced that he'd gotten a job.

She was happy—for him, *and* for her; at least it meant he'd share the financial burden. But oh, no. That little bit of whimsy had flown right out the window when she'd asked where he'd be working, and when he'd start.

"Next week. In New York."

Said as if it were the most natural thing in the world . . . like "Oh, just over in Goethe Square," or something. New York, for Christ sake!

Not knowing whether to be annoyed, disappointed or relieved, she'd laughed. All that fighting with herself, trying to talk herself into having the guts to tell him to pack up, and fate had taken care of it for her.

There had never been any question that she'd go with him. First, she had her job, for whatever *that* was worth. Second, he never asked her. Not that she *wanted* to go with him, but she would have liked to have been asked . . . just so she could have said no. Like not being invited to a party that you didn't want to go to anyway.

So, Gordon had taken all of his things, and, she'd discovered, a *lot* of hers. As a parting gift, he'd given her his cold. Well, she thought, at least it's kept me home from a job I can't stand, though it seemed a meager silver lining.

She sneezed.

She decided that the common cold was a disgusting thing and planned never to have another. Across the room, she could see herself reflected in the full length mirror on the door of the hall closet.

Her dark red hair, which in summer brightened to a strawberry blonde, hung now in matted strings down either side of her pretty, but hopelessly pale face. Dark rings circled around her rich brown eyes, which under better circumstances were startling on a redhead. Her full, rather pouting lower lip had developed a large cold sore, currently in full bloom. Her ordinarily lean face was now far too thin.

Another shiver ran through her whole body, which surprised her, since she was burning with fever.

When she had called in sick for the second day in a row, her boss had implied that she was malingering. She was nearly out of food, and since Gordon had moved out, there was no one to go out and get it for her.

Mary looked out of the window again. The rain had turned to sleet, and of course, the wind was overwhelming. The radio had told her earlier that the highest temperature of the day would be just above freezing. The only good thing she could think of was that there was a little grocery store just across the street, where she'd be able to buy the few provisions she needed.

Sighing, she placed the box of tissues on the coffee table, picked up the soup bowl and spoon, and carried them into her tiny kitchen.

Now, what do I need to get me through until pay day?

She opened the refrigerator.

It was nearly empty.

Well, that settles that. I need everything.

Opening the cabinets, she was further disheartened. In packing up and moving out, it looked as if Gordon decided to take all her food with him. There was no salt, pepper, sugar, cereal, canned vegetables, catsup or mustard. The tuna was gone. He'd even taken the onions.

That bastard.

She sneezed.

Walking back into the living room, she looked out the window. Through the torrential down pour she could just barely make out the name of the grocery store.

Going to the telephone book, she looked up "Jack's Deli," and dialed. A voice told her the number had been changed. She hung up, and dialed the new number. After ten rings, someone picked up and said,

"Yeah?"

"Is this Jack's Deli?"

"Yeah."

"Do you deliver?"

"Do you know what it's like out, lady?"

"Yeah," she answered.

'Are you nuts?" They hung up loudly.

"Yeah," Mary said quietly. She started to cry.

The box of tissues was back on her lap, but now she was dabbing her eyes instead of her nose, and listened to herself sniffling, and the sleet beating down. It seemed suddenly like a sick, grey, completely wet world.

Framed on her wall was a poster that proclaimed in bright, sunny letters the word "MANILA!" It looked warm there.

Of course it was warm there. It was the Philippines.

Her father had sent her that poster in what he liked to call "Gift-cum-Care" packages that arrived sporadically from wherever in the world he was at the time. Mary remembered thinking it cost her nearly forty dollars for the frame, when the poster itself probably wasn't worth more than eight. Still, she enjoyed looking at it. And, it reminded her of her father.

Her Father.

Dad. Oh, Dad, Dad, Dad. I miss you.

Getting up again with some effort and sneezing twice more, she went into her bedroom, got out a small box from her vanity, and sitting down on the edge of her bed, took out a worn envelope.

She had read this letter over and over . . . how

many times? She'd lost count. It was dated late last
November and it was the last letter she'd received
from him so far. She'd written him twice since, but
as yet had had no reply. This, however, was not
unlike him. Mary rarely received more than three
letters a year from him, and perhaps two phone
calls, always made at an hour that was for her, in
Chicago, the middle of the night. She read:

"Dear, dear Mary,

     Sorry as usual, I've not written more or sooner,
and also as usual, this will be brief, as I am up to my
eyes in work.

     Dana and I are really onto something concrete, I
think. It sounds preposterous, but I do believe I've
stumbled on to something very big, and very
different. I may have mentioned we've hired another
assistant, an American girl named Margery Croft,
from Boston. Quite a hot shot in the brains
department, and rather reminds me of you a bit. She
and Lucy are rooming together. I speak of you
often—they've both mentioned that they feel like
they know you already. Lucy still a hard worker, but
she's strange . . . a moody child. I think this girl
Margery will be a healthy influence on her.

     Expect to be leaving Manila for New Guinea
again, this time in the jungles. Will have to take one
of the girls with me, but don't know which one yet.
Would, of course, like it to be Dana, but someone
does have to run things here, and Lucy and Margery
lack the experience. When I return, then
perhaps . . . well, we'll see. I can't give you a definite
date, but I would like to get back to the States, and
you, some time very soon. Once again, plans to
return are sketchy, but it won't be for Christmas,
my darling, so please don't get your hopes up for
that.

     But very soon we'll spend time together and I'll

tell you all about Manila, (and New Guinea, with any luck), and anyplace else you want to know about.

> Until then,
> Much love,
> Dad.''

Not much more information than you'd get on a postcard, really. But Mary knew practically every word by heart even before Christmas had arrived, and with it, an expensive wooden bowl with an intricate mother-of-pearl design in-laid across the rim.

Still, for all the warmth of the letter, it seemed impersonal to her. They knew so very little about each other. Even the time he had spent in Chicago, when he'd given his symposium, she'd still barely seen anything of him, and before long, he was off again to yet another site. No time to become friends. Mary had rarely even mentioned Gordon to her father. Thinking back, she realized then that she never really thought of Gordon as important enough to her, to bother mentioning him to Marc, in more than a casual reference. She certainly couldn't equate her relationship with Gordon with the same importance as, say, her father's relationship with Dana McKinley.

This made her smile. She'd only met Dana twice, but she'd liked the woman right off.

Looking at the top of her vanity, where the wood and mother-of-pearl bowl sat, filled with her jewelry (some of which her father had given her), she got an idea.

Deciding suddenly that on Friday she would go into work, pick up her check and quit on the spot, she quickly walked back into the living room and hoisted the telephone book up on to her lap, flipping through to "T."

As she looked up the number she wanted, her mind quickly ran through her savings and checking accounts. Mary paused for only a moment, wondering about the wisdom of what she was about to embark upon. Then, remembering her credit cards, all paid off and ready to use, she continued to search through the yellow pages, deciding this was not the time to be frugal. Her passport was in order, and she could quickly get the special shots she would require for the journey.

If he wouldn't come to her, she'd go to him.

Mary began dialing agencies, getting information about travel to Manila. She felt better already.

She was going to visit her father.

Bolt upright and wide awake, hyperventilating and thoroughly shaken, she saw the bedroom slowly begin to appear before her eyes, as they became accustomed to the darkness. The air-conditioner hummed reassuringly in the window and, between the slats of the blinds, she could just see now the faint rays of dawn lighting up the eastern sky.

She didn't have nightmares as a rule. In fact, she rarely even remembered her own ordinary dreams. But here it was again. The same horrid scenario, the awful outcome. It was the third time she'd had the dream . . . exactly as it had been the night before Marc and Margery left. Christ, she thought, is this becoming a habit? What would a good psychiatrist say about a recurring dream . . . and one as dreadful as this one?

It was nearly as bad awake, once the relief that it had not been real had passed. That was when the worry started. Where are they now? Were they all-right? What if . . .? What if . . . what?

As before, she talked herself into the firm belief that though clarivoyants probably did exist in the world, she was not one of them. Premonitions were not her province. Fact was. She had no facts. She would presume them to be fine until she heard otherwise. And she wouldn't. No. They *were* fine.

Even so, she did not feel entirely safe in the aftermath of the nightmare. The glowing numbers on her bedside clock read 5:15, and she groaned a little. She'd never get back to sleep now, but she didn't really have to be up until nearly seven.

The space next to her in the big bed was empty and she smiled to herself, aware now that she automatically took the left side, leaving the right for him to occupy. Perhaps tomorrow,or rather, to-night, she would try sleeping in the middle of the bed, just to see what it was like to have that much room.

But she knew she probably wouldn't like it. Sleeping without him beside her wasn't something she wanted to get used to.

A bird began to chirp somewhere near her window; a very loud, annoying bird. Dana McKinley placed her feet firmly on the floor, yawned and decided to make some coffee for herself.

She rose to her feet and stretched, pulling her body up to its full five feet seven inches. Then she walked, nude, from her bedroom through the living room into the small kitchen where she filled a pot with water and put it on to boil, taking down the Melita from its shelf together with a paper filter and the coffee canister.

Free now until the whistling pot would call her

back, she went into the bathroom, turned on the light and got on the scale.

At one hundred and thirty pounds, Dana wished she were lighter, but all things considered, it wasn't too bad. Her weight was not a subject she gave a lot of thought to. She was in excellent health and was quite fit. She saw to that.

Pulling on the wine-colored robe that hung on a hook at the back of the door, she ran a comb through the pepper and salt of her hair, looking at herself in the mirror.

She looked tired . . . but with this nightmare robbing her of peaceful sleep, no wonder. But that wasn't what was bothering her. Once again, there was something wrong with the image that faced her. She put her hands up to her temples, and pulled her hair straight back, holding it there as she studied her face.

That was it. This is what had made her less than happy with what she was looking like lately. She'd only just now taken the time to look and discover it.

There was more salt than she liked and, though she was neither afraid nor ashamed of her age (she was forty-five), she did feel that this ever increasing gray in her hair was gradually "washing out" her complexion, which was ordinarily pale, and the color in her eyes which, before the gray, had seemed much bluer to her. She put the brush down and stared, trying to summon the image of herself with a head full of hair that was once again chestnut brown. It was always cut short, and kept that way, since it was easy to care for and certainly cooler in this climate. So, she reasoned, it wouldn't take too long, if she were to have it "done."

"Oh, what the hell," she said aloud, and decided

then that she'd call her hairdresser that morning and make an appointment.

That reminded her again of the early hour. Even if she called at nine, that was still over three hours away. She didn't want to start to work this early. Besides, she'd need Lucy's help today and the girl wouldn't arrive until close to nine, either. The pot began to howl in the kitchen and she ran out to the stove, turning off the jet. Two minutes later, she sat at her kitchen table with a steaming cup of coffee to her left, a pen in her right hand and her journal (though she had come to think of it of late as her diary) opened before her.

She found it easier to write, and something of a comfort to address these thoughts as if she were composing a never-ending letter to Marc Pemberton. One that would never be mailed. So, she wrote:

Dear Marcus,

Awoke from the same dreadful dream. As it always is . . . you were in danger. Waking up was a relief . . . but I was up at just after five! Can't possibly get back to sleep, so here I am, writing to you again, pretending you'll read this someday . . . who knows? Perhaps you will?

Have decided to dye my hair, darling. I can hear you now . . . I promise I won't come home looking like Lucille Ball. But I think I look mousey and since you're not around, I do feel I need a little something to pick up my spirits.

I do miss you most awfully . . . I'd say 'especially at night,' but it isn't just that. It's always; there is no time when I'm not aware that you are not here.

The work goes well, but am really getting to a point where little else can be done until you return with . . . whatever it is you'll have found. We've managed to date the legend, so we now know approximately how old the culture may be, but if they ARE what you think and the link has been missing all these thousands of years because it isolated its own evolution, then I can conclude that at some juncture, I will have to join you there myself, to observe first-hand, in as much as bringing back a live specimen seems improbable, not to mention inhumane.

I only wish I'd hear from you! Really, Marc, you COULD get SOME kind of correspondence through . . . unless you've already departed from the island . . .

Dana continued to write, and after having finished her third cup of coffee, felt a slight pain in her hand. Looking at the clock, she saw that it was now six A.M. The sun had risen fully and the heat of the day made itself felt.

She put her "journal" away, got into a sweat suit, and did fifteen minutes of stretching, toning, warm-up exercises. Then, she left the house and jogged a mile and a half, came back, showered and dressed, and it was time to start another pot of coffee. For one so concerned with her own health and well-being, she knew her caffeine addiction should be curbed. Six months had already passed since she first decided something should be done. Nevertheless, she wanted more coffee.

At eight-thirty, wearing a pair of khaki short pants and a green and red rayon Hawaiian shirt, she began working in her garden to the rear of the house, near the office door.

This always relaxed her, and also satisfied a creative need in her that was private and calm, as if she were aiding nature in the creation of itself, making its job easier, for a time. And, it gave her a constructive way to occupy her time before starting the work day, which anyway could not begin until the arrival of Lucy Case.

Lucy was at that moment, just closing the door to her own apartment. Turning the key a second time, her hand remained there as it did habitually every morning, for it was always at this point she tried to remember if she'd performed all the mundane little tasks necessary before leaving home for the day. Were the faucets in the bathroom and kitchen turned off? Had she turned off the gas? Was her last cigarette butt crushed completely before she'd emptied the ash tray into the garbage? It was all such a bore but after all, she didn't want flood or fire, especially since she was responsible to Margery as well as herself. Once, two months ago, she had left a tap in the bathroom sink running and it had flooded, ruining a small throw rug at the entrance of the bedroom. No other real damage had been done, but the little rug had been Margery's and Lucy was embarrassed by her own carelessness. She'd replace the rug, but now was extra careful about such things.

She stepped out into the glaring sun and wondered if her decision to forego her usual morning swim was a wise one. Customarily she started the day with a short drive to a nearby beach, and today, the water would be wonderful, since it looked to be another scorcher. Still, she wanted to get to work; not unusual, since she liked her work, but she had not heard any word from Margery for some time, and thought perhaps today there might be a letter or a call for her or Dana. Then too, she'd just got rid of another one of the annoying headaches that plagued

her of late, and it crossed her mind that she might be
spending too much time in the sun.

Once behind the wheel of her little VW, she lit a
cigarette and turned on the air-conditioning, sitting,
smoking, while the atmosphere inside the automobile cooled to something bearable.

She was glad Margery was a smoker. It made life
easier, God knows. Dana was always at both of
them about stinking up the place with tobacco, and
though she was good-natured about her complain-
ing, Lucy would have found it difficult to contend
with the same whining from a roommate. As it was,
they took Dana's displeasure seriously at work, but
privately, at home together, it amused them.

In fact, there was a lot that was amusing, lately,
since Margery moved in. Lucy hadn't realized that
she didn't like living alone, until she didn't anymore.
But that may have just been Margery.

She thought of Marcus and her friend together out
there in the jungle and, though it should have
brought a smile to her face, it didn't. She tried to
analyze this feeling . . . this anger . . . but pinning it
down was hard. First, she hadn't been asked, but
Margery had. Then, she was alone here, and missed
Margery, which would have been the case if *she'd*
gone with Marcus instead; either way, they'd have
been separated. Also, Lucy thought Marcus Pemberton a very attractive man; yet, lately, when she
thought of Margery and Mac left alone, there was
this anger again, and directed not at Margery, but
at Marc.

It was all confusing, and she would be glad when
they were both home and things were settled back to
normal.

Lucy took a deep drag of her cigarette and, deciding the air was cool enough now, started the

engine and began the usual drive to the Pemberton Foundation, and work. Midway through the journey, she was aware that her headache had returned, and drove a bit faster. Dana would have some aspirin.

At last she pulled the little car up in front of the Foundation and walked quickly up the path. She held her front door key poised, ready to use it, but trying the knob first, she smiled. Unlocked as it frequently was, she knew she would find Dana out back in the garden.

Dana was so involved and concentrated on her puttering she did not look up at all until she smelled smoke, _saw_ smoke drifting before her eyes.

"How long have you been sitting there?" she asked of Lucy, who was seated in a lawn chair, puffing relentlessly on her cigarette.

"About two minutes," the girl replied, laughing. "I snuck right past you, you were so caught up in those flowers of yours."

Lucy's rich black hair, tied high on the back of her head, shown nearly blue. She was a girl who spent as much time outdoors as possible and her tanned skin contrasted brilliantly with the ice blue of her eyes.

"You're early," Dana said, rising from her knees.

"I know. I decided not to take a swim this morning." Trying not to sound overly concerned, she added, "Any word from our travellers?"

"Not a peep. I think they must have left for the island sooner than they expected. Coffee?"

"Mmm. Please." She was disappointed, but the day had just begun, and at least she hadn't missed a call. "I wonder how Margery is liking the wilds of the jungle?"

"Hates it, I'll bet." Dana brushed herself off and went back into the house, holding the door for Lucy to follow.

"That would be a disappointment for her. She was so excited about going."

Pouring the coffee, Dana looked close at Lucy. Something seemed wrong, but she made no comment. They carried their cups out into the garden again, taking seats in the wrought iron chairs, painted white. Dana breathed deeply. The sweet, heavy aroma of the many flowers surrounding them made her happy, for a moment. "Doesn't that smell wonderful?"

"I guess so, Dana. I personally believe my sinuses are shot," Lucy whined, pulling on her cigarette.

"Another headache?"

Lucy nodded, closing her eyes.

"Well, no wonder, since you'd prefer breathing carbon . . ."

"Dana, don't start. How many cups of coffee have you had so far this morning?"

"Alright, that's my addiction, I admit it, but . . ."

"Enough, Dana," Lucy said and blew smoke out of her nose, sipping from her cup.

"Did you hear something?" Dana asked.

From the front of the house came the jangle of the doorbell.

"Great ears, Dana," Lucy called as Dana sprang from her seat to answer the door, yelling as she went. "I'll bring back a few aspirins for you!"

It was a boy, and he was delivering a telegram, addressed to "Marcus Pemberton." Although she had Marc's complete permission to open his mail while he was gone, she usually left all but what appeared to be the most important, unopened for him. This, she knew however, had to be read, no matter how she disliked doing it. She gave the boy a dollar, closed the door and crossed to her couch, opening the envelope as she went. She read:

"Dad—

Arriving Feb. 5th, Manila, for as long as you will have me."

There followed particulars about time and flight number, and closed with,

"Love, Mary."

Dana looked at the calendar on the wall. Today was Tuesday, the third. Mary would be here on Friday.

She was fond of Mary, and it had been a long time since she'd seen her. But really, this was not the best time for her to pick for a visit. She'd have to keep her busy and amused until her father returned. Lucy could help in that area. Ben could, too.

How surprised Marc will be! I wonder how he'll take it?

She heard the screen door slam out back, and Lucy called, "News?"

"Yes! But not about Marc and Margery! I'll be out in a minute!"

Looking at the clock, Dana decided it was late enough to call her hair dresser. If she could, she'd try to make the appointment for tomorrow afternoon. She'd be a brunette again by Thursday!

Mary might not notice, but what a return for Marc! His prodigal daughter and a dark haired hussy both waiting for him!

As she picked up the receiver she could just barely hear the sound of Lucy Case, who had returned outside to the garden, now in the midst of a coughing fit. Reminding herself to bring out two aspirins for the girl, she began dialing.

Two days after the ravaging, the ruins of the Pemberton campsight was discovered by some natives from a far off Village, who had come through the jungle to hunt.

They were going to bury the bodies of the two guides, but the Chief realized that murder had been done and that the authorities must be notified.

Though he and his men recognized in these killings an old and dreaded pattern, they said nothing of this to the police.

After investigating, it was determined whose camp it had been, and plans were made to inform the victim's next of kin.

SEVEN

The letter "R" jammed again for the umpteenth
time, so that his name on the By-Line read "Ben
amsey."

Cursing, he backspaced and struck the "R" key
with his index finger. However, having neglected to
push the shift first, he printed the letter in lower
case. Cursing again, and promising himself that
tomorrow he'd take this typewriter in for repair, he
reached for the bottle of whiteout, which had been
used so often in the past two hours that its rim and
brush were encrusted with the dried out liquid.
Applying it as best he could, he blew on it quickly,
shifted, hit an upper case "R," pulled the sheet of
paper from the machine, leaned back and yawned.

The story was finally finished. It was the third re-
write he'd had to do. The first was, as usual, written
with good, terse reportage. In the second, he had in-

jected a quicker pace and underscored the suspense.
But after reading it again, he realized he was
hedging. It still wasn't what Blair . . . or Shiff, had
asked for.

He then had poured himself a stiff bourbon, taken
a deep breath, and set about ruining his story to the
extent that it would please the publisher and sell
newspapers.

Collating the pages into their correct order, he
began reading:

"Fifteen Hours Of Terror

'The still, badly beaten form of Miriam Canlas,
the beautiful, allegedly adulterous wife of factory
worker Roman Canlas, was carried into the bullet-
ridden ambulance only minutes after her rampaging
husband was apprehended by police, following a
fifteen hour shoot-out at the Canlas house last week.
The other hostage, Canlas' sister Rita, screamed in
horror as she was led from the house of death, her
bullet wounds streaming blood behind her, while her
hand-cuffed brother shouted obscenities after her.
What had brought about this gruesome bloodbath?''

It went on like that for nine more pages. It bore
only a fleeting resemblance to the truth.

First, Miriam Canlas' "form" *had* been "still"
when carried out on a stretcher. She was not, however, dead, nor even unconscious. She had not been
"beaten" at all, much less "badly." There was a
small black and blue mark on her forehead. This was
incurred while she had missed her footing on the
stairs as she was being helped from the house by the
police. She'd hit her head on the bannister, having
gone over on her ankle. Unable to walk, they had
gotten a stretcher for her. She had passable good
looks, but was by no means a beauty.

The ambulance had one bullet hole in it from a policeman's gun, the cop missing the window at which Canlas had momentarily stood, and hitting the ambulance. In the fifteen hours, a total of three shots had been exchanged during the "shoot-out," one of these shots being the one that had hit the ambulance. Rita, the sister, *did* have a bullet wound that had grazed the fleshy part of her upper arm, but it was *Miriam* who had shot at her. The sister-in-law had told Roman that his wife had slept with another man. This was a lie. Roman *was* handcuffed when led away, and *was* screaming obscenities at his sister . . . but all in all, Rita probably deserved every name she was being called.

Ben had been there for the last two hours of what had been an all-night vigil for the police and other reporters, waiting for something to happen. Finally, something had. One cop took it upon himself to fire a shot. Canlas fired back. The cop fired again; Canlas, terrified, surrendered. Until that had happened, the hours had been passed, at least by the newsmen, in shop talk and unending card-games, anything to stave off the boredom of the long night's wait.

He couldn't read anymore. This is crap, he said to himself. They'll love it.

Disgusted, he threw the pages down on the desk, switched off his typewriter, and hid it beneath its dust-cover. He belted down the remains of the bourbon in his glass, now turned largely to water. Looking at the clock, he decided he'd have one more drink before turning in for the night. It might help him sleep, or anyway relieve his conscience, for what he'd been willing to do to keep his job. He felt like a whore.

He got up and walked into his kitchen. The bright overhead light was already lit, because it was always lit. The only window in the room faced a brick wall, and there was very little daylight that managed to angle its way down into the dark kitchen.

At the refrigerator, he cursed a third time for not remembering to fill his ice trays. Throwing the plastic into the sink with a clatter, he moved back to his bottle, kept atop the small portable television in the living room, and poured. Since it was not very good bourbon, he didn't really want it "neat"—ice and water took the edge off the bite. But having no choice, he took a sip, shivered, and sat down heavily on the cheap plaid love-seat that served him as his couch.

Stretching his long legs over the coffee table, littered now with newspapers, magazines, three dirty coffee cups, a plate, a fork, and a glass with some milk at the bottom of it, he yawned again.

Well, anyway, if nothing else, there was one consolation: it was good to have the story over and done with. Though he'd had to bastardize the whole set-up, prostitute himself and tell a pack of lies, no one involved in the Canlas incident had been seriously hurt. They were all still very much alive. He'd been a reporter for eight years now, and proud, until recently, of his professionalism, his ability. He'd seen a lot; what reporter hadn't? Yet, he remained uncalloused regarding much that he had witnessed over the years. He wasn't squeamish. He was concerned. And he was proud of that, too.

At that moment, his telephone rang. It was late, and for most anyone else, a phone call at that hour might be a source of annoyance or alarm. However, his work had accustomed him to disturbances at almost any hour, so he merely picked up the receiver as a matter of habit, hardly stopping to look again at his clock which now read 12:30 in the morning, nor to think that it was at all peculiar.

"Ben?" a female voice asked.

Quickly he thought, well, of course it's Ben. Everyone knows I live alone. Who else would it be? But he said, "Yes?"

"It's Dana McKinley."

"Dana! How are you?"

"Not good, I'm afraid."

"What's the trouble?"

There was a pause, and through the line he could hear a deep breath being taken, then slowly released in a long sigh that rushed into the receiver and into his ear, and he knew immediately something was dreadfully wrong.

"Are you alright?"

"For now, I . . . I don't know yet."

"Dana . . ."

"Marcus is dead."

He heard the words but somehow they would not compute in his brain. The man had been strong as a horse, as far as he knew. He couldn't be dead. Ben took a swig of his drink and asked, "How?"

"It was . . ." she began, "he was murdered, they think, and . . ."

"Don't Dana. I'll find out later. What do you need?"

A longer pause now, and he knew she was containing herself. In the interval, his brain was racing. Murdered? No. Who'd want to kill Marc Pemberton? At last she spoke again, saying, "Lucy's been heavily sedated. She's here with me, but she's fallen apart completely . . . Margery is missing too . . ."

"My God."

"Can you come over Ben? Now?"

"I'm on my way."

"Thank you, dear."

"Give me half an hour. See you then."

He hung up and reached for the bourbon bottle again. He would allow himself one more before he left. It would give him time to calm down from the news he'd just received, as well as prepare himself for what was to come . . . whatever that might be.

Marc, dead.

It seemed impossible. Pemberton had always been the most vital, alive, ambitious worker that Ben had ever known. For a great mind like that to be stilled, before it had reached its greatest goal; to be silenced at the very peak of its powers, seemed grossly unfair.

So, what's fair? Ben thought, and realized then that there were tears in his eyes.

Marcus Pemberton had been one of the main reasons Ben had come to the Phillipines. He had been here now for the last two years, after having worked for a large weekly publication out of Chicago . . . a city he liked very much, and still missed.

Originally, coming from a small town in Ohio, Chicago was the top of the heap to him. He'd spent three contented years there, and in his wildest dreams had never thought that fate would take him to Manila, a place so remote and far away, it existed for him only in history and headlines. But that was prior to his contact with Dr. Marcus Pemberton. Before that meeting, Ben had smugly considered himself a reasonably sophisticated city dweller, when in fact he was still a small-town boy.

They had met during Ben's second year in Chicago, when Ben had been covering an archaeological symposium in conjunction with Pemberton's much publicized research.

Ben had been eager and hungry for recognition. From his articles about Marcus Pemberton, he had taken a large step in just the direction he'd wanted. They were widely read, and controversial.

Having attended only one of Pemberton's lectures, Ben had gone back to his typewriter and written a scathing article, lambasting all of the Doctor's work, and reducing a life time quest to the putterings of an historical dilettante.

That was when he had first heard from Mary Pemberton. It had been a phone call in his office, at the paper, the afternoon his article had been published.

"Mr. Ramsey, I won't mince words. I am Mary Pemberton, Dr. Marcus Pemberton's daughter. He doesn't know about this phone call. I just wanted to let you know personally what a son-of-a-bitch I think you are. And an ignorant one, at that."

After soothing her with only mild apology, she'd agreed to let him buy her a drink that night.

They talked a good deal, after he'd gotten her over her snit, and as he'd found out from her exactly how long her father had been working on this theory, he was gradually convinced he had indeed done the gentleman a disservice.

Two days later, he'd met Marcus Pemberton and from that moment had become completely enthralled with the man's work, and what he stood for. Ben not only printed a retraction, but began a three part, in-depth series on the work of Marcus Pemberton's theory of evolution. He had filled it out with a character study of the man and explained, as best he could, what the research involved.

This total about-face of opinion from a journalist had caused still more interest and the series was read, and discussed. Pemberton's belief that the missing link in man's evolution had been somehow arrested, or isolated, and that it existed to be seen in the world even now, seemed a lot of hooey, to a lot of people, Ben included. But through the Doctor's painstaking explanation in laymen terms, Ben had come to believe it himself.

Ben's series, once printed, had made Marcus something of a celebrity, and since in the interviews, there was much mention of funding and lack of it, it had not been long before two major benefactors had come forth with the money. It had sent Marcus and his team to the Philippines, and set up a research laboratory for further delving into man's origins.

As it happened, Ben had received a feeler from the Manila-based newspaper, concerning a position, shortly after Marc had left. He still wasn't sure whether Marc or Dana had had anything specifically to do with the job, but after some talking long distance, he realized that his series had reached them there, and had been well thought of. Many letters followed and soon, he had agreed to work for the paper, arriving some five months after Marc and Dana. He liked them, he liked his job, and the town. He felt at home.

Now, Marc was gone. And in a strange way, so was the job he'd liked so much.

Ben only hoped that Dana McKinley would be strong enough to continue her colleague's vital work.

So, with his thoughts turned now to the living, Ben threw on what clothing he needed and, making sure he had plenty of cigarettes, left his apartment for the drive to the Pemberton Research office.

Lucy Case began to close her eyes, then opened them quickly, fighting the heaviness that pulled at her lids. There in that dark, it was quiet and private, and away from the world she needed to escape from. But then, quite suddenly, she would remember the news, see the horror in her imagination and open her eyes wide again, if only to reassure herself that she was in fact, in Dana McKinley's large bed . . . the bed she had shared with Marc Pemberton . . . and that she, Lucy, was not surrounded by flames in the middle of the jungle, or alone, in her own apartment, and without Margery.

She felt a palm on her brow and then Dana's face moved before her, smiled and said, almost inaudibly, "Sleep, Lucy."

At last the drug had done its work, and Lucy's eyes shut and remained so, as her breathing came evenly.

Dana stroked the girl's forehead once, then adjusted the covers around her and left her there in her room to sleep.

It was now nearly one in the morning and she hoped Ben Ramsey would be here soon. There seemed to be something she should do; some action to take, some way to fight, to fend off the terrible aching in her heart that would not yet allow her the luxury of getting it out. She had shed tears, yes, but she knew herself too well to know that those few were anything near the overwhelming hurt she felt. A hurt that had not as yet been released.

One A.M. now, and the news had come to her, via a visit from the local police, at eleven. Two hours. Her whole life had been completely changed in only two hours. Since that time, the call to Lucy, the girl's arrival, collapse and subsequent call to and visit from the doctor had filled her time and mind with responsibilities. Now, here alone and quiet, there was nothing to do, no one to do for, and she

found herself fighting fear and anger. Organizing
chaos and helping others made it easy to ignore the
duties she had to herself.

Outside, headlights shone through the slats in the
blinds and the crunch of tires on gravel announced
the arrival of a car before the house.

She was on the porch waiting before the car door
slammed, and Ben Ramsey came walking toward
her. His body was lit by the light from the porch.
Dana saw Ben, then, all at once, as different. Not in
looks or size, but in relation to who he was and what
he was to her and to Marcus. Before, Ben had been a
rather nice young man with an interesting job. Now
he had become in her eyes a mature man with help to
give and a self-appointed responsibility to bereaved
loved ones.

"Thank you for coming so quickly," she said.

As he reached the porch, Ben squeezed her arms
reassuringly. His fingers pressed her flesh, feeling
the damp of perspiration over the soft blonde down
on her upper arm. He moved to hold the screen for
her, and they entered the house.

Since they had spoken last, the night seemed to
have grown warmer. Even in the low light of the
living room, Dana's forehead twinkled with
moisture and he could feel his shirt begin to adhere
wetly to his torso.

It was quiet inside. Somehow he had expected
noise. Crying, screaming perhaps. A doctor writing
up a prescription for Lucy . . . for Dana; some
activity. But no. It was just him, and Dana, and the
house.

"Drink?"

"Please. If I can make it for both of us? You sit.
It's hot."

"The air-conditioning!"

"What?"

"No wonder it's hot. I only keep the air-conditioner on in the bedroom at night. Here, let me turn this one on in here."

Watching her, Ben could see she was grateful to have an activity and it was apparent to him her nerves were frayed. He was glad he'd come.

"What are you drinking?"

"You're an angel. Scotch, please, I think." She turned from the window unit and gestured to a small table with bottles and glasses on it. "I'll get the ice. Meanwhile, this should cool us off a bit, in a little while."

She retreated into the kitchen and while he heard cubes dropping into a bowl, Ben poured the Scotch into a glass for her, and bourbon for himself.

Dana usually drank gin. Usually, in fact, martinis. He wondered that she'd chosen Scotch, since there was ample gin and vermouth there before him, but she was back now, and placing a glass bowl full of ice down beside the bottles.

He studied her. She looked very strange; almost changed. Something more than just the circles beneath the red rimmed eyes. He couldn't put his finger on it, but he knew that she looked different to him.

Dana took a seat in an overstuffed chair, snapping on the small standing lamp that stood nearby. Ben took his cue from her and sat on the couch facing her.

"Are you up to telling me what happened?"

She nodded and began, "It was nearly eleven, and I was alone. Lucy had left hours before, and I wrote a bit in my journal, and was just about to turn in for the night, when someone knocked on the door. It was the police." She sipped from her glass as if giving herself time to phrase her thoughts. Then, she continued, "Some hunters told them something was wrong . . . I don't know specifically. Anyway, they located the camp site. It was robbed and burnt, and . . ." she shuddered, "all of the men had been killed. Their throats had been cut."

Ben began to speak, to tell her not go on, but she insisted, "No, I've got to tell someone, now that I've started. Please?"

"Go ahead."

"There's not much more to tell. Margery was . . . is . . . missing. And Marc . . ." she gulped more of the drink, closing her eyes momentarily and whispered, "he was beheaded."

She stared at him, her eyes glistening with tears. He knew it would be awful. But this . . . this barbarity . . .

"It's worse than that, really . . ." she continued. He waited for the words. Worse? How could it possible be worse? She leaned forward and reached for his hand. He stretched and gave it to her across the coffee table between them, and she squeezed his fingers tightly, as she barely squeaked, "His head, Ben. They didn't find his head."

They stayed like that, their hands clutching one another, gripping hard, as if to hold on to each other, gathering strength to continue. Eventually, she withdrew hers and, wiping her eyes, went on with the rest of the story.

"The police stayed with me for a while. I'd called Lucy. I didn't tell her over the telephone. Just asked her to come over. I realized now that that was a mistake. She saw the police when she came in and became immediately alarmed. By the time she'd heard what happened, she was hysterical. The doctor came quickly, and sedated her. She's in my room now. They left, and then I thought to call you."

"I'm glad you did."

"So am I," she smiled briefly.

"Do they know anything, Dana? I mean, why?"

She shook her head. "No, they don't," she answered, accenting the word "THEY."

"Meaning you might?"

Her eyes held his for just a second then moved away.

"It's only surmising, now. I'll have to think about it. As it stands, they're assuming it was robbery . . . possibly involved with some cult of some sort . . . in other words, they know practically nothing, Ben."

He wanted very much to ask her what she knew, or anyway what she suspected. But he knew Dana well enough to know that she'd have told him, if her facts were more substantial than merely "surmise."

So, they sat silently, both retreated into their own thoughts.

For Ben, the reality still had not truly dawned upon him, and he continued to have the feeling that Marcus was only away for a while, and would return soon. but of course, he wouldn't, and this sadness seemed to fill the room as an almost palpable oppression. Many people had loved Marc Pemberton.

One in particular.

"Dana?" he said quietly.

The doctor came back from wherever her thoughts had taken her, and gave him her attention.

"What about his daughter?" Ben continued.

"Mary?" Dana replied, as if she'd never heard the name before.

"Yes, Mary. Has anyone told her?"

A shocked expression passed across Dana Mc-

Kinley's face, and then she practically whispered, "Oh, Ben. Mary."

As if in a trance, she rose and walked to a small wooden table near the front door, from which she picked up her purse, searched through it, unblinking, until she withdrew a piece of paper. She held it, turned it over once, then again, but did not speak.

Ben waited for some explanation, some answer, but she only stood staring at the paper in her hand, until finally, Ben insisted.

"Dana. What is it?"

She sighed heavily and carried her purse back with her, handing the paper over to him. He read it, then looked up at her.

"But this means Mary's due here tomorrow . . . or rather, today."

Dana nodded, then placed her face in her hands and ran her opened palms up until her fingers moved through her scalp. She looked exhausted.

"You have her number?" Ben asked.

She removed her personal phone book from her hand bag and gave it to him.

"She's probably left already, but there might be a chance I can reach her, or track her down."

Ben reached for the phone on a nearby end table, pulled it closer to him, and having found the number, began dialing.

There was no answer, and nowhere else to leave word. He hung up and was about to place the instrument back where he'd found it, when Dana said, almost without emotion,

"Ben, Margery's father doesn't know yet, either."

Margery.

He was so upset about Marcus's death, so filled with thoughts of Mary Pemberton arriving in only a

few hours, expecting to see her father, that he had
almost forgotten about Margery. She may still be
alive. From the look of Dana, she wasn't up to
calling, but knew that if worse came to worse, she
would if she had to. Yet, he also saw the hope that
he'd make the call instead. Someone had to let the
man know his daughter was missing.

He flipped open her phone book once again,
saying,

"Croft, isn't it?"

"Yes," she said.

He found the number and dialed. As the con-
nection was being made through the lines, linking
him up with the other side of the world, he studied
Dana's face again. Then, he realized what, beyond
the pain, was changed about her.

"Your hair, Dana."

"What?"

"Your hair. It's dark."

"Yes," she smiled, a tear glistening in her eye, "I
did it as a surprise. For Marc."

Something heavy landed loudly on the glass immediately to Barton Croft's right, and he pulled
back instinctively. Only then was he aware that
another car had passed them and sent up a huge
spray of water from a deep puddle, nearly covering
one side of the cab. The rain seemed heavier, and he
had hoped that it would have stopped by the time he
left the shop. But it hadn't, and he decided that
he'd stay home tonight with a book. He had planned
on dinner with his best friend Jack, but the thought
of leaving the apartment again this evening wearied
him.

The cab stopped for a light and the rain sounded
louder, as if the roof of the vehicle would cave in on

them from the weight of the water. Through the streaming windshield, he could just make out the awning of his building one block away, and pointed it out to the driver.

Barton was surprised that he was not upset at this delay. Ordinarily, his impatience had been such as to ruin a day or an evening. His blood pressure would soar, contrary to every order Baum had given him, and he would sometimes hyperventilate. But since he had decided to retire, things somehow seemed to bother him less; or, maybe he just felt that they didn't matter, and were hardly worth getting excited over.

He'd spent the better part of the afternoon back at the store. Larry Burbage had called that morning; could he drop by and take a look at a new piece that Burbage was considering for inclusion in their inventory? He wasn't sure it was quite right. Not that it wasn't authentic; not that it was ugly. Merely that it was American Indian, and the store carried a lot of such artifacts already.

As it turned out, it was a magnificent bowl, beautifully carved and painted; wonderfully preserved. Barton had congratulated Larry on his good fortune and taste. It was a real find and a definite asset to the store's already impressive acquisitions.

The call, the visit, hadn't annoyed Barton. On the contrary, even though he'd only just officially turned over the reins to Larry and was now in the ranks of the "retired," it felt good to be needed; good to know his opinion and expertise still meant something of value.

Pulling up to the curb, he paid the driver and the doorman opened his door, leading him to the entrance of the lobby beneath an umbrella, even though the awning kept him perfectly dry.

Walking swiftly to the front desk he asked for his mail and messages, and spent a few moments in pleasant chit-chat with the old lady who ran the switchboard. The elevator arrived, he greeted James, the operator, and looked through the pile of paper in his hand.

Aside from the mail, which looked to be the usual bunch of junk mail and bills, there was a phone message. It had come in that afternoon, just after he'd left for the store. He'd just missed the call. It asked him to please call the Pemberton Foundation in Manila as soon as possible, regardless of the hour.

Bart grinned, letting himself into the apartment he had occupied for the last fifteen years—a place he'd shared for a time with Margery. It was odd, her calling during the day. She didn't as yet know the exact date of his retirement, did she? His last letter couldn't have reached her yet, could it? It wouldn't be like her to call during the day. She was good about calculating the time differences, and they usually spoke in the late evening.

Tossing off his coat, he decided he'd make himself a little drink to warm him up. He knew he had to be careful; he always did, with booze. But he had exercised restraint of late—also part of doctors orders. He stepped out of his wet shoes, loosened up his tie and built himself a mild whiskey and soda, taking it to the large red leather chair in the corner.

Putting the message on the table beside the phone, he took another quick look through the stack of mail before calling.

Good thing too, he thought. Not all of it was bills and junk mail.

A letter had escaped his notice in the elevator. A letter in the familiar envelope, written in the

familiar hand, from Manila. The post mark was over
a month ago; the letter dated a few days before that.
He smiled. She'd probably forgotten to mail it right
away.

"Dear Dad,

"Things have been really hectic or else I'd have
written sooner. Anyway, there's news. Nothing
definite, but exciting.

Dr. Pemberton's told me he'd like *me* to go with
him on the expedition! I'm so happy, dear, that he
trusts me with such responsibility. The awkward
thing is, he hasn't told Lucy yet, and I'm sort of in a
spot, since I know she wanted to go as much as I do.
Also, she deserves it more, what with her experience
and all. I don't know whether to break the news to
her myself, or just wait and let Dr. Pemberton do it.
But, we'll figure that out.

There's still apparently a lot to do, and schedules
to figure out, which is why I say nothing's definite.
We don't know *exactly* when we'll be going, beyond
that the target for departure is in about two or three
weeks. I'll call and let you know as soon as I know
when we leave.

Now, *your* news: I think it's great that you've
decided to retire early. What the hell, huh? You
deserve it. Have you set *your* date yet? Hopefully,
when I call *you* can tell *me* when and *I* can tell *you*?

Of course, the best of all this is that, unless I'm
being awfully selfish, you can come visit me here, as
soon as I get back from New Guinea. So . . . go get
your passport renewed (if it isn't already!). We
expect to be gone no longer than about three weeks,
even if we find what we're looking for (more on *that*
when we talk), so perhaps you can get over here mid-
March? It's gorgeous here, darling. You'll love it.
And March is the *perfect* time to get away to some-

place warm . . . and believe me, *this* place is *warm*!
   Talk to you soon. As always, I miss you very much.
   See you soon?
   All my Love,
   Margery"
   So, that's what the message was about. She was
calling to let him know when she was leaving, and
when she expected to return. He could start making
plans for his visit soon. Maybe even tomorrow, de-
pending on what transpired in their conversation.
   Barton picked up the telephone, and taking a sip
of his drink, he smacked his lips in contentment and
began to return what he thought was a call from his
daughter.

EIGHT

Her cold was better, but not by much, and the stale air inside the cabin didn't help her breathing any.

At least the plane had begun its descent. She could feel the pressure in her ears change even if there hadn't been an announcement to "fasten your seat belts." Fortunately, the two other seats in her row had not been booked. She had been able to stretch out during the night and was now free to move from her preferred aisle seat, across to the tiny window and observe the landing.

Mary had always found that the view from a window seat remained interesting for the first twenty minutes, and the last ten, and was hardly worth having to climb over two other people when she wanted to get up. Mercifully, that had not been an issue on this flight. But she was restless. The movie had been a stupid, middle of the road family thing, and she'd purchased the head sets chiefly to block out the never ending screams of an infant at the back of the plane.

But now, with her face washed and fresh make-up applied, she was feeling tired, but eager. This was the right thing to have done. To be rid of that rotten job, that rotten weather, made her feel light. Calling up her friends to tell them she was leaving had felt good. And informing Gordon particularly pleased her.

Through the window, the blue of the water now became speckled with spots of land, many many islands that grew more and more numerous as they moved closer, until the plane was over solid ground, and then she could see its shadow reflected sharply against the earth that glared in the sunlight. Then, a mild "thump," and they were down, driving smoothly toward one of the gates.

It took some time for the rest of the passengers to disembark, and Mary found it difficult to be patient. Dutifully, however, she stood in the aisle, her tote bag slung over her shoulder. It was warm, so she carried the fire engine red cotton jacket to her pants suit over one arm, along with the thick black wool coat she'd worn through the rain and snow of Chicago.

Having been thanked by a steward and stewardess, she was at last in the terminal, and following the crowd to the baggage pick-up.

Her eyes searched the throng lined up outside the customs gate. There were so many people of so many races . . . all either searching for their own friends and loved ones, or waving madly to those they'd spied amongst the disembarking passengers. Everyone looking back at her seemed bright,

happy . . . even their clothing reflected a warm,
easy, yet energetic mood, accented by vivid colors in
light, warm weather materials.

It was her turn now, and as her luggage was
pulled up and unlocked, she continued to search the
crowd facing her for a familiar face.

Then at last, she thought she recognized someone.
He was a few years older, but then of course, who
wasn't? His black hair was cut quite short, and the
moustache he'd worn in Chicago was gone now, but
she was sure she recognized Ben Ramsey. He obviously hadn't spotted her as yet, for his deep green
eyes continued to move erratically in his search for
her. So, she was free to openly stare at him, study
him, without guile.

He seemed taller, from this distance, anyway. She
figured he was about 6'2", and though his frame
was not thick, the wide expanse of shoulder and
chest gave him an appearance of mass. His plain
white, short sleeved shirt revealed dark hair peeping
out from the "V" of the opened collar, and down
arms and hands that looked strong.

When at last he did see her, his grin revealed
white, even teeth that seemed to deepen the tan of
his skin. Mary made a quick mental note that she
must get some sun soon, so as not to be as pale and
sickly as she now felt. She could shed these heavy
winter clothes for tropical duds, but her pallor
would give her away as a brand new tourist right
away. Still, she wasn't a great one for the sun; she
burnt easily, and besides, it was bad for the skin,
and aged you quicker than need be. But looking
around her, she saw that a little color was called for.

As quickly as the smile had flashed across Ben's
face it was gone, and he looked quite serious as he
pointed to the exit gate. She nodded, just as the

custom's official passed her through, and a red-cap loaded her luggage on a cart.

Mary walked toward Ben, struck again by what an attractive man he had become. Or maybe he always had been. He certainly seemed to make Gordon dim yet further in her memory. She knew her father was fond of Ben, so it was not really much of a surprise that he should ask Ben to meet her. Though she had hoped Marc would be there to greet her personally, she knew the chances of that were slim. He worked, and worked often and hard. Tearing him away from that, even to meet his daughter at an airport, would have been next to impossible, though she knew he probably had intended to come himself and simply gotten involved with whatever he was up to at the moment.

Ben was holding his hands opened wide to her.

"Hi, Ben!"

His arms went around her and she inhaled, smelling heat, and soap. "Hello, you. You're all grown up!"

"Well, I've done my level best, anyway."

She was embarrassed suddenly at hearing her own voice, feeling the cold made her sound adenoidal and stupid. She was about to say something about it when she saw the look on his face. Up close she realized that he had obviously not been sleeping well. Rings beneath his eyes, and creases along his mouth told her he was overwrought, tense and looking now, older than his years.

As if trying to hide it from her, he looked around to make sure the man with the luggage was still behind them, and then addressing them both, said, "My car's over here."

Mary stared at him and she thought he seemed to

avoid her eyes. She still felt something was odd; out of place.

They approached the sliding glass doors that would get them out to the curb, passing a souvenir and magazine shop on the way. Mary nearly walked past it completely. They were almost through the doors when she stopped suddenly. Ben was holding her upper arm and gave a little tug, smiling nervously. She turned and looked back at the little shop.

Lined up on a low table outside were various newspapers, and the front page of two of them had huge photographs of her father's face smiling back at her. She looked quickly back to Ben, whose grip on her had tightened slightly. He was about to speak but by that time, she had pulled herself free of him and started back to the shop.

A headline screamed "CULT MURDER IN JUNGLE CAMP!"

She heard herself cry out, just before she fainted.

"I'll speak to you tomorrow, Ben," Dana told him quietly, and cradled the receiver. Her journal lay on the desk before her, opened to the entry she'd made two days ago. Flipping forward to a new, clean page, she wrote:

My Dearest Marcus, my only Love,

I have just re-read what I'd written . . . when? How long ago? Anyway, where I scolded you for not having written.

I hate it so that it happened . . . this way . . . so very far away from each other. I keep thinking, if only I'd been there. If only you hadn't been so alone through it all.

How am I going to make it through all this? All your work . . . our work . . . and now, does it stop?

And Mary . . . we . . . Ben and I, couldn't stop her. I just spoke to Ben. She's here. In a hospital. Hysterical. What do I say to her? She's coming to stay with me tomorrow. Margery's father went nearly mad on the phone when Ben told him. Lucy is terrified . . . Oh, God, Marc, please be with me. Please help me, because I know somewhere you must be able to hear me, to feel what I'm feeling. I can't be strong for everyone, but it all seems to have fallen upon my shoulders, and but for Ben, I feel like I'm doing it all alone.

Oh, I know this is disgusting self pity, and that I must be strong, but I'm so very, very tired, and yet I know this is only the start of an ordeal . . . and I want to escape . . . to be free of these responsibilities . . . and have a while to lick my wounds, and be alone with my grief. All the things I never said. Never told you. But you knew, didn't you, my darling man?

You knew I loved you more than anything, or anyone. And you must know now, that the rest of my own life, from this day forward, is time spent only waiting to be wherever it is you are, and that then, we will not be alone again. Ever.

Coming back up from sedation Mary's eyes opened and she lay peacefully, waiting for her vision to clear; for things to unblur. There was no doubt in her mind that they would become clear, and that in itself calmed her somewhat more. As the world came into focus her taste buds seemed to come alive, and she wished they hadn't, for there was a terrible taste in her parched mouth. Her eyes were sticky too. She knew she was drugged.

Ordinarily the news would have been crippling; but with Gordon gone, quitting her job, jet lag, and the last stages of the cold added to the trauma, she was in a weakened state at the start, an easy and willing mark for the effects of sedation. She seemed to be coming out of it now, and was afraid of full consciousness—afraid of something she'd been told, something she'd have to think about, and wanted very much to sleep again. She had the feeling that she would never, ever get enough sleep. But she opened her eyes so at least for now, she was grudgingly awake.

First she wondered where she was . . . oh, she knew it was Manila, but what was this room? She thought she was alone and that momentarily panicked her, so that she raised her head from the pillow sharply and then, saw Ben Ramsey asleep in a chair at the corner of the dimly lit room. Hotel room. Yes, I must be in a hotel room . . . my room, and there's Ben . . .

And it came back to her full force, and she was screaming again.

Ben started, snapping out of the chair almost immediately and was beside her bed even before he himself was totally awake.

The doctor had warned him that this might happen, and there wasn't much to do about it except give her another pill. Much as he disliked keeping her doped up like this, it seemed as if there was no other recourse.

She threw her arms around him and held him so tightly he felt his rib cage constricted, making it difficult to breath. Still he let her hang on, sobbing as she did so, huge shudders coming from her. She was, despite her apparent strength, small and frail to him now, and this all seemed ugly and unnecessarily cruel.

After Mary had calmed into simple weeping, he poured a glass of water from the tray beside her bed and gave her a pill. She took it willingly, eager to be free of thought, of pain, and he held her at either shoulder, slowly easing her back flat upon the mattress. She smiled up at him, a small weak and grateful grin, and it touched him deeply. Mary closed her eyes and he blotted the perspiration from her brow with a tissue.

He assumed the nurses had removed her clothing. She was dressed now in a pale green hospital gown. Although she was as comfortable as they could make her, she looked bad. Aside from her usual pale hue, her skin was now ashen beneath the smudged colors of her makeup that stood out upon her face in harsh, clown-like garishness. He wondered why they'd not removed it.

Once he could see her breathe evenly and that she was again sleeping, he went back to his chair in the corner and watched her for a long time. At the airport, someone had summoned a doctor, and the three had ridden together to the hospital where they were now. He'd wanted to get her to the Foundation and Dana, but once admitted, the hospital insisted on at least an overnight stay. He didn't like hospitals . . . didn't want her waking up in one. When he was able to call Dana, they had agreed Mary would stay with her, once she was able.

Leaving it at that, there was little left but to wait until the first shock had passed and she was well enough to leave the hospital which, it was expected, would be tomorrow.

He too was exhausted, and also angry. Once again, his employers had done their job in spades, for of course the newspaper with the screaming headline she'd seen, had been the *Manila-American.* The story was even worse, and he was thankful she'd not read it. Yet. Glad too that he'd not been assigned to cover it.

Dana McKinley's words of advice came back to him once more, haunting him now. But it was rapidly becoming more than just a case of his own personal freedom. It was a matter of conscience as well. How much longer could he rationalize working for them, when they did things like this?

She was resting again, thank God. Calm and quiet.

Ben's head began to nod, and he fell back into a troubled, much needed sleep.

The following afternoon Dana McKinley was on the phone saying, "That's idiotic, Ben. She's perfectly welcome. She must know that."

"Still, she says she feels she'd be an inconvenience to you . . . what with Lucy there too . . ."

"Ben, please put her on and let me talk to her?"

"She's unpacking. She wants me to do the talking 'cause she's afraid you'll persuade her into staying with you."

Dana could hear Mary's voice from somewhere nearby. "Oh, alright," it said, "give me the phone, Ben."

"Dana' here's Mary."

The muffled sounds of the receiver changing hands rustled in her ear and a woman's voice said, "Hello, Dana."

It shocked her at first. The mental picture she had of Mary Pemberton was of a girl just out of her teens. But this voice did not match it; this was a mature, sensible adult on the other end of the line. It instantly changed Dana's mind about putting up any arguments.

"Hello, Mary. You're not going to stay with me?"

"No, Dana. I mean thank you, of course, but I've already checked into the hotel and have my room.

It's better this way." The voice was still slightly groggy, the words pronounced a trifle too clearly, to avoid slurring.

"It's so impersonal . . ."

Dana thought about mentioning the spare beds at Lucy's apartment, but Lucy had made no offer of letting Mary use the place; besides, it being where Margery had lived too . . . who knew how either young woman would feel about that?

"That's exactly why I'd prefer it." Mary was replying, "Dana, I couldn't stand living around all of Dad's things at your place . . . I just . . ." her voice cracked and the receiver exchanged hands again.

"Dana," Ben said, "we'll drive out to see you tonight, okay?"

"Absolutely. If she's up to it. She's allright?"

"I think so. I'm going to try to persuade her to have dinner after she naps . . ." she could hear a protest and Ben saying "Not now . . . but you should eat something later . . . wait . . ." then back into the phone, "Dana?"

"Yes, Ben."

"Look, we'll have dinner here in the hotel and be out to your place by eight tonight."

"Good. See you then. And Ben . . ."

"Yeah?"

"Thank you."

There was little choice in the matter of taking a suggested nap. She was still weary and still drugged on valium. After Ben left she called down to the front desk and asked them to ring her room at 6 P.M. That would give her plenty of time for sleep, before getting ready for the difficult evening ahead.

Leaving the hospital, she'd worn the same red suit

again, and now she stripped naked, throwing it in a heap to the floor. She would never wear it again, she knew. The room was cool; the air conditioning felt good, especially since the intense heat of the streets had been such a surprise. She stretched, yawned, and climbing between the fresh sheets of her new, comfortable bed, gave herself a moment to relax. Grateful for the privacy she now had at last, Mary took three deep breaths, said a silent prayer for her father and was asleep in two minutes.

When the telephone awoke her from a dreamless sleep, she answered it on the fifth ring, thanked the caller and lay calmly, eyes opened, assessing her present condition. She felt better, she decided. Not completely up to par, but certainly on the way. Carefully she sat up, testing her stomach muscles, which responded and performed. She had not pulled the blinds, and for the first time looked to the window that was filled with the last diffused light of the sky. She stood, walked over to it and drew in her breath with a smile, looking out onto Manila Bay at dusk.

There were people lining the street, looking out to the sea, watching the show in the sky. She understood now why the sunsets here were so famous. Even her father had mentioned the spectacular sight in his letters and she suddenly felt comforted; practically serene. Her father had looked out upon this very same beauty that occurred here every night, and she felt somehow joined to him. She was feeling the same things he felt at witnessing this graceful twilight, and experienced the little thrill she always felt when the meaning of it all seemed just within a grasp, and just beyond reach.

She remained at the window, watching the pink sky give way to purple light. The Bay glistened. The

Convention Center turned violet, the Cultural
Center alive with the moving water that sparkled in
its fountains. Lights came on in the buildings and
the pedestrians now began to move on about their
business in the night.

I'm stronger now. I can feel it.

She picked up the telephone and dialed room
service.

"Could you send up a small pot of coffee, please?
Oh, and an order of toast?"

She thought the toast would keep her from eating
like a field hand at dinner.

"Will there be anything else, Ma'am?" the voice
on the line asked.

"Yes," she answered, deciding quickly, "bring up
a newspaper, please. The *Manila-American*."

The bartender placed a fresh drink before him, but
Ben merely muttered a thank you without taking
his eyes from the article he had almost finished
reading.

As he had intended it to read, it would not have
been bad. It certainly started out well enough, and
he'd briefly had the hope that it had seen print
untouched, unaltered. His orders this time had been
to write it truthfully, honestly, with no histrionics.
That had been a surprise, coming from them, but
Shiff knew he was acquainted with Marc.

But as Ben continued on down the page, he saw
what Blair had had them do. Whole sections had
been either cut or entirely rewritten with much
reference to the "horror of The Jungle Night," the
headless corpse, the hacking and slashing involved
in the murders and the abduction of the girl—all
within a supposed "tribute" to the dead archaeolo-
gist.

The surprising, unfamiliar taste of good, top-shelf
bourbon momentarily distracted him. He savored it,
thinking, had Mary read this thing? It was the first
of a three part close-up of Marc Pemberton. He'd
turned in Part Two that afternoon. It would print
tomorrow, and God only knew how they'd slice that
up for their sleazy readership. If they'd leave it
alone, it would be good; work he could be proud of.
But no; silly even to hope for that.

He'd begun it as a dignified salute to a fine man.
Mary's arrival had helped spur him on. Her coming
here brought home so many memories of Chicago
and Marc's help at the outset of his career. It had
come back to him freshly, clearly, and he was able to
get it all down on paper with an eye for the truth,
and Marc's own personal vision.

All that was missing from the pulp trash he now
held in his hands.

He put the paper down on the bar and glanced up
at the ornate clock above the mirror. She was late.
He'd give her another ten minutes then call her
room. Ben hoped she wasn't still asleep.

She wasn't.

After a shower, she thought about what to wear,
as she dried her hair with the portable dryer she'd
packed. She didn't like being forced into this kind of
concern, but it had to be dealt with. She recalled him
saying they would not only meet in the bar downstairs, but eat in the hotel as well. The restaurant
seemed fairly dressy, but she wasn't up to spending
time on her appearance. Winding her hair in a knot
at the top of her head, she chose a dark brown
chiffon blouse and skirt. Two inch heels. No jewelry,
and spare makeup—perhaps a bit more blush than
usual. This was all done quickly. It was her aim to
feel fresh and clean, to look merely presentable. She

wanted to find out more than what she'd read in the
paper, and she was hungry. Vanity was neither
called for nor felt. Yet, her appearance, when fully
dressed, was, though unintentional, both striking
and dramatic.

The elevator operator directed her through the
lobby toward the restaurant and now, she stood at
the entrance, where she spotted Ben looking rather
anxiously up at the clock. She followed his eyes and
saw that she was five minutes late. Then he swiveled
on the bar stool, headed for the house phones in the
corner, just as the Maitre D' approached her and she
gestured toward Ben, who waved her over.

Though she looked tired and somehow thinner
than she had this afternoon, the familiar lilt to her
walk, and the way she had of cocking her head to one
side when greeting you, reassured him that she
would be alright. She had turned into a very fine
looking woman, from the veritable child he'd considered her only a few years back.

"Hello," she said.

'I was just about to call your room," he said.
"Hello. You look beautiful."

"Thank you. I'm sorry I'm late."

"Don't be. Plenty of time."

"Good. I had no idea there was a 'Sardi's' here in
Manila."

"Much less right here in your own hotel!"

"Mmm. I'm glad. I wasn't up to going too far
tonight."

"The drive to Dana's is a pleasant one, and only a
few miles away."

The host beckoned them and they followed him to
their table.

"This place is really lovely, Ben," she commented
as they walked, taking in the walls, lined with cari-

catures of the celebrities who had dined there. Many of the names and faces were unfamiliar to her.

"Local movie and TV stars," he responded to her question, "well, Australian, too, if you'd call that 'local,' as well as Filipino. You should see it during the Festival."

"Festival?"

"Yeah. Last month. In fact, every January. The Manila Film Festival. Almost as big as Cannes."

They were seated now, their menus before them. Ben asked, "Hungry?"

"Famished. I had some toast and coffee from room service, but that's all, since the plane."

"We'll fatten you up on some good Filipino food."

The restaurant was not crowded, and dimly lit, giving her a feeling of intimacy that she was grateful for. He was willing to indulge her in small talk, and she was thankful for that too. She found herself surprisingly on edge, and was unsure that her behavior was alright, looking around at the other female patrons, self-conscious that she may be over-dressed. The waiter came and asked if they'd like drinks.

"I'd kill for a Rob Roy," she glanced at Ben, then added, "but considering what else I'm on, I think a ginger ale will do me just fine." Ben smiled, ordering a bourbon for himself. The waiter departed and Ben leaned toward her over the table.

"I keep forgetting you're old enough to drink."

"I'm even old enough NOT to. Besides, we first met over drinks. Remember?"

"How could I forget?"

"Listen, Ben. Thank you. I know what a nuisance I've been . . . I'm not usually a fainter, especially in public places, regardless of how bad the news is. I was under a strain anyway, and . . ."

"No apologies. It was a horrible shock."

"I'm feeling better now, I think."

"You look it, I'm happy to say."

There was an awkward silence, and he could see there was something on her mind. "What is it, Mary?"

"Well," she sighed, "besides the toast and coffee, I also got a copy of today's *Manila-American* with room service." He started to speak, but she silenced him with a finger to his lips, "I had to, Ben . . ."

"Yes, of course," he interrupted, "but it's been so exploited in the papers . . . and mine . . . my paper is probably the worst offender of the lot." It was suddenly important to make her understand, and he continued, "Mary I swear, they changed practically every word I'd written."

"It's alright," she said, but he was picturing her reading the terrible details in the cold, impersonal wordage of a newspaper report. Even in his own paper, there had been two follow-up stories in today's edition, as well as his Profile article.

The two other items had been reportage with as much sensation as possible; even the plain truth of it was grizzly, and the chance to re-hash what had already been described a day earlier, had not been passed over.

"Well, I will admit it was a shock. I mean, such a pack of lies, Ben. And I didn't expect it to be quite so . . . graphic."

"Fiction, most of it. They get as salacious as possible without knowing the facts."

He felt badly; felt that he had in some way let her down; that he should have been there, when she'd found out the details . . . even told them to her himself, though how he could have done that, he didn't know.

"How did Dana take it?" she asked, shifting the subject away from the news.

He paused, still not sure how to reply. "It's hard to say, Mary. She seemed to take it as well as could be expected, but then, you can't always tell with Dana. She's also had Lucy Case to deal with and . . ."

"The assistant?"

"Yes. Her roommate was Margery Croft."

Mary nodded quickly and Ben took it as a signal not to continue. The drinks came, and for a while they sipped them in silence.

"I can't believe he's really dead."

"Take it slowly."

They wondered what to say next. Both seemed to be walking on eggs, they were so preoccupied with not offending the other.

"How's Chicago?"

"Cold. What else, this time of year? Do you ever miss it?"

"Yeah. The people. The bustle."

"Looks like there's plenty of that here."

He agreed, and picked up his menu. "Since this is all new, may I order for you? I guarantee it to be magnificent."

"Yes, please do. But keep it light, Ben. I'm hungry, but a little unsteady."

"One delicious, steady dinner, coming up," he promised, and she laughed.

He called their waiter and as he ordered, she sipped her ginger ale and thought, He's made me laugh. She felt almost guilty. It seemed wrong to be here with this man, in Sardi's, of all places, laughing, drinking, when her father . . .

"Mary?"

She heard his voice from afar, and realized that

she'd been staring deeply into the center of her glass, watching the amber liquid swirl as she stirred it with a swizzle stick.

"I'm sorry. What?"

"Another ginger ale?"

"Oh," she looked up at the waiter, "No. I think not. Thank you."

The waiter smiled and left.

"Ben," she said at last, "listen, we may as well get this over with. The funeral . . . what do I have to do?"

"Nothing, unless you want to, or unless you wish some changes made. His body arrived two days ago from New Guinea. It's all been taken care of. The funeral's tomorrow. We, that is, Dana and I, assumed you'd want him buried here, rather than dealing with flying him back to . . ."

"Yes, yes. You were right. He loved it here. It's what he would have wanted."

"Are you sure you want me to go on with this?"

She nodded, but he knew this was hard on her, maybe the hardest thing she'd ever done. "No sense in postponing it, if the funeral's tomorrow. I may as well know now. It's inevitable anyway. One thing. Can I see him, Ben? Before the funeral?"

She saw Ben hesitate, obviously trying to form words.

"What, Ben?"

"Mary . . . it's a closed coffin."

"Oh, yes." She remembered then, the newspaper she'd read. It was because of the head. She closed her eyes, fighting back a wave of dizziness.

"You okay?"

"Yes. Please go on. Just keep talking."

"The plans are to pick us up here by limousine tomorrow morning. There'll be a short mass at a nearby church at ten, and then the cemetery at eleven."

Mary took a sip of her drink and a tear in the corner of her eye caught the light and glided across her cheek. She wiped it away and the corners of her mouth turned up in a sweet smile, as if to let him know that she was going to come through just fine. Ben felt a rush of admiration for her, and he put his hand over hers.

"I wish it were all over, Ben."

"Soon. Soon."

Their eyes met and held, then she pulled her hand from beneath his and picked up her glass once more. "What about you?" she asked, "Your nerves must be shot, too."

"His death was a blow, of course. We were close."

"He always thought you had the Great American Novel in you."

"Well, perhaps a halfway decent book, anyway."

"Working on anything now?"

"The third part of the profile on him has to be written tonight."

"Can I read it?"

"I have no choice. All you have to do is buy a paper. The second part appears in tomorrow's issue."

"And a book?"

"Someday, maybe."

The salads arrived, and as the waiter garnished them with fresh pepper, Ben ordered a glass of white wine with his meal, after she'd declined one.

"Dana's looking forward to seeing you."

"I want to see her, Ben. She and Dad . . ."

"Yes. Dana wasn't sure you knew about her relationship with him . . . I mean, the depth of it."

"Oh, she's an attractive woman, and Dad wasn't

made of stone. I didn't think it was a secret. Besides from the way he'd written about her, much less the way they'd acted together in Chicago, it would have been evident. It didn't really take much figuring."

"Have you thought at all about yourself?"

"Me?"

"Yes. I mean, well, after the funeral . . . do you have any plans?"

"No, none really. I'd planned on a two week stay here at the very least. I don't know. I'll have to make some decisions, I suppose. There'll be insurance to settle . . . and a will, I suppose."

"Dana's got the policies and the will . . . but it all goes to you, Mary."

She stared at him, genuinely taken back. "All of it?"

"Yes. Why?"

"Well, I just thought . . . you know . . . Dana . . ."

"Your father was absent minded about things like that. I mentioned it to him a few times . . . just so there'd be something for Dana. Not that she cares for money. She only sees it as something to spend on research . . . they had that in common, too. Anyway, Marc kept putting it off . . ."

"Well, when I see her, we can straighten it out."

"Be careful, Mary. Dana has her pride."

"I know," she smiled, "but she couldn't turn down a sizable donation to the research, now could she?"

He laughed, and they began eating their first course. He liked the woman Mary Pemberton had turned into. Marcus would have been proud.

The meal had been, as promised, delicious. Guinataang Tagunton, which, she learned, was a concoction of small, fresh water shrimps in coconut milk. It had surprised her until Ben told her coconut was a staple of Filipino food. With the first scruptious bite she appreciated how long it had been since she'd eaten, and Ben had been happy to witness the return of her appetite.

They'd talked about him, mostly, and of his work; some of the assignments he'd covered. She found that she liked him. He wisely kept her from talking too much about herself . . . or her father.

Now, with her hair down and blown by the wind from the window of the car, the air felt good and clean. She was pleased he'd decided to forego the air-conditioning. She breathed deeply and exhaled.

As he took a right turn, his body leaning towards her slightly, he looked over at her, grinned, and brought his eyes back to the road.

"Feel okay?"

"Oh, Ben. So much better. Thank you."

"Good. We're almost there."

Up ahead she saw a house, isolated by about a quarter of a mile on either side from any other. There were lights on in the front and in the rear, and as they drew closer, Ben honked the horn with three short blasts. A small light went on inside a closed screened porch, and the opened door of the house revealed a female silhouette outlined in the threshold.

"Ben?" a girl's voice called.

"Yeah. Lucy?"

"Yes. It's good to see you!"

"You too," he replied, slamming the door and coming around to Mary's side of the car. "Glad to see you up and around."

Mary emerged from the car and as the door slammed he took her elbow, and guided her up the short path.

"Aren't you going to lock it?"

"This isn't Chicago, Mary."

She shrugged, feeling just a little stupid. On their right was a sign suspended on a chain between two posts, that read "Pemberton Anthropological Foundation." She had a photograph of her father standing in front of that sign, taken on the day it had been erected.

The screen door of the porch squeaked as they entered, and now Mary could see, dimly lit by the porch light, the girl who stood holding the opened door of the house.

It was immediately apparent that the girl had been through an ordeal, and recently. Though she didn't look much past 25, she too had dark circles under her eyes, and her black hair looked as if it hadn't been washed in a while. Beneath her tan, she seemed pale. The most striking thing about her lovely face was the eyes that were so very light blue.

"I'm Lucy Case," she stated.

"Hello," Mary replied, holding out her hand, "I'm Mary Pemberton."

Closing the door, Lucy took her hand, the ice blue eyes filling up with tears as she whispered, "I'm so awfully sorry."

Mary said a quick "thank you" and Ben put an arm around each of them, moving them on into the house.

So, this was where he had lived.

Mary had often tried to imagine his every day surroundings, and now, here they were. Of course, she'd seen photos too, of the inside of the house; she even recognized a few of the things from Chicago, and from pictures. In the corner, where now an easy chair and hassock stood, the Christmas tree was placed each year. Two small paintings on either wall that framed the tree, in the photos she'd seen, told her that. Still, even from pictures, you couldn't really tell. This room now had a warmer, cozier glow to it than the glare of a flash cube could reveal.

"Dana . . . Dr. McKinley . . . is in here," Lucy said, and moved ahead of them, leading them through the living room toward the back of the house.

NINE

They entered a long, rather dimly lit hallway at the end of which, dead ahead, was a door that a first glance appeared to be closed. However, as they approached, a thin line of light became visible around three sides, and Mary could see it had been left ajar. Lucy's hand went out and slowly pushed the door wide, revealing the room within.

It appeared to be a combination library and office. The bouquet of Turkish Latakia tobacco spiced the air like incense, and Mary reacted inwardly to it. Instantly she knew her father had spent many hours in here.

A very large, detailed map took up most of the wall to the immediate right of a large metal desk. Two other walls were lined with books and in one, where the books ended, there was another door that appeared to open outside into a garden. A table stood close to one of the bookshelves, and on it lay various artifacts, parchments, notes, and what looked to be bones or ivory of some sort, spread out in what seemed like disarray. A few had labels tied to them with wire. The remaining wall had many framed awards, degrees and diplomas hung upon it, and here and there, photographs of people who had been important to the life of Marcus Pemberton. Mary spotted a picture of herself at age fourteen among them.

The desk was placed in front of this wall, and the only light in the room came from a brass lamp with a green glass shade that stood at its corner. A figure sat behind it, motionless, in a large, worn, brown leather swivel chair. She was leaned back and all the lamp light caught were her hands. Their long thin fingers, with nails cut short and filed down, were folded before her in her lap.

"Dana?" Lucy asked quietly.

The chair creaked on its old springs and the woman leaned forward, moving from out of the shadows and into the light. Her face, fully lit now, stared at them, while just above her head a large photo of Marcus Pemberton barely caught the glow from the lamp. Dana McKinley smiled and said, "Mary. Oh, Mary, How very good to see you."

She stood up and extended those long hands across the desk, and Mary came forward to accept her embrace, as Dana added softly, "I'm sorry. I must have dozed off in my chair."

They hugged and both were surprised at the ferocity with which they held each other. Mary, because she now truly accepted that for all intents and purposes, this woman was her father's widow, and her grief was as deep as her own. For Dana, it was much the same kind of emotion, strongly maternal, mixed with relief that another person, another woman, had arrived among them who felt strongly about having *lost* Marc. Many were upset about the manner in which he died, but here was one who's life had been changed by this loss, as had her own. With Mary here along with Ben, she felt that some of the responsibility, real or imagined, had been lifted from her shoulders. "I'm only sorry," she whispered in Mary's ear, "that it had to be like this . . . seeing you again."

When they separated, Dana held Mary at arms length and they looked at each other, knowing that they had become allies, friends. "Why don't we all sit down?" Dana suggested.

Ben pulled a few chairs around the desk and they sat down facing Dana. Lucy remained standing however, and asked, "I could use some brandy. Anyone else?"

"Excellent," Ben smiled, and Lucy left the library through the door they'd entered. When she'd gone, Dana said quickly,

"She's been beside herself with this news. She's very highly strung. She can't sleep, has headaches . . . you know. Lucy's best friend was with your father, and she hasn't been found yet. Anyway, keep that in mind and bear with her?"

"Of course," Mary answered quietly.

"You're looking much better, Dana."

"Thanks, Ben. I've just been able to get a little rest."

Mary stared at Dana behind the desk. She looked not too different from the last time Mary had seen her, but for looking weary. Dana's figure certainly was as trim as it had ever been, and in the beige slacks and pink t-shirt she now wore, she looked younger than the forty-plus years Mary guessed

Dana must be.

Lucy returned with a cut glass decanter of brandy and four snifters carried upon a silver tray. How elegant, Mary thought as the girl placed the tray on the desk. Dana began pouring as Lucy took an ash tray from a nearby shelf and seated herself next to Ben, he being the only other smoker in the room. She lit a cigarette and inhaled deeply, while Ben handed her her drink. She nodded a "thank you" and sipped immediately, not waiting for the others to be served.

Mary accepted a glass thinking, well, I don't have to drink it. Still, it looked good. She allowed herself the temptation and took her first sip; it stung, but she liked it. She looked at Lucy.

The girl had a strange effect upon Mary. It wasn't her being there as much as it was her attitude. The girl's depression was practically tangible, and the air seemed thick with Lucy's anger and fear. And too, though Dana was warm and cordial, indeed even motherly, Mary could not help but take note of the fact that Dana chose the office for them to meet in, when the living room would have seemed, to Mary, more appropriate. No doubt, she thought, this room may have been picked because her father's presence was probably stronger here than in any other part of the house. Nevertheless, it did give the feeling that they were attending a "meeting," and she would have preferred it to have a less formal atmosphere.

They all had their drinks now, and Ben said, "I don't think a toast would be out of order, do you?"

No one spoke, and he continued, "To Marc Pemberton. He liked a good snort once in a while."

"I dare say," Mary agreed, throwing a glance to Dana, who grinned and winked.

They raised their glasses, and were about to drink, when a small, trembling voice squeaked out.

"What about Margery Croft?"

The three of them turned to Lucy, whose glass was already empty. Her hand was shaking, and there were tears staining her cheeks.

"Yes," Mary said to her, "of course. Margery Croft as well."

"You didn't even know her!"

"Lucy," Dr. McKinley put in, "we're all upset enough as it is, thank you."

Lucy took another drag of her cigarette and then crushed it out in the ash tray.

"I know," she sniffed, wiping her eyes as she rose and filled her snifter again, "forgive me. I was rude. I . . ."

"It's alright. Never mind," Mary offered.

Lucy took her seat again, and lit another cigarette.

"Go on," she sighed, meeting Dana's eyes with her own.

Dana stared back at her for a moment, as if to regain the focus of the room, and the attention of the others. After a bit, she turned her gaze to Mary, saying,

"I hope discussing your father's death won't upset you too much, Mary. There's something very important I must talk with you about."

"You'll know if it does, Dana. Besides, it might clear up a lot of questions I have . . . and separate the truth from . . . well, from whatever exaggerations I may have . . . heard."

She shot a glance over to Ben but he simply took her hand and squeezed it, making her know he was not offended.

Dana took a sip of her brandy and stood up. Flipping a switch on the wall, an overhead light illuminated the large map. She picked up a pointer that was leaning in a corner and gesturing with it as she spoke, she exuded an air of a slightly officious instructor.

"To put it as simply as possible, you know that your father and I were looking for a missing link."

Mary nodded, "He'd been working on it for years. At least as long as I can recall, anyway."

"Alright, then. Only a few months ago, all we really had to go on was what every other anthropologist of this century has had available to them. Bits and pieces of this and that, folklore which has been impossible to determine if there was even a shred of truth to, and of course, the sightings."

"Of what?" Mary asked.

At that, Lucy laughed sarcastically, letting a billow of smoke out as she did so. Mary's hand waved the smoke away from her face, and Lucy said,

"Excuse me. I didn't mean to . . ."

"Never mind. It's alright."

"Ben," Dana asked, as he was about to light one of his own, "why don't you open the back door there? The screen door will keep out the insects, and I think we, at least Mary and I, anyway, could use the fresh air. Of course it will make the air-conditioning useless, but that can't be helped."

Ben reluctantly did so, and Mary remembered then about Dana's intolerance to smoking. Lucy leaned in to her then and said, mostly for Dana's benefit, "Smoke makes her nuts. Marcus was forever forgetting to open the door and filled the room up with smoke all the time."

Dana leaned on the pointer like a cane. Her grin made her eyes crinkle in narrow slits.

"She's right, Mary. Though pipe tobacco smells a good deal better than cigarette smoke, I'll admit. And, it could have been worse; I mean, he could have been partial to cigars. But I'd even toyed with the idea of hiding that lighter you'd given him."

Mary laughed, "Well anyway I'm glad he used it. When I'd bought it for him, it took two weeks of my salary."

A cool breeze came through the opened door from what was now the dark night, stirring the thin cloud of smoke that hung suspended in the room. The leaves of the trees rustled, and somewhere, far off, a night bird called.

"Better?" Ben asked, and blew his own smoke in an exaggerated puff toward the opened door.

"Much," Dana clucked, "now then . . ."

"Sightings," Ben offered.

"Ah, yes. Sightings. You know about Big Foot? Abominable Snowmen, that sort of thing? That's what I mean. They've been spotted, or reported to have been spotted, in many heavily wooded regions of the United States, and of course, the Himalayas."

"And you think these things are the missing links?"

"Wait, Mary. I don't want to get ahead of myself here." She took a sip of her brandy and ran a hand quickly across her brow. Then, leaning the pointer against the wall, she walked behind them to the table, picked up a scroll and returned with it to her place before the map.

"A while back we came across this," she held up the scroll, then undid the ribbon it was tied in and unrolled it very carefully, holding it gently with thumb and forefinger so they could see it. Something that resembled handwriting was scrawled across the ancient parchment in an unrecognizable language.

"We, Lucy and I . . . have only just recently been able to date it, and at that, only within a hundred years or so, one way or the other."

She rolled it up again slowly and placed it on the desk.

"We think it was written by a scholar named Pausanias. It's taken some time to translate, but as close as we can come it seems to document a story that may have been the basis for a legend that has existed here in this part of the world, for some time."

Lucy yawned audibly.

"Thank you, Lucy," Dr. McKinley said shortly.

"Perhaps I should lie down," Lucy mumbled drowsily.

"Perhaps you should, dear."

There was silence as Lucy rose, crossed to the door and added, "I'm sorry, Dana. Good night, Ben. Good night, Mary, and I hope to see you again under better circumstances."

"Well, I don't know that it will be better circumstances, but I expect I'll see you tomorrow . . . at the funeral?"

Lucy stared at Mary for a moment, looked down at her feet, then looked back up again, gave one nod of her head, and was gone. When the sound of her footsteps had disappeared, Dana commented softly, "She's had too much to drink on top of her sedation." Mary blushed, wondering if the same could be said of her.

"She's been staying with you, here, Dana?"

"Yes. Margery shared her apartment with her, and the place gives her the creeps, now. She's afraid to be alone in it."

Mary took another sip of her drink, saying, "I can't say as I blame her, really."

"Nor I. Now, then . . ."

"Pausanias," Ben reminded her once more with a grin.

"I'm glad you're here, Ben. I'd never get this told." She picked up the pointer again. "Pausanias tells of a ship driven off course in a violent storm, and wrecked on a small island. At first, Marcus and I thought, erroneously, that perhaps Pausanias was talking about someplace in the Philippines. But, once we'd started investigating, we realized that was wrong. Well, the only other logical area it could have been was here," and she gestured with the stick on the map, "in one of the many islands of New Guinea. After a long process of elimination, we've narrowed it down to this one."

She moved the pointer to a tiny speck on the map. "Satyr Island."

Ben asked, "Why this island, as opposed to all of the others in that area? There must be hundreds."

"Because, for various reasons it's one of the islands that qualify, according to what we believe."

"Which is?" Ben asked again.

"That there is a secret society on this island here," she pointed, "called Savong-khai. It's the largest island in this cluster here, and midway between the coast of Papua, New Guinea, and Satyr Island. You'd barely even notice Satyr Island was there, but it's close enough to Savong-khai to be habitable."

"Dana, two questions," Mary asked, pouring herself a half glass of brandy. She filled Dana's glass, then Ben's, continuing, "What is this 'secret society,' and why have you called that little dot 'Satyr Island'?"

"Back to Pausanias, I'll bet," Ben laughed and took a swig of brandy.

"You're so smart," Dana chided, "Alright, our fisherman are shipwrecked. But they were able to escape the island in a row boat, knowing they could make it as far as Savong-khai, which is in sight across the water from Satyr Island. Apparently, they had pushed off and were well under way, when a woman appeared on the beach, pleading with them to take her with them. Of course, they'd thought the island was uninhabited. The woman swam out to their boat and as they rowed away from the island with her, a creature ran out onto the beach calling to her . . ."

"A creature," Mary observed, "like Bigfoot, or an Abominable Snowman?"

"Yes, exactly, from all reports. But the sad and terrifying thing about this story is, there was a child."

Dana laid the pointer down on the desk and sat behind it, her face lit by the glass lamp. She looked more tired than ever, as she downed the remainder of her drink, rubbing her eyes. She went on.

"The monster supposedly held this infant up for her to see, and when she did not return, the thing drowned the baby in the surf, then walked into the water, and being unable to swim, also drowned."

They all three sat without moving, the effect of the story having silenced them. Then, Ben ventured.

"An infant?"

"Yes. Presumably . . . and I *stress* 'presumably' . . . from the union of the woman and the . . ."

"Missing link?" Mary whispered.

"Perhaps, Mary. At any rate, what it's called when the legend is told by the natives, translates most closely to what we know as 'satyr'."

"Oh, Dana, come on now," Ben said, standing up, obviously attempting to hide the fact that he was visibly shaken by all this, "those are part man, part goat, oversexed sprites from mythology. They can't exist. They never did."

"Well, Ben," Dana retorted impatiently, "I can't . . . or won't . . . argue with you. But whether we call it a missing link, or we call it a saytr, it doesn't seem to me to make a hell of a lot of difference since we don't in any case, know what in fact, it is."

Ben, feeling put in his place, sat down again. He did not look at Mary when she spoke.

"And that's what my father wanted to find out."

"Yes."

"But Dana, why would he, and all the others, be killed?"

"Lucy knows this legend, and that very question is what is driving her mad. We don't know for a fact, that ALL of them were killed."

"Dana, I don't understand . . ."

"If Margery Croft is still alive, then what happened to her?"

Mary sat, incredulous, waiting for an answer, but none came. She looked at Ben, then back at Dana. The night seemed to grow warmer, but it hadn't, really, she knew. Her pulse had quickened and perspiration had broken out across her brow and upper lip. Finally she managed to say, hoarsly.

"Are you implying . . ."

"Draw your own conclusions. That is all we really know, and all I am prepared to say. I think your father made a larger discovery than even he was aware of, and he was silenced."

Mary rose and walked over to the opened door, looking out at the lovely little garden, through the screen. Flying insects flew around the small amber bulb that burned just outside. She ran her index finger down the screen just once. The mixed heavy fragrances of the blossoms wafted in to her. When she turned around, Ben and Dana were both staring at her. Addressing Dana, she declared,

"I am financially able and willing to sponsor an expedition to begin where my father left off. Would you be willing to arrange, and conduct it?"

"You don't beat around the bush, do you?"

"Neither did Dad, Dana."

"No. He didn't."

"Well?"

"I'd be honored," Dana stated quietly.

"Good. There's only one condition."

"What?" Ben asked.

"I go along," Mary answered.

"Hold on a minute."

The two women turned to Ben and he knew he had put himself on the spot. "After all," he continued, "there are people dead . . . murdered . . . I'm sorry, but there's Margery missing, too. Is this wise?"

"Ben," Dana put in, glancing quickly over at Mary, "listen. It wouldn't be just us. We would hire people . . . a guide, people to help us . . . people who know what to warn us about."

"Well, you're paying for it," he said to Mary, "so I won't try to talk you out of it, much as I'd like to. Anyway, it wouldn't work, would it?"

"No, it wouldn't Ben. But, if it's alright with Dana, you can come along with us, if you like."

"No objections here," Dana shrugged. "What about it, Ben?"

Thinking quickly, he weighed the question. Though the jungle would be difficult, disgusting and probably dangerous, still the reporter in him told him it was an opportunity that came along only once in a life time. And, too, there was Mary.

But how would he clear it with the paper? They'd never give him time off and he couldn't put in for vacation time at such short notice. Besides, he only

had four more days vacation coming to him this
year, and a leave of absence would hardly be agreed
to. There was, however, one possibility.

He looked at Dana, then took Mary's hand and
said, "Listen . . . I want to. Probably more than
anything in the world, right now. But I'm a
reporter, Mary."

Dana obviously knew what he was getting at, and
put in, "He's right, Mary. He can't just pick up and
go. He's got a job. A job he hates." She looked
pointedly at Ben, nailing him with, "A job that
compromises everything he believes in . . . but he
can't risk losing it. Isn't that right, Ben?"

They held the stare for a moment, Ben at last
saying, "You mean I lack an indifference to con-
sequences?"

"What?" Mary asked.

"Nothing. A private joke," Dana answered her,
still not taking her eyes off Ben. "Yes. That's what I
mean, Ben. It's still a question of freedom, isn't it?"

"Alright," he said. "The reality is that for now, at
this moment, I still work for that rag."

"That's exactly what Marc called it," Dana commented with a smile.

"Not to me, he didn't. I wish he had. Anyway,
until I make any decision, the only way the *Manila-
American* might be coaxed into allowing me to go
would be in an official capacity."

Mary removed her hand from beneath Ben's. "As
a reporter covering it as a news story?"

"Right," he replied to her, the move not unnoticed.

"And you'd write about it . . . I mean, paint it up
with gore, the way they'd like?"

"No. I'll write the truest account I can, turn it
into them, then . . ."

"Then, what?" Dana asked hopefully.

"Then . . . I might think about quitting."

"Well, it's certainly a step in the right direction, isn't it?" Dana turned toward Mary. "It's up to you of course, dear, but I'd agree to it, if I were you."

They waited for Mary's decision. Finally, she said, "Allright. Ask them, Ben."

"Thanks. Listen, they might say no, and your conscience will be clear."

"And yours?" Dana questioned. "What if they *do* say no? Will you come with us anyway?"

"I . . ." he began, then hesitated and settled for saying, "We'll see, Dana. Let me put it to them and find out how they take it. Then, I'll decide."

"Fine," she replied, obviously not satisfied, but willing to accept his plan. There was a brief silence in the now smoke filled room, broken by Ben asking, "When do we leave?"

"You'll know when I do," Dana answered, obviously pleased with his decision. She turned to Mary, adding, "I'll need Lucy, if she'll come."

"I'll come," came a hard edged voice from the shadows of the doorway and Lucy emerged into the pool of light that encircled the others.

"I thought you'd be asleep by now." Dana was trying to sound conversational, but the annoyance was hard to miss.

"No. I've been listening outside the door, actually. I'll come." She said it again, almost a dare, as if she were waiting, indeed, hoping for someone to object and give her a reason to tell them off.

Ben broke the silence that followed with, "I don't know about anyone else, but I'm tired. And you," he motioned to Mary, "must be exhausted." The implicit reference to what they faced tomorrow did not escape anyone. Tomorrow, she would bury her father.

She took a step toward Dana and held the older woman in an embrace. Dana's arms went around Mary in response, and they remained still, holding each other. Mary had closed her eyes, and when she opened them, she saw among all the other framed photos on the wall behind the desk, one picture she had not seen since she was a little girl. Dana felt the girl's hold loosen and released her, looking into Mary's face.

"What is it?"

Mary gestured toward the wall. "That picture. I was nine when it was taken."

It was a photograph in black and white, taken probably fifteen years ago, picturing a distinguished woman of about thirty in a dark dress. Her hair was parted to one side and fell neatly over her shoulders. She was just barely smiling, a bit self-conscious it seemed, at having her picture taken. It was Mary's mother. Beside her, Marc Pemberton smiled out happily, holding in his arms with some apparent difficulty, a gangly, awkward child, already too big to be carried.

Dana stepped up to the wall and took the picture down, blowing a little dust off the top of the frame. "Here," she said, handing it to Mary, "he'd have wanted you to have this, dear."

Mary reached out and took the photo, studying it now under better light at close range. Her mother had died a few years after this picture had been taken. A tear fell upon the glass and ran off into a corner of the frame. Mary wiped her eyes and smiled at Dana. "Thank you," she said simply.

"You're welcome."

With that, Dana turned her back to Mary as tears came to her own eyes. She reached into her pocket for a handkerchief, letting a short sob escape. When she'd regained her composure and blown her nose, she said thickly, over her shoulder, "I'll see you tomorrow." Her back remained turned to them.

Lucy did not walk them through the house to show them out, but stood motionless as they left, and did not move or blink even after she heard the front door close behind them.

When Dana McKinley turned around, she saw Lucy staring at the map on the wall, her eyes transfixed on the miniscule dot that was Satyr Island.

Outside in the garden, just to the left of the back door, a figure was hiding from the amber bulb over the threshold, recoiled in fear of discovery, as Mary's fingernail ran nosily over the screen less than two feet away. It had been there since Lucy had brought the brandy, listening to all that took place inside, from the legend of Pausanias to the declaration of forming a second expedition. It dreaded having to relay what it had heard to its superiors. The information would not please them.

Now, the reporter's car had started up, masking the sound of footsteps moving away from the rear of the house, through the garden, crushing a few flowers underfoot as the figure made its way across a neighboring lawn in quick retreat.

Ben was driving faster now then he had on the way out and Mary was pleased. The wind, though hot, revived her, and she was glad she'd had enough sense not to drink any more than she did.

The car took the last turns easily and she saw that they had almost reached the main downtown area, and would be at her hotel shortly.

It had been quite a night. She knew already that sleep would not come quickly to her. But then, there was always the valium. Her brain seemed to ache with all the information she had heard tonight, and thinking back over the evening, she wasn't sure she'd remember everything.

Oh, well, she thought sighing, there would be time to digest it all and hopefully understand it too. Of all the things she had heard, what had upset her most was not, surprisingly, any of the references to her father's passing. What stuck in her mind above all else, was the story of the creature, and the baby. The baby. Drowned. Had it been human? Part human? It seemed silly, but she found herself worrying about it not being baptized before it had died.

The car pulled up to the curb outside the side entrance of the hotel.

"Home, sort of," he said quietly, as if not wanting to jar her from her thoughts. She looked at him, saying "thanks" and began to open her door as he moved to open his. "No," she put a hand on his arm, "please don't get out, Ben. I can get myself upstairs."

He settled back in the driver's seat again. "Okay. If you prefer."

"I do."

He took her hand in his and held it gently. "If there's anything you need or want, please call me. You still have my numbers?"

"There is one thing."

"What's that?"

"Marcus . . . Dad . . . he wasn't the only one . . . I mean there were others . . ."

"Yes. There were three other local men that were killed, too."

"Do we know who they were? Their names, I mean?"

"Yes. They were mentioned in the reports. Why?"

"I don't know. I'd like to do something . . . flowers, or money . . . something. They must have had families, too."

"I'll find out and let you know."

She caressed his rough cheek with her fingers, the stubble of beard feeling good as she pressed her palm against it. He was, she thought, a very sweet, very beautiful man.

They looked into each other's eyes for just a moment longer than either had planned, and in that moment, moved in, face to face until their breath mingled together in the air between their parted lips, which met and held in a tender kiss that promised more.

They were both breathing quickly when she'd pulled her mouth from his, opened her door, and whispered goodnight.

Ben watched her walk up the steps and into the hotel, then started the car and drove home knowing that tonight, his life had changed.

Upstairs in her room, the faces of Mary, her mother and her father grinned from within the frame that stood now beside the phone on the night table. Once in bed, she looked at the picture for a little while, said a silent prayer, and turned off the lamp.

TEN

Lamberto Cellion was twenty-five years old and had been working as a chauffeur for five years.

He had moved here to the largest island, Luzon, and settled in Manila, after spending most of his early life on Bacalod, growing up and working on the sugar plantations there. Though Bacalod was a thriving little metropolis, he had wanted to move to the capital city for many years, and many reasons.

The deciding factor in his relocation, however, was that his sweetheart, Theresa Oloroso, had been at the time, a minor, and forced to move there with her father, Jaime.

Lamberto and Theresa had been married the very day she had reached majority, and since then, had been living in the city, not far from her father, who liked Lamberto.

The Cellion's were now a family. Theresa having

given birth to two boys in their four years of marriage. Lamberto did well as a limousine driver, and though they were hardly rich, he and his family wanted for nothing, and could even afford a few luxuries.

Today was to be an easy, fast day. He simply had to pick up some Americans at various places, take them to a church, then a cemetery for a funeral, and return them all to where he had picked them up. Though it would not amount to much on an hourly basis, he knew the man who had died was some sort of famous scientist or something, and Lamberto anticipated being back home with Theresa in the early afternoon, with a handsome tip.

So, he had left their house early that morning and drove in his own car to the garage from which he worked. As usual, he said good morning to the dispatcher in his little office, and as usual, headed for the locker-room, to change into his uniform.

Pulling on his cap, he headed to the office for the keys to the car he was driving that day, wishing the uniforms were made of lighter fabric. Even this early, the sun was already roasting the pavements, and the blast of heat that hit him from inside the car brought yet more fresh sweat to his brow.

He turned on the air-conditioning, started the big vehicle moving, and as it passed the office, he waved farewell to the dispatcher, and headed the car out into the street.

Once he had been driving for about three minutes, he stopped for a light, in a deserted area he always passed through in order to get to the main part of the city.

Lamberto started as he felt something stick him just beneath his jaw on the right side. He knew it was the tip of a knife, when a man's voice spoke to him from behind, where the glass partition separated driver from passenger. It had been opened when he got into the car and he had not thought to close it, nor to look into the back seat. The cars were always cleaned and vacuumed the night after their use, and ready to go for the morning. He wished he had inspected it before leaving the garage. Now, it was too late.

The voice told him to turn left, and he did so, whereupon they found themselves on a long dirt road that bordered a large plot of land, over-grown with grass and weeds.

The voice told him to stop the car; he did so.

Get out, it said; he did so, and the voice followed him, and told him to walk into the tall grass and weeds, and take off his cap, uniform, and shoes.

It was the last thing Lamberto Cellion did, before the first thrust of the knife dug into him.

They dressed in white for funerals here.

Looking around the crowd, she was made aware of what a large part the sun played in their every day lives. The gathering was literally brilliant with white, radiating light, made more so by the rich contrast of green grass surrounding them, and the red carnations they all carried. It was intensely hot and the scent of the flowered crosses and wreathes were everywhere.

Ben had already been picked up by the limousine and it was he who had called for Mary that morning. The day was not starting out well. The car was fifteen minutes late in arriving. Their driver was a native, but, contrary to the Filipino personality, seemed surly, as if he resented doing this and there had been no apology from him, for his tardiness. He'd not even turned around in his driver's seat from curiosity, when Mary had entered the car, much less gotten out to open the door for them when they emerged from the hotel. "Wait'll he sees his tip," Ben muttered angrily as she settled into her seat. No matter, she told herself. She did not want to be more upset than she was already. The chauffeur probably didn't like funerals anymore than anyone else did.

Just the walk through the front doors of the hotel and into the blast of heat that waited in the street made her wilt, and she was grateful for the almost chilly air inside the Cadillac. It's started. This unavoidable day has commenced, and by tonight, this will be a memory, she thought. I can . . . I will, get through this. The car drove off to the Pemberton Foundation, where Ben hopped out and returned shortly with a composed Dana McKinley. Her black sunglasses were stark against the total whiteness of her broad brimmed hat and luncheon suit. Lucy seemed in a somewhat more delicate state, but she'd managed a sober greeting as she climbed in to join Mary.

Once on the road, Dana had removed her glasses and sat staring through the dark, smoke-tinted windows. Lucy and Ben had taken the folding jump seats, and so sat facing their companions. Mary took the chance to study Lucy.

The girl's nails were bitten down to a point where she must obviously have drawn blood. She had at last washed her hair, but only that morning. With the moisture heavy in the air nothing really dried, including Lucy's hair. It lay in wet curls where it didn't hang listlessly over her ears and into her eyes, or stay confined within a black ribbon at the base of her sticky neck. She had been crying again, for her eyes were puffier and more bloodshot now than they

had been last night. It was disturbing, because
Lucy's genuine good looks seemed to underscore
these ravages of grief. But no, Mary thought. It was
not grief that bothered this girl. It was fear.

Dana had obviously done some crying too. But her
grief—and that was the right word—was self-con-
tained, controlled, disciplined. She seemed to be a
professional to her very core, and without being an
unemotional, unfeeling person. Mary admired her
for it.

The church was also gleaming white and once
inside, cool. It made Mary nervous to have the
massive coffin there, just a few feet from her in the
center aisle. She couldn't get it out of her head that
if she wanted to leave, to run out of here and away,
her escape was blocked by the coffin—by her own
father.

The service was over quickly, thank God, and once
again they moved to the cars. The strange driver
still sat motionlessly behind the wheel. When Ben
knocked on the partition, the car started up and
they drove here, to the last stop. The cemetery.

The priest was talking now, and she continued to
look over the people gathered to mourn her father.
She'd met a few of them outside the church, but
knew none of them. Yet they had all, in some way,
cared about him. And here he was, Marcus Pemberton, come to rest in a graveyard in the Philippines
after a life begun in Connecticut. He would have
laughed.

The mourners took their cue from the priest and
stepping close to the coffin, threw the red blossoms
upon it, joining them with the blanket of flowers
that already lay over it. She thought of him, inside
that box—so alone—and she began to weep. But of
course, he wasn't alone; he wasn't even there. What

dwelt inside the coffin was a body. Him—his
essence, his spirit—had departed; and it was she
who was . . . or felt she was . . . alone, abandoned.
The word "orphaned" came to mind, and it was with
that that she pulled herself together, ashamed of her
own morbid self-pity. She dried her eyes and blew
her nose.

Then it was over, and after a few goodbyes, she
felt Ben's hand at her elbow, guiding her back to the
waiting car. It was a familiar gesture, but an un-
pleasant one. She remembered him doing the same
thing to her at the airport. Ben could feel her tense,
and glanced at her. Mary was staring at him as they
walked. Then, gently, kindly, she looked down at his
hand and removed her arm from his grasp. He was
embarrassed, but she smiled, telling him it was
alright.

Since the driver had not previously gotten out to
open the door for them, it was hardly a surprise that
he remained in the front seat now, and stayed there
until Ben's knock once again signalled him to start
the car.

They moved slowly at first, the mighty weight of
the large vehicle crunching over the gravel in the
circular drive leading in and out of the grave yard,
but eventually they passed through the huge black
iron gates, turned left and were back on the smooth,
paved road leading back toward town.

Having all taken their original seats, Ben was
once more facing Mary. He caught her eye, and she
acknowledged his glance with a friendly, thankful
smile. Directly behind him, they could hear their
chauffeur humming a little tune, and though Mary
thought it hardly an occasion for song, at least it
humanized the heretofore stoney driver. They drove
along in silence for a time. Then Ben asked of Mary,

"Do you have plans? For today, I mean?"

"What time is it now?"

"Eleven forty-five."

"Well," she replied, "I think I'd like to go back to my room and lie down for a while, actually."

"Call me when you wake up. Maybe you'll feel like dinner?"

"Maybe," she answered softly.

"Dana, join us later?"

Dana had been looking out the window again. They were now on a shore road, with the beach and ocean a few hundred feet out and down a steep embankment. She turned to them saying, "What? Oh, no, no, I think not, Ben. I'd really like to spend the rest of this day . . . well, alone, you know? Perhaps Lucy will join you?"

Much as Ben liked Dana, at that moment he was sorely tempted to kick her in the ankle, for that suggestion. The last person he wanted to be near was Lucy. He felt sorry for her, but her presence was depressing, and demanded attention that he was not willing to give her.

Mercifully, Lucy declined, as if she knew she was not welcome and had been asked simply because she was there. Ben did not press the issue, but accepted her refusal and said no more about it.

The limousine had picked up speed now and rounding a turn, Ben and Lucy had to put their arms out to lean on the doors, lest they fall off the little seats.

"Driver," Ben called through the glass, "take the turns a little slower, please, will you?"

The chauffeur mumbled something and Ben looked over at Dana. She was still looking out the window, but now she was sitting upright, and her eyes went from the beach to the road below them and then, to the driver. Something was wrong.

The driver was still mumbling something, though, and Dana silently motioned Ben to open the glass partition a crack.

As he did so, Mary become aware that the car had picked up still more speed than was necessary. The palm trees went whizzing by them and from the front seat, she heard what she now realized was not a tune the driver had been humming, but a kind of chant, that sounded like, "Hoo-reh-yeh."

Now, even Lucy was attentive and sat forward to listen.

But the man behind the wheel was barely even seeing the road by this time, his head was so full of a voice that came to him from afar, speaking exclusively to him, unheard by the world around him, ordering, demanding, becoming his own will, as it droned, "From the Book of the Dead we reaffirm our Vow of Death to those who would seek to Destroy and expose The Secret of Hoorehyeh!"

The driver repeated aloud the word "Hoorehyeh," and the voice in his head grew louder, saying, "Will the servant's hand, that they may end the evil that surrounds us!"

The car took a sudden violent lurch to the far side of the road, clear into the next lane, then swerved violently back gain, and Ben heard, "Evil surrounds us!"

"Driver!" Ben shouted, sliding the partition opened fully, but the only voice the driver heard was screaming now inside his head.

"Bring honor once more to our Holy Mother!" and spinning the wheel, left and right again, he yelled back, "Honor our Holy Mother!"

"All Hail our Sacred Nymph of Heaven!" his

brain ordered, and he roared back, "Hail, Nymph of Heaven!"

The road ahead stretched out before them down hill in a series of sharp turns, and the limousine gained speed all the time, the man's foot pressing down and down on the pedal, and his private voice so loud now he was nearly deafened with the chanting, "Honor Hoorehyeh! Honor Hoorehyeh!"

They realized it was past even yelling, for the driver to halt or even pay any attention to them at all. Ben turned around and was about to lean through the partition, when there was a loud click from all the doors. Mary and Dana each tried theirs, but they had been locked in tight by the master switch up front, and they looked at Ben. Lucy began to scream then, when the car lurched into the opposite lane again and stayed there, going faster and faster, and then they could all see, bearing down upon them, a big, old, yellow schoolbus full of children, looming over them. The driver screamed, and the sound of screeching brakes and the poor, tinny honking horn of the decrepit bus mingled with Lucy's screams, as Ben forced himself through the partition, and grabbing the wheel over the driver's shoulder, swerved the car into the other lane just before impact, and they were heading toward a wall of rock.

In trying to avoid the crash, the bus overreached its turn, skidded across the road, teetered for a second on two wheels, and then righted itself before coming to rest just inches from where the road dropped off to the sea below.

The limousine had hit the rock and the chauffeur's body lay slumped over the wheel. Ben, unconscious, was jack-knifed over the divider, his upper torso resting on the front seat, his legs dangling lifelessly in the back, like a discarded doll.

Mary tried to get out, but the doors were still locked, and she was screaming now, too, as were the children from the bus, some of whom were now running about in the road. Lucy was moaning, her hands at her head, blood seeping through her fingers, and Dana was holding her, weeping, looking over to Mary in disbelief as the bus driver ran to the car, yelling at the top of his lungs, and Mary felt the temperature inside the vehicle rise very suddenly, and she knew it was neither the sun, nor adrenalin that caused this overwhelming heat. She saw the smoke rising from the front of the car, growing thicker by the moment, enveloping the automobile, and she began to pound frantically on the glass, hysteria rising inside her as her fists beat the windows, covered over now in black smoke, and her voice joined in the pandemonium of terror and panic.

"Get us out! Oh Christ! Get us out of here!" she screamed.

PART III

SAVONG-KHAI

ELEVEN

The season for rain had past. This was unusual weather and did not help the overall depression that seemed to be mounting ever higher within Lucy. Still, the unseasonable downpour was fascinating, and she could not pull herself away from its hypnotic rhythm. From where she stood she could see the red light of the emergency entrance, four floors below. Cars and ambulances came and went, sending up a spray of water over the curbs. People were carried or wheeled through the doors and out of the wet day into the dry whiteness of the hospital in a muted drama that she observed from behind the streaked windowpane.

Lucy had not felt safe since the first word of the massacre had reached them. Now the danger had moved across the sea, directly into their own lives. Though they had not actually said the words to each other as yet, everyone in the car that day knew it was no accident. Yet her nerves seemed to be holding up, she thought. Though the "accident" had been a shock, at least it had been something she'd seen and known. She could deal with what was known. It was the fear of what had happened to Marc . . . what *might* have happened to Margery, that terrified her.

Her hand came up and touched the patch of gauze bandaging on her forehead. The wound was tender, but no longer painful; more a glorified bump near the hairline on the left. The doctor advised her to leave the bandage on a day or two more. Until then, her floppy, wide brimmed hat would cover it up in public. She didn't mention that the headaches were more frequent now. She should have, she knew, but somehow she was afraid to. She didn't know why she was afraid, and she didn't want to.

When the limousine had swerved for the last time, Lucy had been thrown against the window of a door, sustaining her current injury. By the time they had hit the rocks, she had been on her knees on the floor, and it had been her own body that prevented Dana McKinley from hitting the glass partition.

Police had arrived on the scene very quickly and gotten them all out of the burning vehicle, and into the two ambulances that took them here, to the General Hospital. Mercifully, none of the children in the school bus had been hurt, beyond the trauma of the crash.

Lucy wanted a cigarette, but knew she was not allowed to smoke in here. She toyed with the idea of lighting one anyway; even if Ben had been awake, he certainly wouldn't care; he'd probably want one too. But she refrained and turned her back to the window, looking over at him.

His eyes were opened and staring at her. She grinned and walked over to the foot of the bed.

"How long have you been awake?"

"Five minutes, I guess. You've been at the window a long time. What's so interesting?"

"The rain."

"It's too late for rain."

"You're already talking too much. Buzz for the nurse."

"Why? I don't need the nurse."

"We were told that if you woke up while we're here, to let them know."

"We?"

"Dana and me."

"Where is she?"

"Where else? Getting coffee. Now ring for the nurse."

"Wait," Ben protested, "I've got some things to find out first."

"Ben," Lucy began anew, and at that moment the gray door opened into the gray room and Dana McKinley entered. She'd pushed her way in with her hip, both hands holding paper cups from which steam arose.

"Ah!" she cried, "you're awake!"

Lucy took one of the cups from Dana and tasted it. "Oh, God! Dana, this is horrible!"

Dana sipped at her own and agreed, "Truly foul. But, there's caffeine in it, and that's the point."

"Would one of you two ladies please answer some questions?" Ben insisted.

Lucy put her cup down on the small table next to Ben's bed, saying, "Here, you can have this stuff. I will go and get the nurse personally. Dana, humor this man."

They watched Lucy leave the room. Once the door

had closed, Ben said quickly, "Lucy seems under control, considering."

"I know. It's surprised me as well. Maybe she's one of those who reacts best under pressure, although . . ."

"Well, whatever the reason it must be a relief not to have to worry about her."

"Who says I don't? She could snap back to the depression at any second. I've seen her like this before."

Dana took a seat on the straight-backed chair near the bed. The light from the window showed the rings beneath her eyes, and the lines around her mouth seemed deeper today than usual. On her feet, rubber "cowboy" boots had protected her from the rain, and the wine colored slacks she wore had been tucked into the tops of them. A purple (she called it "plum") blouse was opened at the neck and showed signs of having been rained on, where her yellow rain slicker had not been buttoned completely. The slicker hung on the door knob to the bathroom, a small puddle of water beneath it.

"Alright," she said, "what do you want to know?"

"How's Mary?"

"Hoarse from all the screaming she did in the car. Two broken ribs. She's fine. She's thrown all her energy into our expedition. Refuses to be frightened away."

"Where is she now?"

"Asleep at her hotel, I expect. Leastways if she has the brains I think she does. Lucy is taking her shopping later today."

"She can't be wanting souvenirs?"

"For luggage, Ben. What she has is too large and heavy for where and how we're traveling. She'll need a knapsack or duffle bag. Besides, she'll enjoy a trip to Rustan's. It's like an exotic 'Bloomingdale's'."

"You'll have to drag her out."

"I doubt it," Dana chuckled, "but she might have
to drag Lucy out. She's got guts, though. I'll say
that. She's her father's daughter, allright. I'm proud
of her. She's ready to go."

"Okay, okay," Ben declared with exaggerated
impatience," I hope they have a ball. What's wrong
with me?"

"Concussion." she fired back with amusement,
"You'll live. It's a mild one. You can go home
tomorrow."

"The chauffeur?"

"Dead."

"The bus? The school kids?"

"Hysterical, but uninjured. Their driver is fine,
too."

"What do the police know about it?"

"Not much, Ben. Someone saw the crash from
their house nearby and called for help. But they
said . . ."

The door opened again and a rather plain,
businesslike nurse of about fifty came in. She
bobbed her head in a curt greeting to Dana and
without a word stuck a thermometer into Ben's
opened mouth. He tried to speak, but the nurse told
him to be silent.

Dana smiled, enjoying the sight of Ben successfully shut up by this complete stranger, whose
uniform name plate read "Mrs. Mendoza." She was
Filipino, and her dark hair was pulled up under the
white cap, streaks of gray fanning out from above
each ear. Spotting the paper cup at the bedside
table, she asked of Dana, "Did he have any of that?"

Dana said no, and Ben attempted to speak again,
but the nurse said, "Be quiet." The three sat in

silence and after a bit, she removed the tube from her patient's mouth and read it.

"Well?" he asked.

"Drink your coffee," she replied, "if you can stomach it." She left the room.

Ben started laughing, then winced in pain.

"What is it?" Dana asked.

"Nothing. I'm just sore. Actually, I feel like hell."

"That's how you look."

"Cute. Very cute. Y'know you're not looking ready to win any beauty contests yourself, doctor."

"No, I don't guess I do. Anyway, I know you'll be alright if you can joke about things. I was a little scared for you there, for a while."

"Do you think the driver was stoned or something?"

"God knows. What do you remember?"

"That he was almost completely incommunicative from the time he picked us up. I remember the car sped up gradually . . ."

The gray door moved silently again and Lucy entered the room.

"Did the nurse come?" she asked.

"Yes. We're just trying to piece together what we remember from the crash."

"And," Lucy added, closing the door, "what the police told you?"

Dana turned sharply to face Lucy, obviously not happy with the last remark.

"What, Lucy?"

Ben became extra attentive now, as he watched the two women stare each other down. Lucy spoke:

"They told you *something*, Dana. I know they did. I saw you with them."

After a brief pause, Dana sighed. "Alright. But you've been in a state . . ."

"I'm in a state now, Dana, from NOT knowing. Please."

"Let Ben continue," she said, "I promise you I'll tell you everything, Lucy."

The corner of the girl's lips curled into a quick, satisfied smile. She took a chair from near the window and moved it over to the bed.

"Go ahead, Ben," Lucy said.

"Okay. We were leaving the cemetery and then you," he motioned to Dana, "signalled me to open the sliding glass. I heard the driver say something like ''hooray' . . .''

"Hoo-reh-yeh," Dana corrected him.

"You DO know," Lucy accused.

"For God's sake, Lucy, I said I would explain it shortly! Please be patient. Ben, go on."

He looked from one to the other. Ben was uneasy whenever these two women were at odds, and he could see the familiar fear making itself evident once more in Lucy's demeanor. He went on rather hurriedly.

"I remember thinking that the chauffeur was singing to himself at first, but he wasn't. This was monotonous, like a chant or something. He repeated that word quite a few times, and some other stuff about 'evil' and 'nymphs,' I think. Then, the doors locked, he started swerving the car all over the God damned road, I got brave and tried to get the wheel turned from the bus, and that's all I remember. What happened after that?"

"We hit a wall. A rock wall," Lucy explained.

"Ben, had you ever seen our driver before?"

"No, Dana, never. At least, I don't think so. Either one of you?"

Both women shook their heads, and Ben asked, "Dana, what the hell's going on?"

As Ben reached to the table for the coffee, Dana picked up her purse and withdrew a small pad and pencil. He nearly gagged from the first sip of the dreadful dark liquid, and quickly put it back down. Lucy laughed, "I told you!"

"Christ! What turtle piss! Dana, how can you drink . . ."

Dana took a big swig, smacked her lips and proclaimed, "Tastes fine to me."

"You're a real connoisseur," said Lucy.

"I'm a real caffeine addict. Shall we continue?"

Lucy lit a cigarette for Ben and herself and Dana gave a quick "tsk," but made no other comment before she began.

"It seems this man, our chauffeur, was not employed by the limousine service hired by the funeral parlour. Oh, the limousine was . . . but not the man."

"What happened to our real chauffeur . . . the one we were supposed to have?" Lucy inquired.

Dana hesitated, then said, "He was killed, Lucy. Now . . ."

"How?" Lucy persisted.

"Isn't it enough that he was murdered?"

"No, Dana. *How* was he murdered?"

She paused again, then answered, "He was drawn and quartered."

"Oh, Jesus!" Ben exclaimed. Lucy bowed her head and made the sign of the cross, while Ben took a drag of his cigarette.

"What was his name, Dana?" Lucy asked at last, her head still bent.

"Cellion. Lamberto Cellion. Did you know him?"

"No," Lucy shook her head, "thank God."

"Do they know who killed him?" Ben let smoke drift from his moving lips as he spoke.

"Or why?" Lucy looked once more into Dana's face.

"I'm coming to that. They think our driver . . . the one who caused the accident . . . murdered the real chauffeur. As best they can figure it, the killer hid in the back seat of the limousine, forcing Cellion off the road, killed him, and changed into the chauffeur's uniform he wore."

"But when did he get into the car?" asked Ben.

"Since the garage was locked until morning, it must have been the night before. It's a wonder the killer didn't suffocate in all that heat."

"It's no wonder at all, if he was as crazy as I think he was," Ben said.

"Or mesmerized," Lucy spoke these words softly, and Ben asked her to repeat them, but she shook her head and instead asked Dana, "Who was he? The killer?"

"The police haven't been able to identify him. But, they found two strange things when they examined his body. First, he was a eunuch."

There was silence in the room while Dana waited for some comment from them. They were incredulous, and silent. She went on, "Second, on his body they found a scar purposely 'carved' into his skin. Like this," and flipping over a clean sheet of her pad, she began sketching something with her pencil. When through, she held it up and they saw:

"Where . . . on what part of his body," Lucy asked weakly, "did they find this mark?"

"Under the left shoulder blade."

Lucy rose, stubbing out her cigarette and crossing once more to the window. She let out a great sigh.

"What is it, Lucy?" Ben queried softly.

Lucy turned to address him.

"I've heard . . . only rumors and legends, of course, but I've heard about men who kill . . . as part of a club, or . . ."

"Cult?" Dana offered.

"Yes," Lucy continued, "a cult. They are all supposed to have that sign to identify each other by."

"Like the pyramids for the old Masons?" Ben guessed.

"Yes, something like that," Dana said, "and this sign, Lucy. What is it supposed to represent. Do you know?"

"Don't the police, Dana?"

"I assume so, Ben. But they told me only the actual facts. They wouldn't theorize for me at all, much less volunteer any added information."

Lucy nodded once and lit another cigarette. "I think," she said, "It's supposed to be the Sign of the Ram."

"And this murder," Ben ventured, "was part of a ritual?"

"Not exactly," Dana stood up, dropping the small pad on the bed near Ben's foot. "Our own driver, Mr. Cellion, had to be replaced with the killer for a very practical reason."

"Like what?"

"Why, to kill us, Ben. Or *one* of us, anyway."

The telephone was practically next to her left ear, and when it rang she was nearly deafened. Her heart was pumping fast at the shock of being so suddenly, jarringly awakened, and though she was able to silence the damned thing by the second ring, resentment was already building up at having to cope with a caller, as well as her own fragile nerves, before reaching full consciousness.

A male voice informed her that it was ten o'clock. For a moment, she was confused at someone calling her up to tell her the time. Then, she realized that this was the wake-up call she had requested from the hotel switchboard last night. She thanked the voice, and hung up.

She lay there for a second, feeling mild guilt at having requested to be woken up so late, then dismissed the thought as a waste of valuable time. She had been exhausted, even though all she'd really done yesterday was buy a duffle bag, with Lucy's help, and then transfer her essentials into it. Lucy had taken her extra clothing, in the suitcase she'd come with, and brought them back to store at the Foundation.

Mary stretched and sat up. A sharp, brief pain shot through her left side, and she was reminded once again of her injury. Beyond these occasional stabs, the broken ribs did not give her too much discomfort, and she was at least grateful for that. She decided against room service. She would dress, have breakfast downstairs, and take a morning walk.

Looking out her window, the water of Manila Bay was a rich blue, though the sun was still over the eastern sky, the palms that fringed the Bay a brilliant green in the bright morning light.

After a shower, she decided on wearing a pair of baggy Bermudas, some good, cool walking shoes and a yellow blouse, so light and thin it was nearly, but not quite, sheer. Her hair was still damp, but she pinned it up and stuck a straw hat with a small brim over it.

Once downstairs in the coffee shop, she ordered poached eggs, orange juice and coffee, asking for the coffee as soon as possible. Her voice was deeper than usual; partly because it was still morning, and partly because she had strained it, screaming as she had when trapped inside the limousine. She cleared her throat and drank the water that had been brought to the table by the waitress. Then, the coffee was before her, the steam rising into her face, and she took the first delicious sips.

It was 10:40. Mary wondered if it was too early to call Ben. If the Philippine General Hospital was anything like other hospitals, they probably woke up their patients at 8 A.M., or earlier. Still, she hesitated, and decided to enjoy breakfast first, and make the call closer to eleven. Maybe she would even visit him; he was due, she thought, to be dismissed today. She could help get him home, perhaps. Unless her sense of direction was failing her, the hospital was only a few blocks north from here along Roxas Boulevard, then maybe three or four east to Taft Avenue. She had been surprised, when dismissed herself, at how close the hospital had been to the hotel.

The whole car incident seemed now very long ago, and she was also grateful for the illusion. But for the broken ribs, there was no other reminder of the horror of it. Her voice was raspy, but it did not hurt to speak, and the overall effect was not, she thought, unbecoming. She fancied that she rather sounded like Tallulah Bankhead used to. It made her smile.

Mary was happy that they had all come away reasonably safe from what must surely have been an attempt at murder. Murder. Her father, and now her? Why? It had to have something to do with in-

formation; knowledge that her father had
had . . . and that Dana was on the verge of discovering; perhaps, already had, without being aware
of it?

It looked a good day for a walk. She was gradually
becoming more accustomed the heat and the close,
humid air. Once out on the street, she was relieved
to discover that though still quite hot, there was a
cool breeze coming from the Bay, and the air seemed
sweet and fresh after the rainfall of the preceding
few days.

There was much to see as she walked along
parallel to the Bay, and the hustle and scurry of
moving traffic reminded her vaguely of Chicago.
She passed many hotels, cars driving in and out, full
of tourists from all over the world. But Mary's
thoughts were on Lucy. And Dana.

And Ben.

Perhaps it was because of Gordon; of having
broken up that relationship just prior to her arrival
here, but she found herself thinking of Ben frequently. Mary did not consider herself a "needy"
person, or one who fled from one love affair into
another. This, she knew, was not the case. She was
aware that this attraction to him could possibly
stem from the recent, horrid loss of her father, but
was also aware that, whatever the psychological
reasons may be, the feelings were no less genuine.
She realized the depth of this feeling when she could
not rest without knowing if he, Ben, would be
allright after the crash. Only then had she been able
to concern herself with the realities of her own circumstances.

And there had been that kiss. That magnificent
kiss.

She had walked a long way by now, and was

beginning to feel a little wearied, having strolled
through the Rizal Park, past the Aquarium, and was
now approaching the walled city of Intramour. So,
she decided to have a look.

Having arrived she saw Fort Santiago and there,
San Augustin Church, and the Manila Cathedral.
The Spanish history of the city seemed preserved
here, and she quite suddenly longed for the
tranquility of prayer and decided to go into the
church for a while, to sit in quiet meditation. For a
moment, she hesitated, wondering if her costume
would be acceptable inside the holy place, then
decided that though casually dressed, she did not
consider what she wore immodest. Besides, she
needed to pray. For the safety of the girl, Margery
Croft; for the soul of her own father; for herself, and
her companions here on this adventure that they
were about to embark upon; and for Ben Ramsey
who, she knew, was becoming very important.

That same night at the Foundation, a hand ran
lightly across the spines of half a dozen thickish
volumes standing on the shelf among many others
of like subject matter.

Dana McKinley muttered something softly under
her breath, on occasion pronouncing a title or author
aloud, considering their worth or appropriateness,
then making her judgment with "no, that won't
do," or "too silly," or "too romantic," dismissing it
and moving on to the next. At length, she came
upon one which above all the others, suited her
purposes, and so removing a book entitled
Demonic Mythology, she said, "Here, this should
tell us something of what we need to know."

The room was once again lit only by the light of

the desk lamp, and leaning over to place the book beneath its shade, she opened it carefully, going systematically through the alphabetized subjects it contained.

Lucy was nearby, her face above the lamp that cast strange and ghostly shadows upon her tanned skin.

"What are you looking for, Dana?"

Dana continued her journey through the book, flipping pages after quickly reading one or two, and Lucy had to repeat her question.

"What? Oh," Dana finally answered her, "I'm sorry, Lucy. I'm ... we're ... trying to find out what that mark on the driver's back meant. I could swear I've seen it, or something like it, somewhere before."

The page headings contained words such as "Alchemy," "Beelzebub," "Coven" and so on. Dana had passed through "J" ("Juggler"), gone quickly past "K" and "L," and was well in to the "M"'s ("Magician"), when she stopped finally at the word "Magus," and stared at the page before her.

"There it is," she said, almost reverentially.

Lucy leaned in a bit further and saw on the page a drawing like the Bull's Eye Dana had drawn for her and Ben in the hospital, the previous afternoon. She saw Dana nod her head and she looked at her questioningly.

"I knew it Lucy."

"Knew what?"

"That this meant something more than just a scar. You were right. Look."

Dana gestured toward the caption beneath the illustration. It read, "The Sign of The Ram."

"Good," Lucy declared, "but what does it mean?"

"You don't know?"

"No. I mean, I only knew it was supposed to be an insignia of some sort, but I still don't know what it means. It's a sign of the zodiac, right?"

"The Ram is, yes. It represents Aries."

"I thought Aries was a goat."

"No. That's Capricorn. But it wasn't even the correct symbol for that. As you said, it's the Sign of the Ram, but not the sign of Aries."

"But what does the Ram mean, Dana?" Lucy frequently found herself more impatient with Dana's roundabout way of expressing herself, and Dana felt it.

"Here, look," Dana replied, just as impatiently and pushed the book over toward her assistant. At the top of the page was a photograph of a mask made in the form of a goat, with huge horns, more like antlers.

"Magus," Lucy read aloud.

"Yes," Dana said, "The Magus. The Magician. The Sorcerer."

"Doesn't mean a thing to me, I'm afraid."

"Lucy, have you lived in a tree all your life? The Magus is part of the tarot deck; part of the practice of Wizardry; there was even a novel using it as the title."

"I saw the movie, Dana."

"Alright, alright."

Dana paused for a moment, rethought her words and continued, "Follow me. I'll mix us up some silver bullets and we can talk." It was Marc's phrase, but Lucy said nothing.

They left the library and walked through the length of the house, turning on lights as they went, finally arriving at the kitchen. Dana took down a glass pitcher from a shelf.

"Ice?" Lucy asked at the fridge.

"Please," Dana answered and removed the caps from bottles of gin and vermouth.

She had taken the book with her, and it lay opened on the counter for her to refer to as she began building a batch of martini's, choosing her words carefully as she spoke:

"Now then, this mark was the insignia used by an ancient cult to symbolize a eunuch who served the Hoo-reh-yeh . . ."

"Hoo-reh-yeh. That was the word . . ."

"Yes. It's no coincidence the driver was repeating it. These 'Hoo-reh-yeh' were women, much like vestal virgins, I suppose, and they served at the altar of the Magus . . . or Aman-rah, helping to organize ceremonies involving the acting out of sex lives of the gods."

Lucy was watching Dana intently as she talked, not only caught up in this new information, but wondering if Dana was aware of what she was doing while she spoke. Lucy looked at the little clock on the wall. It was seven o'clock.

Dana had taken the pitcher, stirred it and glanced over a paragraph in the book. Lucy could see a difference in Dana, whenever she had something to work on, or something to puzzle out. The older woman would somehow be more alive, more energetic than usual, and Lucy envied her just a bit for loving the work so much.

Without having to ask, Lucy got out a jar of olives and placed them on the counter, removed two glasses from the cabinet and threw one olive into each.

Dana looked up from the book to say, "Here, they were called 'Nymphs of Heaven.' He said that too! Remember?"

Lucy nodded and Dana began to pour the

martinis. When both glasses were full, she looked
around, ready to pour a third.

She halted, the pitcher held out in front of her,
still waiting for another glass to fill. It dawned on
her, then, why there weren't three of them. Slowly,
deliberately, she put it down upon the counter and
gave a small, sad sigh. Lucy was staring at her, she
knew, and when their eyes met, the girl looked away
quickly, trying not to acknowledge the mutual embarrassment.

The clock told Dana that it was the hour which
she and Marc used to call the 'end of the day,'
celebrated with a pitcher of martinis. She leaned
across the counter and patted Lucy's hand.

"You know," she said in almost a whisper, "he
told me he'd even make a drink at night, on
expedition. Horrible hot martini's, but . . ."

"I saw what was happening, Dana . . . what you
were doing. But I didn't know how to tell
you . . . whether to stop you or not . . ."

"I guess old habits will be hard to break."

Lucy picked up her drink, taking her olive from it
and throwing it into her mouth. "Come on," she
ordered, chewing, "let's you and I browse through
some more of those books and finish off this
pitcher."

Dana had looked deep in thought, a million miles
away. But now she was back, and smiled in
gratitude at Lucy. She could be such a nice girl
sometimes, when the headaches left her alone.

"Sure," she said, and they started back into the
library. Dana flicked off the lights in each room as
they went, and knew that tonight would be the last
time, for a long time, she would be drinking
martinis.

Replacing the receiver back on its cradle, Ben sank down deeply into the pillows at his head and back. He was pleased ... no, more than pleased, that Mary had called, even though he had only spoken to her that afternoon. He was glad she had not visited him. He felt frail and weak and did not like being seen this way.

He was home in his own apartment now, but not for long. They were due to leave soon and he was anxious. The plans were all made, but for a few last minute details, and he was looking forward to it.

When he was conscious and able to take visitors and calls, Mrs. Mendoza had informed him curtly that "a Mr. Blair had left three messages."

He'd looked at her in surprise. "Blair? Not Shiff?"

"I said 'Blair didn't I? A Mr. Shiff called once."

Ben had wondered what was going on; did Blair have a guilty conscience, or did he want to fire him in spite of the accident? He'd still not heard the reaction to the Canlas story he'd written, though Ben certainly thought it was rotten enough for them to eat up with a spoon. He had, however, seen the coverage the paper had given the accident. It didn't make the front page, but page 2, which wasn't bad, the banner reading *"Manila-American* Reporter Injured in Collision With School Bus!" Naturally, it was all fabrication, since the car and the bus did *not* in fact collide. Almost, but not quite. He hadn't even bothered to read the article.

He'd called Shiff first, but apparently Blair had been close-mouthed, saying only he was "concerned" about Ben's welfare. Finding out no more than that, he'd called Blair immediately. He couldn't get any more out of him than that Blair wanted to see him in his office as soon as he was out of the hospital. Of course, Ben had thought, it would never strike you to come visit *me*, but no matter.

There was still the subject of the expedition to be broached. His plans to do so after the funeral had of course been blown all to hell.

So, this morning he'd shown up at the *Manila-American*, ready for a showdown. If they'd let him cover the expedition for the paper, fine; if they'd give him vacation time or leave of absence to go, fine; if not, he'd planned on quitting on the spot, instead of waiting until he got back from New Guinea.

Figuring he'd drop in on Blair later, saving the worst for last, he headed for Shiff's office.

As he walked through the usual hysterical hubub of the city room, his cronies called out their greetings to him, and though he hated what the paper had become, he'd had to admit it was good to be back with his friends, for however long. When all was said and done he was, after all, a newspaper-man.

Walking into Shiff's tiny, smoking office without bothering to knock, he yelled, "Allright, I'm here!"

Shiff's head snapped up from the mountain of paper on his desk. "Hello, you old son of a bitch!" They shook hands and Shiff continued, "Well, you don't look any worse for wear. From what I'd heard, I thought you'd be on crutches, for Christ sake."

Ben laughed. "Don't believe everything you read in the papers . . . especially *this* paper. I'm a little cut up, but I'll live."

"Reserve judgment until you hear what Blair lays on you."

"You know?"

"Not a clue . . . but he had that nasty gleam in his eye the last time your name was mentioned. Something's cookin . . . and I think it's you in the pot."

"I can imagine. Get him on the horn. We may as well get this over with."

While Shiff called Blair's extension, Ben had thought of explaining to him what he wanted. Then he thought better of it. The less Shiff knew, the more innocent he'd be, and couldn't be blamed for having prior knowledge, and thus be thought of as an accomplice in the plan. He knew Shiff would back him up in the request to go to New Guinea with the paper's blessing, but didn't want to pass the buck to his boss. Better to speak to Blair directly and keep Shiff out of it, and clean.

Shiff hung up the phone. "He wants to see you right away. Go on up."

"I'm actually invited up to the inner sanctum? You're right, something's up."

"Let me know what it is before you leave?"

"Sure. Oh, Herb . . . did he say anything about the Canlas story?"

Herb smiled. "Before I tell you, let me give you my personal congratulations. Absolute tripe. True garbage, Ben. I was really ashamed of you. It's being printed as is, without a change. I didn't think you had it in you."

"Thanks. I think. What about Blair?"

"I said we're printing, didn't I? Next Sunday's magazine. He loved it. Of course, he may not tell you that, but now you know."

"Good. That may give me some bargaining power."

"Bargaining power? You're cooking up something too, sounds like."

"Maybe. I'm off!" Ben said, springing to the door. "I'll talk to you when it's over!"

Upstairs where the executive offices were located,

was a far cry from the mayhem that existed throughout the rest of the building.

The elevators opened up on a huge, quiet reception area done in Chinese blue walls and thick matching carpet. Behind the thin, impeccably dressed and coiffed receptionist was a life size, full length color photograph of Harrison McNeil, looking down at you as if overseeing his domain. Few of the staff writers had even been here in the reception area, much less inside Blair's office. You came when summoned. Nobody dropped in.

"Mr. Ramsey, I take it?" the receptionist said in a clipped accent which bespoke the Queen's English. She, anyway, was most definitely not from New Zealand. Ben nodded and began to take a seat on a Chinese Blue couch, when she halted him with, "You may go right in. You're expected."

Gesturing behind her to a Chinese Blue door, all but invisible in the wall to the left of the McNeil altar, she pushed a buzzer beneath her desk, releasing the lock on the door. He opened it and walked in.

Ben didn't expect that Blair's office would be anything akin to Shiff's poor little cubby-hole downstairs, but *this* was ridiculous.

First, the office was so big Ben could hardly see Blair behind the desk on the far side. He sat before a glass wall, sunlight streaming in and glaring off every surface in the room, because the entire room was white. White desk, white rugs and walls, white couch, chairs . . . even a white painting, framed in white, which appeared to depict absolutely nothing but white brush strokes. The only color in the room was supplied by six pillows on the couch. Predictably, Chinese Blue.

The black silhouette against the painful glare of

light said, "Ben. Good to see you."

Wish I could say the same, Ben had thought, starting across the room and certain he had been tracking mud across the virginal carpet.

At length he arrived before the desk, taking Blair's extended hand as Blair said, "Sit, sit."

A panoramic view of the city of Manila now revealed itself, the Bay beyond gleaming in the late morning light. Ben sat.

"The Canlas story," Blair began.

Ben feigned ingnorance, putting his hands up in mock defeat, saying, "I did the best I could."

"No, no!" Blair laughed. Boy, Ben thought, whatever this is about should be a dilly, he's being so God damn friendly. "It was ... *is* ... terrific! I'm glad we had our little talk a while back. Obviously, it set you on just the right track!"

"Obviously. Thank you. Now, may I ask why I'm here? I'm still a little woozy from the accident ..."

"Terrible thing! Terrible thing! You read our story, of course? We painted you up as quite a hero!"

"Yes ... and thanks again, only ..."

"To the point, of course. You must be exhausted. You only got out of the hospital this morning?" Ben nodded and Blair went on, "Then, we'll make this quick and get you home and to bed."

Ben said nothing, but sat and waited, his hands folded calmly in his lap. Blair leaned in across the white desk and taking on a confidential tone, asked quietly, "What about this Pemberton thing, Ben?"

Bingo! This was going to be very interesting.

"What do you want to know?" Ben had asked in return.

"I understand you were acquainted with the victims?"

"Victim. The girl has not been found yet."

"Yes, of course. I'd read your profile of the doctor with considerable interest, Ben. A little too reverential, but that was before our talk . . . and besides, we need a little class now and then. What had escaped me is how *well* you knew him, and his family."

"He was a friend."

Blair nodded in sympathy. "You must be very upset." He paused, then asked, too innocently, "I understand the daughter was here . . . for the funeral?"

"Still is. She was in the limo with us."

"Right. Right." Ben could practically see the wheels going around in his head. "And I hear, through the grapevine, that she's vowed to avenge her father's death by making an expedition to the site of the massacre?"

You hear a lot, Ben thought, and talk like one of your own articles.

"Well," Ben answered, "no one knows who the killer or killers are, so there is, at this point, no one to take vengeance upon, if indeed that's what Mary is after, which I very much doubt."

" 'Mary,' " Blair smiled provactively. "You mean Miss Pemberton?"

"I mean Mary Pemberton, yes."

"A close friend?"

"I've met her twice, Blair. What's your point, please?"

"My point, Ben, is this: I want the *Manila-American* to do an eyewitness, on the scene, indepth report on this bloodbath and its aftermath, and I want you to use your connections with the family to weasle your way into an invitation to go along on that expedition."

Blair obviously mistook Ben's shock and loss of word for outrage. He continued quickly, "Now, I know you may see this as compromising your personal relationship . . . but you're a newspaperman!"

Ben decided to make him sweat a little. "I don't know, Blair. I mean . . . it'll be difficult to get them to agree to have me along . . ."

"You can do it! I know you can. What a story, Ben! 'The Manila-American Solves The Mystery of Pemberton Massacre! A First Hand Close-Up by Ben Ramsey!' Sound tempting?"

"Well . . . oh, may I smoke?" Ben lit a cigarette, Blair shoving a white ash tray across the desk. "Yes, it certainly sounds tempting, Blair. I just don't quite know how I'm going to go about convincing these people I should go. They're not fond of this paper, you know."

"I can make them fond of it."

"How?" As if I didn't know, Ben thought.

Blair leaned back in his chair, obviously very pleased with himself. "I've been authorized by Mr. McNeil to make a donation to the Pemberton Institute in the name of the paper. That is, only as a last resort, of course, and only if they agree to letting you go along."

"Then I think you'd better tell McNeil to plan on spending the money. They need it, and like I said, they don't like you. Us."

"Done."

"How much?"

"Two thousand dollars?"

"Make it five and they'll bite."

Blair hesitated, shifted his eyes about the room, then said, "Oh, alright. Five thousand. But *don't* mention it to them unless you can't convince them any other way, on your own. The money is a *last* resort.''

"You said that already. Agreed. Now me."

"You?"

Sure, Ben had thought. What the hell, I might as well go for a little gravy myself. "Yeah, me. If they do let me go along, I get a raise, and a five thousand dollar bonus, payable half before I leave and half when I return."

"Ben, Ben, I . . ."

". . . And that all rights to the Pemberton series I compose revert to me, not to the *Manila-American*."

"That is not your agreement with this paper. We own all future rights on special material written for this . . ."

"These are my terms."

"You writing a book about this thing?"

"Maybe. Someday. We'll see. Is it a deal?"

There was a long pause, then; "It's a deal. You drive a hell of a bargain."

"Relax, Geoffrey. My chances of getting them to agree to a reporter from this paper going along are just about zero. This probably won't cost you a dime."

"And if you do, it's already cost ten thousand dollars."

"Now, now," Ben had leaned in across the desk, letting a plume of smoke drift from his mouth as he spoke, "you have to spend money to make money, don't you?"

They'd left it at that, and Ben had gotten out of the office quickly, before Blair changed his mind. He could hardly believe his good luck. It had all fallen right into his lap. Hardly any work at all.

He'd gone down to tell Shiff the news, Shiff smiling as he walked in the door.

"Well," he'd said, "I can tell it must be good news from that shit-eating grin on your face."

"It is," Ben answered and told him the outcome of the meeting. They roared over it, shook hands, and said their goodbyes.

When he'd gotten home to his apartment, he'd called Dana and told her the whole story, including the news of the donation. She'd laughed.

"You certainly play their game well, Ben."

"Not for long, though."

"Oh?"

"I'm quitting. I'll give notice the day we get back from the trip."

"But what about the raise? The bonus? What about the story?"

"They'll get the story, Dana. The way *I* want to tell it, or they won't print it at all. And I'll take the raise for as long as I'm left on payroll . . . *and* the five grand."

"You play dirty."

"No, Dana, I don't. Like you said, I play *their* game. The game *they* taught me. I've finally learned how, and I don't want to get any better at it, believe me. That's one of the reasons I'm getting out."

He figured he'd wait a day before calling Blair. It would give more credibility to his having begged, cajoled, and bribed his way into an invitation to the expedition.

Things had broken; changed. Everything was different, now. He didn't feel stale any more.

Though he enjoyed his life here in Manila, . . . things promised to be taking new and exciting turns. Of course, he'd have preferred that these changes had not come about via violent death. But he had to admit the pending trip thrilled him. It had been a long time since the call to adventure had beckoned and he was keen on the experience, even though he knew there would be danger for himself, and all the others.

Since their meeting, since their kiss, he had allowed himself erotic fantasies that had become more and more intense. Mary was always in the leading role of these sexual flights, and he had frankly longed for her. Yet when they were alone at the hospital, they had not been intimate; at least, not physically, coming no closer to embracing than a mere peck on the cheek. It seemed there was always some nurse or doctor or aide, walking in and out of the room on some stupid pretext. He had wanted to take Mary in his arms, pull her body close to him, but he had not. It was exciting though, knowing that she wanted him to do it.

But Savong-khai would be soon, very soon, and there would come a night, one special night, that he hoped would be the beginning of many.

He switched on the television and lit a cigarette. The flickering image on the screen did little to take his mind off Mary.

My Dear,

I did something stupid tonight.

I forgot that you are gone from us. I made a pitcher of martinis for "us"—just like we always used to do at the end of our days. It was the habit of doing it. The habit. I just totally forgot. Oh, God, it was like being hit in the stomach.

We're getting ready to leave in two days. Then, we're off, ten in the morning, from Manila airport to Port Moresby, in New Guinea. A guide is being arranged for us, and a crew to help us into Savong-khai, and thence to Satyr Island. By that time, perhaps the mystery will have been solved. Perhaps we'll know what's become of Margery.

I'm afraid now, Marc. Someone, or something is trying to kill us, and yet I can't let anyone, least of all Mary or Lucy, know my own misgivings. And too, there is the ache, this relentless aching, and all the little reminders . . . like a silly pitcher of martini's . . . that constantly bring back to me that you are gone. When does it stop hurting?

TWELVE

An overhead fan spun listlessly in the center of the dirty room, doing little more than pushing the stale air around in circles. A grimy fish net was decorously draped across the ceiling beams and swooped down to cover the filthy mirror at the back of the bar. The bartender, a huge black man, sat on a stool reading a three-year-old copy of 'Penthouse.' In a hardly visible corner, the red glimmer of an ancient juke box radiated its feeble light, while from within it, "How Much Is That Doggie In The Window?" played for the third time in an hour, Patti Page's voice almost inaudible over the cracks, pops and surface sound in the old recording. Three native men sat at the bar, two of them asleep with their heads nestled in their arms. The third drank his beer sullenly, glancing now and then at a white man who was staring down into his own glass of Scotch.

Drunk and getting drunker, the Scotch drinker leaned his elbows on the rough, splintered wood of the decrepit bar, the fumes of the cheap booze drifting up into his nose.

It had finally stopped raining and, after almost five days in New Guinea, the dampness was getting to him, making his joints ache. He knew there would be heat, but this was truly displeasing and though he did not regret this trip, he harkened back to the civilization and comfort of his home. Only the thought that something had to be done, kept him here.

Yet since his arrival, he had done little more than drink. He seemed insatiable; a thirst having come over him the likes of which he had only experienced once before in his lifetime, when his wife had left him.

Now, for the third time, really, his whole life had been picked up, rattled and thrown back down, and arranging the pieces again was that much more difficult since he was that much older. It was all fantastic, horrible, and finally, almost unbearable.

So, here he was presently sitting in the bar of the only hotel on the island. The lounge of The Jungle Orchid Hotel. It looked like the set for a third rate bus and truck tour of "Rain." The whole of social life revolved around this place and he found no one particularly eager to talk about anything with a drunken stranger, especially one whose questions pertained to a recent mass murder. He had gotten little satisfaction in Port Moresby from the authorities there, concerned as they were with facts that he'd already gleaned from the newspaper reports, which had been profuse.

He'd decided to sit it out here and hope that if some bit of information did come his way, he could remain sober enough to take action upon it. There was more to these killings than anyone was saying. But it was hard to do nothing. Still, for now he had little choice in the matter.

The telephone behind the bar rang just then, and when he heard the bartender repeat the name "Pemberton" into the mouthpiece, he became alert. Maybe he wouldn't have to wait too long, at that.

Before them there was only mountain. They could feel the little plane losing altitude as the tops of the trees came closer and closer. Ben was convinced that they were going to crash and now was sorry he was seated near the window. He didn't like watching what he was positive was about to happen.

Nor could he help himself from doing so. When it seemed that the branches and trunks of trees would come right through the sides of the flimsy plane, there suddenly appeared a tiny field, just beyond the thicket of trees.

But beyond the field, there was nothing. Literally nothing, as it appeared to have been cleared away atop a small plateau, ending abruptly in a steep drop that looked to be some three hundred feet further down into yet more jungle.

The tiny plane landed as if dropped onto the field, and Dana wondered quickly if permanent damage had just been done to her spine. Dried soil and earth swirled around the windows, churned up by the propellers. Though they were now on the ground, Ben knew how short this "airfield" was, and it seemed they were going far too fast to enable them to come to a complete halt before reaching the drop, and plummeting hundreds of feet more.

The scream of the brakes was nearly deafening as the pilot forced them into submission, and at last they came to a stop.

Ben looked over at Mary in the seat beside him. Her eyes were tightly shut and perspiration stood out on her brow and upper lip.

"It's okay," he said.

She opened her eyes and looked back at Ben. He was pale. She looked over to Dana and Lucy, seated across the aisle. They were both pale too.

"My God," Dana said to her, "you're pale, Mary."

Mary laughed.

The door was pulled opened from outside and dirt and dust came whirling in at them, filling the cabin air. Coughing, they were helped out of the plane by the pilot, who was smiling broadly, seemingly proud of having gotten them all back on the ground alive.

Ben could see that the plane had come to rest some six feet from the edge of the cliff, as he walked into the little hut that served as the "Terminal." He shuddered, then smiled, seeing the entrance to the hut.

Above it a stencilled sign painted in red hailed the greeting "Welcome to Savong-khai!". But the sign was peeling and splintered and seemed to promise far more than it had been able to deliver in quite some years.

Once inside the room appeared to be deserted. A very small counter, littered with dusty, grayed and yellowed tourist information, all pertaining to other islands, stood against the far wall. An old beaten up fan spun its blades nosily atop a rusting file cabinet. Then, out of his peripheral vision Ben noticed movement, then noise. He turned.

Standing against the opposite wall was a massive creature stationed beside a pay telephone, his hand still grasped around the receiver that he had just obviously hung up. He must have weighed three hundred pounds or more, and beneath the short sleeved khaki sweat stained shirt, muscles rippled in his chest. The huge biceps were heavily veined and coarse, auburn hair sprouted out over the backs of his hands and on his mammoth arms. There were holes in the skin at the tops of his nostrils.

Before any of them could speak a door behind the counter opened and a small black clerk came out and smiled at them.

"Hello," he said, "You are the McKinley party?"

Dana was at the mud-splattered window, from where she could observe the "ground-crew" (two native teenage boys) throwing their luggage helter-skelter from the plane into big wheeled bins.

"Yes," she called, upon hearing her name, and turned from the window to Mary, trying not to move her lips as she said, "Watch that our bags get off the plane safely." Moving across the creaking wood plank floor to the clerk, she identified herself as "Dr. McKinley."

The clerk seemed surprised at first, but Dana was used to this reaction. People often seemed to think a "Doctor" was going to be a man, though she had to admit, less and less as time went by.

"This gentleman, has been waiting for you, Doctor," the clerk informed her.

All four of them turned to face the huge person across the room by the telephone. For a moment no one moved. Then Dana asked, "Are you our guide?"

"Yes," he nodded once.

She waited for him to continue but he did not, and so she offered, "Well, I'm Dr. McKinley, as I suppose you know by now."

She had expected his name in return, but all she received was another nod and another "Yes."

After a pause, realizing his name was not forthcoming, she introduced him as "our guide" to the others and then said, "Now then, if you'll show us to our hotel, we can talk about the expedition, if you don't mind?"

She began to walk toward the door, the others following her, and the big man smiled and opened the door for them. He mustn't speak much English, Dana thought. That won't help matters. As they passed by him and out into the road each was aware of how very small they felt beside him, even Ben, who was not a small man.

Outside, an antique station wagon waited for them and as they emerged from the terminal, their driver got out of the car, and they all, but for the guide, stopped dead in their tracks.

The driver was nearly as big as the guide and made up for in girth what he lacked in the guide's height. He too was magnificently muscled and also covered in auburn hair, matted down flat against his skin from the sweat that poured freely from him.

The Guide began taking knapsacks and duffle bags from the clerk and handing each piece to the driver, both of them handling the bags as if they weighed nothing. Dana tried to talk to the driver but he had immediately started with the luggage, virtually ignoring her, until she said at last, quite loudly,

"Excuse me!"

The driver took one more suitcase from the hands of the guide. The latter turned to Dana, his fists on his hips, staring down at her. She waited until the driver had loaded the bag into the back of the wagon then asked of him,

"How far is it to the hotel, Mister . . .?"

"It's about a ten minute drive, Doctor," the Guide answered.

"I was asking the driver, thank you," Dana smiled.

The driver looked from Dana to the Guide then back to Dana, and also smiled.

"Doctor, your guide is quite correct. It will take ten minutes or so."

The driver picked up another case lying near the car and the guide continued to stare at Dana, who stared right back.

"What is your name, please?" she insisted.

"Thot," he answered.

"About how *far* is it? In *miles*, please, Mr. Thot."

"Five miles, and it is not 'Mister' anything, Ma'am. It is Thot. Just plain Thot."

The four of them crammed uncomfortably into the back seat, there being no further room up front with just Thot and the driver occupying that space.

After three false starts the motor turned over, and they lurched into motion, the old car obviously straining under the added weight. It was an inferno inside and Mary rolled down the window nearest her for a gasp of some air.

"I suggest," Thot called to them from the seat beside the driver, "that you close your windows back there while we drive along this road."

"I don't see, or feel, any air-conditioning, Mr. Thot," Mary called back.

The man turned around in his seat to face her.

"I have said once, Miss Pemberton, that my name is Thot. Simply Thot. Merely Thot. You are correct. There is no air-conditioning. As to the opened window, I warned you. You may of course do as you wish."

He turned around again to face front, giving Mary the distinct message that she was dismissed.

The road they travelled was unpaved, and as they

picked up speed, the wheels brought up more and more dust and dirt, until enormous brown clouds filled the air about the auto and began to fill the inside of the car, via the window Mary had opened. As the four in the rear began to cough and choke, Mary grudgingly rolled up the window on her side. By the time they had stopped moving she was furious as well as sweltering.

Despite the discomfort, Ben did find it amusing, while Lucy kept her eyes glued upon the driver, obviously not about to trust anyone in the position of hired "chauffeur" ever again, much less one as big and menacing as this one way. This was neither fun nor pleasant, and the only good thing about the day so far was that her forehead was no longer bandaged. A small black and blue bruise was the only evidence of the crash.

Dana, however, seemed oblivious to all but their guide, Thot, and his overwhelming presence.

The doors opened and they fairly fell from the vehicle, to find themselves before a three story ramshackle structure with a thatched roof. The cloud of dirt they had arrived within began to settle about them, and as it did Lucy could discern the words "Jungle Orchid" on a wooden sign nailed above a small porch that served as the entrance to the building.

She leaned in closely to Dana and spoke quietly into the Doctor's ear, "Dana, are you sure this is where Marc and Margery stayed before going out into the jungle?"

"Positive," Dana whispered back, "he called me from here just before they left. It was the last time I spoke to him."

The driver was already hard at work, nearly drenched with sweat while unloading the bags. Thot walked up the three steps of the porch, turned, and gestured to them to follow.

The lobby was a huge room split down the center by a piece of sheet rock braced with two by fours on either side, and there was a distance of some four feet between the top of this divider, and the beamed ceiling. To the left was the "Front Desk," which was exactly that . . . a desk, with a chair behind it, and in that chair sat a large, robust looking woman in a flowered print dress. Behind her was a crude arrangement of boxes, each with an adhesive label stuck to its bottom edge, each label bearing a number. A few pieces of wicker furniture, painted green and yellow, had been placed about this half of the room.

To the right of the sheet rock was a bar and it was immediately apparent that here was the main reason for the existence of the Jungle Orchid Hotel. A bartender was seated on a stool reading 'Penthouse,' while two men slept with their heads on the bar. Five or six tables with checkered table cloths and candles stood in the remaining available space, the red neon glow of a very old juke box dimly lighting the restaurant part of the establishment.

Thot gave a look over to the bar, then looked away quickly, as a white man, obviously feeling no pain, looked up suddenly as the party walked to the front desk. Lucy happened to catch the exchange and she too glanced over to the bar. For just a second her eyes made accidental direct contact with those of the man at the bar. He was drunk.

He might once have been distinguished looking. He might be again. But now, the silver hair had yellowed, and grew wildly all over his head and down the back of his neck. More of it sprouted from a three day growth of stubble on his face. His eyes

were red and rheumy, and he seemed very white, as
if he never went out of doors, but stayed instead,
inside this place, away from sun and light. For just a
second a rush of recognition struck Lucy, then was
gone as quickly as it had come. She could have
sworn for only a moment there, that she knew that
face; had seen him before.

"You have reservations for these people," Thot
said to the woman behind the desk.

She laughed and wiggled her index finger for Ben
to come over. He did so reluctantly.

"For the Ladies," she said, "I have the Royal
Suite, Sir."

She handed him three keys.

"For you, sir, I have the nice room across the hall,
hey?" and she laughed again loudly, for no apparent
reason, banging her palm on the little bell to her left.
An orange plastic beaded curtain rattled noisily, the
cheap shiny strands parted to reveal a small,
smiling native man, dressed in a pink Polynesian
wedding shirt that seemed very warm for the day.
With some difficulty he managed to pick up four
bags of varying size and saying "Follow," he headed
to the left, where a flight of stairs disappeared
upwards into what looked to be total darkness.

Thot and the driver took the remaining luggage
between them and the six of them trailed behind the
little man in the lead.

It was a mystery why they were located on the
third floor since there didn't seem to be very many
other guests in the place, but, Mary thought, they
probably wanted to give us their best, and the
"Royal Suite" was probably it.

"It" consisted of two rooms, one with three beds
in it.It had a bathroom of its own.

"You eat?" the bell boy asked.

"Whenever I have to," Mary replied. He giggled, answered "Very funny," and meant it. He told her that dinner was at 6:30 sharp, in the "dining room" downstairs. Then, he was gone, having thrown all four bags on one of the beds.

Lucy looked at her watch. "Well," she said, "It's five, now. Gives us time to clean up, anyway."

"And have a drink," Ben added.

"Amen to that!" Mary sighed, sitting on the edge of a bed.

"Will you join us for dinner, Thot?" Dana asked.

"I think not, Doctor, thank you. Perhaps, though, I will meet with you beforehand, say in an hour from now, in the bar? We can make further arrangements."

"Excellent," she agreed.

"In an hour, then," Thot said, and leading the driver out of the room, he closed the door as he exited into the hall.

"My God," Lucy said, "talk about big."

"Friendly cuss, too, no?" Ben smiled, picking up his bags, "Well, I'm across the hall, I'm told. So, who's for a drink, and how soon?"

"Not me," Lucy said, falling back on a bed, "I'm taking a shower and laying down until dinner."

"I'll knock on your door in forty-five minutes, Ben, okay?" Mary asked.

"Good," he said. He took his key in hand, left the room, and began looking for his own.

It was indeed, just across the hall from theirs. It had a bed and a window. The key to a bathroom down the hallway hung on a nail near the door.

Ben decided to lay on his bed and smoke a cigarette before venturing out into the hall again for the discovery of the bathroom. He hoped that this all hadn't been a mistake, and that he'd be able to keep hold of his sense of humor.

From two floors below, he could barely hear what he thought was Pattie Page singing "How Much Is That Doggie In The Window?"

It was them. They were here, finally. Finally. Something had happened, at last.

He didn't like that Big One . . . the one that had looked over at him when they'd all come in. He'd avoid him if he could.

As soon as he'd heard their footsteps trodding up the stairs, he slid off his stool and stood listening for just a moment. Once he was sure they had reached the second floor landing, he pulled some money from his pocket, threw it on the bar and walked very carefully across the lobby section, coming at last to the bannister of the staircase.

Looking up, he saw shadows, heard voices, and knew they had all continued on up to the third level. He'd give it time. Wait until the Big One and his friend came back down, then go up and speak to the McKinley woman.

He knew he needed a shave, and the stench of liquor was all over him. He thought about going up to his own room on the second floor and tidying up, but there was time for that later. Now, he had to wait and see that the Big One left, then grab his chance to see McKinley.

He felt good for the first time in weeks, and didn't even notice when the juke box started playing that Patti Page number again.

THIRTEEN

Lucy wanted to get into the shower more than anything else. However she was the only one of the three that had not made plans before the dinner hour. So she deferred to her two companions, and agreed to shower last.

"But if you two use up all the hot water on me I'll scream!"

Since Mary was due downstairs first to meet Ben, she was in the bathroom before the others. Mercifully there seemed to be ample hot water, though it trickled out of the tap rather than showering down.

In the other half of the "suite" Dana had opened one of her bags and changed into a light robe while she chose fresh clothes to wear for the evening. Occasionally she would comment aloud on the trip, the hotel, or whatever, but receiving no more than grunts from Lucy's prone figure, she remained silent thereafter.

Dana continued to be worried. Not over anything in particular. So far, things had not gone badly. Uncomfortable and tiring, yes, but that was certainly to have been expeced. This, what she felt now, was little more than a feeling, and she didn't like it. She was a realistic woman; a rational person, and intuition was not something she held too much stock in. Still, she could not shake this feeling. Too much had gone on. Five people were already dead.

Lucy, was meanwhile grateful that Dana had taken the hint and was now quiet. Beyond the sounds of water coming from the bathroom and the rustle of the trees being moved by the late afternoon breeze (what there was of it), she could dimly hear the strains of a song drifting up from the bar. Thinking of the bar reminded her then, of the man she had looked at when they'd come in. She wished she hadn't thought of him again. Try as she might, she couldn't place him. Still, he had seemed so very familiar to her.

This brief, talkless period ended when Mary opened the bathroom door. The smell of scented soap and powder entered the room before her, and Lucy heard her say, "God, it's so damp, you start sweating again before the water is even dry on your body."

"Hot water, though?" Dana asked.

"Yes, and no sign of it stopping," she said loudly into Lucy's ear. "Who's next?"

"Dana is, thanks," Lucy mumbled, rolling over on her side.

"Thank you, Lucy," Dana said, and Lucy heard the bathroom door close again. Mary opened the duffle bag that Lucy had helped her pick out at Rustan's. She'd never owned anything like this before, not even as a Brownie. My God, I was a

Brownie. Probably the only troop in America to go
bankrupt. It was fun, and made her feel rugged. Of
course, this luggage—or did you call a duffle bag
"equipment" too?—this all looked awfully new. But
then, it was. Certainly not rugged. Not yet. She
looked inside at all the garments tightly rolled,
rather than folded, all very compact, very neat and
orderly. Lucy had also showed her how to pack it.

She had taken one skirt with her, and after
donning fresh under things, tied the white cotton
wraparound securely about her waist, then buttoned
up a blue and beige Hawaiian shirt, not tucking it in,
to allow air up next to her still-moist skin.

She parted her hair, still slick from the water, and
tucking it behind her ears, left it as such. A glance in
the mirror told her she'd look acceptable enough
after applying a touch of makeup to her lips and
eyes. She was trying to hurry. Moments alone with
Ben would, she knew, be few and far between from
now on, and she wanted every possible minute she
could get.

She tiptoed over to Lucy's bed and moved around
until she could see the face of the girl's watch on her
wrist. If she left now, she'd still be ten minutes
early. But there seemed no real reason to stay here
in the room either. Mary thought about knocking on
the bathroom door to let Dana know she had decided
upon leaving now, but thought again, not wanting
to awaken Lucy with her pounding. Slipping into
her open toed shoes, Mary quietly moved out of the
room and into the hallway.

Ben was just pulling on pair of clean jockey shorts
when he heard the knock at his door.

"Mary?"

"Yes, Ben," she answered, and taking his call to
be an invitation, opened the door to his room.

She didn't turn her head or blush. After all, though he was in his underwear, he was still wearing more than what she'd seen some men wear at the beach. She smiled. It was he who was blushing, looking about for something to cover himself with, but before he found it, Mary said laughingly, "I'll wait for you downstairs," and closed the door.

Ben started moving in doubletime, throwing on clean clothes as he came to them in his bag. He'd have a few more minutes alone with her, then.

She had nearly dozed off. Dana was still in the shower and the noise of the running water was soothing. Lucy could feel the tension begin to ease from her legs and shoulders and was happy in a simple way, knowing she'd soon be in the shower as well. She could hear Dana humming.

Then, something gave her a sharp poke in the left side of her back and at the same time, she heard a snap in the mattress beneath her. She sat up with a start, rubbing her back as she turned to touch the spot where she'd been laying. Under the sheet, she could just feel the pointed tip of what must have been a spring poking its way up.

"Dammit!" she muttered, not only annoyed at having her rest disturbed, but immediately thinking about how she'd be able to maneuver herself around that spring, for a night's sleep.

She looked around the room for a phone to call the front desk. There was none. Oh, well, she thought, they probably couldn't do anything about it anyway. But she realized then that if she were able to turn the mattress over, she might be able to get through the night on the underside, before another spring, or the opposite end of the same one, came out to stab her a second time. If that didn't work, there would be no recourse but to ask for another mattress.

Wide awake now, Lucy swung her feet over the edge of the bed and stood up. The room did not seem nearly as bare and stark as it had. Opened knapsacks, plain and frilly undergarments, makeup, shoes, all lay about on the floor and beds in a profusion of color and texture. If it was a mess, at least it looked inhabited. When she had laid down and closed her eyes, all there had been were bags on beds. Now, seeing the uncovered contents, she was proud of them, her companions, even herself. They had packed for this trek with great economy.

Sweat was making her clothes stick to her and it was only then she realized that but for kicking off her shoes, she was still fully dressed. She wanted to get the mattress turned over before Dana got out of the bathroom; Lucy neither liked asking for help, especially from Dana, nor did she like being caught, awkward and clumsy, in the act of turning over a mattress. But the anxiety was adding to the perspiration already caused by the sweat, and the work ahead, though brief, would be arduous enough to have her sweating buckets by the time she was through. The most sensible thing to do, before she began, was to get out of her clothes.

One minute later she was clad in nothing more than a pair of blue panties, a thin sheen of sweat glistening over her tanned nudity. The sound of the water and Dana humming in it, made her long to bathe, but that would be soon enough, and she put her mind to the task before her. She bent at the waist and began pulling back the sheet that was tucked in hospital folds around the mattress.

Then, she heard something, and looked up toward the door of the room.

The man she had seen in the bar stood in the doorway, staring at her.

Lucy pulled the sheet completely off the bed and held it up to cover herself, when the man slammed the door behind him.

Descending the final step of the stair case, Mary instinctively hesitated there for a moment, fighting down the urge to turn around and walk back up the two flights to return to her room. Looking left past the desk and partition into the "Lounge/Restaurant," she didn't really feel comfortable walking in there without a . . . what did they used to call it? Male escort? The white man who'd been at the bar when they walked in was no longer there, but the other patrons were still slouched over it, and now one of them was awake, muttering abuses to himself.

But what really put her on edge was that their guide, Thot, was having a quiet conversation with the bartender, who nevertheless still held the beaten up copy of "Penthouse" in his hand. Thot was seated on one of the stools, which seemed to disappear beneath him, but for the four spindly legs that looked as if they would not bear the weight of his great body too much longer.

The Guide's eyes left the face of his companion momentarily glancing up, and Mary knew Thot had seen her. Well, she thought, Ben would be down shortly, and there was no reason to believe that she wouldn't be left alone while she waited. She feared this giant, but he had been no more than rude, and that in and of itself was nothing to be afraid of. Taking a breath, she walked slowly toward the lounge, smiling at the woman behind the desk as she went.

Choosing a table by the wall facing the bar and the entrance, she searched in her bag and, finding a book of matches, lit the candle. The illumination of the table made the bartender aware there was a customer, and she watched as he excused himself, put the magazine down, and came over to her.

"Dinner is not served for another forty-five minutes or so, Ma'am."

"Yes, I know. I'm meeting a gentleman here for drinks, thank you."

He paused for a moment, and seemed about to say something, but replied only, "Will you order now or wait for the gentleman?"

"Now, please. I'll have a Marguerita."

"Fine," he said.

She watched the big man saunter back behind the bar and saw how he suddenly seemed dwarfed when beside the Guide, again.

Mary looked down into the candlelight. She felt at least calmer now, and thankful for a bit of rest before starting out again. Her thought took her into the unknown jungle, daydreaming about what they might find out there. Her father had loved it. So did Dana. She wondered if she would ever discover, too, what mysterious attraction it held. So far, it escaped her. The Marguerita appeared before her on a tray. A hand set it down on the table and she looked up, saying "Thank you" into the face of Thot. "May I join you?" he asked politely.

"Ummm . . . well, yes, please do . . . however I am waiting for Mr. Ramsey, and . . ."

"And I am waiting for Dr. McKinley. I'll just stay 'til Mr. Ramsey arrives."

Mary looked deeply into his eyes. They were blue, and they were large and, she thought, really quite beautiful. Suddenly her fear seemed stupid to her, and she smiled at him. He had sat down across from her now.

"I'm sorry, Mr. . . . excuse me again, I'm sorry, Thot. I don't mean to be rude."

He smiled back at her. "Nor do I, Miss Pemberton. My size often frightens people at first, or makes them shy. And, I suppose we've gotten off on the wrong foot. I'd like to apologize."

She felt very relieved, and it must have showed, for his smile broadened, and she replied, "Unnecessary, but certainly accepted if that's what you wish. What time do we leave tomorrow?"

"Well, as early as possible, I should think, though I'll have to talk it over with Dr. McKinley, along with just about everything else. But, I may not have the chance again to say privately to you how sorry I am about your father."

"Why . . . why, thank you, Thot," she said, genuinely moved by this expression of concern. Then, she saw Ben coming across the lobby toward them. She waved and he waved back, as Thot stood up. Ben and the Guide shook hands, Ben saying,

"Please, sit. I didn't mean to interrupt."

"It was I who interrupted, Mr. Ramsey," Thot said, "Now may I tell the bartender what you're drinking, and save him a trip over here?"

"Gin and tonic, please," Ben said, a little taken back at the man's cordiality.

"Coming right up. You enjoy your drinks and dinner, and I will see you both tomorrow morning."

Thot turned and walked back to the bar.

"Surprised?" Mary asked quietly.

"I'll say. What did you two talk about?"

"He came over to apologize for the way things started out at the airport. And he gave me his condolences, about Dad. He's really quite nice, Ben."

* * *

"I'm not alone in here, so don't come a step closer to me!" Lucy said, one hand holding the sheet up to her naked body, while the other was stretched out to defend herself. But somehow she felt she wouldn't have to. She had neither screamed nor yelled for Dana and she was aware that though startled, she did not actually feel any fear.

"I know you're not alone. It's her I want to see," he said at last.

"Her? Who?"

"McKinley."

"What for?"

Then something even more peculiar occurred.

The man's eyes began to fill up with tears and he swayed, as if he were going to faint. Taking two steps, he sat down on the edge of a bed, put his head in his hands, and sobbed uncontrollably. Lucy wasn't really sure what she should do next, and found herself confused as to what her reaction was, or what it was supposed to be, anyway. She reached out to her opened suitcase and pulled out a robe which was, thankfully, right on top. She pulled it on quickly, letting the sheet fall to the floor, and was fastening the middle button when she heard him whisper.

"Margery. Margery."

It dawned on her then. His face! She HAD seen it before! Not personally; never in the flesh, but in photographs; one in particular that had stood in a silver frame on the dresser across from her roommate's bed. The photo had been taken a few years ago, so there was much more grey in his hair now, and he was clean and neatly dressed in the picture, but it was him.

"I'm Lucy Case," she said, and he looked up at

her, "I was Margery's roommate."

The bathroom door opened and steam billowed into the room as Dana McKinley, wearing a towel, stepped out and stopped, staring at the strange, unkempt man sitting on Mary's bed. Dumbfounded, she looked to Lucy, who said,

"Dana, this is Margery's father, Barton Croft."

Dana stood completely still. She blinked. Twice. She was then aware that she was clad in nothing more than the towel she had pulled around herself from the shower.

Barton Croft, however, was simply staring up into the face of this woman, wiping tears from his cheeks and trying to control himself and keep from appearing to be a total fool in her eyes.

She did not think him a fool, though. He was, she thought, to be pitied, to be understood. He looked like hell, and in his face she recognized her own torment and grief, unguarded, unmasked.

"Dana," Lucy was saying, and she looked to see the girl holding up her blue cotton wrapper for her. Dana excused herself and stepped behind the outstretched garment, slipping her arms into it while dropping the towel at her feet. She tied a single knot in the sash and turned to face him once again. It had given her the time she needed to collect her thought, and she said now, "Mr. Croft, I'll do anything I can to help you. Please know that. What do you need?"

He let out a long, stuttered sigh and Lucy could see his shoulders relax.

"Just to hear you say what you just said is part of what I needed. I've felt very alone, friendless, really, since the news."

Dana sat down beside him on the bed and though he reeked of Scotch, she placed a hand over his. She looked up at Lucy, who smiled back at her, tears in her eyes.

"Well," Lucy said, "I'm going to grab a shower while I can, if you don't mind."

"No, please do, dear," Barton said.

Lucy went to the threshold of the bathroom, but did not enter. She wanted to say more; felt that she should, but the words would not come. Somehow, though, she thought he understood that, for at that moment he nodded to her and she knew no further words were necessary, for now. She stepped into the bathroom, closing the door behind her. A sharp, sudden pain blinded her for an instant, but she recovered quickly. Removing her robe, she turned on the faucet and tested the water. Please, she thought, please don't let another headache start in, please. Not now.

"Well, Mr. Croft . . . Barton," Dana was saying softly, "let's you and I have a bit of a talk, hm?"

Ben reached across the table and gently took Mary's hand in his. Thot was probably watching them. But she was at ease about the guide now, and almost because she was, he was as well.

The bartender had obviously turned up the speed on the overhead fan to fend off the additional heat that came from the kitchen (wherever it was) in preparation for dinner. However the fan made a tinny, metallic little squeak, but not regularly. Not on every revolution it made, but only sporadically, so that each time it squeaked it had the unexpected effect of fingernails on a blackboard. Sometimes it would go for two minutes or more without a sound, making you think it had corrected itself and would remain silent, when the squeaking would begin again. No one had played Patti Page in a while, because one man at the bar decided upon Theresa Brewer's "Music, Music, Music," which was just starting its second spin.

Ben looked from their entwined hands to Mary's face. He saw that she could barely contain herself, on the verge of laughter as she was.

"What's funny?"

"All of this, Ben. I mean, I love holding hands over candlelight, but it just struck me that there's also a screeching fan that's absolutely no relief for 98 degree heat or better and if I hear 'Put another nickel in, in the nickelodeon' a third time I'm going to kick in that juke box."

"That juke box would probably bring in a small fortune as an antique in the States," Ben said, growing very serious as he added, "but aside from all that, isn't this fun?"

She laughed loudly, and kissed his hand. "I think I could use another one of these," she drained the last of the Marguerita and touched the rim of her glass to his, "so drink up, baby."

"Very cute," he said sarcastically, motioning for the bartender.

"You said that once already," she retorted.

"You off the valium now?"

"Just one before I go to bed. It's too easy to get hooked."

The bartender came over, excusing himself from the conversation he continued to have with Thot.

"Sir?"

"Two more please; and could we see a menu?"

The bartender looked from one to the other and seemed embarrassed.

"Is something wrong?" Mary asked.

"Madame, sir, we don't often get customers for

dinner. Hence, there is only one selection for the meal. No menu, I'm afraid."

"And the meal tonight is . . .?" Ben asked.

"Squid and mussels over a bed of rice sauteed in squid's milk."

"That's wonderful. Thank you."

When the bartender retreated, Mary asked in a half-whisper, "That sounds wonderful?"

"Well, to me it does, anyway. Trust me."

"Oh, I do. It's the squid milk I don't trust."

"Wait'll you taste it."

"Getting hungry, Ben?"

"Mmm, and if they can cook it right, it sounds delicious. You hungry?"

"I guess. The heat's really all I can think about. Beyond tomorrow."

With that, Mary saw Ben's face grow somber. She knitted her brow and leaned in toward him questioningly.

"About tomorrow, Mary . . ."

"What? What's the matter?"

"Well, as far as I can tell we're heading out to find the camp site here . . ."

"Ben, I know that. It's one of the reasons for the whole excursion."

"Mary," he said impatiently, "please let me finish a sentence?"

She stared at him, surprised at his tone, but relented and sat back in her chair, folding her arms before her. "Go on," she said.

"It's just that though Dana was in love with your father, she's a professional. She has a professional's approach to this whole thing. Lucy, too . . . oh, she's young, and upset about Margery, but she's prepared for a jungle situation . . . knows in some way, what to expect."

". . . And you're a newspaperman, and also a pro, and also ready to meet any obstacle, whereas I, the deb from Chicago, could crack up and fall apart under the circumstances?"

She was miffed, and he couldn't blame her. And, too, his own sloppy way of expressing himself annoyed him as well. Words are my profession, he thought, but half the time I blow it when I have to make my point out loud, instead of on paper. I'd do better at this writing her a letter.

At last he said, "You've misunderstood me . . . and please don't get defensive on me. What I meant was, there was a murder . . . several murders . . . committed on that spot. Margery is missing, but there may be . . .," he searched for a way to phrase it delicately, ". . . evidence, Mary. Evidence of horrible things that the authorities may just have left there for the weather, and time, to dispose of."

"Oh." she said.

She knew it was not specifically what he meant, but the thought that her father was decapitated came back to her full force.

The second round of drinks arrived just in time. As they took their first salty sips, Mary saw Dana coming down the stairs wearing white shorts and blouse, her brown canvas bag slung over one shoulder. She spotted them almost at once, and came over to the table, smiling.

She wished for some company to help explain the occurences of the last few minutes. Usually, this kind of a situation presented no problem for her whatsoever. But the day, the heat, and the emotions brought forth from her encounter with Barton had been taxing. She would have liked to have had Lucy there with her now, since she had been present upstairs and witnessed at least part of the strange meeting. It would be easier to explain to them, somehow. Uncertainty was not a state of mind Dana was used to. It made her feel "fragile," an adjective she would not like hearing applied to her by anyone else, yet there was no denying that the word was apt, for now.

Dana looked from the smiling faces of Ben and Mary over to the bar, where Thot was sitting. Her heart sank a little further. It was not a meeting she was anticipating with any relish. She nodded cordially to the giant, silently mouthing the words, "I'll be right over," and took a chair at the table.

"Lucy will be right down," she said to the couple, "and I can only chat for a moment before I have to see Thot. A lot's happened, though."

The bartender stopped Ben from asking what she'd meant. Dana almost ordered a martini, but checked herself, quickly deciding upon a Scotch. The three of them sat then, in silence, the bartender having taken her order and departed. Dana's hands were folded together on the table, and she was staring at them, avoiding the expectant faces of Mary and Ben. Then, she gave her head a brief shake, looked up at them, and said, "Margery Croft's father is here."

"What?" Ben asked, incredulously.

"You heard me. He was sitting at the bar over there when we arrived. Perhaps you saw him?"

"I think I did," Mary offered, not commenting on how seedy he'd looked . . . if that *had* been him.

"Wait a minute . . . let's back up, here. How did this come about?" Ben asked.

"I was in the shower. When I came out, he was there in the room with Lucy. As far as I can tell, he just walked in on her."

"How is she?"

"Fine, Mary, just fine. I think she had a sixth sense about him. They're very much concerned with the same thing . . . finding Margery. She's showering now."

Ben asked, "And where is *he*?"

"He went to his room after he and I had talked a bit. He's joining us for dinner."

"Here you are, ma'am."

Dana looked up into the face of the bartender, who had placed her Scotch down on the table with a dull "clunk."

"Thank you," she said quietly as he turned away. She took a quick sip, then suddenly called after him.

"Yes?" the man asked.

"Would you please tell Thot . . . he's the gentleman sitting . . ."

"I know Thot, ma'am."

"Oh. Good. Well, tell him I'll join him in two minutes, will you?"

The bartender left, and she returned attention to her companions.

"Dana," Mary was saying, "this Mr. Croft . . . he looked in pretty bad shape, if he's the one I mean."

"He is . . . or was. We'll see. He told me he's been here for a week, and hasn't been able to do much of anything but drink."

"Hasn't he found out anything about the massacre?" Ben licked a grain of salt from the corner of his mouth as he spoke.

"He knows about as much as we do, I think. No one here, locally, would speak to him about it. That of course, added insult to injury, and since it was useless to ask any more questions, he thought he'd stick around and see if anything . . . any information . . . came his way through hearsay. Meanwhile, he drank."

"Poor bastard."

"I don't know about that, Ben. His instincts are good, anyway."

"What do you mean?"

"I mean, *we're* here, aren't we?"

Despite the implications, she refused to think of Barton Croft as a bum; obviously what Ben and Mary inferred or suspected. Dana had an inkling of what he'd been going through, and as they'd talked, it became clearer to her. His wife had left him for another man, years ago. All he had was his daughter, and when it seemed that he might have lost her as well, his life began caving in. Barton had come here against the advice of everyone, including his own doctor, who warned that such an adventure could be dangerous to his heart. His blood pressure was high, and his nerves were in shreds. Nevertheless, Barton knew that to sit around Boston, in terror of a phone call . . . yet waiting for its ring, would drive him mad. He'd taken an action to force reaction, and Dana admired that.

He'd said that his original plan had been to go to Manila and question Margery's co-workers at the Foundation, and some of the local authorities. But having thought that much over, he'd decided that he could jump the gun by heading straight to the source, to New Guinea, gleaning what he could from the police at Port Moresby, and meanwhile phone or write his questions back to the people in Manila; Dana and Lucy, in particular. Once he'd realized that the police were telling him nothing he didn't already know, he'd tried to phone the Pemberton Foundation, but received no answers. Dana had explained that regular hours, since the murder, were impossible to keep, and they had no answering machine. He'd probably called at one of the many times when no one was there. She learned that, having found no satisfaction from his phone calls, he had written. That letter was probably there in Manila right now. They had left before it arrived.

"Now then," she said, bringing herself back to the present, "I've kept Thot waiting long enough." She sighed deeply, summoning her will, and rose from the table, saying to Margery, "Wish me luck."

"I think you might be in for a pleasant surprise," Mary smiled back encouragingly. Dana returned the grin with a skeptical, "I hope so," and walked over to the bar.

She had just turned her back to them when Lucy appeared at the entrance. She had piled her hair on top of her head, a yellow ribbon shining through the mass of blackness. A yellow tank top and shorts set off the darkness of her skin. On her feet she wore a pair of plain white canvas shoes, and in her hand a small canvas purse.

"Well," Mary said as Lucy seated herself, "Dana says things have been popping while we've been sitting here getting swacked."

"You mean Barton Croft?' Isn't it wonderful?"

"How did it happen?"

Lucy foraged around in her little purse, withdrawing a cigarette. She was about to return the pack, when she smirked at Ben, and offered him one.

"Thanks," he smirked back, lighting both with his lighter.

It was evident to him that this recent development had changed Lucy's attitude. Of course the short nap, the shower and change of clothes could have helped to refresh her, but he felt that it was far more than simply that causing this pleasing change in the girl. He got the distinct impression that she was genuinely rejuvenated. Barton Croft's appearance upon the scene had very obviously given her back the hope she'd once had, and seemed to have lost.

"Well," she sighed, a rush of smoke blowing from her lips as she emoted the vowel, "I was naked . . . really . . . and I heard the door, looked up . . . and there he was."

"My God, you must have been terrified." Mary leaned in closer to the girl.

Lucy thought for a moment, then replied, "You know, it's funny, but no, I wasn't. Confused, and certainly embarrassed at having been caught with nothing on . . . but frightened of him . . . no. Not at all."

Her statement came forth as a surprise, even to herself, and Ben and Mary both grinned at the charm of its candor. But it was more than a surprise to Lucy. It had been almost a revelation . . . she had never once really feared Barton Croft. Then, she was aware that they were waiting for her to continue speaking, and so she asked, "Where's Dana?"

"At the bar, with Thot." Ben answered.

"Did she tell you about her meeting? Mr. Croft was gone when I got out of the shower, and Dana was just getting ready to leave."

Mary recapped what they'd learned from Dana, and had just finished when Ben leaned in and said quietly, "Good timing. Look who just walked in."

It was, of course, merely coincidence that at the moment of Barton Croft's entrance, the record on the juke box ended, a silence falling over the room that was interrupted only by the occasional rattle and clatter of dishes and silverware from the kitchen.

Thot and Dana, deep in conversation, stopped talking, and the three at the table gave their attention to the man standing at the doorway.

He had obviously shaved and showered. His white hair, still damp, caught the dim lights of the room and glistened about his face, which, though still a might red-eyed and weary, was at least free of the white stubble that had sprinkled it earlier. He looked younger, and the effect was helped by the clean white shirt and pants he now wore.

Lucy waved to him and he came over, rather shyly, as the juke box started up once more, this time with Carleton Carpenter and Debbie Reynolds jabbering out "Abba Dabba Honeymoon." It stopped Barton for a second. He hadn't heard that song in 30 years, and now, here, of all places . . .

Introductions having been made, he asked, "Have you all ordered already?"

"Not food, yet. Just these," Mary said, holding up her drink.

"Well, I think I've had enough for one day already."

"I haven't," Lucy said, and was about to signal to the bar when she saw Dana walking toward them, the bartender and Thot in tow.

"We've had a nice talk," Dana said, regarding Thot, "and the plans are made, for the most part, I think?"

"I think," Thot smiled back at her.

"Now then. A few introductions. First, this is our bartender, Trobi. He will be part of our party."

They all said their hellos and he happily returned their greetings.

"You're lucky, Trobi," Ben joked, "to be able to get off work on such short notice."

"My sister . . . she owns the place," he laughed, "so, I see you all tomorrow, huh? Dinner soon. Another round for now?"

They agreed, Lucy also deciding upon a Marguerita, while Barton added a club soda to the order.

Dana pulled out a chair, and gestured to it, saying, "Do join us, Thot."

"No, I cannot, Dr. McKinley. I must make a few more arrangements before tomorrow. So, I'll say good night."

"Wait," Dana half shouted, "you haven't met Mr. Croft."

Barton Croft began to rise as Thot, taking his extended hand, said, "Please, don't get up, Mr. Croft. A great pleasure. I've seen you . . . around."

There was an embarrassed pause that Croft covered beautifully with, "And now you've seen me practically sober, Thot. Nice to meet you."

They silently watched Thot exit. Once he was out of earshot, Mary whispered, "How did it go?"

"Fine. Somewhere along the line he got his manners back. We leave tomorrow at 8 A.M."

There were alternate gasps and groans about the hour of their departure, and Dana quieted them down with a gesture.

"I have one more question," she turned to Barton, "and I think I can speak for all of us, Mr. Croft, when I say we would be honored if you would join us tomorrow. Will you come?"

Everyone at the table was staring at him, waiting for his response. He looked back into each of their faces and began to speak, but words would not form. Tears began to fill his eyes, and he at last said, "Thank you. Yes. Thank you."

Lucy took his hand in hers and squeezed it, then wiped a tear from her own cheek.

Trobi arrived with the drinks, and Dana grabbed his sleeve as he started to leave. "Stay a moment, Trobi. You're a part of this gang, now. It's too bad

Thot couldn't stay for a while longer."

The big man stood obediently, watching as Dana raised her glass high.

"To Barton Croft. And to our mission."

They all drank. The mood of the day had changed to a relaxed, indeed, friendly evening that held promise for the morning. Trobi, however, did not smile, but stood staring down at the happy faces.

"Dinner is ready, if you are." he said.

They were, and he turned round and walked back past the bar, toward the kitchen. His back was to them. They could not see that now, he too, was smiling.

"Thank you, Barton. Good night." Dana said quietly, and closed the door to the room.

She did not turn on the light, but stood there in the dark for a moment, her cheek against the warped wood of the door, hearing his footsteps retreat down the hall.

The others were still downstairs in the dining room. After dinner, Trobi had sent over a round of brandys, but Dana had given hers to Ben, explaining she was tired, and that with the long day ahead, she wanted sleep more than a brandy. And she'd hoped the rest of the table would take her departure as a reminder that they too would need all the rest they could get. God only knew when there would be a real bed to sleep in next.

Yet, it was their last night in a civilized atmosphere . . . however remote . . . and she couldn't blame them when no one else followed her lead, except for Barton Croft, who had asked if he might see her to her room.

He'd said nothing as they trudged up the squeaking staircase, and though her brain raced for

something intelligent to say, all that crossed her
mind had been either inane, or provocative, and so
she too said nothing.

Now, inside the quiet room, she felt almost
relaxed. Things had gone well—far better than she
had initially expected. Thot had proven to be bright
and cooperative with her, despite their bad start,
and Trobi seemed helpful and friendly. There had
been about the evening a feeling of teamwork; as if
in some way they had all been transformed from in-
dividual egos and wants into a single unit. A team
bonded by a mutual goal. True, she was concerned
about Lucy's very apparent ... indeed, nearly
transparent interest in Barton Croft; during dinner
it had been almost embarassing. Still, emotional
control was evidently not one of the girl's stronger
points, and she couldn't be faulted for her interest in
Margery's father, though it would have to be kept in
check.

Listen to me, Dana almost said aloud. I sound
jealous. But, no, I am not a jealous woman ... I am
not a jealous person. And even if I were, there is no
reason. You are here for Marcus Pemberton.
Remember that.

She remembered then why she had left the table:
to get to bed. If she could get to sleep before Mary
and Lucy returned, she knew nothing could awaken
her until her travel alarm went off at 6:30.

It was then that she heard something. At first she
thought it was her imagination ... but she trusted
herself. There *had* been a noise. It had not come
from the hallway; her ear was practically against the
door. No; either the sound had come from outside,
through the opened window behind her and in the
opposite wall, or it had come from inside the room.

Dana held her breath, straining to hear any other

sound. Very slowly, she turned around, pressing her back against the door.

Only the moonlight beaming through the unshaded window illuminated the darkness. If anyone else was in the room, there were only two places they could be; in the bathroom, the door of which was ajar, or next to the window, out of the light.

She had to think where the light switch was, then remembered that it was a pull-cord that hung from a ceiling lamp in the middle of the room . . . too far away for her to reach from where she was.

Her hand reached in back of her, feeling for the doorknob. She grasped it, and it turned.

"Don't try it." a voice said.

Sweat broke out anew from every pore as she sucked in the air she'd been holding back from her now aching lungs, at once realizing that she was in danger of hypervenilating.

"Walk over to the bathroom door and face it," the voice commanded.

As she did so, she could hear the figure move across the room.

She came to the bathroom door and stood staring at it, her two hands holding on to the knob with all her strength, the opened door creaking from the pressure.

"You will all die. Turn back." the voice said.

The door opened. Light came briefly into the room and was gone, leaving her alone in the dark as the door closed.

Ben sat on the edge of his bed, the piece of torn paper in his hand.

He had already decided to say nothing about it. It

could only upset anyone else who saw it, and since, now, things seemed definitely improved, what was the sense? But he was glad to have Barton Croft along for the ride ... another man, directly involved in the whole situation, seemed to lessen his own responsibilities. Nevertheless, he questioned the wisdom of not at least telling Dana about what he had found taped to the mirror in his room.

The silence that surrounded him was so total, that the soft knock on his door scared him half to death.

Stuffing the note under the flat, shapeless pillow on his bed, he reached the door in a single bound, opening it to reveal Dana McKinley. She held her forefinger to her lips to insure his silence, and slipped into the room. He closed the door quietly as she sat down on his bed.

Dana turned her head twice, surveying the place, and said, "What a horrible little room."

"You're right," he agreed, reaching for the quart of Scotch he had remembered to pack. "Want a drink?"

Without hesitation, she said, "Yes."

"No glasses, I'm afraid. Here, have a pull."

Dana grabbed the bottle with both hands, took two hard swigs, and passed it back to him.

"Well done," he said, and took a slug himself. "You're upset. What's the matter?"

"There was a man in my room, when I came upstairs ... no, no ... he didn't hurt me ... didn't even threaten me, really. But he gave me a warning."

"Dana, start from the moment you walked into the room."

She related the incident to him, leaving out nothing. She ended with, "I waited til Mary and

Lucy came in . . . they said you'd come up with them, so I knew you were here."

"Did you tell them you were coming to see me?"

"No. I suppose I should have . . . I could have made up some excuse . . . but, you see I *was* coming to see you . . . it seemed too close to the truth . . . Oh, I don't know. I guess I'm just not thinking quickly enough. Anyway, I said I'd thought of some things Barton should know about tomorrow . . . to wear light clothes or something . . . I don't know, Ben . . ."

"It's alright, as long as they believe you."

He knew then that he had to tell her about the note. Reaching across her, he took the note from beneath the pillow. Ben held the bottle out to her.

"Here. Take another slug. You're gonna need it."

Dana obeyed, taking the bottle from him. She brought it to her lips and tipped it. "Okay," she finally gasped, "What?"

He was holding a sheet of ragged paper in his hand, a burning cigarette he'd just lit poised between his fingers. "I found this on the mirror when I came in."

She took it from him, passing the bottle back.

The paper was brown, as if it had been haphazardly torn from the end of a paper bag. On it was written, "YOU WILL ALL DIE. TURN BACK."

"Oh, God," Dana whispered, "these are the same words he said to me."

"Then, whoever he is . . . it's not him we have to fear."

"What do you mean?"

"Well, I think it's exactly as you said. It's not a threat. It's a warning."

"But . . ."

"Dana, he could have killed you easily. He didn't.

He could have killed me just as easily. But he didn't. Someone's already tried to get us all, remember? No. He wants us to turn back for our own safety. I think he's on our side. But who?''

FOURTEEN

"Excuse me, but I don't believe I ever did find out your name," Dana was saying to the driver as she handed him her knapsack. "You disappeared so quickly last night, with Thot. I thought I'd see you downstairs at the bar, or at dinner."

"Kara," he replied in the deep.sonorous voice that fit so perfectly with his appearance. It did not seem to be the voice from last night, but she couldn't be sure. Then, she wondered if he was saying something to her in his own language, and deciding to make certain, asked, "Your name is Kara?"

He nodded, and the huge arms lifted the heavy bag and placed it with care into one of the three land rovers at their disposal.

It was 7:45, the sun already high and yellow in the sky, the heat becoming more intense by the moment. When she had stepped out onto the steps

of the Jungle Orchid, only seconds ago, Kara's
powerful bulk was dry beneath the kahki's he wore.
But now, sweat was already beginning to break out
in patches across the beige cloth covering his wide
back, and a dew of perspiration dotted his face.

She extended her hand to him. "I'm Dr.
McKinley, as I suppose you already know. I realize
it's a little late for this, but I've neglected thanking
you for your help. If, in the next few days, we seem
ignorant to you, please bear with us?"

Kara smiled shyly, almost guiltily, nodded as he
shook her hand and, excusing himself, walked to
another land rover, making a great show of securing
the ropes that seemed quite secure as they were.

Dana was grateful for the early start, though in
fact she'd have preferred it even earlier. Still,
everyone seemed tired yesterday, and an evening of
relaxation, of getting to know their new companions
was, she felt, therapeutic.

As Mary had predicted, Thot certainly had been a
surprise last night. She'd expected him to be as curt
and rude as she'd found him at their arrival, so had
approached him on the defensive. But his grin was
so wide, his handshake so eager, that she'd been
immediately disarmed. Then, he introduced her to
Trobi, explaining that the bartender had been hired
on as a hand. He, Trobi, seemed from the first,
happy to be included.

The first thing was to see a list of the provisions
that would be needed. But for a few items, Dana
found it complete, and Thot informed her he would
pick up those items that night, after their talk, or
early in the morning; his cousin owned the shop. The
station wagon he had picked them up in at the
airport had been his cousin's too. It began to amuse
her, that they all seemed related in one way or

another. This was a *very* small town.

For the journey, he had secured three land rovers; two to carry the four passengers and two drivers, and one for a driver with the provisions and bags.

It was then she'd told him of her idea to invite Barton Croft, if he'd come. Thot had replied that since three jeeps were necessary already, one more person would not be a problem. Making a few notations for additional materials, he'd continued on with the agenda for the first day.

Near noon, they would be stopping at a village to rest and eat, and afterwards, continue on, arriving at the Pemberton campsite around four. They could proceed directly across the water to the Island if they chose, but, he thought, quite rightly, that they'd spend the night there. Dana had concurred readily. She'd be able to investigate the grounds, and also they would be fresher for an early start the following morning.

As he talked, she'd been impressed with his organized, concise manner, and the way in which he expressed himself. It seemed he'd taken everything into account.

"That's fine, Thot," she'd said.

"Thank you, Doctor."

"If I may, I get the feeling you don't live here all the time."

"Oh? and why is that?"

"Well . . . you seem to have an air of . . . poise, I suppose . . . that comes from dealing with a lot of people."

"You mean 'sophisticated' people?"

"Thot, I didn't mean to offend you, I just . . ."

"No, Doctor. I know what you meant. I am used to dealing with all sorts, you are right. Though these people here on Savong-khai may seem quaint to you, there are things about them that should not be underestimated. But, to answer your question . . . I was educated in Australia. I live half of the year in Port Moresby, half here, where I was born." Dana thought he was about to say more, but he stopped, seemed to consider his words momentarily, then merely said, "We should leave early tomorrow, I think."

He had abruptly closed the subject, and shut the door on her overtures of friendship, making it known politely that his personal life was not for discussion at any length. Well, so be it, she thought. He's certainly entitled to his privacy.

It was at this point that Barton Croft entered the dining room.

"Come," Dana had said to Thot, "and meet the additional member of the party."

The brief exchange between Barton and Thot had been mildly embarrassing, but moreover, Dana had gotten the feeling Thot already knew who Barton was. Not surprisingly, really, considering Barton had been asking questions about the massacre. Still, she thought it odd.

Dana looked at her watch. It was ten to, and not a sign of any of them. She knew the other women were up; they'd all had coffee sent to their room earlier. But Ben . . . and Barton? Where was Barton?

She smiled to herself then, and leaned on a spindly "pillar" holding up the roof of the porch of the Jungle Orchid. She realized in an instant, that she was not only impatient to get going, but looking forward to seeing Barton Croft again this morning. She blushed, which she knew was not in character for her at all. Then, she put these thoughts out of her mind, Marc Pemberton's image coming to her once more, reminding her where she was, and why. For all

the sudden and seeming camaraderie, someone had
been in her room . . . and the same person had given
the same warning to Ben.

She heard voices behind her and turned to see
Mary and Ben coming toward her through the
lobby. She was again a little amazed at how fresh
Mary managed to look, wearing her shorts and blue
polka dotted cotton blouse with an air of easy
elegance. Once again, the straw hat was stuck on her
head, her red hair pulled up beneath it. Ben too wore
shorts, and Dana noticed with admiration, the
strength of his bare, well muscled legs. It was becoming obvious that they were very much attracted
to each other, and Dana found herself wondering if
they'd made love yet; then caught herself, thinking,
there I go again. Sex has started off my day . . . Oh,
Marc, I do miss you.

Ben was carrying both his bag and Mary's, and
they were laughing. Lucy was just one flight behind
them on the staircase, Trobi behind her carrying her
bag. They reached the lobby just as Ben and Mary
passed through the door to the porch. As they did
so, Lucy began looking around, absently rubbing
the palms of her hands against the cloth of the long
legged gray trousers she wore. Turning to Trobi, she
said,   "Listen,   I've . . . I've   forgotten
something . . . take the bag out, please? I'll be there
in a minute."

He agreed, and she watched him enter the bright
sunlight where Kara was loading one of the jeeps.
Then she quickly ran over to the bar, peeping into
the now darkened dining room, not yet opened for
what little business there might be. Even the
horrible little juke box was mute. Looking around,
and satisfied now that it was empty, Lucy gave a
quick glance to the lobby area, then pushed the old

squeaking screen door and joined the others on the porch.

It was Mary who noticed how busy Lucy's eyes were, searching the porch, then over the railing and out to the dusty path where the land rovers stood ready.

"Lucy?" Mary asked.

"What? Oh, hi. Gorgeous day, no?"

Mary shot a quick look to Ben, then agreed with her. After a moment, Lucy asked, "Where's Mr. Croft?"

"He's running a little late," Ben answered, "I looked in on him earlier. He'll be down very soon."

"Oh, good," Lucy said breathlessly, with apparent relief, "I thought maybe he'd changed his mind."

Dana glanced at Lucy then. She seemed once again to be the youthful, energetic young woman she'd been before the news of the attack. She'd even bothered to apply just the slightest bit of makeup, which seemed impractical for such a day.

The screen door squeaked, slammed and rattled in its frame, announcing Barton Croft's entrance.

He too seemed in fine form. The eyes were no longer red rimmed, a night's sober sleep having done him a world of good. He was clean shaven again and was, as the night before, clothed completely in white, though this time, the pants were short.

"Good morning," he called to all. Such was his exuberance that they all returned his greeting and he fairly skipped down the steps to hand Trobi his bag. He turned smiling up at Dana.

"Slept well?" he asked.

"Fine," she replied, laughing.

"What's funny?"

"You. You're a new man."

"No, it's the old me. But I know what I'm doing now. Lest I forget, let me thank you again, Doctor."

"You can save it until after this is all over, and then see if you still want to thank me. For now, you can call me Dana."

"Good," he pronounced, as Thot came out of the hotel.

"Everything is taken care of," he said, handing the receipts of paid bills to Mary, "so if everyone's ready, I suggest we take off."

Mary looked through the papers quickly, then stuck the receipts into her purse, saying, "If you don't mind, I'd like to ride with you, Thot . . .at least for the first half of the trip. I think I've got some questions here. Money questions . . . I'm not too good with figures, or to be honest, with some of this handwriting."

"Of course," he grinned, "it will be a pleasure."

Mary and Ben climbed into the first car, Thot driving. Obviously, Dana was meant to be seated beside Thot, but she hung back for just a moment, realizing that of course, Lucy and Barton would have to ride together in the second, with Kara driving. She climbed in next to Thot, and turned around to look at their little caravan. Trobi was just getting into the drivers seat of the last land rover, loaded up with the luggage and equipment.

Barton was looking straight at Dana in the first jeep. The waves of heat rising from the hot metal of the vehicles hood made her image shimmer, as she smiled back at him. Lucy, beside him, donned a pair of sun glasses and a canvas hat. She tapped him on the shoulder, removing a pair of very good binoculars from her bag. She handed them to him.

"If you'll hold these, we can share them. There

should be a lot to see," she said with a beaming smile.

"Ready?" Thot's voice came to Dana, returning her attention to business at hand.

"Oh, yes," she answered, turning face front and sighing very deeply, "we're ready."

Their engine started, then the second and third, and they lurched forward, slowly, haltingly at first over the rocky gravelled path, until it had widened into some semblance of a road, and they had begun the second leg of their journey.

The little jungle village was quiet but for a few animals and birds that went scurrying about, from shade to shade, across the square. Then, dimly, the hum of motors could be heard, and as it grew louder, people began to emerge one by one, and in couples, from their tiny houses.

At last, the hum grew into a roar, and three land rovers zoomed up and over the steep slope that brought them into the village.

As they entered the little town, the first thing they saw was the Spirit House. Of the few buildings it was easily the largest and tallest, and also built on something of a hill, and so towered over everything else. It was very like a huge, wooden tent, the central post of which was a high totem pole, from which large decorated brackets shot out, left and right, in support to the side, which travelled on up to the pinnacle of the triangle, standing some forty feet above them. The entire structure was roofed in palm frond, and this sloping roof continued on down until its bottommost edge touched the ground, the roof becoming the sides of the building. Within, tree trunk, the bark still remaining upon them, held up the back ends of the house.

The three land rovers roared up the incline, two of them in imitation of the showy, noisy entrance of the first, driven by Thot. They stopped before the Spirit House, while the villagers came running to greet them.

The Pemberton expedition disembarked, while the three vehicles were driven away, only Trobi returning shortly to watch the native celebration, the Sing-Sing. They had traveled for nearly four hours, stopping only once along the way. But that stop had been brief, everyone seeming to be of the same mind about moving on, for various reason; anxiety, discomfort at the unbelievably bumpy road and eagerness to get it over with, or simply because within the moving vehicles, some breeze was created, alleviating the monumental heat. Mary had been most surprised at the speed—or lack of it—they were forced to travel at. Because the roads were little more than grass cleared away from the soil, the journey was bumpy, dirty, and slow going. Alone, a driver could have made far better time, if he or she didn't care about risking a wrenched neck or slipped disk—but traveling with this many people necessitated patience. They had been fortunate that the rain had stopped a while ago, giving the thirsty ground time to soak it up and dry in the baking sun. After a heavy rain, these roads would be impassable; virtually miles of mud. But Mary, and even Dana, had been impressed by the timing. As slow as they had been moving, it had obviously been taken into account, for their arrival at the village had been as promised, precisely at noon.

Now, the people had gathered in a large circle; practically the entire village.

Their bodies were swathed in the skins of cus-cus, an animal not unlike the possum. All wore hair ornaments or elaborate headdresses so that, seeing them from afar, they appeared to be an enormous, varied aviary of every conceivable kind of bird, in every possible color of the spectrum. The feathers were, among many others, from the Bird of Paradise, cassowary and cockatoo, all moving independently of each other, combined into a quivering gaggle of humanity.

Though Mary was sure this was largely being "staged" for the benefit of the "white tourists," it was nevertheless an extravaganza of sorts.

Thot and Kara had removed somewhere to see about lunch while Trobi and the other five sat on straw mats beneath the palm trees, out of the insistent rays of the noonday sun. Only a few minutes before, this little clearing had been empty. In what seemed like moments, an "event" was taking place.

The town people continued to talk and make ready, now and then adjusting the necklaces of shells that rattled noisily around their weathered necks, or bending their heads to tickle a friend with the rainbow of plumage in their headdresses, laughing as they did so. Then, with no apparent hush, pause, or signal, all voices became one, the conversation blending directly into song, and the Sing-Sing had begun.

The dancers came forward, smiling, moving sensuously, rhythmically, feet gliding or stamping, their knees and thighs making the grass and leaves of their skirts undulate as if stroked by an unfelt wind. In the song, in the voices, Mary could distinguish at least two harmonies under a simple, forthright melody, all sung accapella, and she found herself swaying to the beat, moving up against Ben or her right, as she did so. He smiled and leaned into her, shoulder to shoulder, moving his body with hers so that they swayed to the same syncopation. They looked at each other then, but were no longer smiling, and the perspiration stood out on their flushed faces. She took his hand and held it, returning her attention to the Sing-Sing.

Soon, it had ended, and the people disbursed, presumably to their homes.

Once the crowd began to thin, Mary spotted Thot on the other side of the clearing, speaking with Kara. She had not as yet had the opportunity to say what she'd wanted to Thot, and as Kara moved away from him toward the Spirit House, she squeezed Ben's hand, saying, "Listen, I'll meet you at lunch. I've got to talk with Thot, and I think I see my chance right now."

"You could have asked him about the money while we were on the road."

"Show him receipts while he was driving? On that road? Besides . . . there are other things I'd like to find out."

He was about to caution her, but then realized she'd only become offended by his over-protectiveness. He said only, "Be tactful."

"I am the soul of tact. See you later."

And she was up, dusting herself off as she sauntered into the blazing brightness of the clearing, her hair seeming to ignite in red and gold, as a breeze caught and played with it about her ears. She shook her head, pulled her hair up off her neck, and stuck the straw hat firmly upon her head, as she called Thot's name.

The huge figure turned. He was sweating, and a thin layer of dust coated his skin and clothing.

"Hello," he greeted her, "did you enjoy the Sing-Sing?"

"Yes. Really wonderful and colorful. Thanks for arranging it, Thot. Where were you?"

"Arranging more. Luncheon is almost ready. I've even managed to get some beer. But I expect you'd like to go over those receipts now?"

She hesitated a moment, then ventured. "Yes . . . a few of them, anyway. And other things, too."

"Oh. Alright. There is a table and chairs in the Spirit House, if you'd like."

She agreed, and two minutes later a few sheets of paper were laid out before him on a heavy wooden table. He picked up each one in question as he went, explaining: "This figure here . . . forgive me, but I was in a hurry when I wrote it . . . is a 'five.' Also this one. This receipt is for the gas I bought to carry with us for the vehicles. There are two bills Mr. Croft ran up as your guest at the hotel . . . on Dr. McKinley's instructions . . ." he continued on, Mary watching his face rather than the bills. She knew for the most part, what most of them were for; and she felt that Thot knew she knew, seeing through her ruse as an excuse to talk. At last, he finished, collected the bills into a pile and pushed them back across the table to her.

"There now. That should answer most of your questions."

Mary folded them up and stuck them in her shoulder bag, thanking him. "Of course," she added, "I am curious about some other things."

"Like?"

"The massacre."

He blinked, then met her stare with his. When she neither responded nor backed down, he said, "Well?"

"What do you think happened to Margery Croft?"

"I think, Miss Pemberton, that she was murdered, like the others. I am sorry."

"Then what became of her body?"

"It is possible," he said, wiping perspiration from his forehead with his arm, "that it was taken away and . . . it is hard to explain to one who is not used to the ways of certain sects . . ."

". . . or cults?"

It stopped him for only a second, and he went on, ". . . or cults, if you will. One, in particular that I can think of, has not completely abolished cannibalism from their rites."

Mary's face drained of color, and she sat back heavily in her chair.

"I am sorry," he repeated.

When she could speak again, she said, "I supposed this is stupid of me, but I'd not even thought of that. Alright . . . that would explain the missing body . . . but why her, and not the others? Unless it was some sort of a sex thing."

"I do not know the intricacies of these religions. Why it was she, could have any number of answers."

Mary breathed deeply, preparing herself for what she was about to ask. "Why then, was my father's . . . why was he decaptitated, and . . ."

"I know this is difficult for you," he interrupted, then finished her thought for her with, "and I know, just as there was some cannibalism here once, so was there the practice of head shrinking."

He stopped, pausing for her to accept his words, looking for what her reaction would be. Tears welled up in her eyes, but she nodded for him to continue.

"It has been many years . . . a century, nearly, since any of this has been practiced even remotely . . . but there are strange, minor religions and bizarre rituals. Also, we speak here of two whites. They could be perceived as 'trophies,' in certain beliefs."

Thot withdrew a handkerchief and handed it to her. As she wiped her eyes, he added, "I regret to have upset you. There is no . . . delicate way to explain the things you ask, but I have tried."

Recovering gradually, she returned his hanky. "Thank you. There's no need for apology. You were most considerate, Thot. You've at least set my mind at ease about one thing."

"What?"

"I've had this horrid fear that . . . that his . . . head . . . would still be . . . somewhere. That I'd find it . . . trip over it, like a scene from a horrible black comedy. But you've set my fears to rest, as terrible as the alternative you've offered is."

His hand patted her twice, and speaking softly, offered, "Then I am glad. And I will help again, when you need me."

He rose then, his shadow falling across her face. "I will see to the food."

She watched him walk away, while she remained at the table, her hands folded before her.

She was praying silently.

Lunch had been more like a feast, spread out in the shade on the ground, huge leaves laid down in various scalloped, fanned designs, that served as a "tablecloth." The food was much, varied, and delicious. A choice of sinugbang kitong (broiled fish), soup made from stewed shrimp and clam, curacha (deep sea crab), with a variety of fresh fruit and homemade cakes, were more than satisfying.

To drink, there was coconut milk, and as Thot had promised, beer, and it was even cold!

Lucy had brought one over to Barton Croft, but he

gracefully declined, and handed his to Ben, who accepted it willingly; indeed, gratefully. Thot, Trobi and Kara sat across from Ben, Mary and Dana, having put the local "Mayor" of the village at the head of the "table."

The "mayor" was about fifty, and had been one of the leaders of the dance, during the Sing-Sing. He had not removed his costume, and the feathers of his headdress shook as he moved, while talking in his native language with Kara and Trobi, as Thot interpreted the gist of conversation. "His Honor" was on his second brew, and he would gesture now and again with the bottle of San Miguel Dark he drank from.

But Mary had not been the only one present whose thoughts had that day turned to Margery Croft.

Lucy had been trying since that morning, to find a way to bring up the subject with Barton. She wanted, not only to find out more about what Margery's life at home had been like, but also to engage Bart in conversation concerning so much mutual affection. When they had finished their lunch, she was pleased when he'd asked her if she'd like a bit of a walk.

Excusing themselves from the others, they started out through the bright and dusty clearing, strolling down the hill they had ridden up earlier.

"We'll be leaving in about thirty minutes," Dana called after them, and Barton turned around and called back,

"We won't be late!"

Dana watched their departure until they had disappeared below the close horizon of the hill. She had an impulse to join them, to follow along ... to chaperone. But it was ridiculous; she, Dana, was being ridiculous. She returned her attention to the Mayor, still shaking his beer bottle and his feathers as he spoke.

Down the road, a cool breeze, rare and welcome, came through the nearby brush and ran over their hot bodies like a veil of chiffon. Lucy breathed, the air sweet and musky with a wild perfume, and she realized then that in some perverse way, she was as close to happy as she had ever been. She laughed, and the sound brought Barton back from the thoughts that had carried him to Margery's tenth birthday in Boston, the year he'd turned forty years old.

"Something funny?" he asked, looking at Lucy.

"Not especially. But it's beautiful here, and nice to be away from so many people for a while."

"I suppose," he said with a sigh. "I've spent a lot of time away from people these last weeks. I rather enjoy the company."

"Good."

They walked in silence together for a few steps. Then Lucy said quietly, "I'm sure we're going to find her, Barton. Alive. And take her away."

He did not answer, but continued walking on beside her, his eyes cast down to his feet.

"I'm glad," he replied at last, "because I feel the same thing." He looked up at Lucy and said, "You know, she wrote me about you?"

"Good things?"

"She was very fond of you. You were kind to her . . .'showed her the ropes,' is how she put it, I remember."

"Oh, Barton, that was so easy to do. She enjoyed it all so."

"Lucy . . . did she . . . had she a boyfriend at all?"

"You know . . . we dated some, but there was no

one serious. We'd tease each other a lot . . . she liked young men. I mean, our own age. I'd call her a cradle robber, though, and she'd get back at me with jokes about Marc Pemberton.''

"I thought he and Dana . . .?''

"Oh, they were. But Margery knew how attractive I thought he was . . . used to accuse me of having a father fixation or something. It was all just teasing.''

"How old was Dr. Pemberton?''

"About fifty, I'd say.''

"You find men of fifty attractive, do you?'' He was obviously flattered and pleased.

"Yes, I do. And you know, you're not unlike Dr. Pemberton.''

"No?''

"No. I'm sure Dana sees it too.''

Lucy felt her heart sink when she saw his face fairly light up with a beaming smile at her last remark.

"You do?'' he asked eagerly.

"Yes, I'm sure of it,'' she continued, deliberated for a moment, then decided upon saying, "After all, she did find some excuse to visit you last night.''

"What? When?''

"After we all came upstairs. She told us she had to see you . . . to make sure you'd wear the right clothes today, something silly like that.''

"Lucy,'' he said rather sternly, "the last time I saw Dr. McKinley last night was when I said good-night to her at her door after we'd left the dinner table together.''

"Oh . . . uh . . .'' she stammered, immediately regretting what she'd said, "I suppose I was wrong. Maybe it was Thot she went to see.''

"Thot left before we did, Lucy.''

"I'm not a liar, Barton."

He looked at her for a moment, then put his arm around her shoulder. "Of course not. Where she went is her own business."

"I guess it is," Lucy replied, not wanting to return to the subject of Dana McKinley. She bent, without breaking her stride, and picked up a stone, throwing it lazily into the brush. It landed a few feet into the lush greenery and created a flurry of activity in the undergrowth. A second later, three hornbills took to the air. It startled them both at first, but it passed and they began to laugh.

"My God," Lucy gasped, "we're both so jumpy!"

"Yes," he agreed, catching his breath, "this could be a wonderful place, under different circumstances."

"Mmm. I guess. I've never been fond of the jungle, myself. It's different, now, though."

"How?"

She tried for a lie, but nothing believable would come to her, and feeling completely idiotic with her truthful reply, stated simply, "You, I guess."

Barton looked at his watch. "We'd better be getting back now," he observed, trying not to sound as self-conscious as he knew he appeared, "we wouldn't want them to leave us behind."

"No," she said, reaching into her bag for a cigarette.

But as they turned round on the path, she wondered who was lying about last night. Him . . . or Dana?

It was already two o'clock, and the best that could be said for the journey so far was that the sun was no longer directly overhead, thus giving them a reason to hope for relief.

Ben was not in any sort of good humor. He wanted the jeep to move faster, but knew of course that any real speed was virtually impossible; even at what seemed to be a snail's pace, they were all nevertheless covered in the dust that the wheels had churned up, and sent in billowing clouds around them. It was even worse for the vehicles that followed, having to drive through and into the wake of the preceding jeep. They could even taste the air.

On occasion they'd pass another little village, so tiny it made the one they'd lunched at seem a thriving metropolis, and Ben would at times find himself childishly envying the people he'd see along the road. They looked happy, unconcerned with murder and mayhem—and they were able to deal comfortably with the heat. Their little houses with frond roofs ideally created natural air-conditioning, making the most of whatever breeze came along and sending it, pulling it, in and around the rooms. The cane walks that led your eye up to the front doors seemed to invite you in. He even envied them their grass skirts, though he imagined that the rough strip of tree bark that served as the belt from which the grass was strung, probably scratched a good deal. Still, it seemed a small price to pay for being so cool.

He wondered if there was any of the San Miguel left; but if there had been, surely someone else would have had one in their fist. No one did.

They'd stopped very shortly, to let a herd of pigs cross, their swineherd waving to them as his animals squealed and grunted their way from one mass of forest to the other. Fortunately, they'd come to rest in heavy, merciful shade. Ben had turned around to see the others.

It didn't look as if Barton and Lucy were getting

on too well. Barton sat forward, his elbows on his knees, staring out to the left, while Lucy held her binoculars up to her eyes, coming around to Ben's face looking back at her through the lenses. He waved and she laughed, but there was no response from Barton.

At last they were moving again, albeit slowly. The road had widened some, and where the jungle gave way to more open space, wallabies could be seen cavorting in the distance, while at other intervals, wild dogs, thin and strange, stranger than hyenas, prowled through the trees and fields in packs. There were spots where the road, such as it was, became overgrown with vegetation, and when they'd rumbled through such areas, hornbills, cranes and egrets took wing, as if suddenly released from hidden cages beneath the tall grass.

Dana, seated next to Thot, would ocassionally question, or comment to their guide. But Mary sat in the back beside Ben, and it was she that could see Ben's face, furrowed with concern.

Ben knew her eyes were on him, but he did not acknowledge her interest. There was more on his mind than just the discomfort they were enduring.

It was not only the warning that Dana and he had received last night. But something else . . . a little thing, had happened over lunch, that gnawed at him.

The Mayor had been talking, and Thot would translate what he said. When the conversation had come around to their motives and destination, the Mayor had looked at the three white people, and back at Thot, then spoken.

Thot had hesitated, then translated what was said as, "The Mayor says that Satyr Island is a cursed place. He says people here, on Savong-khai, have disappeared many times, last seen crossing the water to the Island. He says there are those who seek to protect it from invasion. He warns you to turn back."

They had all been silent, Dana at length coming up with a gracious thank you for the Mayor's concern.

But what had bothered Ben was the expression on Trobi's face. It was deeply troubled; shocked, even. But his eyes were on Thot, not the Mayor. Ben made a mental note to privately ask Trobi one question, later on.

Meanwhile, he fingered the small shark's tooth the Mayor had given to him, to "The Man." It was, he learned, a good luck piece to fend off evil, and to give courage and strength to its owner in time of danger.

The land rover halted abruptly, and Ben snapped back to the here and now.

The dust in the air began to clear and he saw then that they had stopped on top of a steep hill. Below them and to the right, was more lush, green jungle. But some way off was a clearing surrounded by heavy vegetation, and beyond, at the outer edge of the ring of trees, silver water could be seen before disappearing behind a rock wall that the side of their land rover had nearly scraped.

"There," Thot said pointing, and they began their descent down to the site of the massacre.

FIFTEEN

Trobi and Kara were the last to make their way through the forest, carrying with them the bulk of supplies that they had removed from the land rovers. So heavy was the vegetation here that the jeeps had to be left out on the road, which had become, at that point, almost one with the jungle. The tree branches and bushes snapped into their faces as they went, but they knew they would not be long on foot.

Up ahead, following Thot's lead, Dana could feel, even hear, her heart as they drew closer to the spot.

She knew that they may be on the brink of some discovery; some meaning to what now was the senseless death of innocent people. It struck her almost immediately that the word "discovery" had come to mean something entirely different to her, than its definition of only a month ago. Once, the

very thing she was doing at this moment would
have filled her to the brim with an anticipation
regarding the research she and Marc had worked so
exhaustively on over the years. Her thoughts would
have been on the hope that perhaps *this* time they
would find the evolutionary proof they believed
existed. But now, brushing branches back from her
face and tripping now and again in her haste to keep
pace with Thot, she realized that the research meant
little, until she had . . . what?

Then the word came to her, and in that moment
she learned a little bit more about herself, and how
this thing, this hideous violence, had changed her.
Because the word was "avenged." She would
avenge the death of her lover, and then continue on
with her work, and find alone what they'd sought
together.

Dana gave a quick sigh of relief. It was, in its way,
good to know what you were about. She had known
for some time that her motives had changed, and
giving a name to them at last made her more confident, though she was hardly proud of this rage.

Just behind her, Ben's chief concern was how the
others would react to being here, in the place where
it had happened. He was fairly sure that he himself
may be upset, but since the emotions tied in with
Marcus Pemberton were not as strong as the others,
he felt his duty would lie in helping calm his
companions. Lucy already seemed tense, and
though he thought Dana and Mary could keep a grip
upon themselves, he hardly knew Barton Croft, but
the man had nearly crumbled beneath the news of
his daughter's abduction.

Ben could hear little cries of pain and curses
coming from various voices that followed behind
him. Without turning, he knew that Mary and

Barton, having worn short pants like himself, were being whipped and scratched about their bare legs by the forest they now invaded. He knew because looking down, he saw several cuts and one particularly mean gash on his own. It had been foolish to attempt this without covering for their legs, but at least it had made the journey itself cooler. However, he did notice that Lucy and Dana, as well as Thot and his men, had had the good sense to wear long pants.

As they continued on, he could barely hear a sound that crept up to them so gradually, that one did not really "hear" it, as become aware of it; a white noise that came rhythmically to him, louder all the time, until he recognized it as the sound of the sea: they must be getting closer to their destination.

Then, Dana came to a halt, and peering beyond her, Ben could see Thot stooping before what seemed a wall of tree and fern. His great arms began slashing through it with a long, curved knife, and as he did so, more and more light appeared to them, until he had cleared an area large enough, and stepped through it and out of sight.

One by one, they came up to this entrance which, to Barton Croft, appeared to be like a hole in the world, through which one stepped into another existence, like walking through a mirror and coming out on the opposite side.

By the time Trobi and Kara had stepped through, the others were standing in a semicircle, silently looking at the campsite. It actually existed. They were standing here, on the very spot.

It had happened.

Up to now, the idea had been so unreal that the actual fact of human slaughter was kept in abeyance by the lack of tangible proof. Prior to this, it had been "news," a story they had heard. Now, there was proof. It was not as if there were bits of gore hanging from the branches; nothing of the dreadful horror that had happened here was immediately apparent. But there seemed to be a solemn stillness about the place that made you want to whisper in reverence . . . in deference . . . to the lives that this place had claimed.

It's only a little clearing in the woods, Mary was thinking. Just a spot where a little grass grew, surrounded by lush jungle, and cut off by that jungle from the nearby sea, which could be heard but not seen. In the dust on the ground, many footprints were still visible; she wondered if any of them had been her father's. Small holes in the ground at various places around the area told her where the tents had been pitched. She looked over to Barton Croft. There were tears in his eyes. Dana seemed stunned, numb. Lucy was pale beneath her tan.

It was Thot who spoke first.

"I suggest, Dr. McKinley, that we make camp here now for the night. Tomorrow, we can go across to the Island."

The Island, Dana thought. There was yet another place. It did not end here, she reminded herself. It ends on the Island. Whatever the answers are, they are there.

"Yes," she answered Thot.

At a signal from him, Trobi and Kara sprang into action, giving Ben and Barton orders, while Lucy and Mary began unpacking what would be needed.

By 4:30 that afternoon, the little clearing had once more been transformed into yet another campsite, not unlike the one that had stood there some time ago. There were only three tents this time, not four.

It had been decided that the lighter they traveled, the faster they'd move, and keeping this in mind, some privacy would have to be sacrificed. Mary, Dana and Lucy had consented to share a tent, and now that it had been erected, they saw that it was going to be quite cramped. Still, it was only for tonight and possibly tomorrow night. They could certainly make do for that length of time. Trobi and Kara shared the second tent and Ben and Barton were in the third. Thot had told them that unless there was bad weather, and none was expected, he would sleep out doors. Besides, Trobi and Kara alone were more than ample occupants of their tent. Thot could not possibly have fit inside it comfortably, considering his size together with that of the other two.

The heavy work having now been done, they began to think of leisure, and of being cool. The work, the heat, the tension, needed relief; especially here, where they were now, reminded at all times of their own mortality.

Thot had announced that he and his men were going down to the beach for a swim, and explaining that it was just through the trees, following the sound of the surf from there, he, Trobi and Kara vanished into the brush.

Lucy wanted to ask Barton for another walk, to clear up what she knew to have been a faux pas on her part, but when he'd seen her coming toward him, he declared rather too loudly that he would use this time for a nap before dinner, which Thot had promised to cook that night. This gave Ben the excuse of wanting Bart to have the tent to himself, which was not entirely untrue. But asking Mary for a swim was certainly part of his consideration.

Feeling dejected, or rejected, Lucy lifted the flap

to her tent and found Dana changing into a bathing suit. There was an awkward moment's silence, then Dana spoke: "Mary's gone down to the beach already and . . ."

"Yes. I saw her. With Ben."

"Naturally. They're cute, no?"

"I suppose so. You're going to the beach too?"

"Yes," Dana replied, "I think we can afford a little time to cool off. It'll feel good."

Lucy lit a cigarette and sat down on a rolled up sleeping bag.

"I wish you wouldn't smoke in here, Lucy. You know I don't usually mind, but these are such close quarters for us."

Lucy silently took one more drag from the cigarette, then crushed it beneath her heel saying, "It's alright. You going alone?"

"To the beach? Yes. Why?"

"I thought you might be going with Barton Croft."

Dana stared at Lucy, accepting the dare in the girl's eyes, but saying, "You heard him say he was taking a nap."

"The whole world heard him say that, but he meant it for me."

"You like him?"

Lucy nodded and shrugged. Dana bent down toward her. "Listen, Lucy," she said softly, "don't go after him so hard. He's got his daughter on his mind, dear."

Lucy raised her head quickly to meet Dana face to face. "Mind your own business!"

Dana was not used to being spoken to in that manner; also, she felt somehow wronged by the remark, misunderstood. True, she found Bart Croft attractive, but it was hardly competition she felt concerning Lucy. She was under just as much pressure as any of the others, and after all, Marc Pemberton had been her lover . . . and here they were now at the place where he'd been murdered. And what was all this going on, anyway . . . this jealousy? What had any of it to do with finding out the truth?

Dana had tears in her own eyes as, saying nothing, she left, leaving Lucy weeping on the floor of the tent.

Ben ran the last few feet and threw himself down onto the towel he'd spread upon the hot sand. Water ran off him into the towel and already he could feel the heat of the sun, even this late in the day, evaporating what remained on his glistening, hard body. A shadow came across the sun and said, "You beat me, you rat! I thought you'd let me win!"

Mary took her place beside him on her own towel, grabbing a comb from her bag and dragging it through her tangled hair.

"No chance," he answered, stretching, feeling his muscles come alive from the swim. He lifted himself up on his elbows and looked out to the beach and sea. The sand was dark, and covered with rocks and pebbles, they having found one of the few small spots smooth enough to rest upon. Though he had a few little bruises on the soles of his feet from the coral in the water, the view was a colorful spectacle from here; the water, lovely and blue. Farther out, he could see Thot, Trobi and Kara swimming and cavorting, spending as much time beneath the surface of the water as on top.

"Look at them," Mary laughed. "They're like seals."

"Mmm. Thot said that snorkling is very popular

with the tourists. Of course, I don't guess those three need snorkles or sissy stuff like that."

"You sound jealous, Ben. They're natives."

"Oh," he rolled over on his stomach and looked up at her, "I know. But they . . . he . . . I mean, puts me off, sometimes."

"Well, he seems to be doing his best to please us."

Ben did not acknowledge her statement.

"I mean," she went on hopefully, "they're out there probably trying to catch the dinner he said he'd cook for us tonight."

"Mmm," Ben murmured again, noncommitally.

"Ben, he *is* going through an awful lot of unnecessary trouble. He said he'd even gotten entertainment for us after dinner."

"Sure. Frank Sinatra."

They lay there silently. He made her furious sometimes, but he made her laugh, too. She stared down at him, taking in his body, traveling down the broad shoulders and through the valley between them that ran down his muscled back, acknowledging to herself how much she wanted to touch him. She wished he'd look at her, so he could read it on her face, in her eyes, and give him her assent, but he lay there with his eyes closed against the sun, breathing evenly.

"Ben, are you scared?"

"Yes," he replied, not opening his eyes.

"You don't sound it."

"I am, though."

"I am too."

His eyes were still closed, but his hand reached down to find and hold hers. He squeezed it then, and looked up at her.

The sun was very bright and her hair seemed like wet fire, aglow around her face. Most of the water had already dried off her body, but for a few drops that trickled down from behind her neck, over the swell of a breast, and disappeared below the line of red cloth that was the top of her bikini. Moving closer to her, he placed a hand behind her neck, smoothing the remaining moisture over her skin, following the same path as the drop of water he'd watched, until his hand rested gently, firmly upon first one, then the other breast, and she drew closer to him, and he to her, their faces coming together, lips parted in a kiss that had them gasping for breath.

"You realize," he said at last, "that I'll have to spend the rest of the time on this beach lying on my stomach."

"Flatterer," she said, happy at his arousal, "Maybe one of these nights we can go for a moonlight swim?"

He smiled and took her hand. "When?" His face was serious.

"Soon," she said, just as serious. "I promise."

She felt good; at least, certainly better than she had in a long time. This man was good, and she'd needed to feel a man near her, for her, who might help her defend herself from whatever danger was abroad. The security of that knowledge helped her fight the awful, sick-making violence that was in the air, here in this place, which her own father could not defend himself against. Somehow, Ben's love would help make her strong in the face of the hatred they found themselves in the midst of.

It was then that she saw Dana. The Doctor was standing almost at the edge of the forest, atop a small dune. In her hands, cupped before her, something caught the light of the sun and flashed brightly, hurting Mary's eyes. She thought at first that it was a small mirror that Dana held. Mary called out to her, but the Doctor did not look up. She remained staring down, almost entranced by the shiny object.

"Excuse me, Ben," Mary said quickly, and slipping into her shoes to protect her feet from the burning sand, she was off, heading toward Dana. Ben watched her walking hurriedly away from him, noting the sway of her ample hips and the firm roundness of her bottom as it moved within the bikini pants. Her long legs were strong, her calves and ankles working as they traveled across the irregular terrain. Ben let his mind wander to the future, where they were naked together in the moonlight, their bodies wet after the promised swim. It was only the sound of a woman crying out that brought him back to the present.

Mary was just running into the trees toward the encampment, Dana calling her name as she turned to watch her go.

"Dana!" Ben waved an arm to her.

The Doctor turned again, saw Ben, and came over, sitting herself down on the towel Mary had left. Ben could see she was shaken and practically shivering in spite of the heat.

"What is it?" he asked.

Dana looked out to sea as she held out her opened palm to him.

"This," she said flatly, little expression in her voice.

In her hand lay a cigarette lighter. He picked it up, and she said, "Look at it closely. There's an inscription."

Flipping it over in his hand he saw, etched into the silver;

"M—FOREVER—M."

A chill ran through him suddenly; a chill not

unlike what he knew now Dana must be feeling. He looked back into her face, but her eyes remained set on the water.

"I was on my way here. I saw it shining in the bushes. It belonged to Marcus. It was a gift from Mary."

He knew it, of course. He'd recognized it almost immediately. Marcus had often lit his cigarette for him with it.

Without a word, he began to rise, thinking only that he must get to Mary, but Dana's hand stayed him.

"No," she commanded, "she doesn't need you . . . or me . . . right now. It's too private, Ben. Let her alone."

In an instant he knew Dana was right, and he eased himself back down, placing the lighter on the towel. For a while they sat without saying a word, each of them concentrated on their own thoughts and fears. The sound of the water moving easily into the shore and the occasional cry of a bird were the only sounds, while out in the water, Thot and his men swam contentedly . . . "like seals."

After some minutes, Dana said, "Trobi told me that some of this area was explored for the first time only thirty years ago."

"I know. I keep forgetting that. Still," he sighed, "there are things that seem . . . stranger than they should be."

"What do you mean?"

"Little things." He was already sorry he'd said this much. Now, he had to go on.

"Well . . . the threats aside . . . this area from all reports was gone over with a fine tooth comb after the discovery of the killings. Why did one of us find the lighter, now?"

She looked at it, lying carelessly there on the towel, as if it had no meaning or significance at all; just a pretty good, expensive hunk of gold that lit cigarettes.

"And there's something else, Dana."

"What?"

"I don't want to jump the gun on this, so let me ask a question and we'll leave it at that?"

She nodded, and he continued, "During lunch, when the Mayor was speaking, did you notice anything?"

She thought back over the episode, which seemed a year ago, now. The Mayor spoke, Thot had translated, and they had been warned . . . again.

"I don't think so," she answered.

He was silent, thinking it over for a moment.

"Well?" she urged him impatiently.

"I don't know, Dana. Maybe it's just my imagination. But I think I saw something. I've got to ask Trobi something tonight."

"What, Ben?"

"How many languages he speaks."

Dana looked at him curiously, but he said no more. She returned her gaze to the shoreline, and out into the sea where the men still swam.

Beyond the three figures, across the water, was Satyr Island, its black sand and dark jungle silhouetted against the deep pink of the evening sky surrounding it.

It's like its alive, she thought. Waiting for us.

Night had fallen quickly, and they sat around the camp fire, smoking and drinking foul coffee. They had eaten the tasteless, overcooked fish that Thot had so proudly presented to them, caught freshly that day by him and his men, and with their bare hands, it would seem. But the discovery of the lighter had gradually come to occupy their thoughts, and now that they all knew, a pall had settled over the group. That being the case, none of them had had much of an appetite anyway, and it seemed to Barton Croft that Thot was disappointed the meal had not gone over better. They knew the big man meant well, but his sudden forced congeniality in the face of the news was more annoying than anything else. While serving the supper to them, he had gone on at some length about the "entertainment" he had arranged for after dinner, and they knew that having endured the meal, they were not yet free, waiting for this "entertainment" to happen.

They'd all changed from their bathing suits, and from the fire's glow, their faces took on the bright orange hue from the comforting light. Since the clearing was cut off from the ocean by the trees, no strong breeze disturbed the steady flames, though an occasional breath of fresh sea air wafted through. Animals cried out in the night and the darkness that came at them from the jungle was total, like a wall of black that seemed to move in on them, the camp fire fending it off with what was almost bravery. Mary had been silent through dinner. When Dana had returned from the beach, she'd given the lighter to her. Mary had put it in her shirt pocket, and would now and then check to make sure it was still there. Against his better judgment, Ben took Dana's advice. He left her alone.

Barton couldn't help but feel somehow outside the situation. There was so much he didn't know. He looked across the flames to Dana. Her short dark hair had frizzed from the salt water, but she did not seem to care. The light accentuated the planes and

angles of her handsome face and Barton realized
that he was not only taking in that face, but also her
body, watching her small, high breasts rise and fall
with the slow breaths she took.

He remembered Lucy then, and shot a quick
glance to her. The situation was ridiculous, and he
was angered that he should feel self-conscious . . .
even guilty, about being caught looking at a woman,
by a girl who fancied him. Fortunately, Lucy was
intent on the flames, looking deeply into them, lost
in her own thoughts.

Suddenly, a loud crash came from the jungle
somewhere near him. Then another, and still
another, until he realized it was not a crash, but the
beat of a primitive drum. From over his head, something whizzed by and landed in a billow of dust and
dirt, just short of the flames.

Lucy screamed; Ben got quickly to his feet, ready
for a fight. But Trobi and Kara remained seated,
and Ben realized he was being laughed at. This,
then, must be the "entertainment." Angered and
embarrassed, he sat down again, watching the
"show."

It was a man. That much was certain. Black, thin;
very tall.

He stood completely still for about ten seconds,
his arms poised over his head, one leg raised, only
his head moving slowly around to draw them in, not
unlike a Tai Chi pose, allowing them to view him
fully. He was naked, but for a piece of tattered loin
cloth that barely covered his genitals, and the
flames flickered light on and off him, making his
body seem animated despite its eerie stillness. He
was covered evenly in a thin coating of brown dust,
that here and there were streaked with black
rivulets as the sweat from his body broke through it

and turned the dust to a thin, runny mud, trickling down his armpits and chest. But the horror of it was his head . . . his face. It was covered in an almost formless, dark brown mound, as if it had been baked into a helmet around him . . . a mask of mud that only had the suggestion of a ridge of brow, of nose, of mouth.

The drum had not stopped its incessant beating from just beyond the campsite, and between the beats, a foot would pound down onto the ground while the other replaced it in the air, alternating in a purposely awkward, angular dance as if he were a marionette whose strings were in the hands of a puppeteer gone mad. He moved slowly, in a circular motion, stopped before each of them, a harsh, hoarse scream emitting from the closed mud lips, before he danced on, spending particular time before Dana, and then Mary. By the time he had come full circle and stood once more before Barton, all of the dust that covered him had been turned to mud by the sweat he had raised from his dance, and from the heat of the fire and the humid night. He began to spin in place, faster and faster, drops of his perspiration fanning out and spraying anyone within ten feet of him, then stopped abruptly, frozen in the same position he had begun in, once again turning his head to each of them. Then, he screamed, leaped into the air, and was gone again, swallowed up into the jungle.

No one spoke. No one moved. They were completely stunned, not sure what had just taken place, or what it meant. It had happened so quickly, so unexpectedly, that it had been over and done with before their senses had absorbed the event.

The sound of clapping came from behind the bushes, and Thot stepped through them into the clearing, a small, brightly decorated drum at his waist, hung from a shoulder strap. Applauding and smiling, looking into their faces, he tried to entice them to join in the applause. But they all continued to sit there, dumbfounded and motionless, until his clapping slowed to silence, and he stood there not knowing what to do or say.

A strangled little noise came from the circle, and all eyes turned to Dana, whose hand was at her mouth, her eyes filled with tears and her shoulders shaking until she could no longer hold the uproarious laugh that burst forth from her, and continued uncontrollably. At first the group was silent with embarrassment, until unstoppable giggles infected Ben, who began to chortle, while Lucy tried restraining her own sudden fit of laughter. It wasn't long before they had all dissolved into helpless gales of hilarity, the sound of the laughter ringing out in the silent jungle . . . an affront to its dignity; mystery. The idea that something so primal . . . feral, even . . . could be deemed as "entertainment"; that it could be intended to take their minds *off* the primitive, tribal violence that entangled them, seemed not only ridiculous, but hilarious. It came as a welcome relief of mounting tension, and seemed to lend reality to the bizarre.

"I'm sorry, Thot. It was wonderful . . ." Dana managed before what she knew were moronic giggles overtook her, ". . . really . . . I don't know what's got into me . . . Thank you. Where is he? Bring him out so we can thank him . . ." her voice rising at the end of the sentence into further laughter, and she feared she was on a jag. She was wiping her eyes as Thot answered.

"He has gone by now, Doctor. If I know him as I

think I do, your laughter has driven him off, back to his own people. You are fortunate I do not follow suit."

With that, he turned and strode through the center of the camp, almost walking into the fire in his haste to be away from them. Gradually, the others became quiet, guiltily stealing furtive glances at each other that did not hold for more than a second . . . any longer would have set them all off again.

"Touchy, isn't he?" Lucy remarked to Kara as he followed his leader. Dana winced, knowing instantly it was the wrong thing to say.

The Other big man replied, "Yes, Madame. In this case. We went to some trouble to engage a Mud Man to dance tonight."

He too made a hasty exit, and just in time, as Lucy stifled a snicker, looking after him.

Now Trobi was all that remained of the trio, and Dana sat down beside him. "Will you explain, Trobi?"

"Yes," he began, "he was a Mud Man that Thot had paid this afternoon in the village. He . . ."

"But," Dana interrupted, "how did he get here? He didn't ride with any of us."

"He did. We hid him in my jeep, among the baggage. Thot wanted it to be a surprise."

"Oh, it was that alright . . . . and then some. But why?"

"The Mud Man's dance is a Ghost Dance. He pretends to be a conquered soldier who comes back from the Land Of The Dead to haunt those who killed him. Tonight, he was supposed to represent the spirit of your Dr. Pemberton. It was for good fortune, tomorrow, on the Island."

Or to scare the hell out of us, Dana thought, but said:

"Thank you Trobi. I do feel like an awful
fool . . . is the Mud Man still around, do you think?"

"No, ma'am. It is as Thot said. He was probably
returned to his people."

"On foot?"

"Yes, ma'am. He will run most of the way, I
think."

"What can I do to apologize?"

"Thot will be better later on, ma'am. He is, as the
lady said, 'touchy.' But in his absence," Trobi raised
his voice to be heard by the whole camp. "I must ask
the gentleman to please come and discuss guard
duty for tonight."

"Guards?" Lucy asked. "What for?"

"The fire must be maintained to keep animals
from the camp. And . . . but never mind. Gentlemen,
please?"

SIXTEEN

Barton was to take the first shift, then Ben. Later, Trobi would discuss the rest of the night's guarding with Thot and Kara.

So the evening wore on into the night. Trobi excused himself to join Kara and Thot at the shoreline. Three boats were kept sheltered nearby, for travel to Satyr Island, but these boats had to be inspected and repaired, if necessary. Gradually, the rest of the party began to turn in, the lamps inside the tents going out or dimming. Trobi gave Barton a rifle.

"Just in case," he said, and started off to the beach, leaving Barton leaning against a palm tree, the rifle across his lap.

Trobi had not gotten far when he heard rustling in the brush behind him, and a whispered voice call his name. His eyes searched the darkness, till they

301

found Ben Ramsey approaching through the brush.

"What is it, Mr. Ramsey?"

"I have to talk to you, Trobi. It won't take long," Ben answered softly, coming closer. "I have to ask you a question."

The campsite was very quiet and the stillness it-self was unnerving. Barton watched the flames of the firelight, the sound of its crackling the only noise in the night beyond the slow, easy, rhythmic waves landing gently on the nearby shore. Even the forest animals were quiet, but for an occasional hoot or scream.

From the women's tent, the flap moved and he saw Dana come out and wave to him. He waved back, and she sauntered over.

"Would I be interfering with your duties as a guard to sit with you for a bit?"

"I'd welcome the company."

"Good. I was hoping you'd say that."

She sat crosslegged next to him. He was smiling broadly, and was aware that he felt almost like a schoolboy; thrilled and shy, at once.

"We haven't had much of a chance to talk," she said.

"No. I'm glad you came over. Aside from wanting to talk with you, it'll help pass the time out here."

"How long are the shifts?"

"Mine's only an hour, and then Ben relieves me ... but I think they've let me have the easy watch, and a short one, too. Though I think Ben is on for only an hour, too. The others take two hour shifts ... as far as I can figure out. Just as well, really. I wouldn't know what to do with one of these," he raised and lowered the rifle, "if my life depended on it."

It was silly, she knew, but that last statement far from pleased Dana. "Didn't anyone show you how to use it?"

"No. I think they assumed I'd know. Being a man, I mean. It wouldn't bother me, except I know this guard duty isn't just to frighten animals away."

"You're right, of course," she sighed. "What tipped you off?"

"Oh, the way Trobi almost said more, then decided against it. I think he thinks that someone's trying to stop us, or scare us from going over there tomorrow."

Dana saw that she had underestimated him. Without full knowledge, he'd guessed the truth. Someone was out to stop them. The car wreck, the man in her room, Ben's note, the Mayor's warning: tonight, Marc's lighter planted for them to find. And there was still this long night ahead of them.

"And are *you*?" she asked.

"What? Scared? I'd be a liar if I said 'no.' But I can get through the next hour. Hopefully anyone who sees me holding this won't stop to think it's just a prop. Tomorrow isn't here yet."

He smiled again and she averted her face, color coming up her neck to her cheeks as she smiled at her own Victorian reaction. She looked at him again, still smiling, and his hand rested on hers. She did not withdraw.

"You're a fine woman, Dana. Margery thought so too."

"That's good to know. I liked Margery."

"And me?"

Dana did not answer, at a loss for words with him.

"I'm not drunk now, you know," he offered.

"No," she stammered, "it's not that, Barton. Surely you must know . . . here . . . with Marc gone . . . it's like dancing on his grave. We don't know each other at all. Not yet, anyway. It's impossible. And, there's Lucy, too."

"You've noticed that, have you?" he asked worriedly.

"Who could miss it? She's got a big crush on you, and she's always been a little jealous of me, I think. This has only brought it out."

"Has she said anything to you?"

"Oh, she's implied this and that . . . and this afternoon she told me to mind my own business. I'm worried about her."

"I never encouraged it, Dana."

"Oh, Barton, of course I know you didn't. She's frightened, she's upset about Margery, and you, being Margery's father . . ." there were tears in her eyes she hastily wiped away, "I've done more crying today than I have all year."

Barton moved to put an arm around her shoulder, but she reached away to toss a twig into the fire, avoiding his touch.

"I'm sorry," he said.

"It isn't you."

"When this is over . . . back in Manila . . ?"

Her first reaction was anger; didn't he understand? She hadn't gotten over the horror of Marc's death yet . . . and she was already thrown into the very spot where he had been murdered . . .

But then, she thought of Margery . . . and that this man before her had been nearly crushed in the aftermath, and was only reaching out. At last, she answered, "Yes. I'd like that, Barton."

He heaved a relieved sigh.

Mary was awake in her sleeping bag, angered that sleep would not come. Tomorrow would be exhausting anyway, even with a full night's sleep. But sleep evaded her, and her hand closed more tightly around the cigarette lighter she had given her father. His face came back to her behind her closed eyes, and she tried to remind herself, He is calm, now; he is at peace, now. She rolled over onto her other side facing the entrance of the tent. There seemed to be light coming from somewhere. She opened her eyes.

Lucy was standing at the entrance of the tent, peering out a small opening she had made in the flaps. She was watching something, or someone, in the clearing.

Mary saw that Dana was not in her sleeping bag, and knowing Barton had first watch, she put two and two together, and realized what Lucy was peeking at. Oh, Lucy, she thought, pitying the girl. She knew how she felt. She, Mary, felt that way about Ben.

Ben.

He had the next watch, didn't he?

Sudden movement made her look up. Lucy had quickly closed the flap and scurried over to her sleeping bag. Mary could hear footsteps approaching their tent, and by the time Dana entered, it looked as if Lucy were sleeping.

Dana undressed, while Mary and Lucy lay there pretending to sleep. This is insane, Mary thought. She wanted to speak, but had to wait, wanting to convince Lucy she'd been awakened by Dana's entrance, and so had been asleep during Lucy's spying. Fortunately, Dana tripped getting out of her pants, and made enough noise to warrant Mary being awakened by it.

"I'm sorry, Mary. Go back to sleep," Dana whispered.

Mary sat up, rubbing her eyes.

"Is Ben on duty yet?" she asked sleepily.

Three boats had been pulled from the sheltering
jungle, inspected for damage, found acceptable, and
loaded with the few provisions needed for the
journey in the morning.

That much had not been a lie.

But a fourth boat stood on the shore further down
the beach, closer to the water. Three figures were
gathered around it. Even the moon was an accom-
lice, withholding it's light behind dark and heavy
clouds, aiding them with the cover of darkness.

Trobi sat in the sand nearby, watching them. He
knew what they were discussing; knew what he had
gotten himself involved in. He did as he was told.
Out of love for the Faith; dedication to the Secret.
But he did not take relish in bloodshed, and so had
not felt it necessary to become a part of the talk that
now took place.

At length, the small figure who had been the Mud
Man pushed the boat into the water and began
rowing, filled with promises of honor and reward,
assured that soon he too would bear the Sign of the
Ram in his flesh. Almost immediately darkness
closed in on him, and the only evidence that he was
there became the rhythmic slaps of the oars. Trobi
watched, then listened. Such was the power of the
night, to make a man invisible, not to be seen again
until tomorrow, on The Island.

The business done, the meeting over and the
orders given, Trobi walked down to the shore and
joined the two huge creatures there.

"Are you through with me?" he asked of Thot.

"Yes, for all the help you were," Thot replied.

"I was not needed for this!"

"Keep your voice down!" Kara ordered.

Thot shot a look to Kara, then back to Trobi. "We are all edgy. Be calm, both of you," he said. "Tomorrow, all will be safe again and the secret kept. Come," Thot put a massive paw around each of their shoulders and began leading them up the beach, "we may rest for the night. All is done."

"Not all," Kara pulled away and stood apart from them. "There is still one more thing. Tomorrow may still be avoided, if they are turned back."

"As if you wanted tomorrow avoided," Thot smiled at The Other. "You think, Kara, I do not know you have waited for this moment? Hoped for a chance like this?" They stood staring at each other, and Trobi looked from one to the other suspiciously.

"Do it," Thot said finally.

Kara sauntered over to one of the boats as Thot moved Trobi toward the jungle, saying, "You and I will go back to the camp, now, Trobi. I must not be late for guard duty."

He laughed quietly as they walked, and Trobi turned around once, looking over his shoulder to see the shadow of Kara remove a sack from the first boat, and carry it off into the night like an animal with prey.

They had been talking politely for quite some time now; far more politely and more guardedly than they had since they'd first met. There were two reasons: the first, was what had passed between them on the beach that afternoon, before Dana's appearance; the second was, she'd brought a blanket out here with her, when she'd come to talk to him during his guard duty. She wasn't finicky about her clothes, he knew; so, the blanket wasn't to keep her slacks from getting dirty while she sat here on the ground with him.

Ben looked at his watch. Ten more minutes remained before . . . who? Thot, he thought, was to be his relief. As if she'd read his mind, Mary asked, "How much longer?"

"For what?" he asked, practically daring her.

"Should I have the decency to blush, Ben . . ." she answered, accepting the dare, "or say I meant when is your watch over?"

It was very quiet and very hot. His hand came up to her brow and wiped off a sheen of perspiration.

"This is hell for you, I know."

Her lip was trembling, and the embers of the fire cast a dim glow in the rim of tears that lined her eyes. She looked at him, memorizing his face, his lips, making her need felt, giving over to the vulnerability she trusted him to see. He could feel the blood surging through him, deserting his limbs, his mind, working to arouse his own need for her.

She turned quickly at hearing something from the far side of the camp.

"Here comes Thot and Trobi," she said with a smile.

He returned the grin, looking deeply in her eyes, and said, "We're going for that swim. Now."

"Yes," she answered simply.

Thot had almost crossed the clearing, Trobi having gone into his tent without a word. Ben called softly, "You're early. Thank you."

"My pleasure. Is everything quiet?"

"Fine. We were just talking."

"How nice," Thot said to Mary, "Good evening, Miss Pemberton."

"Good evening, Thot."

"Well, I've just come from getting everything in

order for tomorrow. It's all ready to go. Get a good night's sleep, you two."

"Oh," Ben said, handing the rifle to Thot as he stood, "we're going down to take a swim."

"Excellent. A very hot night, tonight."

As they passed through the camp and on into the undergrowth that led to the beach, Thot could see a small light coming from the women's tent.

Dana heard footsteps go past, and knew the guard was changing.

She looked over at Lucy, who slept soundly. Dana was glad that the dim battery operated lamp she'd lit was not disturbing the girl. She hoped tomorrow, to smoothe things over between the two of them.

For now, Dana wrote in her journal, leaning on an arm as she bent over the lined pages of the book, while Lucy opened her eyes and stared at the older woman, hating her.

But on the beach, the hatred that had brought them all together was for the moment set aside.

They had joined hands as they walked and came to a stop just two feet above the water line, looking out to the vast expanse of sea and sky that stretched before them, lit only by the thousand stars in a night whose moon would only peek out on occasion from the lace of clouds that drifted before it. The long dark hairs of his arm brushed gently against the soft blonde down of her own, and she moved her own arm ever so slightly beneath his, feeling it tickle deliciously.

He turned his head to her and looking up, she was about to speak when he placed a finger against his lips. She kissed the tip, then took it gently between her teeth and barely applied pressure, before she took his hand in hers and he moved into her, his back to the surf, standing tall before her. Very slowly he lowered his head as her lips parted once more and they joined in a kiss that grew from tenderness to passion, as his tongue explored her welcoming mouth.

They were both breathing heavily, and even the slight breeze that blew in from the sea did little to cool their minds, their bodies. His palms and finger-tips barely touched the swell of her breasts, her hardened nipples pressing against the center of those palms, begging for the strength in them, the pressure of them, until at last it came, and she pulled her mouth from his to gasp for breath while his hand squeezed and kneaded.

Taking her into his arms and pulling her face to him, he kissed her again, feeling the heat of her breath in his own mouth. Moving his arms in front once more he began loosening the buttons of her blouse, as she moaned just once. When at last the final button was undone, he removed his mouth from hers, stepped back half a step, and taking the two edges of the garment between the fingers of either hand, he peeled back the cloth from her body, so slowly that she shivered, the cotton resisting his gentle tugging, clinging as it did to her moist skin. She was revealed to him in the light of the stars, which caressed her beauty in an aura of gold that gleamed on the slopes and curves of her full breasts, her firm stomach.

"You're so beautiful," he whispered, not touching her, but staring down at her body, as he slid the blouse down her arms, letting it fall to the sand next to the blanket that had been by now forgotten about.

She raised her hands to his face, his cheeks, the

roughness of a day's growth of beard scratching at her palms that he was kissing now. She let them slide down the front of him, opening his shirt buttons, nails digging into the hard flesh of his pectorals, the hair running through her fingers as they continued to travel down, unbuckling, unbuttoning, unzipping, until she looked down at him as he had on her, murmuring, "You're beautiful, too," and grasped him.

They went easily to the sand, kicking free of their clothing until they were naked against each other, awash with sweat and aglow with starlight, their hands, their mouths, learning the other's body, until he entered her, and they rocked and swayed with pleasure in each other, slowly, tasting the salt of their bodies, and the wet succulence of an unending kiss.

Dana put her pen down and turning back the page, she reread what she had just put down on paper. It had taken a while to begin, to gather her thoughts, but now, there was a clarity about her approach to things that she felt she had not hitherto possessed. She read:

"Dear Marc,

"It has been a while since I wrote here. I could say it's because we . . . I've . . . been very busy, preoccupied . . . what have you. And it wouldn't really be a lie. Things have been mad for the past few days, and so much has already changed.

"But I've avoided writing because it's so difficult to face you . . . here . . . knowing now that you will never, ever really read this . . . that I write to a phantom . . . and that . . . accepting that . . . is so hard . . . so hard. There is guilt, and disloyalty in everything I feel . . . so I avoid Barton Croft.

"Until tonight, I had successfully convinced myself that all this was mere flattery . . . how could it be otherwise . . . with you just gone? But it isn't just that. I can't just play nursemaid to everyone . . . and that's not what he wants, thank God.

"Now there's Lucy . . . presenting such a problem . . . underlining everything I suspect and fear within myself by her own ridiculous crush on him . . . as if she's transferring her own fear into a false sense of protection from Margery's father.

"Tomorrow, we face God knows what . . . and this could very well be the last time I write to you . . . now, in this life. But tomorrow we may find out the truth . . . for your peace . . . for Margery . . . for Barton . . . all of us.

"I have loved you like no other."

Lucy lay there still, her eyes opened and intent on Dana as she read. She watched as the Doctor sighed, closed the book and put it into her bag.

When Dana turned to make herself comfortable in the sleeping bag, she happened to glance up, and in that second catch Lucy's eyes on her. They immediately closed, and it had happened so fast, Dana wasn't sure she'd seen it. The girl certainly looked, now, to be asleep. Still, she was sure she had seen Lucy staring at her while she'd been reading . . . even while she'd been writing?

At that moment, a loud, horrid scream, piercing, bloodcurdling and desperate, ripped through the quiet night.

Dana was up on her feet at once, quickly donning a robe. She grabbed a flashlight and was out of the tent by the time the second terror-filled scream came, vibrating from the base of her spine to the back of her neck as she ran through the brush toward the sound.

Behind her she could hear other running feet, male voices, Lucy's voice, all following her as she followed the sound of the horrified voice. Sticks and thorns grabbed at her long robe, tearing at it while she pulled to be free and move on through the jungle.

Up ahead, she could see two figures and drawing closer, she saw Ben holding a hysterical Mary in his arms. A folded blanket had obviously fallen from her arms and lay on the ground. Sand was in her hair and on her blouse. Her hands were clutched into Ben's naked chest, holding on to him as if her legs would not support her.

Ben looked up suddenly like a startled deer caught in the lights of an oncoming automobile, shielding his eyes from the glare of Dana's torch.

"Who is it?" he cried out.

"Dana," she answered, and Mary began to scream again.

Barton came from behind Dana, and walking over to the couple, took Mary by the shoulders and lifted her, with some difficulty, away from Ben.

"Come," Barton said softly, and led her sobbing, back through the jungle to the camp, holding her tightly as they went.

Ben's face had lost all of it's color. The hair on his chest was matted with Mary's tears, and his own sweat.

"What was it?" Dana asked.

"I can't explain it, Dana. But . . ."

"What, Ben? For God's sake!"

"Alright," he said, "give me the torch."

She handed it to him. He took three steps over to

her; turned her a half step with his hands on her shoulders. Then, standing beside her, he said, "Give me your hand."

She did so. He squeezed it hard, and pointed the light ahead of them, just off the side of the path.

"Oh, my God!" Dana whispered.

Within the circle of light was a wooden stake stuck into the earth.

Impaled upon it was a severed human head.

Dana felt herself falling into Ben's arms, and he heard her cry, "Oh, Marc."

Then, she fainted.

PART FOUR

THE SECRET OF SATYR ISLAND

SEVENTEEN

The worst thing, after the first horrid shock, was the responsibility of deciding what was to be done with the head.

In one way it allowed him to feel . . . what would you say . . ."useful?" "Helpful." Barton was calming down Mary with Scotch he had fortunately remembered to bring. Dana was still out cold, which was worrisome, but at least required no attention. Lucy seemed in a stupor, managing to act and react to stimuli about her, particularly from Barton, but rather like an automaton, emotionless, as if she were switched on to automatic. She refused any aid from Ben.

Trobi and Kara had wisely stayed out of it, having retired again to their tents when it was evident there was nothing to be done. So there had been only Thot to contend with, and that confrontation had taken enormous shows of will from both men. It was as this point that they eyed each other with new suspicions, fears, and a kind of twisted respect that told the other, this was someone to be dealt with.

Thot knew the answer to the question long before it was posed. Nevertheless, for the satisfaction of Kara, he asked, "We return then, tomorrow?"

Ben met him eye to eye, replying, "Is that what you want?"

"I am your employee, of course, Mr. Ramsey. I have no personal wish in this matter at all."

Ben knew differently, and felt insulted by this patronization. However, as sorely tempted as he was to say as much, he said instead, "Dr. McKinley would want us to continue on. We will proceed as scheduled."

The two stood for a moment looking at each other.

"I think you are making a mistake," Thot said finally.

"But," Ben added, "since you are my employee and have no personal feelings in this matter, you'll do as you're told, won't you?"

There was a brief pause, then a soft "yes," and Thot walked off into the jungle night, leaving Ben totally alone in the clearing, his shadow looming large from the glow of the fire that had been re-kindled.

He decided it was best to simply take action now, without consulting Dana or Mary about it. Weighing the alternatives was horrible enough for him. In their condition, it was unthinkable to ask either of the women to make a decision such as this.

It was hideous, macabre, to even think of taking the head back to Manila . . . to bury with the body. Still, it did cross his mind that there were stories . . . ghost stories . . . of corpses in search of

their own disembodied parts . . . tortured creatures
. . . vanquished warriors seeking revenge,
wandering the earth without peace . . . spirits at
large in the world to be called up by mystics . . .
Witch Doctors . . . Mud Men . . .

No, this is insane. Mad. Ghoulish. He would subject no one to a further journey with this . . . thing
. . . as added cargo. It was, after all, merely mortal
remains. It felt nothing.

So, finding a spade, a length of burlap from the
floor of one of the land rovers, and a flashlight, he
set out along the narrow path. Nearby, he wrapped
the head of Marc Pemberton in the burlap, and
covered it over in the hole he had dug. Silently, he
said a prayer, and a final farewell to his brave friend,
then walked back to the camp and sat before the fire
until it died, and dawn had broken.

The early morning sun revealed them, all of them,
on the beach, standing before the three boats, ready
to embark.

"Do you know how to row?" Thot asked him.

Is it going to be like this for the rest of this
journey? Mary asked herself. Since she had arisen,
there seemed an undercurrent between Thot and
Ben. Despite what had happened, despite her
nerves, she knew this was not her imagination. It
was as if they were in some secret, private competition with each other suddenly, and it was beginning to make itself known to the others.

"Just on the lake, back in Chicago," Ben was
replying, "but . . ."

"This before us," Thot gestured, "is hardly a
lake."

"Well, it's hardly an ocean either, Thot, and
though I never quite made it to Canada in a row

boat, I did quite alright, so please set your mind at ease.''

I don't know if I'm going to be able to stand this, she thought, looking from Thot's angered face, to Dana, who seemed not to hear. So much was frightening now, not the least of which was this terrible silence from Dana. Before last night, Mary had looked to Dana as an example of control; of determination and rational thinking. To see that even Dana McKinley could be so vulnerable—so outwardly, *nakedly* vulnerable, for all to see—made Mary lose what little faith she had in her own strength.

But I musn't, she told herself. If not for my own sanity, my own well being, then for Dana's. She had been there for me, now I must be there for her. Though she hoped Lucy would come round, she too was in shock, and Mary knew the girl could not be depended upon for too much. So it all seemed to fall now upon Ben; at least, for a while. And Thot. How terrible and guilty he must feel, how terrible for them all. Trobi had seemed truly upset; in fact, still appeared deeply troubled. Kara was, to her mind, the only one among them that looked to be un-affected. But who knew what he would be thinking?

They were getting into the boats now, and as she took her place behind Ben, she knew positively that he had done the right thing. They must go. They must cross the water to Satyr Island. They must.

So the boats pushed off the beach of Savong-khai and slid into the surf, the salty spray hitting them, making them damp, and for a time, cool.

Mary sat between Trobi and Ben, Dana between Barton and Kara, while Lucy rode alone with Thot, in the last boat. She did not row, but she did not need to; Thot had made the journey before, and

alone, and though the others had the advantage of
speed, his own strength moved them along at a
steady, unbroken pace. Up ahead, Lucy could see
the still figure of Dana, staring toward the far shore.

She was not glad, despite her envy. If anything,
the mental anguish of Dana McKinley demanded
yet more attention from all, including Barton. Lucy
had accepted that she had lost him now, but her
attitude toward Dana's situation bordered upon
gloating. She had only to keep herself from
revealing how she felt. Strangely, Lucy had surprised herself, at her own reaction to last nights
horrific find. After the initial shock, it had been easy
to realize that Marcus Pemberton had been dead for
weeks. Mary and Dana, in fact all of them, responded as if the killing had taken place last night.
How had they thought Marc had met his death? In
her mind, Lucy had seen the massacre, played it
back over and over again, enlarging upon it,
amplifying it each time she brought it up, until the
picture before her was so violent, so awash with
gore, that the discovery of the head seemed nearly
mundane, in spite of it being Marcus Pemberton's.
What she had envisioned for Margery Croft now
took place in the dark of her heart and mind, having
passed beyond imagination into a place where
things occured, but were only heard, far off, crying
out in pain and frustration.

While Lucy pondered the machinations of her own
brain, the breeze, for there was now a breeze, and the
spray, began to revive Dana McKinley. The sound
of the oars in the water, the cry of the birds from the
island, and there, the island ahead, growing larger
by degree, seemed to come at her from afar, as if out
of a black, toxic cloud that was dispersed by the
sharp points of their boats, into the bright light of

the new day.

It came to her then as strange that her mind, so confused only a moment ago, should now begin to clear, and her senses once again sharpen. She looked around her as if awakened into an unfamiliar, but not foreign place, and at first, thought this new and welcome clarity came from the distance that had been put between her, and Savong-khai; the further she travelled from that place of death, the more the madness pealed away. But the heavy breeze had given way to what could now be termed a mild wind, and with the increased rocking of the boat, Dana knew that it was not the *leaving* that was clearing her brain, but the *approaching*; that she was growing stronger with each stroke of the oars upon the water and there, ahead, was the sharp, gleaming rock of the reef, that dared them penetrate and finally invade the smooth black sand beyond it. She recalled now why this was important, and looked to the Island as an adversary at long last met, knowing her life was not complete until this scene in her destiny was played out to the finish, whatever it may be.

The clear blue sky surrounded them and met the water, the surface of which began to be dotted with white, the waves coming more frequently as they drew closer to the waiting reef. Trobi and Kara manuevered their small crafts through and around the dreadful sharp rocks that jutted out of the water, or more treacherously hid beneath, to gnaw from below. Thot, behind them, admired the expertise they demonstrated and he was proud, for they had learned what they knew from him.

Mary held on to the edges of the hollowed-out tree as it rode the waves, both hands fiercely gripping the wood, holding herself upright while they pitched

and rocked, the sea water and wind flattening her
hair against her head, her little straw hat now
bobbing in a pool of water that sloshed to and fro
inside the boat, at her feet. Looking up, a mass of
gulls screamed about them, either in welcome or
warning. The sky, as if in imitation of the churning
brine was also dotted now with white, until the
clouds and the gulls merged in movement and the
boats were caught up in one last wave that carried
them up and over, and they had landed with a certain thud upon the gleaming jet black sand of Satyr
Island.

Dana had jumped from the boat and in helping to
pull it further ashore, saw Barton's face, and for the
first time that day, concerned herself with more
than her own thoughts or the death of Marcus Pemberton. Though Barton had the aid of Kara in
getting the canoe onto the sand, his face was
flushed, and his breath came heavily. By the time
she had gotten close enough to speak quietly to him,
the work was done, and he was seated on the edge
of the boat, composing himself.

"Are you alright?"

He looked up at her. "I should be asking you that.
Yeah, I'm alright, I think. My heart gives me a
fright now and again."

Barton smiled, relieved that she seemed somewhat recovered. He had not spoken to her this day,
wanting to leave her alone with her grief. But now,
he was glad to see that she had put it aside . . . laid
it to rest, as it were, and decided to go on with the
business of her life, and this adventure.

They had been walking for some ten minutes when
they came at last upon a clearing that was nearly
pastoral. The gigantic trees towered overhead and
around, like pillars in a massive cathedral, fingers of

gleaming sun groping through the leaves onto the dewey emerald ground. Fruit grew for the picking, and pools of fresh water sparkled, inviting them to drink and be cooled.

Here, they made camp.

It was almost ten, according to Barton's wristwatch.

They had finished setting up the camp, and he had made up his mind to spend some time with Dana this morning, if she'd have him. But at that moment, he saw her throw back the tent flaps and come out into the clearing across from him. He called to her and had started toward her before her gesture was able to halt him, arriving in time for Lucy to greet him as she too emerged from the tent. Mary was talking from inside, saying,

"But we only just got here, Dana. Why don't you both try and get some rest. Take a swim or something. You're pushing yourself too hard." By the end of the sentence, Mary had appeared at the tent entrance, looking out to her two companions. "Oh, Barton," she said, "I'm just trying to convince these two that we've got a little time. Not everything has to be done right away."

Barton studied her as she spoke. Mary had regained her composure quickly, under the circumstances. She looked thinner, even overnight, and there were deeper rings beneath her eyes now. But all in all, he thought she was holding up quite well. He had the feeling that there was, to her resiliency, an element of "being brave for the others" . . . but if it helped her to deal with the horror, then, he thought, more power to her.

Dana answered her rather curtly with, "Mary, I appreciate your concern, but I personally do not wish to stay here in this place any longer than is absolutely necessary ... and, I am also anxious to see if I can locate whatever it was Marcus wanted. The quicker I can do that, the quicker we can all get out of here." She turned to Lucy, asking, "Are you ready?"

Lucy looked at her, then back to Mary. Before the latter could say anything, Lucy turned her head to Barton. Their eyes held for just a moment and he knew she wanted him to say something ... show some concern, for *her*, for Lucy. But he remained silent.

"Yes," she said to Dana.

Mary and Barton were left at the tent entrance to watch the two women go off through the trees, the rustle of the branches and leaves as they passed through them growing dimmer as they went, until at last there was silence, but for the far off cries of the distant gulls.

Mary stared then at Barton's face. It was lined and flushed, and concern for Dana had hardened his already sharp features further.

It's taking its toll, she thought. On all of us ... even Thot and his men were looking uneasy and drawn. What must this all be like for him ... for Barton? In a way, the worst (please God, let this have been the worst) had happened for her, and for Dana. But for Barton, coming all this way on the slimmest of chances would be bad enough ... adding to that the horrors of last night must be filling his brain with all sorts of fears for the fate of his daughter.

He looked back at her then and gave her a reassuring smile that filled her with admiration for him. Mary took a step forward, wrapped her arms around him, and hugged him hard. Barton continued to smile, stroking her hair, as he sighed with resignation, telling himself that soon this would be over for them all.

The day wore on, hot bright, and exhausting. The absence of Dana and Lucy laid on an extra layer of anxiety to the already frail nerves of everyone left behind in the camp. While they were all in sight of each other, there was at least the certainty that they were still safe. But with two gone, the minds of those remaining became occupied with the thoughts of when those two would return; obsessed with how long they had been gone, and testy and impatient for their return.

It was no easier on Dana and Lucy, since conversely, being separated from the camp made them both secretly worry what they'd find upon their return, much less what could befall the two of them here, alone.

Mary had argued that at least one of the men should accompany them, that two women alone in a jungle couldn't possibly be safe. However, Dana had insisted. She felt that they would certainly be safe enough, considering the island was so very small. But the two actual motives for her wishing to be left alone she left unsaid. The presence of the others, on this, the final "dig" of her association with Marc Pemberton, had for her some symbolic, nearly sacred meaning. If she'd had her way, she would now be totally alone, even without Lucy. That, she knew, was impossible. It would appear strange and ridiculous for her to take off alone. Hence, Lucy. Lucy was, after all, the most likely companion for her.

The second motive was that bringing anyone else along seemed a dreadful waste of time; of theirs and hers. She would have felt obligated to make some "show" of exploring, discovering, for the benefit of the laymen in the group.

But with only Lucy, no pretense need be made, and Dana was convinced that there would be nothing to be found on this island.

They had been wrong. The heat was coming at them from all sides; even, it seemed, from the ground, and the foilage was thicker, greener, lusher, snapping into their faces as they walked . . . and they had been wrong. Dana wiped sweat from her brow and sighed. This wasn't the island they needed. This was not, she was sure now, where any secrets to evolution were being kept. She had wanted to be right, for Marc's sake—for her own sake. But they'd been mistaken. Another island in New Guinea, perhaps? Or, maybe one they'd overlooked, back . . . a hundred years ago . . . in the Philippines?

Dana tried to think rationally. She wanted to be sure that this decision forming in her brain was not made or caused by her eagerness to be gone from this place. But as she and Lucy continued to walk, they saw nothing to excite them, nothing to question, beyond normal human curiosity at seeing something new and unknown . . . but not pertinent to their search.

Still something gnawed at her. If this was *not* the place that she and Marc had thought; if there were no secrets to be found here, no illumination to their research—then why had Marcus been stopped from reaching it? And what had become of Margery Croft?

Lucy knew . . . had known for some twenty minutes now, that this was an exercise in "going through the motions." It was just evident, without being said; something almost acknowledged, between the two of them. They had worked side by side for some time. They knew each other well. In one way, she couldn't blame Dana. Lucy wanted to get out of here just as much . . . perhaps more than Dana. But there was Margery . . . there was Barton. Margery had disappeared and there was not a clue to what had become of her. This island deserved a thorough search, if only to determine that Margery was not here. And if she wasn't, then Barton would be distraught . . . and he would need help . . . perhaps from another woman . . . a younger woman . . . about Margery's age . . .

Barton closed his eyes against the glare and laid his head back onto the slope of sand he had piled up beneath his head. His hand rested on his stomach, his skin hot beneath his touch, even though the sun was beginning to make its descent. The day was becoming gradually cooler as evening approached. There was little for him to do but wait until Dana's return—and for the search for Margery to begin. But they would need daylight for that—and it was fast fading.

Then, he had fallen asleep. A dangerous thing, in this sunlight. But from the look of the sky, and his own skin, it had not been for too long, and he had kept his hat on, and a shirt. He wondered vaguely what would be going on back at the camp. Had Dana and Lucy come in, and had they found anything?

It had not seemed right to let them go off on their own, but he would hardly have been much protection. But, if they had found something, it would have been satisfying to be there at the moment of discovery. Not that he cared much about their professional interests in anthropology, but perhaps they might find evidence of Margery. It seemed impossible that she should just disappear into thin air. Even if the worst had happened, there must be some trace, some hint of where . . . and how.

He wanted a drink, and knew he must be careful; must beware of himself, and his own self-destructive tendencies. Drinking only meant a need to escape from the fear he felt for himself, or the others, and for his own little girl. Fear that must not be escaped, but faced; reckoned with.

Barton's stomach growled angrily and he smiled, happy that his body had literally voiced another, healthier need. It would be time for dinner soon. He picked up the few belongings he had come with and stood facing the jungle. The walk back to the camp was just enough to make him weary, and the sun had tired him already. He wished briefly that he were able to just snap his fingers and be there back at the camp, without the drudgery of picking vines and branches out of his face while raising and lowering his legs to avoid growth that choked the meager pathway. But, resolutely, he started up the dunes toward the jungle, the muscles in his calves moving, working, trudging through the black sand. He'd walked only a few steps, when he stopped.

In that sand, coming toward him, were foot prints. Huge foot prints.

They came from the jungle, and stopped just a yard or so from where he stood now. When he had arrived at the beach, the sand before him had been smooth, undisturbed, clear down to the water's edge. He could see his own foot prints now, just to the left. But these others were enormous; large spaces between each gargantuan foot, and the indentations were deep. Very deep.

He looked off to his right, and there were another set leading away, into a different part of the jungle further down the beach. He followed them, not sure of what he would find . . . or what he would do when he found . . . it.

These prints were too big to even have been made by Thot, or the other two men, much less Ben. These prints were made by something that dwarfed even the giant guide.

Barton's eyes did not leave the ground as he followed the prints up the beach, coming closer to the jungle. Almost hypnotized, he parted the first of the many bushes that grew gradually wilder, thickening into another and another, giving way to the trunk and bark of the trees that were the forest. But though there was still much sand between the foliage, the prints had stopped. Vanished.

Turning, he looked back down the beach. There were his own prints alongside the thing he followed, and here he stood, amidst the bushes, and between two huge trees . . . the first trees . . . the beginning of the jungle.

He looked up. Above him, the pink and purple of night made the dark green of the upper branches seem black. Here and there, stars began to wink between the leaves of a roof made of lace. All was still. All was silent. But there was no other answer.

Something . . . something *big* . . . had come from the jungle, down the beach, and stood not six feet from his head as he'd slept. Since he had not been harmed, or even disturbed, whatever it was had seemingly done nothing more than look at him. Watch him. Study him? Then, it had retreated back into the jungle. Since the prints did not continue in the sand further into the forest, there was no place else it could have gone, but up, into the towering network of branches that spread over the island like a canopy. Or a net.

"We'd better get back," she whispered, lifting her body away from his, her nipples just barely touching the curly black hairs of his chest.

Barton had asked them to join him on the beach, but they had declined, wanting to find someplace ... this place ... to be alone. Waiting until after Barton had departed, they struck off on their own in a different direction.

The sky had grown darker since the last time he had looked up. More stars were visible, though the sun had not quite set as yet, and the horizon had burst into a magnificent array of color, texture and shadow, as the clouds made their final appearance of the day, lit from below with pink and amber.

"Look at that," he said softly, and she turned her face to the sea, rolling on to her side.

"My God. It's gorgeous."

"I've only seen one other sunset in my life to compare to it."

"Where?"

"On a boat, coming from Nantucket returning to Martha's Vineyard. I was a kid, on vacation with my folks. The sky had every color in it ... even green. I knew as I was watching it that I'd never forget it. And I'll never forget this, either."

He remained looking out to sea, but his hand found hers and gently held it.

"Nor I," she answered, stole a brief glance at him, smiled, and turned to the sunset once again. She was glad that he was such a tender, considerate lover, rough only when the passion between them demanded it. She was unconsciously running the finger tips of her left hand up and down her own torso, as if to keep herself sensitive to touch . . . his touch.

For Ben, it was only a matter, now, of facing the fact, fight it though he might, that he was in love with this woman. Her beauty, her bravery, were a constant source of sexual excitement to him, and though he felt fiercely protective of her, yet her good brain, her intelligence, lessened greatly his fears and worries for her well being; he was happy to love a woman who could take care of herself. He felt it made his "job" as a "male" easier, and he relaxed into this, confident for a time, in their existence together as beautiful creatures; two naked animals beneath the sky, with no roles to be played. Just being. Alive.

Ben's body had responded to his thoughts, and he felt her stroke him, then roll on top of him once more.

"Again," she murmured, her face coming down to his as their mouths met and opened to each other.

After they'd loved, she ran her tongue along his neck, tasting the salty mixture of sea and sweat, then nestled in his arms. He laughed.

"What's funny?"

"I'm hungry too."

She licked him again. "Good. Is Thot cooking again tonight."

"I think so. I'd rather eat you."

"Fresh," she snickered, "you're dirty and fresh."

"And hungry."

They dressed in the quickly fading light of the day and arrived at the camp before darkness had completely come.

Dana was laying down in her tent, considering her decision made that afternoon. Though her eyes were closed, her brain refused to rest, and she was eager only to be gone from Satyr Island. Yet, there was still the search for Margery to be made—and that would have to be tomorrow. One more day in this awful place, she thought.

Lucy sat near the fire, watching absently as the evening meal was being prepared, occasionally glancing up to look over at Barton.

He was waiting outside the tent. He had not dared mention what he'd seen. It might alarm Dana and Lucy, and his instincts told him the other men were no longer entirely trustworthy. Ben was the only possible ally for him, and even Ben might think him a silly old fool. But only until he could show Ben those foot prints.

Thot had announced dinner, and the smell of frying filled the air; not a pleasant smell, but they were all hungry, and it was welcome.

There was time only for Barton to say to Ben, "I must speak to you alone, after we eat. I've found something."

EIGHTEEN

They had not thought that another ceremony would be taking place quite so soon, but they were nevertheless excited to be of service once again. There were only two boats this time. Though nine participants were required to worship and perform the sacrifice, four of those were already on the Island. These latest arrivals rode three in one boat, but only a pair in the second, filled as it was with the necessary tools to carry out the night's work.

The sun had long disappeared beneath the water, but tonight the moon shone brightly above them. Their powerful arms worked with rhythmic certainty the oars that slashed through the floating field of glitter, carrying them ever closer to the blackness of the Island. But as they grew nearer, a small dot of light, deep, deep within the trees, became visible, and they knew where they must go once they reached the beach.

The dot of light had cooked a meal, and now illuminated the camp in a reassuring glow. Ben smoked a cigarette, one arm around Mary's shoulder. Thot was seated nearest the fire, and Barton suddenly had an image of a huge sea lion whose eyes were intent upon Dana.

"No," she was saying to him, "I . . . we . . . found nothing of any real interest. But perhaps later on . . . we'll discuss it again after I've looked around a bit more."

Lucy was incredulous at this. She was sure Dana had decided to return to Manila. Why was she not saying as much?

With a rush of sensation, Lucy felt that growing feeling of resentment well up inside her again; a feeling that was becoming so familiar. She had had enough of these exhausting emotions, the blinding headaches, and they had nearly overcome her when out in the brush with her superior. She'd been thankful, when they'd returned to camp, that Ben and Mary were absent; even glad, in one way, that Barton had not been about. This latter relief in itself came as another kind of surprise. She previously had not thought it possible to be happy not to be near him. But she knew now that even devotion such as hers needed a rest. Upon their return, Dana had immediately lain down, and the three hired men were nowhere in sight. Lucy was almost alone in the camp and she decided to use the unexpected luxury of this privacy by simply sitting and thinking, quietly and undisturbed. But after a time, thoughts of Barton crowded her tired brain again, and she began to wonder where he was; what he was doing. She'd then decided to take a walk, and try to get him off her mind. But she'd returned even more nervous, just before the others arrived back.

She started suddenly, afraid the expression on her face betrayed her treasonous thoughts to her boss, and looked quickly over to Dana, who had indeed shot her a look of wonder, or perhaps distrust; Lucy was finding it difficult to interpret the input of the others around her. This, she knew, and so wisely remained silent, lest she reveal too much of herself.

"Well then, Dr. McKinley," Thot answered Dana, "I will await further instructions. Meanwhile, I hope you all found the meal satisfying?"

They all nodded or mumbled some lie, for the food had been greasy and, once again, tasteless. But they were full and grateful to some degree, for that much.

"If you will excuse me," he said, rising from the ground to his full height, "there are things to do. Kara, please come with me."

Kara rose and Trobi began to speak, but his two gigantic companions walked past him and out into the trees, disappearing into the night and the jungle. The snub did not go unnoticed by the rest of the group. There followed an embarrassed silence.

"Where are they going?" Mary asked at last.

"They know this jungle, they . . . I don't know," Trobi replied, but Dana thought she saw fear momentarily flash across the dark, handsome face.

"Barton," Ben said to the older man, "why don't you and I go and talk over that business?"

Barton smiled at him while Mary inquired, "What business is that?"

"Aren't you the curious little thing this evening?" Ben replied, mimicking, 'Where are they going?' 'What business?'. She laughed and hung her head in mock shame, deciding to joke, rather than take issue with the "little thing" remark she realized had made her quite suddenly angry.

"Sorry," she said, "I'm just especially inquisitive.

I guess it's none of my business."

Ben looked at her, guilty that she seemed, despite the cover-up, displeased with his teasing. He had patronized her, he knew. Since she was paying for this trip, it certainly was her business . . . at least, to ask. He was about to apologize, when Barton put in,

"No, no, Mary. It's quite alright. I wanted to ask Ben where I might be able to purchase some good, old pieces once we returned to Manila. Thought I might pass them on to my old shop back in Boston . . . and deduct this trip for taxes in the bargain."

Dana looked surprised and said, "I thought you'd retired?"

"Well, I have, officially. But I've still got a bit of the bug left. Also, Ben thought there might be an article in it . . . Chamber of Commerce sort of thing."

"Ready?" Ben said to him.

Barton was about to reply, but then his eyes linked with Dana's and something in her look told him they must speak. She did not look pleased and it worried him. He too had wanted an opportunity to say a few things to her, but the moment to be alone together had not arisen, since he had stood guard. Now, he decided, he must make that moment, despite anyone else knowing.

"I'll meet you down at the beach, just through there, Ben," and he pointed to a section of the undergrowth, "if that's alright?"

"Fine. Shall we say ten minutes?"

Barton nodded, "I'll be back in a bit."

"Me, too," Ben said to Mary, and struck off into the trees.

Lucy watched Dana and Barton cross the camp

and enter the women's tent, and was about to follow, when she felt a hand on her arm. She turned, and Mary said, "Let's talk."

Dana bent and lit the kerosene lamp that stood on the floor beside her sleeping bag. Straightening up, she turned her face to Barton, the lamp creating sharp, brilliant contrast of light and shade upon her strong features. He smiled at her.

"You seemed upset."

"Yes. I was."

"What for?"

"Well," she took a deep breath, let it out slowly, and continued, "since you ask, I suppose it's none of my business either, and I realize what I'm about to say is extremely judgmental on my part, being as it is . . ."

"Dana, please get to the point?"

"Why? So you can keep your tax deductible date?"

She turned her back on him, folding her arms in front of her in a gesture that was uncharacteristically petulant. He paused, then said, "So, that's it."

She nodded and he knew she was weeping. Barton took a step toward her, moving in close behind her and put his hands on her upper arms. She tried to shrug them off, but he tightened his hold. "Listen to me," he said, but she shook her head and struggled for release. Barton turned her around, and she averted her tearstained face. "Dana, listen, I know what that must have sounded like. I know. But I had to think of something quickly. I have to talk to Ben . . ."

"About antiques!"

"No! About . . ." he realized he was shouting and brought his voice down again, "about something

I . . . something I wanted Ben to see.''

Dana looked up. "What?"

With the light on her face, the tears glistening in her eyes, on her cheeks, she looked very beautiful to him, though he hated seeing her unhappy.

"I'll let you know later . . . soon."

"No. Tell me now."

"Dana, please. It could be nothing, and if it is you'll have concerned yourself for no reason at all."

"But . . ."

"Please, trust me?"

"Barton, it's not that I don't trust you. It's that I know more about this situation than anyone else here. You may not be aware of the effects of what you may be doing, not telling me."

"If I thought for a moment I was putting any of us in jeopardy, I'd tell you in a minute. I promise you, tonight . . ."

"Alright, alright," she nodded repeatedly, and it appeared that she was relieved, resigned. She had done her duty. She had protested and warned. If he refused to comply, it was out of her hands.

"What's the matter?"

"Oh, Barton . . . I'm so . . . just so tired."

"I know."

"No, you don't . . . Oh, I know you mean well enough . . . but you see, we . . . Marc and I . . . we were wrong. I'd wanted this to be the place . . . his death and Margery's disappearance would at least have meant something; if today, I'd found even a shred of evidence that bore out what we'd researched. But there was nothing . . . it's all been for nothing." Her voice trailed off in a weary whisper.

"Not for nothing," he offered. "And we're soon gone. Soon, it's over."

"And then?"

He looked deeply into her eyes. For a moment there was no sound but for their own breathing. He wiped the trace of a tear from beneath her eye. She gave him a quick smile that he returned, then bent his head and kissed her tenderly. Dana's lips parted and she pressed against him, giving herself over to the kiss.

Mary watched Lucy saunter off, having said her piece.

When they had begun to talk, Trobi had excused himself and began to clear away the utensils of their meal. He had been publicly embarrased already, and decided it would be wiser to vacate the area before he was asked to leave.

It had not been a pleasant conversation. Mary did not, at the outset, know what she had planned to say. But her motive for the impromptu talk had really been to keep Lucy from barging in on Dana and Barton. She knew they needed time together, and she'd seen the chance to give them that time. But in doing so, it necessitated a conversation with Lucy. Mary had heretofore tried to avoid any confrontations with the girl. It seemed clear that Lucy was disturbed, really disturbed, and though she liked her, under the circumstances dealing with her was more than she'd felt up to. As it turned out, her initial instincts had been correct. Mary had been told off in no uncertain terms, when all she'd done was offer her assistance, if it were needed. Lucy knew now that her mental state was obvious—even discussed among the others.

Were they questioning her sanity? Her dependability?

"What do you propose to do about it?" she had

challenged.

"Lucy," Mary reached out a calming hand that was pushed away, "I only mean you seem agitated, overwrought. If you want to talk, I'm here."

"I'll just bet you are!" she yelled, and walked away.

Just as Lucy had reached the women's tent, Mary saw Barton emerge. He stopped abruptly at seeing Lucy, and they exchanged words quickly; heatedly, it seemed. Then, Barton marched off hurriedly in the direction he pointed Ben in earlier. Lucy entered the tent, and Mary leaned on an arm, staring after the girl. "Maybe if I slip her a valium later, she'll calm down. We're all going crazy. Jesus, what a day," she thought.

Ben had removed his shoes and stood now at the water line, allowing the surf to wash over his bare feet as he looked out to the sea. It was a beautiful . . . no, a glorious night, and a welcome change from the previous one in which huge black clouds had moved across a darkened moon. Now however, the moon was full and large, and every star in the sky seemed to be visible. Though it was hardly a new idea, Ben was struck yet again with wonder, knowing that this very same moon shone over Manila, and over Chicago. Perhaps not as brightly, and at another time, but the same thing, the same object. The thought seemed to calm him, to give him some link with home. It was reassuring. Despite how remote and desolate a place this was, it was nevertheless one of a piece with the world, and keeping this in mind aided in his striving to fight off the feelings of displacement that seemed to be growing inside him.

At about the time he realized he was becoming

impatient for Barton to show up, he heard the quiet,
rapid rush of feet in the sand behind him. Turning,
he grinned to see Barton hurrying down the dunes in
an awkward attempt at running. But by the time he
had reached Ben and was close enough for his face to
be seen by the light of the moon, Ben could see the
older man was upset. He fairly fell into Ben's arms,
and was breathing heavily from the short run.

"Easy, Barton, easy!"

"Where are they?" he said, running a little down
the beach and back, searching.

"What?"

"The footprints!"

"What do you mean?"

"That's what I needed to speak with you about! I
didn't want to alarm anyone else, especially Dana,
and . . ."

Barton, calm down, for God's sake!"

Barton had been making continuous circles, but
he suddenly stopped short. Ben was right and he
knew it. He did have to calm down. It did him no
good whatever to become so upset as to be unable to
communicate. Barton took three slow, deep breaths
and nodded to signify he was alright again.

"Late this afternoon," he began, "I came down
here for a swim and some sun. I was laying down,
facing the water . . . anyway, I suppose I must have
dozed off. I didn't know for how long, but it couldn't
have been more than a few minutes; I wasn't badly
burnt or anything when I woke up, anyhow. But
when I started back up the dunes to return to the
camp, there were footprints, Ben. Huge footprints.
Not human. Footprints that hadn't been there
before, when I'd gone down to the beach."

"Show me where they were."

The two men walked a few yards from the water's

edge to approximately the spot where Barton had lain that afternoon. From that point on up and into the jungle, the sand displayed prints, but certainly human; indeed, small and human. The remainder of the ground was smooth, but for the prints made by Ben, and later Barton himself.

"But they were here! I know they were, Ben."

"It's alright. They ARE here," Ben gestured to the third set.

"No! Not them! These were huge, inhuman and . . . Wait! There are others! Over here!" he whirled and scurried madly across the sand to the retreating footprints he'd followed that afternoon. They too were gone, but he continued along, gesturing for Ben to follow him, until they reached the spot where the prints had vanished, explaining as he went.

"It's not my imagination. Whatever it was came out, stood and watched me, then headed back here and climbed."

"I know. It's alright," Ben reassured him. He did not doubt that Barton had seen these prints. It was the part about them not being human that worried him. The old man could perhaps have gotten a bit more sun than he was used to, even in just a few minutes; especially in this kind of sun.

But Barton read the uncertainty on Ben's face. "No, it's not alright Ben. These little prints . . . these human prints . . . they were made to cover up . . . or made during the wiping out of the other tracks."

"But what *was* it, Barton? And why would it just come out and look at you?"

"Not all animals need to attack. I wasn't harming it. It probably just wanted a sniff. Besides, that's not what worries me. Someone obviously wanted those tracks hidden. But who? And why?"

Ben immediately thought of Trobi, and of the lunch in the village. Barton was getting more upset just from speculation. The frustration alone had already brought color up to his face and Ben could almost see the man's blood pressure rising.

"Barton, listen. Remember the village . . . we got warned off this island by the Mayor?"

"Of course."

"Did you notice anyone's reaction?"

"Who in particular?"

"Trobi."

"Trobi? No. Why?"

"Well, when Thot translated what the Mayor told us, I happened to look over at Trobi. He seemed genuinely surprised; really shocked. So, later, I asked him if he spoke the dialect of that tribe. He said he couldn't speak it fluently, but enough to understand it."

"You mean he heard the warning before it was translated?"

"I mean there was no warning at all."

Barton stared at him, not sure at first of what it meant. Ben continued, "I mean, Barton, that the Mayor probably wished us good luck and a safe trip . . . something like that."

"Thot lied."

"Or Trobi . . . but I'd say Thot, myself."

"And the rest . . . I mean finding the head and all . . ."

"I'm afraid to even think what that means. Obviously something to frighten us off. Also, there was an accident back in Manila, the day of Pemberton's funeral. We all could have been killed. It's all being done to stop us; get rid of us."

"But Ben, if he, or they, had the head, then he

must have been a part of the massacre."

"Or knew about it anyway," Ben said, nodding.

"It's fantastic. I mean, the matter of luck or chance involved, lying to us in front of witnesses. He took quite a risk."

"Not really. He either assumed or knew Kara and Trobi didn't speak the local dialect, or was sure of their silence, their cooperation. Certainly none of us would have known. The only thing that tipped me off was the reaction to the unexpected; something Thot couldn't have predicted."

"Then you think one of them wiped out these prints?"

"Who else?"

Barton looked down at the black sand beneath their feet. The moon and stars reflected their gentle light in the tiny grains, and he was briefly reminded of his childhood, and of what he used to call 'fool's gold.' Strange that he should think of that now. He stared at one of the prints before him.

"I know they are the most likely, Ben," he observed, "but look there."

Ben followed Barton's gaze to the ground where one of several perfect prints of a bare foot was stamped upon the sand. He saw immediately what Barton was getting at. The prints, though large enough to be made by a male, were far too small to match the feet of either Trobi, Kara, or Thot.

"So who?" Ben asked.

They stared at each other, their minds racing. The print was too small to be either of their own, and they had eliminated the possibility of the three other men.

"Barton . . ."

"No. No, it couldn't be . . . could it?"

"Which one?"

Neither wanted to name her, but there seemed no other logical explanation. Finally Ben said quietly, "Jealousy?"

Barton sighed deeply and leaned against a tree. "It's hardly a secret, is it? How she feels about me?"

"You mean she'd follow you down here?"

Barton nodded, "I wouldn't put it past her."

"But when, Bart? She went out to explore with Dana."

"I was here, late, and they were back by the time I returned to the camp."

"But why?"

But before Barton could venture a response, Ben looked suddenly startled, moving from one foot to another.

At first Barton had thought Ben had been struck, but when he saw him running, he knew he was alright and he followed. When he'd caught up to him, sweating and breathless, Ben gestured to the sand. "Look!"

Coming from the sea were two sets of footprints spaced evenly apart from each other, and leading off into the nearby jungle. Examining the underbrush close by, they saw that much of the smaller plant life and shrubbery had been crushed, and many of the tree branches broken and snapped off at chest level and above. They kept walking and there, ahead of them, they saw the cause.

Two long boats sat in hiding amidst the cover of the jungle night. The oars sat propped up against the sides within the boats. Barton bent and touched one.

"Still wet."

"Barton . . ." Ben said softly, but did not go in. Suddenly, he was very scared.

"These aren't the boats we came in . . . are they?" Barton asked.

"No! And they're all alone back there!"

"Come on!"

Together, they set off toward the camp, more frightened than they had ever been before.

NINETEEN

The situation was growing impossible, and an end to it was imperative. When Lucy had entered the tent, she'd glared at Dana, who still had tears in her eyes. An explanation was more than she felt capable of, nor did she feel it owed. She left Lucy alone, and walked to the edge of the camp, breathing deeply. Enough, after all, was enough, she thought and after composing herself, Dana returned to the tent and asked if Lucy would join her and Mary outside. There had been no reply, but once Dana had reached the center of the camp, Lucy was crossing towards her.

"I think it's time I told you something," Dana said.

Now, Mary, Lucy and Trobi sat on the ground near the fire which flared brightly again as Dana threw a stick into its center. They waited for her to go on, but she had paused for effect, to Mary's admiration and Lucy's annoyance. Trobi was merely politely silent, being concerned as he was that Thot and Kara may be displeased with him. They had not returned as yet, and the longer they were absent the more ill at ease he became.

"Well?" Lucy said impatiently.

"If it's alright with you, Mary . . . I've decided we may just as well head back to Manila. Tomorrow."

This was not a surprise to Mary; she knew it was coming. In a way it was almost a blessing. It seemed apparent that their nerves could not stand too much more. The only real disappointment was not finding out the truth about her father's death. But this, she knew, would also be a difficult pill for Dana to swallow.

"Whatever you think best, Dana," she replied, "but I don't have to tell you that it's giving in, to whatever wants us gone from here."

"No, you don't have to tell me, Mary. I thank you for your trust in me up to now, and I hope I can maintain that trust. Of course, I'll have to discuss this further with Barton. It does mean abandoning hope for Margery . . . but honestly, I don't think there is any. She's gone," there were tears in her eyes again, "I'm convinced of it now. I'm afraid what will happen to any of you now, because of me."

"Oh, really!" Lucy was on her feet, legs spread, hands on hips. "You don't want Barton's happiness, do you? You don't want anyone to steal him away! Margery, or . . ."

"Lucy, you are losing your mind."

Mary winced, the remark coming so soon after her own words with the girl. Dana had said it very calmly, very quietly, and Lucy was stopped abruptly in mid-sentence, as if she had been slapped.

But Trobi was relieved. These people were going home; going away. The warnings had worked, and the feeling of impending violence . . . of doom . . . began to lift from him. He did not know what his own future or fate was, in relation to Thot, but at least these people would be spared. They had come dangerously close to discovering the secret; but they had not discovered it, and therein was their salvation.

They were watching. They were all around them and they were watching.

Two had stayed back near the beach and now, six black, naked figures crouched down, their eyes once more intent on The Leader, who, with The Other, was concentrating on the small party gathered around the fire. He waited, fighting back the anticipation of yet more glory to the Gurds, while his chief companion was soaked in sweat, not from the heat of the night, but from the thrilling expectation of the Kill. The breeze from the ocean had grown stronger still and now was more like a gentle wind that rustled through the brush, masking any noise they may themselves have made.

The lady doctor threw a twig into the flame and it brightened, illuminating the four faces in the clearing. It was going to be different this time. They were more than just sacrifices, now. There would be joy in this, for at least two of the giant phantoms hidden within the night. The doctor was too smart for her own good, and the girl . . . that uppity, snot-nosed girl . . . no, this would not be as cold blooded as the one before.

Just then, the girl stood up quickly, and was yelling something. The Leader drew his blade and made ready. The Other followed suit, and poised

now on their haunches, they were ready to spring at
the first signal.

With salvation on his mind, Trobi became distracted by the glint of something in the black jungle
that had caught the light of their fire and flashed
briefly.

A scream, high and shrill, came from the blackness and in what seemed only a second, the quiet
camp became a hell of noise and blood.

Something landed with a heavy thud just to
Mary's left and she turned to see a creature,
marginally human, black, its face painted in reds
and yellows, swathed in sweat and sparkling from
the fire, bones protruding through the tops of its
flaring nostrils. It pulled her to her feet as she began
screaming.

Another had grabbed Dana by the neck and had
an arm twisted around in back of her, in so much
pain she could not scream, even when they were
forced to watch, to witness, the advance upon Trobi.

The Leader stood in the center, near the flames,
observing, overseeing. The three that remained held
Trobi, two at each arm, and the third, The Other,
Kara, was holding him by the hair on his head. The
Leader raised his blade high and moved toward
Trobi while his captors bent him forward, and the
great black arms of Thot swung and sliced.

A mass of blood shot forward and one small drop
landed upon Lucy's cheek. She felt it there, felt it
more intensely than the strain and pressure from
the arms around her, binding her, enslaving her. She
watched Trobi's head roll across the sandy ground,
its face frozen in a grimace of horror, now merely a
thing, no longer alive, no longer human. She looked
at the two other women. Mary had fainted in the

arms of her assailant; Dana was screaming uncontrollably, her body quivering, her nervous system
seeming to have gone mad. She was silenced with a
blow on the chin from the clenched fist of the
Leader, and as she went limp, her legs were grabbed
and she was swooped up and carried, almost
cradled, by the huge thing that had captured her.

Through it all, Lucy made no noise or movement,
and now the crackle of the fire and the flow of the
breeze through the jungle were the only sounds. It
had all been over in less than two minutes. The twig
that Dana McKinley had thrown into the flames had
not as yet been fully consumed.

The six creatures then looked at the still figure of
the girl who stood with a small smile on her lips, and
one tiny red dot on her cheek, ready to be led.

The two that had been ordered to remain near the
beach were both nervous at having been left on their
own to do this. One of them had arrived only just
that night in one of the two long boats. He had performed adequately in the past and was in this
instance the superior. However, it was the first time
in his life he had ever been "boss," and he didn't like
it. But, he knew enough about leadership not to let
the other one know his misgivings. His lieutenant
was the Mud Man, freed of the mask, and if not
clean, at least no longer covered in dirt. He knew he
had been chosen for this task as part of his initiation,
and would be judged by his companion. He had
already wiped the beach smooth, obliterating the
prints Barton had seen in the sand. Successfully
passing this "test" would insure full membership
into the society, and then he too would wear the sign
of The Ram that was etched into the skin of the
others.

They were hidden in the foliage, just off the path that led back to the camp sight. The wind had picked up more so that the trees above and the bushes that surrounded them were in constant movement and emitted an insistent rustling that was without pause, as if the jungle night was screaming out a whispered word that was unintelligible. The sound of it was so loud, they did not hear the approach of the two white men until they were almost upon them, and thus were forced to attack before completely ready.

Barton was the first to see them, a full eight seconds before they sprang. He simply did not know them for what they were; didn't recognize them as human. All he saw was their eyes, peering out from the darkness and momentarily lit by a moonbeam that had been permitted to pierce the undergrowth by the obliging wind, which had moved a bush to and fro before the hidden face that, for the moment in question seemed to flash, as if a light were being repeatedly switched on and off, and on again. At first, he thought they might be large cats lying in wait for fresh prey. Quickly, however, he realized that these were far more dangerous.

The blades were held high over their heads as they leaped and landed, screaming as they went.

The immediate area went mad. Small animals and birds which had fled from the attack at the camp began screaming, running, and taking flight once more in terror.

It had been decided that the Mud Man would take care of Barton, since they were more matched in size. He landed before the older man, screaming with the blade twirling around his own head, like a deadly human helicopter. Barton bent at the waist and, hurling himself forward, rammed the top of his head into the stomach of the wiry assailant. A loud "oof," combined with the thud of impact was heard, and the blade flew up and fell with a dull "clank" against some nearby rock.

Ben did not have such immediate results. His attacker had come from behind, and though Ben had managed to free himself from the grip around his neck, he had slipped and fallen in doing so, and was now on the ground, ducking, swerving and rolling away from the weapon, never finding the time or the footing to get back on his feet. Quickly, he realized that if he continued scurrying in a circle, the giant above him, having to deal with his own girth and constant movement of his entire body, was forced to alternate from foot to foot, so that in each movement there would be a second where his weight was not centered on the broad balance of his legs and feet. Ben grabbed one of the huge feet and twisted as he began to raise himself up, and the killer teetered over and landed with a crushing "boom," like an enormous bowling pin.

Barton had found the Mud Man's weapon and had brought it up over his own head to strike. But in that moment, looking down on the poor, frightened creature at his feet he froze, knowing that now he was about to shed blood, about to take another human life. In that pause, their eyes met and held, and something beyond enemies, beyond color or motives passed between them, and it all seemed to Barton insane, and futile.

But the Mud Man had begun to move, to attack once more, and Ben seeing what was happening called out "Barton! Strike!" The older man was still frozen. Ben ran over just as the Mud Man had begun to stand up, and kicked him in the rib cage. Ben heard a "crack" emit from inside the body, and with a groan, the Mud Man was on the ground again. Ben grabbed the blade from Barton's hand and with a fierce, angry blow, brought it down on the neck of the Mud Man.

The other was now on his feet and was just a moment too late to save his companion before reaching Ben. With no weapon Barton felt helpless, and useless as he watched the two other men stand off in what looked like a duel. But there was no style or elegance in this sword fight, as each man was unskilled in blade-to-blade combat, and went at each other now with blind, savage rage. They lunged, whirled, stabbed, and occasionally the sound of steel crashing against steel rang out through the forest. But the black giant had tried to readjust his grip and just then, Ben struck a blow, sending the others weapon flipping end over end into the brush. Ben did not waste time in watching its flight, but began to strike again. His attacker faked a move to the left and Ben went for it. By the time he had realized the false move, the huge thing was off in the opposite direction, running as fast as his girth would move him. But before he disappeared completely, Ben and Barton saw, carved into his shoulder blade, the Sign of the Ram.

Barton came over to Ben. There were cuts on his hands, and his shirt was torn in several spots, blood mixed with sweat matting the cloth to his body. Barton helped him to a tree where they sat upon the ground, leaned up against the bark, panting, catching their breath.

"You alright?" Barton asked.

"I think so. None of these cuts are too deep. Jesus, did you see that guy's back?"

Barton nodded, "Disgusting. It looked like it had been done on purpose."

Ben was about to go on, then hesitated. Barton doesn't know, he thought. Somehow Ben assumed Dana had clued the man in more fully; it appeared he was wrong. Barton was staring at him. "What is it, Ben?"

"Let me catch my breath a second."

They were silent, listening now to the overwhelming peace of the jungle that enveloped them. What had just occured had had no effect on the watching night; nature made no judgment, held no opinion, knew no right, no wrong. They were to simply survive, or not. Ben thought what strange things the mind does. For all they had just been through and for all they may be about to face, his cigarettes had dropped out of his shirt somewhere, and had been lost in the fight; he wanted one very much, and was annoyed at the inconvenience. Searching through his pockets, he felt something smooth and sharp. Drawing it out, he fingered the small tooth the Mayor had given him, "the Man," for luck. So far, it had worked. Then, he smiled at his own foolishness. Still, they were, after all, alive.

At last he said to Bart, "Ready if you are."

Barton paused. He wasn't sure. Ready . . . but for what? "I think so," he replied.

"Good," Ben said, getting to his feet with Bart's help, "I'll explain about the guy's carved up back on the way."

The two men picked up the weapons that had been left them and looked down upon the dead form of the Mud Man. He lay on his stomach, and the light of the moon fell softly on the man's sweaty back, where he had hoped one day to wear the Sign of the Ram.

They proceeded on without a backward glance.

** * *

According to the legend, the entrance was made from the sea from which all life sprang. So the little boats were just now passing through the last of the terrible reefs, and having maneuvered safely through it once more, had commenced to be paddled around the island to the opposite side where the Gods awaited them.

Thot had heard the clang of steel blades crashing against one another from inside the forest, as they had shoved off from further down the beach. It did not please him, or move him; his thoughts were upon the pleasure of his Masters. The murder of Barton and Ben simply meant the elimination of intrusive danger, and in that alone was there some small relief.

The women were silent, and a good thing, too. With Mary and Dana in one boat, Thot and two aides rowing, there was no more to spare. Traveling would have been impossible if they had had to deal with the extra movement of hysterical women. Both were unconscious, and lay at the bottom of the boat, neatly bound at the wrists. The other boat was less crowded, with only Kara and the two aides rowing, Lucy their only "passenger." But she was awake, and though bound in the same manner as the other women, she sat erect, hands folded on her lap, staring straight ahead, the reflection of the moon glittering in the water dancing upon her face. She was nearly serene.

Staring at her in the other boat that followed his, Thot was filled with wonder. Three mates at once! That alone was an overwhelming achievement. Never had this been accomplished before . . . and he, Thot, had done it. But to have one come to them without resistance, giving of herself for them, was the triumph, for him. He was almost smug, it was working out so beautifully.

They would need further assistance once they had arrived on the ceremonial beach. By that time the Mud Man and his captain would have done their work and traveled by foot through the center of the island, to help in setting up what would be the largest sacrificial altar in the long legend of the Island. This night would add new glory, perhaps even change, or add to, the dogma of the ceremony. Thot had made history.

He stood, his silhouette alone towering above the others against the phosphorescent night, nearly naked, as were all these creatures, the soft auburn hair on the enormous bodies gently moving in the wind that had built up even more. What clouds there were raced across the face of the friendly moon, and the boats bobbed up and down, circling the island with difficulty, rowing, as they were, counter to the current that pulled at them in obedience to that high, full, yellow moon.

They had never been too far from the actual shoreline of the beach, and now they were within sight of the ceremonial grounds. As the arms on the oars carried them closer, the wind picked up their scents, and carried them in to the shore. In waves at the beginning, so that at first it was merely a suggestion of what was arriving. But gradually the scent grew stronger and closer, and the things that made their home in the black jungle became aware, then agitated, and finally aroused. Their huge heads lifted and their nostrils flared, taking in the smell that the wind brought to them from the sea. As each was called by the aroma, they began to make their way toward the beach, coming from their lair, lowering themselves down from the towering trees delicately, in spite of their considerable size and weight, and they saw from behind the shelter of the forest, the two small boats that now began to turn and let the sea carry them forward.

Lucy was no longer listlessly staring out before her, but had suddenly become alert, as if she had heard something, or felt something. Whatever it was, she now leaned out to her left to see past the hulking form of the working oarsman in front of her. Her neck stretched out and she peered into the darkness of the approaching island, knowing something was there, waiting for her. Then, in a flash of self-awareness that came to her from very far away, she knew that she was waiting for it too.

She was both eager and impatient to be with them, among them. She would find Margery there and join her willingly, even joyfully. She would be more and more a part of her friend's life, for was she not now, already? Did she not love the father of the girl . . . because . . . because why? Because Margery had come forth from him . . . wasn't that it? Wasn't that the truth? she asked herself. That if she could in some way obtain him within herself, she would be as close to Margery as possible. She would own some of the very seed itself that had gone into the creation of her friend, and in so doing, posssess the girl more completely than any physical union with her could express, for she had, within her, some of the beginning.

But that had failed, hadn't it? She had not had him properly; there was Dana. Dana. It was Dana he wanted. She hated Dana. Lucy looked to the other boat, but both figures were still dormant, and barely visible over the edge.

Yet, ahead of them was the island. Their destiny

was there . . . her destiny was there, with Margery, sharing in whatever life she had there, and making it her own. Their own.

The canoe lurched, dipped, then rose half out of the water as it hit a huge black rock that suddenly lunged from what had become a tempestuous surf. The water was not deep here, but the reef was hazardous and snaking through and around the dreadful, sharp rocks was a frantic, arduous ordeal for the exhausted rowers, who were in constant motion, pushing off from one jagged mass in time to avoid careening into yet another in their path.

But soon they were clear and rode the last waves into the shore of black sand, the wind now high and full behind them as they dragged the boats onto the shore, and began at once to make ready for the sacrifice.

The ritual usually took place just before dawn, but things being as they were, Thot thought it best to begin immediately. Quickly, the torches were dug into the sand, and once more the same thirty foot circle of beach became the stage on which would be played the last act of three lives. But never, to any of their memories, had the number been so high, nor the preparations so lengthy. Instead of four stakes there were twelve, each tied with the ropes that would bind the hands and feet of the women. The single vial atop each wooden box was there. Then the torches were lit, and as if on cue, the wind began to come up with gusto from the beach, and the flames cast macabre shadows across the strange landscape.

Thot had filled two large shells with sea water and poured them over Dana and Mary, reviving them. Upon looking up from the bottom of the boat, the first thing Mary saw was the huge, naked, painted figure of Thot towering over her. She began to scream, and Thot regretted having awakened her.

Kara stood near Dana; he too was nearly naked, and she saw in his face the deep hatred he bore in his heart for them, and the joy with which he would observe whatever terrible fate he was sending them to. She looked over at Lucy, and it was then that she became truly frightened. The girl was standing on the beach, bound as Mary and she herself was bound, but she was totally calm, even smiling. She was looking up the beach, past the glimmering torches into the trees.

"*Lucy!*" Dana screamed.

Lucy did not turn, but answered her with her eyes remaining on the jungle. "They're taking us to her," she said.

"Who?"

The wind was strong now and their clothes and hair whipped and billowed about them. Dana could barely hear over the howling.

"She's there! In there! She's always been. She's not dead, Dana. We're going to her!"

Oh, my God, Dana thought, she has lost her mind. Completely. She looked over to Mary, who had stopped screaming and was staring at the girl, and Dana knew Mary had reached the same conclusion, and that Lucy was beyond their help. It meant that part of their battle against this torment had been lost, and the quick acceptance of that fact was essential for their future well being; Lucy was no longer an ally.

Dana looked from Mary up again to Thot, then to Kara, whose face was twisted with loathing for them. She was dirty and exhausted, and felt as if she couldn't push her brain to think for another second . . . but I must, she told herself, I must! But, oh, sweet Jesus, what are we going to do?

Simultaneously, Kara and Thot bent and picked up each woman, standing them on their feet. Then each drew their blades, and Mary screamed again, thinking she was about to be struck; but as her garments were ripped and torn from her and from Dana, the scream dwindled into a whimper as their clothing fell about them upon the sand in shredded rags, and they stood naked, vulnerable, and very alone.

Lucy turned and saw her two compaions standing nude, the light of the flame and the moon illuminating the planes and valleys of their bodies.

"How beautiful," she observed softly, and began removing her own clothes until she too stood naked before them. Thot and Kara exchanged looks of surprise and relief, both knowing now the extent of the third woman's dementia. Dana and Mary were lifted into huge arms and carried up the beach where the four massive, nude guards were posted near the stakes. As the women were carried closer, one of the torches looked to be in danger of being extinguished by the high wind, and the guard nearest it turned to lengthen the wick before the flame went out entirely.

Dana and Mary were set once more upon their feet while Lucy walked up the beach, and took her place between them, still fixed upon the jungle.

"Margery," she whispered.

But Dana did not turn or move, or answer. She was staring at the guard's naked back; at his left shoulder blade, and the Sign of The Ram that was carved there into his flesh. Then from the jungle, a loud, scream came forth from the throat of something not human, ripping through the silence of the night.

* * *

A single tear rolled down Barton Croft's cheek as he stood in the empty clearing where the campsite had been. He had smothered the fire that had been left to burn, and the last of it smoldered, not quite dead, stealing as much air as it could from the strong wind; trying to stay lit, and alive.

A dark green blanket lay over the headless form of Trobi. Ben had found the head in the brush but could not bring himself to touch it, and so had left it there. Marcus Pemberton's had been very different; Trobi's was recently done, fresh, and still slimy with gore. Besides, there was not time for burying it, or the body. A quick prayer had been said. Then they took action.

Ben searched through the tents and there, leaning against a center post, forgotten and abandoned, was the rifle. He was thankful, at least for that. Then he thought, no, it had not been forgotten. Thot sent those two to kill. The rifle could be left, because Ben and Barton were not expected back at the camp. They were expected to be dead. There was ample ammunition, and slinging the strap of the weapon over his shoulder, he picked up a canteen and stepped out into the clearing again.

The wind felt good, though it added to the wierd, unclean atmosphere of violent death that clung to the place, bathed in strange lunar light.

Barton had the blade in his hand and looked fierce, and sad, and determined. Ben could only guess what the man would be thinking, but he admired him, and knew he could be depended upon.

Of course, when they had gone back to find the hidden long boats, they were no longer there, and they had then looked out to sea. Silhouetted in the moonlight they saw two boats and the passengers, but could make out only one female form. There seemed no time for a decision, but one had to be made. They would return to the camp, on the off chance that two of the women might still be there. All they found was Trobi.

"Alright," Ben said, "if they haven't destroyed the boats *we* came in, we can use one of them and follow."

"How, Ben?"

"What do you mean, how? We get in the boats and . . ."

". . . And what? We've lost sight of them by now and we don't know where they're headed. They've left the island, and we don't know for where."

"I've a pretty good idea . . . and I don't think they've left the island, Bart."

"We *saw* them, Ben! We saw them leave!"

Ben put an arm up to Bart's shoulder, "Calm down and listen to me. *What* did you see?"

Bart thought for a moment, replaying the scene in his head. He said, "I saw two boats with people in them . . . one of them was a woman, and they were being rowed . . ." he stopped abruptly and looked at Ben.

"Right," Ben answered, "they weren't rowing out to sea, were they? They were rowing off to the left . . . *around* the island, not away from it."

"But why? With the reef as dangerous as it is, to have to get out and then back . . . just to make us *think* they were leaving?"

"No. They were leaving, but not to another island, and not to just circle around and return to this spot after we're gone. No. I'm sure they've gone to the other side of this island."

"Then where are the two other women, and which ones are they?"

"I don't know Bart. There's only one answer. If they're not here, then somehow, they must be with them . . ."

They both realized that this meant the women lay at the bottom of the boats. Barton ran a hand through his hair and paced back and forth, finally crying out, "If they've hurt them, Ben . . !"

"Hopefully we can prevent that, if it hasn't happened already. Let's find our boats."

He started out into the brush, but Barton called his name, and he turned.

"Listen, Ben, if they *did* go to the other side of the island, and since they've had such a big head start . . . wouldn't it be faster for us to go on foot, through the *center* of the island!"

Ben smiled broadly. "I'm an idiot . . . of course, you're right. We should arrive shortly after they do, and we'll come up behind them, too. And this," he gestured with the rifle, "will come in handy . . . especially if we're not seen."

"Let's go," Bart said.

So, they set off into the jungle, into thick lush growth, pathless and overgrown at first, then thinning out some, allowing them at least the luxury of walking without having to cut their way through the foliage. Sometimes, they were even able to break into short runs, before the growth became too thick again, and slowed them down.

Sweat poured off both of them, streaming out and down from every pore and was cooled by the wind that made itself felt, having penetrated deeply into the core of the island, making their skin clammy and cold, for all the heat of the night. They travelled on like this for some twenty minutes. Then they saw that the going was gradually becoming easier. This part of the forest had been cleared, and travelled before. And recently.

Not too far off, they could perceive something, unable to name it . . . or them . . . but it seemed they were certainly structures of some sort . . . not occurences of nature, but built. But they were up in the trees that lay ahead of them, some perched in the uppermost branches and too high and far away, while others were dangling like huge earrings, but still too distant to be seen as anything recognizable.

There seemed also to be much activity, not caused by the wind rustling violently through those trees . . . but movement. Things, moving. But too far off.

They slowed down, and realized that whatever the things were, they were moving away from them, and then . . . there! Wasn't that the sound of the sea? They were near the beach at last, and began to quicken their pace, drawn on by anxiety and now, curiosity.

They were closer. Close enough at least to discern what these structures were, that hung from the trees. Closer, in fact, than even they knew.

A horrid, agonizing roar cut through the white rush of wind through the trees and nearby surf, and they held their ears in pain. It came from just above their heads.

They looked up.

TWENTY

The sound of his own heart beating in his chest grew louder in his ears, replacing the first cry of the Gods that had been sounded from the jungle and had now died away. Thot would have been happy but for the absence of the Mud Man and his officer. They would certainly have been here by now. Perhaps they had deserted? But that did not seem likely, inasmuch as the two had come this far with little complaint. The only other alternative was that they were dead or wounded and unable to get across the island. Either way, these thoughts put a somber note to what otherwise should have been an ecstatic celebration. For, though it was important to him that his own disciples were present, it was far more important that the two whites were no longer alive.

The wick of the failing torch had now been lengthened, and the brightened flame flashed and

cast yet more wild, flickering light across the sand,
the stakes, and the nude figures of the three women
that stood with their backs to the sea. Thot heard
Dana cry out, "Look, Mary!" in an attempted
whisper, and he turned his head to them, his gaze
following theirs to the shoulder blade of the guard
who was turning once again to face them.

Mary saw, before Dana, that she had been heard,
and her eyes darted to Thot's face. In spite of his
concerns, he smiled.

"Yes, look," he said, and then called out an
unknown word in an unknown language. In response, the four guards pivoted in a clumsy about-
face. Kara did not move, but stood on the other side
of the group, to the right of the silent Lucy.

On all of their backs beneath the left shoulder
blade, the circular bull's eye was etched into the
dark skin.

Mary began weeping, but Dana faced Thot,
stating, rather than asking, "You and Kara, too."
He nodded, and she continued, "The chauffeur . . .
you know, of course, about the auto crash . . .?" He
nodded again as she went on, ". . . he was a eunuch."

Thot held her stare for a moment, then nodded a
third time. "You understand now, don't you,
Doctor?"

"Yes, I understand. My God, I understand."

"What?! For Christ's sake, what!?" Mary cried
out.

As if in answer to her, another plaintive cry came
from the dark before them, where the light of the
torches would not go. They all looked to the jungle.
The wind was wild, moving the whole forest to and
fro. But from within, other movements, counter to
the winds direction, could be perceived and now and
again, a small scream, a yelp, a grunt, came to them.

"Your father was right, Mary" Dana said, awed by the realization of what was taking place, "he did find a missing link . . . of sorts."

With that, Thot called out to the others once more, and they turned in unison to face the women.

Mary did not at first comprehend. But Dana was staring at Thot, scrutinizing him, taking in every angle and curve and plane of the huge head, then moving on to the first guard, concentrating on his face, looking deeply into his eyes, roaming over the massive hulk of flesh and muscle that was his body. In disbelief, Mary swung around to look at Kara, hard lines and shadows making his face appear as if carved from rock in the mad illumination of the torches. He stared back at her, the small, mean eyes glaring back into her own, and all at once, she knew.

"It's them, isn't it?" Mary spoke softly, almost in a whisper, the way she did when she was in a church.

Neither woman looked to each other, but stared at these creatures before them, seeing them differently than before . . . seeing them, really, for the first time, as what they were.

"Yes," Dana answered at last, "It's them. It is, isn't it?" she said to Thot. "It's been you all along."

"You should have known when you heard the word 'hoo-rey-yeh,' doctor. It is borrowed from the Ancients."

"I'm an anthropologist, not a linguist . . . or an historian. What do you mean?"

"The definition is loosely translated as 'nymph of heaven' . . . a woman, raised to serve, copulate, and bear the young of the various species."

"Species of . . .?"

"Go ahead, doctor. Say it. Don't be afraid of a word. It won't bite you." He laughed loudly, and three roars in quick succession came from the jungle. His face grew serious once more, and he said, "Apes."

"This is insane!" Mary screamed, fear and horror welling up within her until she could bear no more. She spun around and started running across the sand toward the water. But realizing she would be too weak to swim away with any speed, she veered off to the left, down the beach. Kara was after her in a moment. She moved fast despite her weakened state, and for a frightening second, he thought he might lose her. But then he drew close enough to fly full lenth across the sand behind her, catching her heels in his arms, pulling her down. They both landed with a heavy, painful thud, the rough sand scraping and burning them raw. Before she could struggle free, he was on top of her, his huge form covering hers, his skin against her skin, wet, hairy, and pungent. She lay beneath him helpless, in submission, and then was pulled to her feet and dragged, breathless and limping, back up the beach toward the torches.

Immediately, Thot screamed orders and all but he and Kara began to work. Mary was delivered into the arms of one of the guards while the other three took charge of Dana and Lucy. Throwing them upon the ground, they were tied, spreadeagle, to the stakes, Dana at the center, Mary and Lucy to her left and right. The binding was tight, and Dana could feel the circulation being cut off from her hands as the ropes rubbed and bit into her wrists.

But she stopped struggling when Thot appeared, looking down upon her, his huge legs on either side of her naked body. He bent down, leaning in close to her face, the odor of his breath coming at her in warm gusts as he said, "Frightened?"

"Of what? Rape? From *you*? From *them*?!"

"Of being killed. Torn to ribbons by . . ."

"Stop it!"

"The Book of the Dead states," he went on in a low, almost sweet tone, "that during a ceremony portraying the sex life of the Gods, the Nymphs of Heaven were taken by a horde of baboons, mandrils, gorillas and orangutangs, made drunk and inflamed by the scent from the female of their kind, poured upon the naked flesh of the humans."

Dana spit in his face.

He straightened up suddenly, pulling himself to his full height, towering over her, erect and powerful.

"There is no female of *your* kind, though, is there?!" Dana screamed as Thot wiped his face with a gigantic paw, *"That's* it, isn't it? THAT's the reason! You're a society of males, aren't you? What's the rest of it, Thot? You permit every perversion except mating with your own mothers? Or have you tried that too and failed? You're all castrata! Why?"

He stared down at her, helpless as she was, and he decided. She would probably be dead soon, anyway.

"If we mate with our human mothers," he began without emotion, "mutations . . . horrid mutations come forth and die at birth. You are correct. The union of woman with our fathers brings only males . . . us. Me. We are castrated early, to keep from being tempted by the human female. To keep from causing more mutated infants. But we are sacred, here among these islands, and some, who are not of us, but wish to serve, may join us in worship, after a test."

"And help supply you with females."

"Yes!" he screamed suddenly, his arms flying out left and right, his head raised to the sky. "She is

promised to us!" he cried out, as if angry at the
starry night, "SHE! Who will save us and evolve us
to a higher form! ONE Female Child! The Christ!"

He was enraptured, lost to anything further she
might say. Tears ran down his face, so totally was he
carried away, abandoned to hot frustration and mad
joy.

Dana looked at Kara. He was staring at his leader
intently, but the hate that lived there behind his
eyes was, for this moment, gone, and replaced by
pity. He looked down at her, and she asked of him,
"Are we to be killed?"

"If you live through the mating," he answered,
matter-of-factly," you will be kept alive until it is
determined if you carry life. If not, you will be killed.
If you do, you will live on and raise your young, with
the others."

Lucy began laughing, and whispered a prayer of
thanks. She knew then, for certain, that Margery
Croft was still alive.

From a huge, thick branch of a gigantic tree, a
wooden cage was suspended by heavy chains. The
bottom of the cage was a round block of wood, and
swayed back and forth in the wind, some six feet
over the heads of Barton Croft and Ben Ramsey. It
squeaked and creaked as it moved, the bough
straining beneath its burden. The forest was dense
here, and the bright moon had difficulty in penetrating through the heavy canopy of branch and leaf
that towered still higher above. Farther off, from
where they knew the beach must be, animals
scrambled in sporadic bursts, and the steady
creaking of the cage swaying in the wind was, they
realized, coming from all around them, not just from
above.

But the dim blue-green forest light revealed little to them of their immediate surroundings. All they knew for certain was that something above them had cried out as if in agony. Something inside that cage. Then they heard a soft, mournful whimper, and a thumping sounded on the wooden floor from within it.

Ben cursed that they had not thought to bring a flashlight with them, but of course, light would have revealed them travelling through the wood. But now it was imperative to have that light. They looked around them, peering through the darkness and came upon a hand torch, just near Barton's feet leaned up against the thick bark of the enormous trunk of the tree.

Barton lifted the stick high and gently knocked with it three times on the bottom of the cage. After a pause, three knocks came back in return from inside. They looked at each other, incredulous, and Ben began to search frantically for matches. They were limp and soggy from the dampness of the night and his own body, but at last the torch took the flame and flared brightly.

Now they saw that spikes had been driven into the trunk at evenly spaced points, creating a ladder of sorts, up as far as what appeared to be a gate in the cage. Ben held the torch higher still, and they craned their necks to see what was there behind the bars, but whatever it was sat in the center, just out of sight.

"Climb up," Bart said, gesturing to the spike ladder. Without reply, Ben stepped onto the first rung, grabbing hold of another above his head, and tested them for support of his weight. They held firm, and with the torch out at arm's length, he climbed up four rungs, bringing himself just past the floor of the cage. He brought the torch closer and raised his arm slightly as he looked in.

What remained in darkness became black shadows that sharply defined the white skin, the gaunt cheeks, the parched lips, of a naked human being; a woman, whose eyes were wide with terror, and curiosity, and madness. Her hair was long, so long she sat upon it, thickly matted, and filthy. She was covered in grime and her breasts were caked in a crusty white substance that had dried over the nipples and swollen curves, that looked to be sore and tender. Her fingernails had grown beyond control and curled outwards and away, like the gnarled roots of a wild plant, and there, resting within her hands, was an infant thing, asleep in the cradle of her arms that rocked with the rhythm of the swaying cage.

She looked down at her young, then into Ben's face, then back down at the infant. She stared at Ben again for perhaps ten seconds. In that time, he thought perhaps she knew him from somewhere, for the look was familiar, and friendly. Seeming to make a decision, she began slowly to edge herself forward on her buttocks, getting closer to him. From below, Barton called up, "What is it?"

But Ben did not answer. Barton was looking up seeing Ben staring hypnotized into the cage, as slowly, tentatively, one small hand curled its fingers around a single bar and gripped it firmly. The two men were very, very still. Barton heard something—a gurgle—come from inside the cage, and watched as Ben's face broke into a wide smile. Barton heard another sound then, and could have sworn it was the laughter of a very young child.

"Ben!" he cried out again softly.

With difficulty, Ben removed his gaze from the

cage and looked down at Barton. There were tears in his eyes, and he said, "It's a woman, Barton. A woman and a baby."

"What? What are you talking about?"

Ben was looking into the cage again and replied, "Come up," without another downward glance, moving higher on the trunk to make room. Barton scrambled quickly up the rungs, and as he came in sight of the interior of the cage, Ben said, "Look."

She was a native woman, probably about twenty-five years old, though in her condition it was hard to tell. She did not recoil, but remained close to the edge at Barton's approach, the infant pulling at a bar, exercising its meager strength.

"My God," Bart murmured.

"Where do you think she came from?"

"Abducted, no? From the mainland, or Savong-khai or . . . what does it matter? She could have come from any nearby island."

"Look at the baby, Bart. Look close."

Barton brought his finger up the cage and rubbed the tiny knuckles of the little fist.

"How old would you say it is?" he asked Ben, who was staring at the older man.

"Under a year," he replied, and watched as Barton looked more closely at the child's hand, curious now in a different way.

"Male?"

"Male. I could tell when she brought him over to the bars."

Ben knew that Barton had barely heard this last sentence, as he'd brought his face very close to the cage and was peering in, transfixed, at the baby. The child looked up at him with huge dark eyes, and the mother brought her own face down and in, nearly nose to nose with him. Barton was still rubbing the back of the baby's knuckle with his fingers. He turned his head to face Ben.

"This . . . isn't human . . . is it?"

They both turned to look down once more at the infant. The mother smiled.

"I don't think so," Ben answered softly and felt something warm tickle the hairs on his outstretched arm that gripped the top rung in the trunk.

The woman had reached her own arm out through the cage and ran her hand over his, and up. She and Ben looked at each other and after a pause, she continued the caress, her palm gracefully stroking his cheek and jaw.

From very close—too close—another roar came, at once beckoning and warning. The woman pulled her hand quickly back inside and the child, startled by the noise and the sudden movement, began to wail as his mother shied away, retreating once again to the center of the cage. Simultaneously, screams came from everywhere, all around them.

Certain they were about to be attacked, Barton started down the trunk and had just set his foot on solid ground, when he looked up in answer to Ben's cry.

Ben was holding the torch out and he turned his back on the cage, to face the opposite direction, further into the forest. "Jesus!" he said, awed by what he saw.

Not ten feet away there was another cage hanging from another tree, and within it, another woman. The flames reflected in her poor, glaring, insane eyes, and she stood, legs spread, staring and screaming, at the two men. At her feet was a child of about two years of age—a huge child, with the beginnings of orange fuzz just beginning to sprout through its large shoulders. They could see another torch lying at the foot of the tree, which had had spikes driven into its trunk as well. Barton ran over to it, picked up the torch and ran back to Ben, who touched the end of it with his own. The torch in Bart's hand sprang alive, and holding it up he ran to the other cage.

But upon coming to rest his foot on the first rung he saw, in the added light of his own torch, that just beyond, there was yet another cage, and inside, another woman, this one alone, but at least six months pregnant.

Ben jumped down from his post and joined Barton. Together, they jogged through the area . . . the lair . . . their torches allowing them to see what they still could not quite believe. There were at least ten more such cages, all with hand torches laying at the base of trees, all the trees with spike ladders driven into them. The cages were swinging wildly from the motion of the captive women within them. Most were on their feet, but a few remained seated on the floors of the cages. Some were pregnant, others had their offspring with them, while two were neither pregnant, not yet mothers, but merely caged. All of them were screaming now and the children had picked up the call and cried the piercing scream of what was now like some mad nursery.

"But where are the mates? They're unguarded!" Barton yelled over the din.

"They must be down at the water!"

They realized then that no time could be lost, and Barton cried, "Let's get down there!"

Ben had just extinguished his torch, and Barton was about to do the same, when crying out, shrill and hoarse in desperation, one female voice made itself heard distinctly above all the others. The men froze as they listened.

It was calling out for help, sobs breaking up the words, English words, and Ben saw Barton's face drain of color, of blood, and he staggered, as if about to faint—for he had heard the voice of his daughter.

"Barton, come on!" Ben urged.

But Barton's head was turning back and forth, his eyes searching the cages.

"*No!* I can't! Not yet! We've got to look for her!"

"Bart, she'll be safer in the cage for now. We've got to get down to the beach!"

"Then you go, Ben!" Barton yelled back, suddenly angry, "*You* go! But I'm not leaving this spot until my daughter is free. I'll do it alone if I have to!"

Ben thought quickly, looking through the trees toward the sea. There was still much movement out there and it appeared through the shadows that a large congregation of shapes were gathered at the edge of the jungle, looking out onto the beach. As long as they remained there, he reasoned, and did not actually emerge from the cover of the jungle onto the sand, there was still time. How much, no one knew.

"Okay, let's go! Where is she?"

When the two men discovered her, they realized they had gone right past her in their initial search, so changed was she now.

Margery Croft lay on her side at the bottom of a cage, one arm reaching out to them for help. She was naked and emaciated, red scratches, deep and sore-looking, marring the formerly smooth, tanned skin. The long straight nose was also cut, and her brown hair had lost the golden sheen it once held, robbed of the sunlight here deep in the forest. Her eyes were glazed over, and though she whimpered and begged,

tears rolling down her filthy cheeks, she knew them
only as men . . . human beings, of her own species,
but devoid of identity.

"Margery," Barton called gently to her. She
looked down on him and smiled, but he knew immediately tht she had no idea she was looking once
more into the face of her own father who had come
so far to take her home.

Ben had climbed up the spikes and, taking the
sword from Barton, smashed the wooden bars of the
locked cage, reaching in for her. She pushed his arm
away, though, and signalled him to vacate the
entrance. He climbed down the tree and she pulled
herself to the cage door. In trying to place a foot on
one of the spikes, she fell nearly twelve feet, her
landing cushioned by the undergrowth of the jungle
floor.

She was, however, almost immediately on her feet
and walking, albeit with a limp, and Ben and Barton
were amazed at her strength and resiliency.

Barton's instinct was to go to her, to hug her and
hold her, but though she was obviously grateful to
them for her freedom, distrust for them was in her
eyes. She doesn't know me, Barton thought. Whatever has happened to her, her mind is affected.
Though he thought he could save her now, he wondered if this damage to her reason was permanent;
could he bring her back to sanity . . . to reality, one
day? Then Bart realized that she had been spared,
like the others, because it had not been determined
as yet, whether or not she was pregnant. Her body
was, if anything, painfully thin, so it told them
nothing yet, and would not for at least another
month or so.

A month! She would have lived like this until they
were sure there was no pregnancy . . . and then,

what? Killed? And if she was . . .?

"Oh, God, no," he whispered, the appalling possibilities seeming to explode in his head as he stared at Margery's naked form. Ben took off his shirt and carefully, slowly handed it to Margery. She stared at it for a moment then took it, smelled it, and put it on, buttoning only the middle three buttons.

"Easy, Bart, easy," Ben said softly. Barton had his hands up to his temples, and was hyperventilating. Though Ben was concerned about the man and the woman, he was eager to get down to the beach.

"I'll be alright," Bart said after a moment. But before he could fully regain his composure, they saw Margery tense, her head snap toward the sound of the ocean as if someone or something had called her name. She looked at the two men wild-eyed, ran her thin, cracked fingers through the matted mass of dried, split hair on her head, and was off suddenly, running madly through the wood toward the beach.

"Bart!" Ben screamed, and was after her in a second, the rifle now in hand and ready for whatever might occur.

Bart's vision at last cleared, and he followed some distance behind Ben, running as fast as his age and health would allow, the sword tightly grasped in his fist.

But for an occasional squeal, they were fairly quiet, and only the motion of the very latest arrivals at the perimeter of the beach gave evidence that there was more than merely tree and brush to the jungle. From where he stood, empty vials still overturned and held in his outstretched hands, he could even discern some of their eyes glimmering in the far off fire light, observing, waiting for their cue to come again.

The three women pinioned upon the sand were covered now in the same fluids that earlier had covered Margery and all others who had been captured there. Kara had kneeled, as had the others, and they were all panting loudly in unison as part of the ritual, while Thot was screaming over the wild wind that whipped the flames "Make these females fertile for the Seed of the Race of Gurds!"

Mary screamed madly, sure that her brain would take no more of this, while Dana wept because she was certain there was no help coming . . . certain too that Ben and dear Barton were dead and that soon, if they were lucky, they would be too. Lucy lay in complete submission, eyes closed, breath coming evenly, waiting . . . waiting . . .

Ben had trouble keeping the woman in sight. She ran remarkably fast and darted in, out, and through the underbrush, around the huge trees and, for a horrid second, he lost her. He stood completely still, trying to listen for her steps through the growth up ahead, but all he heard was the sea, very close now, and the wind howling in a duet that joined the screaming voice of Thot, whose garbled voice seemed to come at once from different directions, carried as it was upon the ever shifting but always powerful air currents blowing across sand; whipping, beating. But scrambling up a rocky hill just behind the last row of trees that lined the beach, he caught sight of Margery again, and ran to join her, further on up.

So far he had been correct. They had seen no living thing at all between the lair and here. Now, climbing up the steep embankment, he could see Margery

dimly lit by the thinnest shaft of moonlight. She did
not turn when he came up behind her, though he
knew she knew he was there. She continued to stare,
rapt, out to the trees that skirted the beach just
beyond.

From not far behind, Barton drew near, almost
breathless, and saw the two standing atop the hill.
The thought of the steep climb ahead of him hardly
cheered him, but he must, he knew, reach them in
time. To be caught alone at ground level if an attack
should begin, would mean certain death for him. At
last, he came through the foliage at the bottom of
the incline and, looking up, began to climb, hauling
himself over exposed root and rock toward the two
figures at the pinnacle. He wanted to call out for
help from Ben, but they were now too close to the
beach, and he was afraid he might be heard and thus
give away their position, and presence.

As he approached the last six feet of the hill
Barton saw Ben turn to see him struggling up.
Margery still would not turn and Ben reached out
and down to help Bart up the last of it, until finally
the three of them stood, puffing and anxious,
looking down from their hill at the strange
gathering before them.

A line of trees stood before them, lit from behind
by the firelight upon the sand, and appearing very
much like a scrim at the back wall on a stage during
a play—almost, but not quite, real. It stretched left
and right as far as their eyes could see, some sixty
feet from the bottom of their hill. At first, nothing
beyond the blackness of the trunks and branches
was noticeable, standing out as silhouettes against
the sand of the beach beyond, which glowed and
twinkled in the flashing light of the torches. But as
their eyes became more accustomed to the sight,

Ben and Bart began to see now what Margery had seen from the first; what held her, senseless to all else around her. Within those black shadows were heads, arms, legs, feet and torso that nestled motionless on the ground, in the shrubbery and the trees, clutching the trunks and bark, dangling by arms and tails from the overhanging web of branch, perched, alone, or in groups.

There were hundreds of them. All apes, all wild, and all completely still, mesmerized by what took place out, past the jungle, just fifty feet from where they waited in the darkness.

Since their backs were to them, Ben and Barton were free for the moment, to study them as best they could from this distance, without fear of being seen. The direction of the wind was in their favor too, coming inland from the water so that their own human scents would not reach the beasts. It was amazing how very, very still they all were, lined up, respectful of each other, not blocking any of the other's view, as if they were at Mass, and the beach was their altar.

But looking out there on that altar, Ben's pulse began to race anew. He could hear Mary sobbing, watch her struggle from within the confines of the ropes that bound her to the sand. She looked to be covered in something—like blood, only thinner. Still, he was sure the women had not been wounded. Dana moved every now and again, but only Lucy remained still, while the guards, strangers, and Kara, knelt near each of the women, and Thot was on his knees as well, his hands held out over Dana's body.

Thot and his workers were all nearly naked, loose cloth hung across their waists, their faces painted yellow and red. It was hard to tell from this far off, but Ben was almost positive that bones had been inserted through the tops of their nostrils like minute tusks, protruding from the massive faces. Leaves, twigs and vines were tangled in their hair.

It was then that Barton noticed stirring from the center of the watching congregation, and held his breath as a huge animal stood up, stretching to its full height. It sniffed several times at the night air blowing in from the sea, across the altar, pounded its chest violently, and roared, loud and demanding.

Ben looked out onto the beach. Thot was still kneeled over Dana's body and he heard her cry out, "NO! Oh, God!" Ben tried to see if she was being hurt in any way, but as best as he could tell, Thot was running his hands up and down her naked form and, it appeared, was rubbing in the oily, gruesome substance that covered her, in motions that were more like a slow massage than anything overtly erotic. It had, however, its effect on the apes, all of whom had now grown restless, sniffing at the wind.

Ben held his rifle poised, but knew there was little he could do. Even if every shot fired stopped something in its path, there were far too many of them to even hope of escape, even if rescue were possible.

There was sudden struggling from Margery. Ben saw her moving back and forth, leg to leg, lifted upon the balls of her feet. Then another roar came from the apes, as Mary was rubbed over with the vile fluid, and another animal stood and pounded its chest. Thot had moved on to Lucy. Having covered her as well, he screamed, "Hear them, Oh Nymphs of Heaven! You are confirmed! You are in favor with the Gurds, made ready as Holy Vessels for the Race to Breed, for the Gurds to feed their hunger! We honor you!"

All three women, slicked down with the oily stuff,

glistened like long, wet, pink seals upon the black
sand. Thot stood now, his hands and upper arms
drenched and running with the juices he had spread
over his captives. From around him, Kara and the
others chanted, "It is done. She is so honored."

Kara also rose to his feet and came to Thot. Together, they murmured, "Be fertile, bride." Lucy
groaned.

Another roar came from the apes, and another and
another.

From their place on the hilltop, Margery suddenly
screamed a horrid, inhuman cry full of hate and
pain. Barton turned to see her eyes wide and red.
She screamed again. He tried to silence her, but she
pushed him off and crouched down to defend herself
from them, as Ben came at her as well. She dodged
as he leaped, and her face turned quickly to the
beach, eyes darting back and forth. Barton was
close, maintaining his balance over the rocks.
Grabbing his arm, she pulled him in to her, to wrest
the sword from his hand.

"NO!" he cried out, knowing she was headed
down the hill, and reached to grab at her. They
struggled briefly, and he knew he was losing his
balance once again. He felt something happen, then,
inside his body—inside the heart that had all at once
given up on him. Margery did not know that her
next act was not necessary, as he had already begun
to die; he felt something hard and cold enter into the
middle of him and withdraw just as quickly. There
was in that instant an incredible pain that, coupled
with the hot death racing in his chest, overwhelmed
him totally.

Ben was too late. He watched helplessly as she
drove the blade to its hilt into her father's body and
pulled it out viciously. Barton fell to his knees,

clutching his stomach, and father and daughter's eyes met for one moment. It seemed to Ben that there was recognition on her face as she watched him dying. Margery looked at the blade in her hand, covered in his blood, then back at him, her eyes following his body as it fell face down onto the earth.

She screamed again, turned, and ran down the hill to the beach.

There was no time to think. The entire population that watched from the trees would soon be on the beach. Ben had to get there before they did. He was off, following closely behind Margery.

She jumped, leaped, fell and recovered. When she'd approached the first of the animals, she raised the sword and began swinging left and right, screaming for blood, for murder, a wild, barely human thing gone mad. It happened so fast that she'd managed to get through them and land upon the sand before she could be stopped.

Ben had almost the same good luck, but by the time he arrived, the apes saw him coming. Those nearest him were confused, not knowing whether to go for him or follow the woman out onto the beach and protect what they knew was theirs, lying there on the sand. Taking advantage of that split second, he began to shoot at anything that moved, the rifle barking through the jungle, echoing across the beach, across the water. Three of the huge things lay on the ground when he'd jumped through, clear of them for the moment, and tumbled across the dunes.

He bounced up immediately to his feet and raised his rifle, but too late; Kara had been the closest to her, and Margery had swung her blade again, this time across Kara's chest.

In the moment that Kara hit the sand, flat on his

back like an enormous tree, Margery pulled the steel
from his skin as he fell and swung around to face the
rest. But the other four had seen the apes, one by
one, begin tentatively to move out from the shelter
of the trees onto the beach, knowing it was not yet
their time, but knowing too that something was
very wrong. Three of their kind lay dead. A
female . . . a mate . . . had escaped, and Man en-
dangered their species.

The sight of the hulking shadows hobbling over
the dunes had sent the four guards fleeing in
opposite directions, knowing there was no time to
cast off in the boats.

Now with them gone and Kara dead, there
remained only Margery, blade held before her,
facing Thot who likewise now held a blade.

All three women trapped in the sand had called
out to the girl, but it was only Lucy's voice, soft and
joyful, that caught her attention at last and brought
her glance down to where they lay.

Lucy looked up at her. She was smiling, and the
two young women exchanged friendly, polite
"hellos," as if they were meeting for lunch. The
agony and horror that had brought them to this was
suddenly swept behind a merciful veil drawn over
that memory, existing now only in the long-ago.
Bending, Margery managed to cut the ropes and
free from bondage the left hand of her friend before
Thot struck, and she fell forward across Lucy's
stomach.

Ben raised his weapon and fired, bringing Thot
down with one shot like a felled buffalo. Pain seared
through the chest muscles of the huge thing. He lay
on the beach, his hand, soaked in the ritual "oil,"
coming up to hold his breast, his own blood now
matting the orange hairs covering his torso.

After the initial shock had passed over and through him, Thot realized how totally alone he was. Another pain ripped through him and he shivered, knowing for the first time how badly wounded he was. He looked up the beach.

The bravest, or perhaps the most foolhardy of the animals, had removed from the jungle and Ben turned barely in time to sidestep a crushing blow from the first of the marauding creature. Its magnificent body, its roaring head, came at him like a wall of black, violent sound. As he leaped from its path, he fired a shot, and it fell.

The shot had frightened the others that lined the trees, screaming, gnashing their teeth, pawing at the air, running out four or five feet, then running back to join the others, brave for a moment, then sobered by the memory of the rifle and what it could do.

It bought Ben the time he needed to get down the beach, reaching Mary first.

The stench that rose from the fluids that covered them was potent, and he gasped for air, fumbling with the wet knots at her wrists.

"The sword, Ben!" she screamed, hysterical, joyful, furious, all at once, as she bent her neck back and gave a quick look up the beach where the apes had moved another few feet toward them. The night had gone insane, the wind whipping, raging through the flame, through the jungle, the long hair of the animals blowing about their heads and bodies.

Ben stretched across Dana to the body of Margery Croft, the sword still clutched tightly in her fist. With her free left hand, Lucy was stroking the dry, listless hair of her friend who lay across her own naked body. She did not look up or even acknowledge Ben as he wrested the blade from the dead girl's fingers.

Quickly, with four sharp blows at each wrist and leg, Mary was freed. The ropes were still tight around her limbs, and she tried loosening them to bring back circulation. She fell twice, attempting to get to her feet.

"Run!" Ben screamed as he sliced through Dana's bonds, and Dana yelled, "Yes, Run, Mary! Run! Get to the water!"

Mary hesitated for a second, but the wind came up strong again in a mighty gust, and the apes moved further down the beach. Ben fired straight up at the sky, and the beasts retreated once more, but not so far this time. There were more coming from the trees all the time, like an army.

Dana rose to her feet and she too fell, unable at first to bring back life to her tortured legs. Ben grabbed her, his bare chest now covered with the gore that had drenched the women.

The scent had been carried up the beach by the wind and the apes seemed, all at once, to become enraged, hysterical, screaming, pounding their chests, roaring as they advanced. Ben pushed Dana ahead of him and watched long enough to be sure she was able to make it to the sea. Beyond, Mary stood at the edge of the water, surf feathering out in a phosphorescent fan as it hit her from behind, watching for the two to join her.

"It's the scent, Mary!" Ben could hear Dana yelling from behind as she ran toward the girl, "Get into the water and wash off the scent!"

With his last few waking moments, Thot's foggy brain, shot through with pain from the wound in his chest, registered what had just been said. Realizing in one horrible second that he too, was covered in the scent . . . and he was dying, but not dead yet. Ben did not see the huge thing roll over in unbearable agony, and begin to drag himself on his stomach through the sand and down toward the surf.

For now the apes had begun the attack, and the first of the horde struck out at Ben, nearly hitting him in the temple with its powerful fist. He dropped the sword and fell across the sand, reaching once again for the rifle. There was no time to get to his feet; he fired from the ground and hit it, but it continued to come. He fired again, then rolled away quickly as it fell forward next to him.

But another was already practically upon him, and he was now too far away from sword, and Lucy. He fired again and saved himself once more, but the apes had found the girl, lifted the dead body of Margery Croft, and thrown it down like a stuffed dummy, roaring, pounding their chests. More and more were coming down the beach, to Lucy.

There was nothing more to do. He heard her scream when for a moment the madness seemed to clear away from her eyes and she looked up, knowing her fate.

He raised the rifle one final time, aimed, and put a bullet through her head.

The shot rang out and the two women standing in the water watched as the apes returned again, as if to retreat once more into the jungle, terrified by the deafening report.

Ben threw the rifle down and turned. There, not twenty feet away, were the boats that had carried the women around the island. Frantic, barely able to think beyond escape, he ran toward the nearest one, slamming against it at full speed.

He began to shove at it, trying to slide it down the beach and into the water. It wouldn't budge, and with each heave, his footing slipped in the sand, unable to get the leverage he needed. He turned and looked up toward the jungle. The things were still there at the perimeter, but closer now, gaining courage as no more gunfire kept them at bay.

Digging his feet deeply into the sand, spreading his legs wide, he heaved. He pushed again. It moved. First an inch or two, then easily, gliding through the sand quickly as he ran it into the surf.

As his foot hit the water, the women pushed off, swimming out through the crashing waves toward the rocks of the reef. Ben jumped into the boat, grabbed an oar and began paddling violently toward them.

Thot watched them disappear through the spray of white water and began moving as quickly as his wounded body would allow, knowing he too must wash himself free of the scent that would be responsible for killing him before the bullet would do its work.

The apes saw him moving and the scent coming from the only thing left alive on the beach seemed to torture them. Insane from the overwhelming erotic odor, they screamed in fury, hobbled as one across the dunes just as Thot's lurching figure reached the cleansing sea. He moved out past the surf and stood, the water shoulder high on his tortured frame, allowing the ocean to wash him.

The apes stood lining the shore looking out, but not daring to venture into the water, screaming in agony. The pandemonium of Hell filled the early morning air.

Dana and Mary had reached the last of the rocks and clung to them, their eyes on Ben, who now

maneuvered the canoe close enough for them to
clamber over the slippery reef. Mary fell once and
cut herself, opening yet another fresh wound, but
they reached the boat, falling into it as Ben used an
oar to push off from the reef and began rowing them
out.

The red and amber liquids the women had been
drenched in had washed off into the sea, cleansing
them but trailing behind them in their wake.

Thot too had been bathed by the ocean and those
same oils had also mixed with the sea, enflaming yet
another kind of creature.

As Ben rowed frantically, his eyes still on the
island, he, Dana and Mary perceived the figure of
Thot standing in the water, too weak, too wounded
to pursue, his massive head sticking up above the
surface like some curious sea monster.

Ben felt something graze the side of his oar, but
by the time he looked down, it was gone. He gazed
past the little boat and saw a sharp fin gliding
silently through the water, toward the beach.
Toward Thot.

It was shortly joined by another, then a third and
fourth, until a dozen such fins followed, all slicing
with silent grace through the calm water, not
interested in the boat, but intent on making their
way to Thot.

The two women and the man watched as Thot
screamed, knowing what was coming at him. He
turned to the shore, but the apes were still there,
waiting for his return. Advancing from the sea, the
sharks approached.

The first fin reached him, and the water exploded
with violent splashing. His scream was cut off as a
tail fin appeared briefly above the white foam, and

he went down beneath the surface and was gone. The rest came then to join in the feeding.

Dana turned her face away into Mary's breasts, sobbing. Ben continued rowing, slower now, but without ceasing. They could reach the other side of the Island before dawn, rest, and from there, proceed safely back to Savong-khai.

Ben looked back to the shoreline. The apes had moved back up the beach now except for one which stood closer to the water's edge.

It was motionless. Its thin pelt shone orange in the twilight before the dawn, and in its massive arms it held an infant high over its head, the tiny voice of the child wailing in short, hysterical bursts.

The creature cried out as if calling to them in a longing, agonized plea. Then it was silent, holding its baby high, watching as the three in the little canoe disappeared over the horizon, away from the secret of Satyr Island.

ELECTRIFYING HORROR AND OCCULT

2343-1	**THE WERELING**	$3.50 US, $3.95 Can
2341-5	**THE ONI**	$3.95 US, $4.50 Can
2334-2	**PREMONITION**	$3.50 US, $3.95 Can
2331-8	**RESURREXIT**	$3.95 US, $4.50 Can
2302-4	**WORSHIP THE NIGHT**	$3.95 US, $3.95 Can
2289-3	**THE WITCHING**	$3.50 US, $3.95 Can
2281-8	**THE FREAK**	$2.50 US, $2.95 Can
2251-6	**THE HOUSE**	$2.50
2206-0	**CHILD OF DEMONS**	$3.75 US, $4.50 Can
2142-0	**THE FELLOWSHIP**	$3.75 US, $4.50 Can

MORE BLOOD-CHILLERS
FROM LEISURE BOOKS

2329-6	**EVIL STALKS THE NIGHT**	$3.50 US, $3.95 Can
2319-9	**LATE AT NIGHT**	$3.95 US, $4.50 Can
2309-1	**EVIL DREAMS**	$3.95 US, $4.50 Can
2300-8	**THE SECRET OF AMITYVILLE**	$3.50 US, $3.95 Can
2275-3	**FANGS**	$3.95 US, $4.50 Can
2269-9	**NIGHT OF THE WOLF**	$3.25
2265-6	**KISS NOT THE CHILD**	$3.75 US, $4.50 Can
2256-7	**CREATURE**	$3.75 US, $4.50 Can
2246-x	**DEATHBRINGER**	$3.75 US, $4.50 Can
2235-4	**SHIVERS**	$3.75 US, $4.50 Can
2225-7	**UNTO THE ALTAR**	$3.75 US, $4.50 Can
2220-6	**THE RIVARD HOUSE**	$3.25
2195-1	**BRAIN WATCH**	$3.50 US, $4.25 Can
2185-4	**BLOOD OFFERINGS**	$3.75 US, $4.50 Can
2152-8	**SISTER SATAN**	$3.75 US, $4.50 Can
2121-8	**UNDERTOW**	$3.75 US, $4.50 Can
2112-9	**SPAWN OF HELL**	$3.75 US, $4.50 Can

BISHOP'S LANDING

Dr. Albert Conrad, a clinical psychologist, had been researching the causes and effects of phobias and panic-fear reactions. He developed an experiment to flesh out his research, but he needed stable volunteers.

After much searching, Dr. Conrad found four willing subjects. He took them to a supposedly haunted house in Bishop's Landing for the study, scoffing at the whispered warnings of the frightened townspeople.

The house was waiting. The Evil was patient, and would soon rise to shred the study of fear with such unearthly terror that the survivors would envy the dead!

2053-x $3.50

Make the Most of Your
Leisure Time
with
LEISURE BOOKS

Please send me the following titles:

Quantity	Book Number	Price
_____	_____	_____
_____	_____	_____
_____	_____	_____
_____	_____	_____
_____	_____	_____

If out of stock on any of the above titles, please send me the alternate title(s) listed below:

_____	_____	_____
_____	_____	_____
_____	_____	_____
_____	_____	_____

Postage & Handling _____

Total Enclosed $ _____

☐ Please send me a free catalog.

NAME _____
(please print)

ADDRESS _____

CITY _____ STATE _____ ZIP_____

Please include $1.00 shipping and handling for the first book ordered and 25¢ for each book thereafter in the same order. All orders are shipped within approximately 4 weeks via postal service book rate. PAYMENT MUST ACCOMPANY ALL ORDERS.*

*Canadian orders must be paid in US dollars payable through a New York banking facility.

Mail coupon to: **Dorchester Publishing Co., Inc.**
6 East 39 Street, Suite 900
New York, NY 10016
Att: ORDER DEPT.